THE OLD SPIES CLUB
AND OTHER INTRIGUES OF RAND

EDWARD D. HOCH
(Photograph by Michael Culligan)

THE OLD SPIES CLUB

AND OTHER INTRIGUES OF RAND

EDWARD D. HOCH

Crippen & Landru Publishers
Norfolk, Virginia
2001

Cover painting by Carol Heyer

Cover design by Deborah Miller

Crippen & Landru logo by Eric D. Greene

ISBN (limited edition): 1-885941-59-5
ISBN (trade edition): 1-885941-60-9

FIRST EDITION

10 9 8 7 6 5 4 3 2 1

Crippen & Landru Publishers, Inc.
P. O. Box 9315
Norfolk, VA 23505
USA

www.crippenlandru.com
CrippenL@Pilot.Infi.Net

Again for Patricia, in this Grand Year

CONTENTS

INTRODUCTION

I have now published 79 stories about Jeffery Rand, all growing out of a 1965 short-short in which the character's name was originally Randolph. As with many of my series in this period, its form and direction were guided by Fred Dannay, editor of *Ellery Queen's Mystery Magazine*. He suggested shortening the name to Rand and beginning each title with "The Spy Who … ". The James Bond novels and John le Carre's *The Spy Who Came in From the Cold* were both popular at the time, and Fred felt that a spy who specialized in codes and ciphers would fit right in.

Originally Rand was director of the Department of Concealed Communications, a British institution that I hoped would take its place alongside John Dickson Carr's Department of Queer Complaints and Roy Vickers's Department of Dead Ends. After eleven years and 32 stories I decided it was time for Rand to retire. In an era of one-time pads and computer-generated ciphers I felt the job might become a bit boring for both Rand and the reader. Rand had met and married Leila Gaad, a young archeologist with an Egyptian father and a British mother, which was one more reason for him to shun the spying life. Little did I know that his retirement would stretch out more than twice as long as his years of active service!

This collection of fifteen Rand stories concentrates on the relationship between Rand and Leila, and his life after retirement. They meet for the first time in "The Spy and the Nile Mermaid," and meet again in "The Spy in the Pyramid" and "The Spy at the End of the Rainbow," all of them reflecting the years during which Russian troops were actually stationed in Egypt. Since writing these stories I've learned (from one of Berton Roueche's excellent medical essays) that swimming in the Nile can be very dangerous to one's health. And I also learned that climbing to the top of a pyramid isn't nearly as easy as I've portrayed it to be. Still, this is how it was with Rand and Leila in their exuberant younger days.

Leila came to England in "The Spy Who Took a Vacation" and they were married soon after. She took a position as a professor of archeology at Reading University outside London and they bought a house there. But Rand was a long way from any real retirement. London was constantly summoning him back for special assignments all over the globe, and Leila proved to be a great help. She follows him to Moscow in "The Spy and the Cats of Rome," and they return to

Egypt together in "The Spy in the Labyrinth." Leila is actually kidnapped in "The Spy Who Was Alone," and goes on a solo assignment to New York in "The Spy Who Wasn't Needed." They travel to Scotland together at the end of the Cold War for "The Spy and the Healing Waters," and back to their favorite locale again for "Egyptian Days." In "The Man From Nile K" a Russian claiming to be one of Leila's old lovers turns up in Reading.

She plays a smaller part in four of the last five stories included here, but each was chosen for the special reason. "Waiting For Mrs. Ryder," included in *The Oxford Book of Spy Stories*, is perhaps my strongest blending of espionage and deduction. Sue Grafton chose "The Old Spies Club" for inclusion in *The Best American Mystery Stories 1998*, and its title seemed the perfect one for this collection. "One Bag of Coconuts" won the Anthony Award at Bouchercon as the best mystery short story of the year. And "The War That Never Was" is a favorite of mine.

For long-time readers of this series, I must add a word about Rand's first name. He is "Jeffery," or more exactly "C. Jeffery Rand," as first mentioned in the introduction to my early collection *The Spy and the Thief*. Over the years, it's often appeared in some stories with the more conventional spelling of "Jeffrey." Because the spelling becomes important in one of the stories included here, we have tried to make it uniform throughout this volume.

For Rand's old fans and new ones, I hope you enjoy these tales, spanning nearly thirty years of my writing career. A full checklist of Rand stories can be found at the back of the book. My special thanks to Sandi and Doug Greene for bringing them together in this handsome new edition, and to Janet Hutchings, my *EQMM* editor for the past ten years.

Edward D. Hoch
Rochester, New York
April 2001

THE SPY AND THE NILE MERMAID

It began, as so many of Rand's special assignments did, in the book-lined office of Security's graying Chief of Staff, Henry Hastings. He had acquired new duties, and new responsibilities, since the retirement of Colonel Nelson, and Rand was troubled to see that they were already aging him.

"Mason has been killed in Cairo," he told Rand, coming directly to the point. "I want you to go out there and take his place."

"Is it a job for Concealed Communications?" Rand asked.

"It might be and it might not be. But damn it, Rand, I don't have anyone else to send! Perhaps you can wrap it all up in forty-eight hours."

"You want me to find out who killed him?"

"That, of course. But more important, you're to contact someone known as the Scotsman. I gather he's quite a character around the city. Wears kilts and everything. Mason had some business with him which we must complete."

"All right," Rand sighed. "I'll go. You said it might be a job for Double-C. What did you mean?"

"Mason was stabbed to death in his hotel room. He seemed to be writing in a notebook at the time. This is what he wrote." He passed Rand a single sheet of loose-leaf notebook paper. Across it, near the top, had been printed in pencil the letters:

J A S O N D

Rand studied it for a moment. "Jason D. The name of his killer?"

"Perhaps. But it could also be the name of a yacht, or stand for Jason five hundred—interpreting the D as a Roman numeral. I show it to you because it's the only clue we have to his death. You might keep an eye out for someone named Jason D."

"Did you check the files?"

"Nothing. It could be a new man, or a known agent using a new alias. Or, as I said, it could be merely the name of somebody's yacht."

"You're thinking of Jason and the Argonauts? The Golden Fleece?"

Hastings shrugged. "Someone might have decided it was a good name for a boat."

"If this was a dying message, wouldn't the killer have taken it away or

11

destroyed it?"

"The stab wound was right to the heart. Mason didn't have time for any dying message. He wrote these letters before he was stabbed."

"Mason, Jason ... Could it have been a variation of a name that he was using himself?"

"If he was, it was completely unauthorized."

"What sort of man was he?' Rand asked. "I knew him only slightly."

"Good, plodding, a bit on the unimaginative side. The sort who gets himself killed by trusting too many people."

"How long had he been in Cairo?"

"He was assigned to the general area of the Middle East, but he had a girl friend in Cairo. He spent a lot of time there with her."

"Unmarried? Mason, I mean."

"Wife in Liverpool, but that didn't seem to bother him."

"What's the girl's name? In the event I need to look her up?"

"Forget the girl. It's the Scotsman you have to look up. You leave tomorrow."

"Very well," Rand agreed. There was no arguing with Hastings in one of his moods.

Cairo in June is a hot unpleasant city, with the temperature hovering in the mid-nineties and no chance of any rain to wash away the odors of the narrow streets and ancient buildings. In the old city especially, the sights and sounds and smells are of the past, of a time when a much simpler life existed in the city on the Nile.

Rand spent the first afternoon of his visit in Old Cairo, stopping at the Coptic Museum to see again the little pagan altars and shrines that had fascinated him on previous visits. Somehow the Coptic religion had always symbolized Cairo for him—evolving from paganism to Christianity just as the city itself had evolved from the veiled Orient to the bustle of modern life.

He was to meet the Scotsman after dinner at the Hotel Phoenix, not far from Cairo University and the Zoological Garden. Rand stopped there after eating, killing some time among the caged beasts, and then drove on to the hotel in his rented car.

The Scotsman, whose name was Kirkcaldy, was waiting for him in the cocktail lounge. He was easy enough to recognize, with his colorful kilt and large fur sporran hanging down the front. He rose, beaming and flush-faced, offering his hand. "You would be Mr. Rand."

"That's correct, Mr. Kirkcaldy."

"No one calls me that! I'm just the Scotsman around here— something of a local character, I suppose. But here—come up to my room. You'll be more comfortable there."

Rand followed him up the broad staircase to the second floor, watching the muscles of his legs beneath the plaid kilt. He noticed something else, too—a flat black knife tucked into the top of one of the Scotsman's stockings. "Don't you believe in elevators?"

"Stairs are good for the leg muscles. That's the trouble with London —too damn many lifts, no chance to walk upstairs."

He unlocked the door of his room and Rand followed him inside. "Is that knife you wear standard equipment?"

"This?" The Scotsman's hand moved with a blur that Rand couldn't follow. The knife hit the far wall and stuck there, vibrating.

"You're fast," Rand conceded.

"One has to be. We don't call it a knife, though. It's a skean dhu, a formal part of the Highland Scottish dress."

"You knew Mason?"

"Yes. He was killed with a knife, but not by me."

Rand cleared his throat. "What about a man named Jason D?"

The Scotsman sat down. "Never heard of him."

"There are a great many Russian technicians in Cairo these days."

"Yes."

"Could one of those be Jason D?"

"Perhaps. Anything is possible."

"Hastings, back in London, thinks Jason D might be the name of a yacht. The name Jason has certain maritime associations in legend."

The Scotsman frowned. "You're working for Hastings?"

"I work for myself. I didn't know you were acquainted with him."

"I'm not, but Mason mentioned the name. You're here to take Mason's place, get yourself killed as he did?" He rose and retrieved the knife from the wall.

"I'm in for forty-eight hours, and then out again. Mason was after some information. Now I want it."

The Scotsman sighed. "I only gave Mason a name, nothing more. He was to make contact with a man named Kharga, a minor official in el-Sadat's government."

"And the information he sought?"

"As you no doubt know—the next six months' delivery schedule of Russian planes to el-Sadat. With the power balance the way it is in the Middle East such information is invaluable. Israel would pay dearly for it, and the Americans would be anxious to obtain it as well. How will London use it?"

"I don't make policy, Kirkcaldy. You should know that. Just put me in touch with this man Kharga, and then I'll be on my way."

The Scotsman smiled. "You were asking about a yacht named the Jason D, or does that no longer interest you?"

"Is there one?"

"During World War Two a number of German spies, equipped with a radio transmitter, operated from a houseboat on the Nile. The Russians apparently liked the idea, and their chief security man in Cairo is now living on quite a luxurious houseboat. He keeps tabs on all the Russian technicians and their families who have come here recently. It is possible that he heard of Mason's activities."

"Does the houseboat have a name?"

"That I do not know. It could be the Jason D, or that could be its code name."

"Who is the security man?"

"His name is Lev Dontsova. He likes the good life, but that doesn't mean he's not dangerous."

"Thanks for the tip. What about Kharga?"

"Tomorrow. I'll get word to you where he'll be."

They shook hands and Rand left the Scotsman in his room.

His hotel was across the river from the Phoenix, and as he drove along El Tahrir Bridge toward the center of the city, he thought about the Scotsman and his knife. Kirkcaldy was not a paid agent of the British government. In fact, his status in the whole operation was somewhat vague. For himself, Rand always preferred to know which side men were on. Someone was paying the Scotsman, and he wondered who it was.

He opened the door to his room and instantly became aware that someone was inside. There was no time to draw a gun. He saw a figure move, silhouetted for a split second against the dull nighttime glow from the windows, and he leaped forward with a running tackle that carried them both to the floor.

The softness beneath him erupted almost at once into a girl's high-pitched scream. He covered her mouth with his hand and asked, "Just who in hell are you?"

"I—I wanted to see you," she gasped when he released her mouth. "I told the chambermaid I was your wife and she let me in."

He got up and turned on the light. She was a small dark-haired girl with the pleasing high-cheekboned features found so often in the Middle East. She might have been 25—no more than that, and probably less. "I'm too old to be tackling people in hotel rooms," he told her. "And I'm also too old to be your husband."

"But you are a friend of George Mason's?"

Mason. He remembered what Hastings had said about a girl friend in

Cairo. "Yes, I'm a friend of Mason's," he answered, with less than complete honesty. He'd hardly known the man. "He spoke of having a girl here, but he never told me your name."

"Leila Gaad. I'm an archeologist, associated with Cairo University."

"How did you happen to meet Mason?"

"There was something in the newspaper about my swimming in the Nile and he sought me out. This was nearly a year ago. We've been friends ever since."

"Swimming in the Nile?"

"Skindiving, really. I have a theory that some small tombs from the First Dynasty might be submerged there, but they were only of wood in those days, and so far I've found nothing but some early artifacts. The water is so muddy it's very difficult to find anything down there."

"Mason was interested in archeology?"

"No, he was actually interested in a houseboat on the river. He wanted me to swim out and attach something to its side."

Rand nodded. "A listening device of some sort. Did you do it?"

"Not at first, but—well, we became friendly over the months. Finally I did it for him, but the device never worked right. Just before he was killed he asked me to swim out and replace it."

"Did you do it?"

"I was going to, this week. And then he was killed. That's why I came here tonight, to see you. I have another boy friend who is terribly jealous, but if doing the job would somehow hurt the people who killed George I'll do it. We had a lot of good times together, and I owe him that much. They shouldn't have killed him, no matter what."

She spoke with a mixture of sincerity and detachment that surprised him. He doubted if she could really have been in love with Mason, and yet she seemed to have cared about him very much. "Do you have any idea what he was working on?"

She shook her head. "We rarely talked about his work. It might have been the men on the houseboat, but I don't know."

"Did he ever mention a man named Jason D?"

"No, I don't think so."

"How about the Scotsman?"

"No, but I saw him with a person wearing a kilt, just two nights before his death. It was his birthday, and we were going out to celebrate. I asked about the man, but George just said it was business. I was interested because my mother was Scottish. She married my father, an Egyptian, during the war."

"Was that the last time you saw Mason before his death?"

She nodded. "I gave him a birthday gift—a gold pencil with the University crest and a little engraved pyramid on it. The Archeology Department had some made up, and I use them as personal gifts to my friends. We had dinner and went back to his hotel room for a few drinks. I left sometime after midnight and that was the last time I saw him."

"He allowed you to go home alone after midnight?"

She blushed nicely. "Actually, it was closer to morning. The sun was rising."

"I see." He toyed with his room key, uncertain where to go from here. "Do you have the device Mason wanted attached to the houseboat?"

She nodded. "In my room."

If Mason really did have a method of eavesdropping on the occupants of the houseboat, Rand knew London would want him to follow through with it. In a sense, it might even fall within the province of Concealed Communications, especially if he could listen in on radio messages to Moscow.

"Could we go down to the river tomorrow," he asked, "and take a look at this houseboat?"

"Certainly. What time?"

He remembered the Scotsman. "Let me call you. I may have to meet someone first."

After she'd gone he sat for a long time by the window, looking out at the lights of Cairo by night. It might be as she said, that she only wanted to help get back at the people who had killed Mason. But he had learned long ago that hardly anything was what it seemed in this business.

The telephone next to Rand's bed rang sharply at seven a.m., waking him from a deep sleep. He rolled over and answered it. "Yes?"

A familiar voice came over the line. It was the Scotsman, but he didn't identify himself. "The person we spoke of will be at the Qait Bey Mosque exactly at noon. All right?"

"Fine," Rand said. "Thank you."

He had no idea where the Qait Bey Mosque was, and had to consult a guidebook. It was on the eastern edge of the city, quite close to the quarries, and seemed to be part of a cemetery. Rand had no picture of Kharga, and wondered how they would know each other.

He drove out to the Qait Bey Mosque just before noon, taking the highway which ran past the great sprawling Citadel. Behind him, and to his left, the familiar slender minarets stretched toward the sky, reminding him of Omar's *Rubaiyat* and all the wonders of the Middle East. He saw after a time that he was indeed entering a cemetery grounds, and that the mosque of Qait Bey was actually a tomb—a great domed structure of fantastic and intricate beauty.

Rand waited near the main entrance, studying an undulating arabesque design, until at last a short youthful Egyptian appeared from somewhere and touched his arm. "Mr. Rand?"

"Yes. You would be Kharga?"

"Would you accompany me while I walk about the grounds? The minaret here is especially restrained and subtle."

As they walked, Rand told the younger man, "I'm a friend of the Scotsman. And of George Mason."

"Alas, I was never destined to meet George Mason." He turned his handsome brown face toward the sky. "The Angel of Death met him first."

"He was to purchase some information from you."

The Egyptian nodded. "Numbers, only numbers."

There was no one near enough to overhear, and Rand said, "The delivery schedule of Russian planes to Egypt for the next six months."

"For a small additional sum I could also furnish the number of technicians expected to arrive from Moscow monthly during the remainder of this year."

"How much more?"

"The sum agreed upon for the plane schedule, plus an additional fifty percent. That would seem fair."

"It's a great deal of money."

The young man brushed the black hair from his eyes. "Mr. Rand, there is a great deal of risk. Sadat dismisses his generals when Israel triumphs on the battlefield. Some he even has shot. Can you imagine the fate of a poor clerk? I fear for my life every waking moment."

"Why do you do it then? Do you hate the Russians?"

He smiled. "No, only that I love money."

Rand sighed and handed him an envelope. "The rest when you give me the information. I would like to leave tomorrow, so it must be soon."

Kharga nodded. "In the morning. I will make a final check to see that the figures have not been changed."

"Where?"

"I will call your hotel. The Scotsman says the phones at your hotel are not tapped."

"Who pays the Scotsman? Whom does he work for?"

"That does not concern me. I do not know."

"Have you ever heard the name Jason D?"

"No," he replied, looking genuinely puzzled. "Is he here in Cairo?"

"I think so. I think he killed Mason." Rand watched a bird circling high above them. "I'd like to find him before I go home."

He phoned the number that Leila Gaad had given him and heard her soft voice answering. "Feel like a swim today?' he asked.

"It's you. The Englishman."

"That's right."

"It's getting late in the day."

"I thought toward evening might be the best time."

"My boy friend—"

"I know. He's jealous. I'll pick you up in twenty minutes."

She was silent a moment, considering. Then she said, "Very well. I'll get my gear ready."

He picked her up at an apartment near the American University, and they drove south along the Sayialet El Roda, a narrow arm of the Nile. Leila was dressed in shorts and a brief fringed yellow top that left her tanned midriff exposed. She was full of a youthful vigor that was always attractive to middle-aged men, and Rand had no difficulty in understanding Mason's having been attracted to her.

"Is that your skindiving gear in back?" he asked.

"That's it. I've become something of a familiar figure down this way, so my antics don't attract much attention any more. The device George gave me is in this box."

When they finally came to a stop, a few miles south of Old Cairo, he opened the box and took it out. A listening device with short-range radio transmitter—and the whole thing magnetized to stick to a ship's hull. It was well-made and expensive, and Rand doubted if British Intelligence was supplying them as standard equipment. He turned it over and noted that it had been manufactured in the United States.

"Will you turn your back while I climb into my gear?" she asked.

"Is this the place?"

"We're opposite the Pyramids of Zawiet el Aryan. According to my studies, this is the least likely place for any submerged tombs to be located."

"But then why are you—?"

"Because this is where the houseboat is, foolish!"

He looked out then at the muddy Nile waters and saw a large squarish shape glistening in the afternoon sun. He whistled softly and simply stared at it. "That's quite a boat! The Russians aren't hurting for money."

"Lev Dontsova likes the good life, but that doesn't mean he's not dangerous," she said.

Rand looked back at her. The words had an oddly familiar ring, as if she were quoting someone. "Who told you that? Mason?"

"Yes, that's what he said."

"Someone else said it, too. Just yesterday." Something was wrong here, and he was trying to put his finger on it. "How did you know I was in Cairo, at that hotel last night? How did you know I was a friend of Mason's?"

"I—" The line of her mouth hardened. "If you want me to swim out there, I'd better get started. It will be getting dark soon."

"Go ahead." He wondered if the whole business was a mistake, if he wouldn't have been better off sticking to his transaction with Kharga instead of involving himself with this girl and the Russian houseboat.

In another two minutes she was ready, and she stepped from behind the car wearing a two-piece black bathing suit that showed off her young body well. She had a diver's knife belted to one tanned thigh, and wore an air tank with twin breathing hoses on her back. She took the listening device from him and waved one arm. "Wish me luck," she said, adjusting her eyepiece. Then she was gone, arching her body into a perfect dive off the river bank.

Rand watched her for a moment, until she disappeared beneath the muddy waters and was lost from view. He marveled that she could find her way beneath that opaque surface, but he knew she was down there, somewhere, and he hoped the people on the houseboat hadn't seen her go in.

The hot June sun was almost to the horizon, and he knew it must be late. He checked his watch and saw they still had another hour before darkness. They had parked on the western bank of the river, to have the setting sun at their backs, and while this might have helped shield their activities it also reflected off the houseboat windows, making Rand's own observations difficult.

He sat in the car and smoked one of his American cigarettes, watching the minutes pass by on his watch. She was taking too long, and that worried him. Still, there seemed to be no sign of activity or alarm aboard the houseboat. A few cars passed on the highway, and the sun dipped a little farther, until its lower edge was actually touching the horizon.

A big foreign automobile rolled off the highway and came to a stop behind his car. Rand turned and started to go out to meet the newcomer, but he wasn't fast enough. It was a bulky Russian with a gun, and he had the gun pointed at Rand's stomach.

"American?"

"British," Rand corrected, trying to smile.

"We go." He motioned toward the river, and Rand saw that the houseboat was moving in to pick them up.

Lev Dontsova was a slim long-haired man with sharp features and a general appearance somewhat like the old magazine illustrations of Sherlock Holmes. He even wore a satin smoking jacket as he stood up to greet Rand's arrival. The houseboat had anchored close enough to the river bank for a gangplank to reach across the water, and Rand had walked on with the gunman right behind him.

"I really must protest this outrage," he told Dontsova. Leila stood to one side, dripping wet, her hands tied behind her back. But she seemed to be uninjured, and once they had tied her hands they hadn't bothered to remove the knife from its sheath on her thigh.

"We are the outraged ones!" the Russian stormed in passable English. "This girl tries to put a bomb on our boat!"

Rand sucked in his breath. "You know damn well it's not a bomb." He turned to Leila. "Are you all right?"

"Yes, I guess so."

"How did they spot you?"

"They came off on the side opposite you, two of them, and grabbed me in the water. Then this man radioed to shore and had you picked up, too."

"A bomb," Dontsova repeated. "Our friends the Egyptians pass out long prison sentences for such acts."

"It's a radio transmitter and you know it. You probably have a detection device aboard that spotted it when she swam close enough."

"Then you are spies, not assassins?" He allowed his lips to twist into the hint of a grin.

"We are archeologists," Rand insisted. "She was diving for a lost tomb."

"A pretty mermaid like this? Looking for a lost tomb? I doubt that."

"All right," Rand said, taking a wild chance. "We were sent by Jason D."

The Russian looked blank. "Jason D? Who is this? Another Englishman?"

Rand moved over to the girl's side. "If you don't know that name, you surely must know Taz, one of your top intelligence experts." Rand had met Taz on three occasions, most recently in Moscow, and they were friendly enemies, respectful of each other's abilities.

"I know Taz."

"Then you know enough not to harm us."

"Spies take a certain risk. They know what to expect."

"Like Mason? Did you kill him?"

"The Englishman? No, no! We are here not to kill, but only to aid the defense of the United Arab Republic."

Rand had maneuvered into the position he wanted. His right hand dropped fast, hitting Leila's bare thigh and yanking her knife free of its sheath. Then he whirled, bringing the blade up fast, and struck at the man with the pistol. He caught him in the wrist and the gun flew out of his hand. Dontsova shouted something in Russian, but already Rand was behind the wounded man, catching him around the neck with one arm while he held the knife ready with the other.

The door of the cabin burst open and a burly man in swimming trunks came running in response to Dontsova's shouts. They stood eyeing each other for an instant, while the bleeding man struggled in Rand's grasp. "I'll kill him,"

Rand warned.

Dontsova sighed and held up his hands. "What is it you want?"

"Untie the girl and let us leave."

The Russian shrugged. "We meant no harm. You, after all, were the one who came to cause trouble." He walked over and untied Leila, then stepped back. "Go on, go! You are both free!"

"Pick up the gun," Rand told the girl. When she had done it he released the wounded man and moved backward toward the door.

"Perhaps we will meet again," Dontsova said with a smile.

"Maybe," Rand agreed. Then they were on the deck and he slammed the door behind them. They ran across the gangplank and up the river bank to the car, but no one followed. The Russians had apparently finished their activities for the day.

Back at her apartment, Leila Gaad gave him a fleeting kiss on the cheek. "I can't thank you enough," she said.

"I did get you into it, after all. The least I could do was get you out again."

"I wasn't fast enough in the water. I should have used my knife on him."

He thought of George Mason, dead from a stabbing. "There are too many knives in this affair already."

"You asked me a question earlier. You asked me how I knew you were in Cairo, and a friend of George's. I can tell you now."

"You don't have to," Rand told her. "I know." He left her standing there and went back to his car.

Kharga phoned again in the morning, quite early. Rand listened to his voice on the phone and suggested, "Couldn't you just read the numbers to me?"

Kharga coughed at the other end. "You still have another envelope for me."

"I was forgetting. Where will I meet you? I want to be on an afternoon plane to London."

"At the eastern end of El Tahrir Bridge there are a pair of stone lions. I will be at the north lion, nearest to the Nile Hilton Hotel, at noon."

"Very well." Rand hung up and dressed quickly. He had one more person to see before he finished his work at noon.

The Scotsman stood up to greet Rand, holding out a hand. "I'm glad we could meet again before you left Cairo," he said. "Was your mission successful?"

"Very successful," Rand said. "I'm meeting Kharga at noon to get the information."

"I understand there was some trouble last evening aboard the Russian houseboat."

"News travels fast. There was some trouble, but nothing I couldn't handle."

"Lev Dontsova is very angry. Good thing you're leaving today."

"Before I left I hoped to wrap up the Mason killing."

"You know who did it?"

Rand looked the Scotsman in the eye. "You killed him, Kirkcaldy. You've been running agents for the Americans. It was an American plan to attach that listening device to the houseboat, and you were using Mason to get to the girl. You needed her for the dirty work."

"Oh, come now, Rand! Isn't that rather far-fetched?"

"And you're carrying the murder knife with you right now, in your stocking top," Rand went on smoothly. "The girl could only have known of my arrival if you told her, and she used the same words to describe Dontsova that you had used earlier to me."

"You've been too long in the sun, Rand."

"Do you deny that the Americans pay you? The device was made in America."

The Scotsman sighed and began pacing. "Damn you, Rand! You make a fellow's job extremely difficult. Yes, the Americans do pay me, and yes, I was running Mason as an agent. He'd been in the Middle East a long time and had acquired some expensive girl friends—Leila Gaad in Cairo, and another in Baghdad. So he took money from your people and from the Americans, too. The Americans didn't mind, since it was all the same side, but I don't think London knew. Mason was intent on getting the figures from Kharga, but I was after a longer-range operation. I figured Mason's girl could swim out to the houseboat—"

"She did, twice. But it wasn't that easy. Why did you kill Mason?"

"I didn't, damn you!"

"I think your code name is Jason D."

"I never heard of Jason D until you first mentioned it to me."

"Leila mentioned a jealous boy friend. That could be you—and you could have killed Mason in a fight over her."

The Scotsman chuckled. "Now, now, old fellow. You can't have it both ways. If I were Leila's lover I wouldn't have needed Mason to make contact with her, would I?"

Rand hesitated, uncertain. "The knife—"

"The knife I carry is for throwing. Mason was stabbed with a direct thrust, from quite close up. The wound went directly to the heart, remember, which means it had to go up from under the ribs."

"But—"

"Why not ask the girl about it? She's quite good with a knife."

"You know a lot."

"More than you when it comes to Cairo, old boy. Go back to London where you belong."

Rand had a great deal more to say, but there seemed no point to it then. The Scotsman had beaten him, at least for the present. Besides, it was almost time for his noon meeting.

He parked the rented car at the Nile Hilton and hurried across the street to the wide shaded walk that ran along the river. The bridge of El Tahrir was straight ahead, so close to the water that passing boats had to lower their masts to go under. The water was just as muddy here, but calm and majestic somehow. This was really the Nile, in all its grandeur.

The lion he sought was on its perch, silent in stone, and the short young Egyptian was waiting at its base. "Sorry I'm late," Rand said. "There was some unfinished business."

Kharga nodded. "You have the other envelope?"

Rand handed it over and asked, "You have the figures?"

"In my mind. Write them down as I talk." Kharga was speaking fast, keeping an eye on the bridge approaches. "In July the Russians will deliver fifteen planes. In August—"

Then Rand saw her, waiting in a little car near the bridge. Leila Gaad. For a moment he thought she was waiting for him, but then in an instant he knew the truth. "Jason D," he said interrupting.

"What?" The small man stared at him.

"Jason D. It was you all along. You're Leila's lover, Kharga. You killed George Mason."

The Egyptian blinked his eyes and looked around, seeking escape. He pushed out with his hands and caught Rand off balance, sending him toppling backward. Then he was running up the short flight of stone steps to the street and the waiting car.

Rand recovered quickly and sprinted after him. For an instant he thought he would overtake him, but Kharga turned at the top of the steps, his back against the lion, and drew a short deadly dagger. Rand saw it coming, flashing in the noonday sun, too late to draw his gun. From the car Leila saw it happening too and screamed.

Then a black-hilted knife thudded into the Egyptian's chest. He stiffened, a look of shock and surprise spreading on his face, and fell forward.

The Scotsman came up the steps behind Rand. "Lucky thing I followed you. Didn't I tell you my knives were for throwing?"

An hour later, in the emergency waiting room at Cairo University Hospital, Rand faced the Scotsman and Leila. Her face was tear-stained, and she was close to hysterics. "I don't care," she mumbled. "I won't believe he killed George. Not over me."

"I'm afraid it was just that," Rand told her. "With all the spies and intrigue around it was only a love triangle that caused his death. I knew as soon as I saw you waiting for Kharga, and realized he was your jealous boy friend. You told me you'd given Mason a birthday gift—a gold pencil with a crest and pyramid that you used for personal gifts. I suppose you'd given Kharga one too, and he recognized it in Mason's hand. Of course we already knew that Mason was writing with a pencil just before he was stabbed, and it seemed logical that he'd be using his new birthday gift. Maybe Kharga asked where he'd gotten it, or maybe he knew already. Anyway, he was just as jealous as you said. He must have suspected another lover for a long time, and here he was, suddenly face to face with the man in a hotel room. He took out his dagger and stabbed Mason, poor chap."

"He claimed Mason never made contact with him," the Scotsman insisted.

"I know. That's where Jason D comes in." Rand took out the carefully folded piece of notebook paper. "You see, Mason's penciled message never did say Jason D. Rather, it consisted of the letters JASOND, spaced equally across the top of the page. He was writing it as he faced his murderer, as he waited for Kharga to give him the figures on Russian planes and technicians for Egypt during the next six months."

They looked blank.

"But don't you see?" Rand asked. "JASOND—Mason's quick and simple abbreviations for July, August, September, October, November, December. He wouldn't have written those letters if he wasn't in the very act of receiving the information from Kharga when he died. And since Kharga denied even seeing him, that made Kharga the murderer."

Leila shook her head, but now in despair rather than disbelief. "And all because he recognized the pencil," she said softly. "What do the doctors say? Will he live?"

Rand and the Scotsman exchanged glances, and he said, "I'm afraid there's not much hope. And unfortunately I never did get the information I needed from him."

But now it was the Scotsman's turn to smile. "I just might be able to help you there, Rand. There is a cook on Dontsova's houseboat who has recently proved to be most cooperative ... "

THE SPY IN THE PYRAMID

"**D**o you remember Miss Leila Gaad?" Hastings asked, leaning forward across the desk. "The young archeologist from Cairo University who helped you in the Nile Mermaid affair?"

Rand nodded. "Of course. She was of great assistance." He still remembered her soft voice and blushing face, and the fleeting kiss she'd given him at one point in their adventure. "What about her?"

"She's part of a scientific party studying the Great Pyramid of Cheops. We think something's happening there, something that interests the Russians. A Red agent recently left London to join them in Egypt."

Rand perked up at this. "Do you know who?"

Hastings shook his head. "Our informant could only say that Moscow requested an Englishman who could pass himself off as an archeologist. We don't know who they sent, but if Russia has a man there, we should look into it too. When I heard Leila Gaad was a member of the party, you seemed the right man for the job."

"What about Double-C?"

Hastings smiled. "Concealed Communications can get along without you, at least for the short time you'll be away. That's one of the penalties you pay for building up such a fine staff."

Rand gave him no argument. The London weather was turning bad, and a few days in the company of Leila Gaad just might be fun.

Cairo in October was almost as hot and dry as Cairo in June, and the political climate had also changed little since Rand's last visit. He still saw Russians everywhere in the Egyptian capital—technicians and businessmen and occasional airforce officers—brought in to help the buildup against Israel. War seemed very close.

On the morning after his arrival Rand rented a car for the ten-mile drive to the Giza plateau west of the city. Crossing the Nile at the Giza Bridge he could already see the twin pyramids of Cheops and Kephren looming large on the horizon, and as he drew closer Mykerinos and the other smaller pyramids came into view.

Cheops was the largest pyramid in Egypt, a prize of ancient grave robbers and modern scientists. Looking now over the plateau on which the pyramids rested, Rand could see a group of native Egyptians toiling at its base. There was a scattering of tourists too, and off to one side a camp of canvas tents and desert vehicles that marked the party he sought. Rand stopped the first Englishman he encountered and asked, "Is Leila Gaad around? I'm an old friend."

The man was tall and slim, with the stony-faced look of an army officer. He studied Rand for a moment and then replied, "She's over by the Sphinx with some people."

There was something bizarrely casual about the way Rand crossed the stretch of sand to the classic statue of the lion-woman. Large as it was, the Sphinx seemed dwarfed by the nearby pyramids. Three people stood in its shadow, studying the great stone face with its broken nose. He recognized Leila at once, a small dark-haired girl with the pleasing high-cheekboned features he remembered so well.

"Hello there. Sorry to interrupt, but I thought I saw a familiar face."

She turned to him, smiling, and when she spoke it was the soft familiar voice he'd known more than once in his dreams. "Mr. Rand! So good to see you again!"

"I'm in Cairo for a few days, and the University said I could find you out here."

"Yes, we're hard at work. This is Sir Stafford Jones, a countryman of yours who's financing our project, and his wife Melinda."

Sir Stafford was a wispy middle-aged man who seemed worn out in contrast with the youthful vigor of his wife. Melinda was Leila's age, still under 30, and it developed they'd known each other slightly at Cairo University. She was Sir Stafford's second wife, and the marriage was new enough so that apparently he had not yet learned to cope with her youthful high spirits.

"Girl drags me over here to look at the Sphinx, Mr. Rand, and what does it mean? All I see is a lion with the head of a woman. What *does* it mean?"

Leila smiled. "The most likely explanation is that the Sphinx is half lion and half virgin, symbolizing the junction of the constellations Leo and Virgo in the fourth millennium B.C."

Melinda joined in, agreeing. "The Egyptians knew a great deal about the stars. Some say the Great Pyramid itself was a sort of observatory."

"That's one of the theories," Leila agreed, "though not one I favor."

"Just what is your work here?" Rand asked.

"Professor Danado is in charge. He's trying to continue the experiments of Dr. Luis Alvarez, the Nobel Prize winner, in recording the passage of cosmic rays through the pyramids. By the use of a computer to analyze the recorded tapes it's possible to discover the location of any unknown chambers."

"Interesting," Rand admitted.

"The threat of war put a stop to Dr. Alvarez's work, but Professor Danado obtained permission from the government to carry on. He's a fascinating man. You'll have to meet him."

When they'd returned together to the road Sir Stafford said, "Melinda and I must be getting back to our hotel."

Leila seemed disappointed. "So soon?"

"We'll be out again tomorrow," Melinda promised. "Good meeting you, Mr. Rand."

"Odd couple," Rand commented as they drove away.

"Mismatched," Leila agreed. "But he's paying the bills so I have to be nice to him. Now tell me how you are, Rand—you look simply smashing!"

"For a man past forty I'm holding up pretty well," he grinned. "Have you been swimming in the Nile lately?"

She made a face. "How did I ever let you talk me into that?"

"I have a way with pretty Scottish-Egyptian girls."

"You remembered!"

"My business is remembering. When can I meet your Professor Danado?"

"Right now. Come on."

"He's not the thin Englishman with the stone face, is he?"

"No, that's Roger Pullman, our foreman. He handles the native labor we use to string wires and such. You should see them climbing the side of that pyramid!"

She led Rand across the sand to the base of the Great Pyramid. Close up, he could see that the individual tiers of stone were of irregular height. But some were three feet or more, making a climb to the top a more difficult task than he'd imagined. "There are two hundred and one stepped tiers in all," Leila explained. "Want to try climbing?"

"No, thanks. It's really quite ugly close up, isn't it?"

"It wasn't always. The original covering was a full mantle of polished limestone, which must have been dazzling in the sunlight. But following some earthquakes in the thirteenth and fourteenth centuries, the Arabs stripped off the mantle and used the precious limestone to rebuild their cities and construct a number of mosques in Cairo. Without the limestone the core masonry has gradually weathered."

"You know a great deal."

She grinned at him. "My business is remembering, too. Come on, I'll take you inside and introduce you to Professor Danado."

He followed her up the side of the pyramid until he thought his legs would give out. She had actually gone up only 50 feet when they reached the entrance, but it was high enough for Rand. "You expect me to crawl through there?" he asked.

"It widens out farther along. Be careful, though. The descending passage has a slope of twenty-six degrees."

Somehow Rand managed to follow her down and then up, climbing like a monkey through the low narrow passageway. At one point there was a screech and fluttering of wings as something flew by his face. "What was that?"

"Just a bat," Leila reassured him. "These passages used to be full of them."

"Look," Rand gasped, "what are you doing to me?"

She held up her flashlight and smiled back at him. "Nobody comes to see me because they just happen to be passing by a pyramid, Rand. I know what your business is, remember? I'm the girl who swam the Nile and almost got herself killed for you. We've had some strange things going on here, and now you turn up. I want to know why."

"What sort of strange things?"

"Oh, an odd little Egyptian named Hassad showed up looking for a job with the work crew. We didn't need any more men so we sent him away. The very next day a stone fell on a workman and almost killed him. Hassad returned in less than an hour and got his job."

"Coincidence," Rand suggested. "Unless someone here wanted Hassad hired badly enough to drop the stone on the other man."

"Is that why you came? Is there an enemy here among us?"

"Enemy is a relative term. An enemy of what?"

They had emerged from the narrow ascending passage into the pyramid's Grand Gallery. It was still a steep climb, but now Rand could stand upright, admiring the high-ceilinged passageway lit by battery-operated torches. When they reached the King's Chamber at the top, two men were waiting for them. Leila made the introductions. "Professor Danado of Cairo University and another countryman of yours, Graham Larkey."

Larkey was a nondescript Englishman who would have looked more at home with a bowler hat and a cane. But it was Danado who focused Rand's attention. He was a tall bearded man who gave the impression of age and wisdom while seeming to hide a ripple of muscles that would have put most athletes to shame. Rand guessed him to be still in his thirties, and in perfect physical condition.

"Always glad to have visitors," Danado said, shaking Rand's hand with a firm grip. "We've been running wires here for weeks, but we're almost ready to begin."

"Just what are you doing?"

"We have a spark chamber in the lower vault, beneath the pyramid. It will record cosmic rays from outer space as they penetrate the pyramid walls. Computer analysis should pinpoint any unknown rooms or passages. Dr. Alvarez has been quite successful with the technique on other pyramids."

"It's a big place," Rand said, understating the obvious.

Graham Larkey coughed. "Big is hardly the word! There are two and a half million blocks of limestone and granite in this pyramid—enough to build a wall around France, as Napoleon once observed, or to construct all the churches in England."

Professor Danado nodded. "Whatever its original use, as observatory, tomb, or temple of initiation, the builders performed an incredible task."

"It must have taken centuries," Rand decided.

"Only twenty years, according to Herodotus. But the manpower would have been fantastic."

After another hour inspecting the Queen's Chamber and the lower vault, Rand was eager for fresh air and daylight. They climbed down to the ground, with Larkey in the lead, and headed for the grouping of tents some hundred yards away. "Almost time for cocktails," the Englishman explained. "We must observe the amenities, you know."

The stone-faced man whom Rand had met earlier appeared from somewhere to talk in low tones with Professor Danado. After a moment Larkey joined them, leaving Rand alone with Leila Gaad. "When did Roger Pullman join your group?" he asked.

"We've only been here two weeks. Everyone came at the same time. I believe Pullman and Larkey arrived from England together. Do you think one of them—?" She was interrupted by Danado's return.

"Pullman says there's trouble with the work crew. I'll have to check on it. Meantime, Graham will furnish you with some fine London gin in his tent."

Graham Larkey prepared drinks for them, keeping up a constant flow of conversation about the pyramid. He even had a small wooden model, about a foot high, that he handed Rand for inspection. "Of course you can't tell too much from this," he said. "But the proportions and angles are correct."

"You really think there are more secret chambers?"

Larkey shrugged. "Danado is convinced of it." There was a growing roar from the sky above the tent, and Rand looked out to see a pair of Russian-built Egyptian jets streak by overhead, bound for the Cairo airport. "Don't mind the noise, Mr. Rand. We've got used to it."

"Of course you'll be staying the night," Leila said.

"I hadn't planned to," Rand replied.

"Nonsense! We have plenty of room. I've urged Sir Stafford and Melinda to stay too, but they must have their running water and other conveniences."

There was more talk while Larkey poured another batch of drinks, and presently Rand decided to stay the night. He was not unhappy at the prospect. Leila had managed to point out a dusky Egyptian workman who was the mysterious Hassad, and Rand decided it might be wise to keep an eye on him. If Hassad was an enemy agent he'd been placed there by somebody already present—most likely Pullman or Larkey, the only Englishmen on the scene.

Leila saw him to his tent at ten o'clock. "It's been a hard day. Sometimes we drive into Cairo for the evening, but after all that climbing you'd probably rather turn in."

"I think so," Rand agreed. "But I'll keep an eye open."

"Do you have a gun?"

"Will I need one?" he countered, not wanting to admit to the firm bulge under his armpit.

"I hope not."

"You mentioned strange happenings. What, besides the stone falling?"

She hesitated, then said, "All this wire strung up and down the pyramid. Dr. Alvarez's technique doesn't need that much wire."

"Have you asked Professor Danado about it?"

"No. I'm sure he has his reasons."

Rand nodded. "I'll see you in the morning."

He settled down to read a book about the pyramids by the light of his battery-powered lamp, but within an hour Leila was back at the flap of his tent. "It's Hassad," she whispered. "I saw him sneaking around. I think he's heading for Cairo."

Moving fast, Rand slipped a loose-fitting shirt over his holster and hurried across the sandy darkness. There was enough moonlight for him to make out the shadowy figure of Hassad some 50 feet ahead, moving toward the road. It seemed a simple task to trail the man, but suddenly the figure ahead of him vanished from view. Startled, Rand stopped dead, scanning the ground. Nothing moved. He went forward slowly.

Suddenly, a snakelike arm shot out, tackling him around the ankles, and Rand went down. Before he could free his gun the Egyptian was on him, tumbling him into a shallow excavation below the surface of the plateau. Rand saw the silver flicker of moonlight on a dagger's blade and jerked to one side as it descended.

He felt the steel slice through his shirt sleeve, then he got an arm free for a judo chop at his assailant's neck. Hassad grunted and dropped. Rand pulled himself free and stood up. When Hassad didn't move, he bent down to roll him over. The man was dead. He'd fallen on his own knife.

Rand's first thought, in a business where no one could be trusted, was that Leila Gaad had lured him into a trap. He was still nursing that suspicion as he went quickly through Hassad's pockets. Then his probing fingers encountered a tube, a cigarette holder with something inside it. He dropped it into his pocket and headed back to the tents.

Leila was waiting for him. "What happened?"

"A little trouble. Hassad's dead."

"You killed him?"

"An accident. He came at me with a knife."

"Should we tell the others?"

Rand thought about it. "Better not. I don't particularly want to get hung up with the local police." He took out the metal cigarette holder and saw that it had a piece of paper rolled inside.

"What's that?" Leila asked.

"I found it on him."

He unrolled the paper and revealed a message, apparently in cipher: PMION CTRAD INGCA YDWEA LARTO IROAR RORSS EWERC EAAIR AKCCR EOVER BASES.

"Can you read it?"

"With time and a little luck. That's my business."

"What do you want me to do?"

"Go back to your tent and get some sleep. And try to act surprised when they find Hassad's body in the morning."

When he was alone, Rand set to work on the cipher message before him. It appeared to be broken down into five-letter groups for transmission—a common practice—and the very fact that Hassad had been carrying it told him a great deal. The Egyptian was a courier, taking the message from someone at the pyramid to his superiors in Cairo, where it would no doubt be transmitted to Moscow. Hassad had tried to protect the message with his knife.

Rand stared down at the twelve groups of five letters each. Sixty letters in all. He checked the letter frequency first, and came up with 10 r's, 9 a's, 7 e's. But in such a short message, letter frequencies could be misleading. More interesting was the end of the message, where the words *over bases* appeared together. Coincidence?

After an hour's work Rand put the paper carefully away and went to bed. It was not as easy a job as he'd hoped.

He awoke before dawn and went back to work on the message, but still it would not yield its secret. When he heard the others moving about he joined them for breakfast, waiting for the workmen to discover Hassad's body. Over coffee and eggs Professor Danado was expounding some of the theories of pyramidology, including the somewhat far-fetched ideas of Menzies and Smyth. They were dining in Larkey's tent, and Danado said, "Hand me that pyramid model, Rand, and I'll show you what I mean."

Rand passed the wooden pyramid to him and Danado continued, "They believed that each of the passages, and the very dimensions of the pyramid, contained a chronological history of mankind. Some even claimed the Great Pyramid predicted the Second Coming of the Lord, and the end of the world."

"Rubbish!" Roger Pullman exclaimed, and Larkey nodded agreement.

As Rand listened to the talk Leila slipped into the seat at his side. She'd gone for a fresh pot of coffee and now she leaned over to whisper, "Hassad's body is gone."

Rand nodded, hoping she hadn't been overheard. Someone had decided to hide the body, for reasons of his own. He glanced down at the fingers of his left hand and saw a fine film of white dust. Sniffing, he was reminded of a schoolroom. He wondered why there'd been chalk dust on the side of Larkey's model pyramid.

Sir Stafford Jones and Melinda arrived promptly at ten o'clock for what seemed to be their daily inspection of progress. While Danado showed them around, Rand prowled the campsite, seeking a likely place where Hassad's body might have been hidden. Finally he climbed up the side of the pyramid, resting every few tiers, and inspected the wires that Danado's crew had been stringing. The place would be perfect for transmitting short-wave radio broadcasts, but then so would the tall buildings in Cairo. It seemed unlikely that spies would wire the Great Pyramid simply to use it for a transmitting tower.

"Hello there—out for a stroll?"

He glanced down and saw Melinda Jones, fetching in a yellow pants suit, clambering over the stones below him. Rand held out a hand. "This is a tough climb."

She paused beside him, panting for breath. "Are you going all the way to the top?"

"Hardly! I'm just about done in."

"I can't imagine why my husband is so interested in a pile of stones!" She opened a fresh pack of cigarettes and lit one.

"Perhaps because it's the largest pile of stones in the world."

"You may be right. Stafford has always been attracted to superlatives."

"Even in women," Rand observed gallantly.

"Thank you, sir!" She dipped in a little bow.

"But yesterday you also seemed quite interested in this pile of stones, speculating on its use as an observatory and such."

"Oh, I'm interested in everything Stafford does. I wouldn't have married him otherwise. But he has a great deal of money and I only hope he's spending it wisely here."

They climbed higher, looking out across the sands at the buildings and mosques of Cairo. "A marvelous view," he said.

"Perhaps the ancient Egyptians thought they could see the whole world from the peak of the Great Pyramid."

After a time they went back down and found Professor Danado deep in conversation with Sir Stafford. They broke apart when Melinda and Rand approached, and the talk shifted to lighter topics. Whatever was going on here, Sir Stafford obviously did not want his wife involved. Rand said a few words and then drifted off to find Leila.

He found her checking measurements at the base of the pyramid, aided by an Egyptian workman. "I saw you up there with Melinda," she said.

"Nice girl. Wonder why she married Sir Stafford."

"Money and power. In college Melinda always wanted both."

Rand was inspecting some of the graffiti left by tourists along the base of the pyramid. "They write anywhere, don't they?"

"Graffiti has a long and honorable history here. Most of the early explorers left their names on the walls of the pyramid. Even Mercator, the mapmaker, carved his name in one of the inner chambers."

Rand waited until the workman had moved off and then asked, "Leila, what do you think is going on here?"

"I have no idea, except that it's unlike any other project I've ever been on. Professor Danado seems to assign me tasks like this just to keep me out of the way."

"What about Pullman and Larkey?"

"Pullman works with him, but not Larkey so much."

"Have you ever seen Larkey marking up his model pyramid with chalk?"

"No. Why?"

"Just wondered. There was chalk dust on it this morning."

He glanced toward the main tent and saw that Melinda and Sir Stafford were leaving. "Let's say goodbye to them," he suggested.

"Fine progress," Sir Stafford was saying. "Fine, fine!"

"I do hope it's finished soon," Melinda complained. "I can't wait to get back to London. My body just isn't suited to this heat." She turned to Roger Pullman. "Mr. Pullman, do you have a cigarette? I need something to revive me after climbing halfway up that pyramid."

"Certainly," he said, handing her one. But even Melinda's charms couldn't change the stony expression on his face.

"We'll be out again tomorrow," Sir Stafford assured them.

Danado nodded. "I should be just about ready then."

Rand watched them walk across the plateau to their waiting car. Melinda was talking to her husband, gesturing with the unlit cigarette, perhaps repeating her wish to return to London soon.

That evening, after an agreeable dinner with Danado and Leila and the two Englishmen, it was decided that Rand would spend another night with them. He knew he couldn't remain indefinitely without attracting even more suspicion than he already had, but he hoped that one more night would give him the time needed to crack the cipher message. In his tent he spread the paper out flat and scanned it once again: PMION CTRAD INGCA YDWEA LARTO IROAR RORSS EWERC EAAIR AKCCR EOVER BASES.

Sixty letters. He started writing them in columns, and after a moment a slow smile began to spread over his face.

"Rand!" Leila burst into his tent. "They've found Hassad's body. It was buried in the sand near one of the smaller pyramids."

"It doesn't matter now. My job is about finished."

"The cipher?"

He nodded. "Let's go see Professor Danado, Pullman, and Larkey."

They met in Danado's tent, where the lamps had been lit as dusk settled over the area. There was a new urgency about the professor, and his bearded face betrayed the hint of a troubled man.

"What do you know of Hassad's murder?" he asked Rand.

"It wasn't murder. He fell on his own knife while trying to kill me last night."

"And you hid the body?"

"Someone else did that." Rand glanced toward Graham Larkey.

"Just what is your business here, Mr. Rand?"

"This." He laid the slip of paper down on the table before them.

Danado's eyelids shot up. "You can read this?"

"Yes."

"What does it say?"

Rand turned to Leila. "Could you get me the model pyramid out of Larkey's tent, please?"

The Englishman bristled. "What do you want my pyramid for?"

"To unscramble this message, the same way it was originally scrambled. You see, this is a transposition cipher rather than a substitution one. The letters retain their true identities but are merely mixed up. The chalk dust on the wooden sides of that model pyramid tipped me off that the model served as the device for enciphering the message. In most transposition ciphers the message is written in a square grid, and the letters are then read vertically instead of horizontally. Here the four sides of the pyramid were used—like this."

Rand began chalking the message on the side of the pyramid:

<pre>
        P
       M I
      O N C
     T R A D
    I N G C A
</pre>

He turned the pyramid and did the same on the second side:

Y
D W
E A L
A R T O
I R O A R

The third side:

R
O R
S S E
W E R C
E A A I R

And the fourth:

A
K C
C R E
O V E R
B A S E S

"Now, we read it a line at a time, starting with the top letter *on each side*—P, Y, R, A. Then to the second line *on each side*—M, I, D, W, O, R, K, C. And so on. When all sixty letters are written in their correct order, and separated into the obvious words, we have a message that reads: *Pyramid work conceals secret radar tower covering Cairo area air bases.*"

"Very interesting," Professor Danado said quietly. His hand came from beneath the table, and it was holding a gun. "Now will you please raise your hands?"

Rand took a step backward and obeyed. He'd learned never to argue with a gun. "All right. You seem to have the upper hand."

Danado shifted the gun an inch to include Graham Larkey. "You too, Graham. Put up your hands."

"What is this?"

"Did you send this message?"

"I don't know a thing about it! What's this business about a radar tower?"

"A very clever plan," Rand interjected. "The Great Pyramid is, in a sense, a building more than forty stories high, towering over the city of Cairo. From this position radar could cover the movement of all aircraft, the firing of all missiles. Any radar in Israel is restricted, of course, by the natural curvature of the earth. Low-flying planes are safe from detection, except by radar units mounted on other aircraft. But a secret radar station hidden in the Great Pyramid would be an important weapon for Israel—the ultimate in espionage."

Larkey's mouth hung open. "Does he mean, Professor, that you're an

Israeli agent?"

"I'm doing what has to be done. And what about you, Larkey? Did you write that message?"

"Hell, no! Pullman borrowed the model last night. Said he wanted to figure something out."

"Pullman?"

They suddenly realized that Pullman was no longer with them. He'd slipped out at the very beginning of Rand's explanation. "Put that gun away," Rand told Danado. "I may not be with you, but I'm certainly not against you. If Pullman is the spy—"

He was interrupted by the blaring of an auto horn from somewhere on the road. Danado hesitated only an instant before pocketing the gun. "No tricks, Rand! Let's see what's happening."

Outside, in the hazy twilight close to night, they saw two figures running from the road. Rand recognized Sir Stafford and Melinda. "Take cover!" Sir Stafford shouted. "The Egyptians know everything! Army units are right behind us!"

As if to punctuate his words, a line of fast-moving troop carriers came into view on the road, their spotlights scanning the desert plateau. From one of the other tents a figure appeared, and Rand saw that it was Roger Pullman. He carried an army .45 automatic and there was a look of triumph on his usually stony face. "Stay right there!" he shouted. "You're prisoners of the Egyptian government."

Professor Danado, stepping behind Rand, pulled his gun from his pocket. He fired twice as Pullman's first shot went wild, and dropped the Englishman in his tracks.

"Good shooting!" Sir Stafford exclaimed.

"But I don't like being used as a shield," Rand grumbled.

Melinda ran over to the body. "He's dead. Was he a spy?"

"You should keep your wife better informed," Danado told Sir Stafford.

"The less she knew, the better. Sorry, dear." He glanced over his shoulder. "Those army units seem to be surrounding us. Any suggestions, Professor?"

Danado debated only an instant. "To the pyramid! We'll be safe in there from small-arms fire and they wouldn't dare use artillery on it."

They ran toward the towering pyramid, Melinda and Leila in front, followed by Graham Larkey. Rand, Sir Stafford, and Danado were bunched together at the rear, as if no one wanted to present his back to the others.

"That was good work on the cipher," Danado admitted as they reached the pyramid and started the climb to the entrance. "Too bad you didn't come up with it sooner, before Pullman sent it."

"I stopped Hassad from delivering the first message," Rand said. "But there must have been a second one."

They stared down from the pyramid at the line of troop carriers and half-tracks taking up positions around them. An amplified voice cut suddenly through the night. "The Egyptian government calls upon you to surrender at once as enemies of the state!"

"Now what?" Sir Stafford asked Danado.

The bearded professor did not answer. Instead he knelt on a slab of stone and took careful aim with his pistol. He fired at the nearest spotlight and hit it squarely. As the light died there was an answering burst of small-arms fire from below. A bullet zinged off the rocks above Rand's head. Then there was a barked command from below and the firing ceased.

"They'll send troops up the other sides to encircle us," Danado decided. "We can go inside, but we've no way out."

"Al-Mamun's passage," Larkey suggested. "That's below us."

"They know about that. They're Egyptians, remember? This is their thing." Danado took aim and hit another spotlight. This time there was no answering fire.

"There's one way out," Rand said. "Get on that radio."

Danado frowned. "What radio?"

"This is no time for games. You must have short-wave contact with Israel. Otherwise what good would a secret radar station be?"

"You're right, of course," Danado admitted.

"Tell them we need help."

"What can they do? Start a war just to save us?"

"Remember that commando raid by helicopter last year? They carried off a whole Egyptian radar station from Shadwan Island. Maybe they can get us out."

"Rand, we're ten miles west of Cairo!" Danado protested.

"It's that or spend a few years rotting in an Egyptian jail."

Danado drew in his breath and nodded. "Take this," he said, handing Rand the gun. "Use it if they start up this side of the pyramid, toward us or al-Mamun's passage. I'll be back." He retreated down the shaft into the heart of the pyramid.

"I'm scared," Melinda said. "How in the world did I get involved in this?"

"All my fault," Sir Stafford said. "I've been financing this project on behalf of Israel. But I couldn't let you know. It had to look like a scientific project, to keep the Egyptians from getting suspicious."

"What about Pullman?" Larkey asked. "Who was he?"

"A spy in the pay of the Russians," Rand explained. "That's what brought me here."

"But what made the Russians suspicious in the first place? The radar station isn't even in use yet."

"That's a very interesting question," Rand admitted.

There was a crackling from below and then another call on the loudspeaker for their surrender. Rand fired a shot in the air, just to keep them on their toes. He hoped they'd wait till daylight to storm the pyramid, but he knew it was a dim hope.

Suddenly Danado was back, panting for breath. "They'll do what they can," he said. "We're to climb to the top."

"All the way?"

"All the way. We'd better get started."

It was a difficult climb in the dark, made even more difficult with the women along. Before they had gone halfway they could hear the first soldiers starting up after them. Rand was beginning to sweat, helping Leila over the tiers of stone while the others helped Melinda. "How much farther?" he gasped to Danado after they'd been climbing nearly an hour.

"My count makes this the one hundred and seventy-eighth tier, and there are two hundred and one in all. Let's rest here and then go on to the top."

Behind them, still far down, there was a scrambling over stone. "They think they've got us cornered," Larkey said.

"If those helicopters don't come they'll be right." Sir Stafford scanned the eastern sky, but there were no lights visible.

"You mean we're going to have to go up rope ladders or something after a climb like this?" Melinda moaned.

"I only hope we get the chance," Danado replied. "Egyptian jails can be unpleasant. Come on, rest period's over."

Slowed down by the effects of the climb it took them nearly half an hour more to reach the top. Then, standing on what seemed the roof of the world, Rand felt more helpless than ever. The climbing below them seemed to have stopped, but now new and more powerful searchlights had arrived and were sweeping their beams across the face of the pyramid.

Then suddenly a sound of sirens reached their ears, coming from the direction of Cairo. "Air raid," Danado said. "This may be it!"

As they stood waiting, four men and two women atop the Great Pyramid of Cheops, Rand heard at last the whirling of blades above their head. "Helicopters coming in!"

Two large troop-carrying copters emerged from the night and hovered above them, rotors chopping at the air. There were a few shots from the ground, but they were high enough to be out of accurate range. A light shone down from the nearest copter, and a rope ladder snaked down.

"We're going up," Danado said. "Ladies first."

The troops on the ground had stopped firing, but only because jet interceptors were already taking off from the nearby air base. Rand could see their fiery tails as his turn came to climb the rope ladder. He wondered if this would be his end, hanging here in the sky above a pyramid.

But he made it to the shelter of the helicopter along with the others and stretched out panting on the floor. "Good show," an Israeli with a British accent told them. "Didn't think you'd make it."

"We haven't made it yet," Sir Stafford advised him. "Those are Egyptian jets out the side window."

The jets moved in close, but did not open fire. They seemed to be waiting for something. Rand pulled Leila close and whispered in her ear. He was taking a chance, and he hoped he was right.

Suddenly, as the helicopters turned northeast toward home, Melinda Jones made her move. She yanked open the door of the pilot's compartment and pointed a tiny gun. "We're not going back to Israel," she announced. "We're landing at Cairo airport."

"Melinda! What in hell is this?" Sir Stafford took a step forward and she turned the gun on him. In that moment, her face grim with determination, Rand really believed she would shoot her husband.

But then Leila pounced on her back, fists flying, knocking the gun aside and forcing Melinda to the copter's floor. Rand moved in to scoop up the gun.

"Tell them you're landing," he ordered the pilot. "But when the jets start down, reverse yourself and take off, straight up. At their speed they won't be able to turn quickly enough to follow."

The man obeyed instructions, and the craft shot suddenly upward with the second helicopter following. A burst of antiaircraft fire hit near enough to jar them, but then suddenly the skies seemed quiet.

"What about Melinda?" Sir Stafford asked. "I can't believe it!"

"I think you'll find she was planted by the Russians, sir. If you'll pardon me, you were just the right age to be looking for a young wife. With your reputation for financing causes she must have been suspicious of this pyramid thing. She needed an agent on the inside, actually part of the group, so she asked the Russians for help and they sent Pullman. He, in turn, arranged for Hassad to carry messages to Melinda in Cairo. The cipher message was meant for her, after Pullman had learned about the secret radar station."

"How did you know?" Danado asked. "You warned Leila to jump her when she pulled the gun."

"When the firing stopped I figured it meant one of their people was aboard. That meant she'd try to force us to land. As for its being Melinda, consider the facts. Someone told the Russians to send Pullman. Someone got Pullman's second message and told the Egyptians tonight. But how did Pullman deliver the message after Hassad died and Pullman hid the body?

"Well, Hassad had the first message rolled up in a cigarette holder. Pullman simply varied the technique slightly and rolled the second message in a cigarette. You'll remember that Melinda asked him for a cigarette today at the pyramid, even though I'd seen her just open a fresh pack of her own. *And then she didn't light it!* She carried it unlit in her hand. That had to contain the second message."

"Smart," Melinda said from the floor. "But you're not out of it yet."

"Yes, we are," Danado corrected her. "We've just crossed Suez. We're safe now."

"But you didn't win!" she spat. "You didn't get your damned radar station!"

"Neither side won," Danado agreed. "Another draw decision in a long and fruitless war."

Rand walked to the front of the copter where Leila sat. "Are you all right?"

"I guess so. This time was worse than swimming the Nile."

"Sorry about that."

"And they probably won't let me back into Egypt."

"We have some fine old ruins in England," he said, "if you want to try them sometime."

She smiled up at him. "I just might do that."

THE SPY AT THE END OF THE RAINBOW

Rand was in Cairo looking for Leila Gaad when he first heard about the End of the Rainbow. It had been nearly two years since they had fled the city together by helicopter with half the Egyptian Air Force in pursuit, but a great many things had changed in those two years. Most important, the Russians were gone. Only a few stragglers remained behind from the thousands of technicians and military advisers who had crowded the city back in those days.

Rand liked the city better without the Russians, though he was the first to admit that their departure had done little to ease tensions in the Middle East. There were still the terrorists and the almost weekly incidents, still the killings and the threats of war from both sides. In a world mainly at peace, Cairo was still a city where a spy could find work.

He'd come searching for Leila partly because he simply wanted to see her again, but mainly because one of her fellow archeologists at Cairo University had suddenly become a matter of deep concern to British Intelligence. It was not, at this point, a case for the Department of Concealed Communications, but Hastings had been quick to enlist Rand's help when it became obvious that his old friend Leila Gaad might have useful information.

So he was in Cairo on a warm April day. Unfortunately, Leila Gaad was not in Cairo. Rand had visited the University to ask about her, and been told by a smiling Greek professor, "Leila has gone to the End of the Rainbow."

"The end of the rainbow?" Rand asked, his mind conjuring up visions of pots of gold.

"The new resort hotel down on Foul Bay. There's a worldwide meeting of archeologists in progress, and two of our people are taking part."

It seemed too much to hope for, but Rand asked the question anyway. "Would the person accompanying Leila be Herbert Fanger, by any chance?"

The Greek's smile widened. "You know Professor Fanger, too?"

"Only by reputation."

"Yes, they are down there together, representing Cairo University. With the meeting in our country we could hardly ignore it."

"Are the Russians represented, too?"

"The Russians, the Americans, the British, the French, and the Chinese. It's a truly international event."

Rand took out his notebook. "I just might drop in on that meeting. Could you tell me how to get to the End of the Rainbow?"

Foul Bay was an inlet of the Red Sea, perched on its western shore in the southeastern corner of Egypt. (For Rand the ancient land would always be Egypt. He could never bring himself to call it the United Arab Republic.) It was located just north of the Sudanese border in an arid, rocky region that all but straddled the Tropic of Cancer. Rand thought it was probably the last place on earth that anyone would ever build a resort hotel.

But that was before his hired car turned off the main road and he saw the lush irrigated oasis, before he caught a glimpse of the sprawling group of white buildings overlooking the bay. He passed under a multihued sign announcing *The End of the Rainbow*, and was immediately on a rainbow-colored pavement that led directly to the largest of the buildings.

The first person he encountered after parking the car was an armed security guard. Rand wondered at the need for a guard in such a remote area, but he followed the man into the administrative area. A small Englishman wearing a knit summer suit rose from behind a large white desk to greet him. "What have we here?"

Rand presented his credentials. "It's important that I speak to Miss Leila Gaad. I understand she is a guest at this resort."

The man bowed slightly. "I am Felix Bollinger, manager of the End of the Rainbow. We're always pleased to have visitors, even from British Intelligence."

"I haven't seen all of it, but it's quite a place. Who owns it?"

"A London-based corporation. We're still under construction, really. This conference of archeologists is something of a test run for us."

"You did all this irrigation work, too?"

The small man nodded. "That was the most expensive part—that and cleaning up the bay. Now I'm petitioning the government to change the name from Foul Bay to Rainbow Bay. Foul Bay is hardly a designation to attract tourists."

"I wish you luck." Rand was looking out at the water, which still seemed a bit scummy to him.

"But you wanted to see Miss Gaad. According to the schedule of events, this is a free hour. I suspect you'll find her down at the pool with the others." He pointed to a door. "Out that way."

"Thank you."

"Ask her to show you around. You've never seen any place quite like the End of the Rainbow."

"I've decided that already."

Rand went out the door indicated and strolled down another rainbow-colored path to the pool area. A half-dozen people were splashing in the water, and it took him only a moment to pick out the bikini-clad figure of Leila Gaad. She was small and dark-haired, but with a swimmer's perfect body that glistened as she pulled herself from the pool.

"Hello again," he said, offering her a towel. "Remember me?"

She looked up at him, squinting against the sunlight. "It's Mr. Rand, isn't it?"

"You're still so formal."

Her face seemed even more youthful than he remembered, with high cheekbones and deep dark eyes that always seemed to be mocking him. "I'm afraid to ask what brings you here," she said.

"As usual, business." He glanced at the others in the pool. Four men, mostly middle-aged, and one woman who might have been Leila's age or a little older—perhaps 30. One man was obviously Oriental. The others, in bathing trunks, revealed no national traits that Rand could recognize. "Where could we talk?" he asked.

"Down by the bay?" She slipped a terrycloth jacket over her shoulders.

"Bollinger said you might show me around the place. How about that?"

"Fine." She led him back up the walk toward the main building where they encountered another man who looked younger than the others.

"Not leaving me already, are you?" he asked Leila.

"Just showing an old friend around. Mr. Rand, from London—this is Harvey Northgate, from Columbia University in the United States. He's here for the conference."

They shook hands and the American said, "Take good care of her, Rand. There are only two women in the place." He continued down the walk to the pool.

"Seems friendly enough," Rand observed.

"They're all friendly. It's the most fun I've ever had at one of these conferences." Glancing sideways at him, she asked, "But how did you manage to get back into the country? Did they drop you by parachute?"

"Hardly. You're back, aren't you?"

"But not without the University pulling strings. Then of course the Russians left and that eased things considerably." She had led him to a center court with white buildings on all sides. "Each building has nine large suites of rooms, and you can see there are nine buildings in the cluster, plus the administrative complex. Those eight are still being finished, though. Only the one we're occupying has been completed."

"That's only eighty-one units in all," Rand observed.

"Enough, at the rates they plan to charge! The rumor is that Bollinger's company wants to show a profit and then sell the whole thing to Hilton." They turned off the main path and she pointed to the colored stripes. "See? The colors of the rainbow show you where you're going. Follow the blue to the pool, the yellow to the lounge."

The completed building, like the others, was two stories high. There were four suites on the first floor and five on the floor above. "How are you able to afford all this?" Rand asked.

"There's a special rate for the conference because they're not fully open yet. And the University's paying for Professor Fanger and me." She led him down the hall of the building. "Each of these nine suites has a different color scheme—the seven colors of the spectrum, plus black and white. Here's mine—the orange suite. The walls, drapes, bedspreads, shower curtain—even the ashtrays and telephone—are all orange." She opened a ceramic orange cigarette box. "See, even orange cigarettes! Professor Fanger has yellow ones, and he doesn't even smoke."

"Who's in the black suite?"

"The American, Harvey Northgate. He was upset when he heard it, but the rooms are really quite nice. All the black is trimmed with white. I like all the suites, except maybe the purple. I told Bollinger he should make that one pink instead."

"You say Professor Fanger is in yellow?"

"Yes. It's so bright and cheerful!"

"I came out from London to check on the possibility that he might be a former Russian agent we've been hunting for years. We arrested a man in Liverpool last week and he listed Fanger as one of his former contacts."

Leila Gaad chuckled. "Have you ever met Herbert Fanger?"

"Not yet," he admitted.

"He's the most unlikely-looking spy imaginable."

"They make the best kind."

"No, really! He's fat and over forty, but he still imagines himself a ladies' man. He wears outlandish clothes, with loud colors most men wouldn't be caught dead in, even these days. He's hardly my idea of an unobtrusive secret agent."

"From what we hear, he's retired. He used the code name Sphinx while he was gathering information and passing it to Russia."

"If he's retired, why do you want to talk to him?"

"Because he knows a great deal, especially about the agents with whom he used to work. Some of those are retired now too, but others are still active, spying for one country or another."

"Where do I come in?" she asked suspiciously. "I've already swum the Nile and climbed the Great Pyramid for you, but I'm not going to betray Herbert Fanger to British Intelligence. He's a funny little man but I like him. What he was ten years ago is over and done with."

"At least you can introduce me, can't you?"

"I suppose so," she agreed reluctantly.

"Was he one of those at the pool?"

"Heavens, no! He'd never show up in bathing trunks. I imagine he's in the lounge watching television."

"Television, this far from Cairo?"

"It's closed-circuit, just for the resort. They show old movies."

Herbert Fanger was in the lounge as she'd predicted, but he wasn't watching old movies on television. He was deep in conversation with Bollinger, the resort manager. They separated when Rand and Leila entered the large room, and Bollinger said, "Well, Mr. Rand! Has she been showing you our place?"

"I'm doubly impressed now that I've seen it."

"Come back in the autumn when we're fully open. Then you'll really see something!"

"Could I get a room for tonight? It's a long drive back to Cairo."

Bollinger frowned and consulted his memory. "Let me see … The indigo suite is still vacant, if you'd like that."

"Fine."

"I'll get you the key. You can have the special rate, even though you're not part of the conference."

As he hurried away, Leila introduced Fanger. "Professor Herbert Fanger, perhaps the world's leading authority on Cleopatra and her era."

"Pleased to meet you," Rand said.

Fanger was wearing a bright-red sports shirt and checkered pants that did nothing to hide his protruding stomach. Seeing him, Rand had to admit he made a most unlikely-looking spy. "We were just talking about the place," he told Rand. "What do you think it cost?"

"I couldn't begin to guess."

"Tell them, Felix," he said as the manager returned with Rand's key.

Bollinger answered with a trace of pride. "With the irrigation and landscaping, plus cleaning up the bay, it will come close to seven million dollars. The highest cost per unit of any resort hotel."

Rand was impressed. But after a few more moments of chatting he remembered the reason for his trip. "Could I speak to you in private, Professor, about some research I'm doing?"

"Regarding Cleopatra?"

"Regarding the Sphinx."

There was a flicker of something in Fanger's eyes. He excused himself and went with Rand. When they were out of earshot he said, "You're British Intelligence, aren't you? Bollinger told me."

"Concealed Communications, to be exact. I know this country, so they sent me to talk with you."

"I've been retired since the mid-sixties."

"We know that. It took us that long to track you down. We're not after you, but you must have a great many names in your mind. We'd be willing to make a deal for those names."

Fanger's eyes flickered again. "I might be interested. I don't know. Coming here and talking to me openly could have been a mistake."

"You mean there's someone here who—"

"Look, Rand, I'm forty-seven years old and about that many pounds overweight. I retired before I got myself killed, and I don't know that I want to take any risks now. Espionage is a young man's game, always was. Your own Somerset Maugham quit it after World War One to write books. I quit it to chase women."

"Having any luck?"

"Here?" he snorted. "I think Leila's a twenty-eight-year-old virgin and the French one is pure bitch. Not much choice."

"Exactly what is the purpose of this conference?"

"Simply to discuss recent advances in archeology. Each of five nations sent a representative, and of course the University thought Leila and I should attend, too. There's nothing sinister about it—of that I can assure you!" But his eyes weren't quite so certain.

"Then why the armed guards patrolling the grounds?"

"You'd have to ask Bollinger—though I imagine he'd tell you there are occasional thieving nomads in the region. Without guards this place would be too tempting."

"How far is it to the nearest town?"

"More than a hundred miles overland to Aswan—nothing closer except native villages and lots of sand."

"An odd place to hold a conference. An odder place to build a plush resort."

"Once the Suez Canal is back in full operation, Bollinger expects to get most of his clientele by boat—wealthy yachtsmen and the like. Who knows? He might make a go of it. Once it's cleaned up, Foul Bay could make a natural anchorage."

They had strolled out of the building and around the cluster of white structures still in various stages of completion. Rand realized the trend of the conversation had got away from him. He'd not traveled all the way from London to discuss a resort hotel with Herbert Fanger. But then suddenly Leila reappeared with another of the male conferees—a distinguished white-haired man with a neatly trimmed Vandyke beard. Rand remembered seeing him lounging by the pool. Now he reached out to shake hands as Leila introduced him.

"Oh, Mr. Rand, here's a countryman of yours. Dr. Wayne Evans, from Oxford."

The bearded Dr. Evans grinned cheerfully. "Pleased to meet you, Rand. I always have to explain that I'm not a medical doctor and I'm not with the University. I simply live in Oxford and write books on various aspects of archeology."

"A pleasure to meet you in any event," Rand said. He saw that Fanger had taken advantage of the interruption to get away, but there would be time for him later. "I've been trying to get a straight answer as to what this conference is all about, but everyone seems rather vague about it."

Dr. Evans chuckled. "The best way to explain it is for you to sit in at our morning session. You may find it deadly dull, but at least you'll know as much as the rest of us."

"I'd enjoy it," Rand said. He watched Evans go down the walk, taking the path that led to the pool and then changing his mind and heading for the lounge. Then Rand turned his attention to Leila, who'd remained at his side.

"As long as you're here you can escort me to dinner tonight," she said. "Then your long drive won't have been a total waste."

He reacted to her impish smile with a grin of his own. "How do you know it's been a waste so far?"

"Because I've known Herbert Fanger for three years and never gotten a straight answer out of him yet. I don't imagine you did much better."

"You're quite correct," he admitted. "Come on, let's eat."

He checked in at the indigo suite he'd been assigned and found it not nearly as depressing as he'd expected from the color. Like the black suite, the dominant color had been liberally bordered in white, and the effect proved to be quite pleasant. He was beginning to think that the End of the Rainbow might catch on, if anyone could afford to stay there.

Over dinner Leila introduced him to the other conferees he hadn't met—Jeanne Bisset from France, Dr. Tao Liang from the People's Republic of China, and Ivan Rusanov from Russia. With Fanger and Northgate and Evans, whom he'd met previously, that made six attending the conference, not counting Leila herself.

"Dr. Tao should really be in the yellow suite," Rand observed quietly to Leila. "He would be if Bollinger had any imagination."

"And I suppose you'd have Rusanov in red?"

"Of course!"

"Well, he is, for your information. But Dr. Tao is green."

"That must leave the Frenchwoman, Jeanne Bisset, in violet."

"Wrong! She's white. Bollinger left indigo and violet empty, though now you have indigo."

"He implied that was the only suite empty. I wonder what's going on in violet."

"Nameless orgies, no doubt—with all you Englishmen on the premises."

"I should resent that," he said with a smile. She put him at ease, and he very much enjoyed her company.

After dinner the others split into various groups. Rand saw the Chinese and the Russian chatting, and the American, Harvey Northgate, walking off by himself. "With those other suites free, why do you think Bollinger insisted on giving the black one to the American?" Rand asked Leila as they strolled along the edge of the bay.

"Perhaps he's anti-American, who knows?"

"You don't take the whole thing very seriously."

"Should I, Mr. Rand?"

"Can't you find something else to call me?"

"I never knew your first name."

"C. Jeffery Rand, and I don't tell anyone what the C. stands for."

"You don't look like a Jeffery," she decided, cocking her head to gaze up at him. "You look more like a Winston."

"I may be Prime Minister someday."

She took his arm and steered him back toward the cluster of lighted buildings. "When you are, I'll walk along the water with you. Till then, we stay far away from it. The last time I was near water with you, I ended up swimming across the Nile to spy on a Russian houseboat!"

"It was fun, wasn't it?"

"Sure. So was climbing that pyramid in the middle of the night. My legs ached for days."

It was late by the time they returned to their building. Some people were still in the lounge, but the lights in most suites were out. "We grow tired early here," she said. "I suppose it's all the fresh air and exercise."

"I know what you mean. It was a long drive down this morning." He glanced at his watch and saw that it was already after ten. They'd strolled and chatted longer than he'd realized. "One thing first. I'd like to continue my conversation with Fanger if he's still up."

"Want me to come along?" she suggested. "Then we can both hear him say nothing."

"Come on. He might surprise you."

Fanger's yellow suite was at the rear of the first floor, near a fire exit. He didn't answer Rand's knock, and they were about to check the lounge when Rand noticed a drop of fresh orange paint on the carpet under the door. "This is odd."

"What?"

"Paint, and still wet."

"The door's unlocked, Rand."

They pushed it open and snapped on the overhead light. What they saw was unbelievable. The entire room—ceiling, walls, floor—had been splashed with paint of every color. There was red and blue and green and black and white and violet and orange—all haphazardly smeared over every surface in the room. Over it all, ashtrays and towels meant for other suites had been dumped and scattered. Fanger's yellow cigarette box was smashed on the floor, with blue and yellow cigarettes, green and indigo towels, even an orange ashtray, scattered around it. The suite was a surrealistic dream, as if at the end of the rainbow all the colors of the spectrum had been jumbled with white and black.

And crumpled in one corner, half hidden by a chair, was the body of Herbert Fanger. The red of his blood was almost indistinguishable from the paint that stained the yellow wall behind him. He'd been stabbed several times in the chest and abdomen.

"My God," Leila breathed. "It's a scene from hell!"

"Let's phone the nearest police," Rand said. "We need help here."

But as they turned to leave, a voice from the hall said, "I'm afraid that will be impossible, Mr. Rand. There will be no telephoning by anyone." Felix Bollinger stood there with one of his armed security guards, and the guard was pointing a pistol at them both.

Rand raised his hands reluctantly above his head, and at his side Leila Gaad said with a sigh, "You've done it to me again, haven't you, Rand?"

They were ushered into Bollinger's private office and the door was locked behind them. Only then did the security guard holster his revolver. He stood with his back to the door as Bollinger took a seat behind the desk.

"You must realize, Mr. Rand, that I cannot afford to have the End of the Rainbow implicated in a police investigation at this time."

"I'm beginning to realize it."

"You and Miss Gaad will be held here in my office until that room can be cleaned up and some disposition made of Herbert Fanger's body."

"And you expect me to keep silent about that?" Rand asked. "I'm here on an official mission concerning Herbert Fanger. His murder is a matter of great interest to the British government."

"This is no longer British soil, Mr. Rand. It has not been for some decades."

"But you are a British citizen."

"Only when it pleases me to be."

"What's going on here? Why the armed guards? Why was Fanger murdered?"

"It does not concern you, Mr. Rand."

"Did you kill him?"

"Hardly!"

Rand shifted in his chair. "Then the killer is one of the others. Turn me loose and I might be able to find him for you."

Bollinger's eyes narrowed. "Just how would you do that?"

"With all that paint splashed around, the killer must have gotten some on him. There was a spot of orange paint on the carpet outside the door, for instance, as if it had come off the bottom of a shoe. Let me examine everyone's clothing and I'll identify the murderer."

The manager was a man who reached quick decisions. "Very well, if I have your word you'll make no attempt to get in touch with the authorities."

"They have to be told sooner or later."

"Let's make it later. If we have the killer to hand over, it might not look quite so bad."

Rand got to his feet. "I'll want another look at Fanger's room. Put a guard on the door and don't do any cleaning up."

"What about the body?"

"It can stay there for now," Rand decided. "If we find the killer, it'll be in the next hour or so."

Leila followed him out of the office, still amazed. "How did you manage that? He had a gun on us ten minutes ago, and you talked your way out of it!"

"Not completely. Not yet. His security people will be watching us. Look, suppose you wake everyone up and get them down by the pool."

"All right," she agreed. "But what for?"

"We're going to look for paint spots."

The American, Harvey Northgate, refused to be examined at first. And the Russian demanded to call his embassy in Cairo. But after Rand explained what it was all about, they seemed to calm down. The only trouble was, Rand and Leila could find no paint on any of them. It seemed impossible, but it was true. Rand's hope of reaching a quick solution to the mystery burst like an over-inflated balloon.

It was Bollinger himself who provided an explanation, when the others had been allowed to return to their beds. "I discovered where the paint cans and the rest of it came from. Look, the side exit from this building is only a few steps away from the side exit to that building still under construction. Just inside the door are paint cans, boxes of towels and ashtrays, and even a pair of painter's coveralls."

"Show me," Rand said. He looked around for Leila but she was gone. Perhaps the day really had tired her out.

The resort manager led Rand to the unfinished building. Looking at the piles of paint cans, Rand had little doubt that this was the source of the vandal's supplies. He opened a box of red bath towels and a carton of blue ashtrays. "Anything else here?" he asked.

"Just drapes. Apparently he didn't have time for those."

"What about the carpeting? And soap and cigarettes?"

"They're stored in one of the other buildings. He just took what was close at hand. And he wore a painter's coveralls over his own clothes."

"I suppose so," Rand agreed. The splotches of paint seemed fresh, still tacky to his touch. "What I'd like to know is why—why risk discovery by going after that paint and the other things? He had to make at least two trips, one with the paint cans and the second to return the coveralls and probably gather up a few other things to throw around the room. Who knew these things were here?"

"They all did. I took them on a tour of the place the first day and showed them in here."

"Coveralls," Rand mused, "but no shoes. The shoes with the orange paint might still turn up."

"Or might not. He could have tossed them into the bay."

"All right," Rand conceded. "I'm at a dead end. We'll have to call in the authorities."

"No."

"What do you mean, no?"

"Just what I said. The people here don't want publicity. Nor do I."

"They're not archeologists, are they?"

"Not exactly," Bollinger admitted.

"Then what were Leila and Fanger doing here?"

"A mistake. Cairo University believed our cover story and sent them down for the conference. Fanger, a retired agent himself, knew something was wrong from the beginning. Then you came, and it scared one of them enough to commit murder."

"You have to tell me what's going on here," Rand said.

"A conference."

"Britain, America, France, Russia, and China. A secret conference in the middle of nowhere, policed by armed guards." He remembered something. "And what about the violet room? Who's in there?"

"You ask too many questions. Here's a list of all our guests."

Rand accepted the paper and scanned it quickly, refreshing his memory:

First Floor: Red—Ivan Rusanov (Russia)
    Orange—Leila Gaad (Egypt)
    Yellow—Herbert Fanger (Egypt)
    Green—Dr. Tao Liang (China)
Second Floor: Blue—Dr. Wayne Evans (Britain)
    Indigo—Rand
    Violet—
    White—Jeanne Bisset (France)
    Black—Harvey Northgate (U.S.)

"The violet suite is empty?" Rand questioned.

"It is empty."

Rand pocketed the list. "I'm going to look around."

"We've cut the telephone service. It will do you no good to try phoning out. Only the hotel extensions are still in operation."

"Thanks for saving me the effort." He had another thought. "You know, this list doesn't include some very good suspects—yourself and your employees."

"I would never have created that havoc. And my guards would have used a gun rather than a knife."

"What about the cooks and maids? The painters working on the other buildings?"

"Question them if you wish," he said. "You'll discover nothing."

Rand left him and cut through the lounge to the stairway. He was anxious to check out that violet suite. It was now after midnight, and there was no sign of the others, though he hardly believed they were all in their beds.

He paused before the violet door and tried the knob. It was unlocked, and he wondered if he'd find another body. Fanger's door had been left unlocked so that the killer could return with the paint cans. He wondered why this one was unlocked. But he didn't wonder long.

"Felix? Is that you?" a woman's voice called from the bedroom. It was the Frenchwoman, Jeanne Bisset.

"No, just me," Rand said, snapping on the overhead light.

She sat up in bed, startled. "What are you doing here?"

"It's as much my room as yours. I'm sorry Felix Bollinger was delayed. It's been a busy night."

"I ... "

"You don't have to explain. I was wondering why he kept this suite vacant, and now I know." He glanced around at the violet furnishings, deciding it was the least attractive of those he'd seen.

"Have you found the killer?" she asked, recovering her composure. She was a handsome woman, older than Leila, and Rand wondered if she and Bollinger had known each other before this week.

"Not yet," he admitted. "It might help if you were frank with me."

She blinked her eyes. "About what?"

"The purpose of this conference."

She thought about that. Finally she said, "Hand me a cigarette from my purse and I'll tell you what I know."

He reached in, found a case full of white cigarettes ringed in black, and passed her one. "Is the house brand any good?" he asked. "I used to smoke American cigarettes all the time, but I managed to give them up."

"They're free and available," she said, lighting one. "Something like Felix Bollinger himself."

"You were going to talk about the conference," he reminded her.

"Yes, the conference. A gathering of do-gooders trying to change the world. But the world cannot be changed, can it?"

"That all depends. You're not archeologists, then?"

"No. Although the Russian, Rusanov, knew enough about it to fake a few lectures after Fanger and Miss Gaad turned up. No, Mr. Rand, in truth we're nothing more than peace activists. Our five nations—America, France, Britain, China, Russia—are the only ones who have perfected nuclear weapons."

"Of course! I should have realized that!"

"We are meeting here—with funds provided by peace groups and ban-the-bomb committees in our homelands—to work out some coordinated effort. As you can see, we're no young hippies but sincere middle-aged idealists."

"But why only the five of you? And why out here in the middle of nowhere?"

"A larger meeting would have attracted the press—which would have been especially dangerous for Dr. Tao and Ivan when they returned home. We heard of this place, just being built, and it seemed perfect for our purpose."

"Do you remember who actually suggested it?"

She blushed prettily. "As a matter of fact, I did. I'd met Felix Bollinger in Paris last year, and—"

"I understand," Rand said. "You sent out some sort of announcement to the press to cover yourselves, and Cairo University believed it."

"Exactly."

"Which one of you did Fanger recognize?"

She looked blank. "He didn't admit to knowing any of us."

"All right," Rand said with a sigh. "Thanks for the information."

He left and went in search of Leila Gaad.

He found her finally in her room—the last place he thought of looking. The orange walls and drapes assaulted his eyes, but she seemed to enjoy the décor. "I think I've found our murderer," she announced. "And I've also found a concealed communication for you to ponder."

"I thought this was going to be one case without it. First tell me who the killer is."

"The American—Northgate! I found this pair of shoes in the rubbish by the incinerator. See—orange paint on the bottom! And they're American-made shoes!"

"Hardly conclusive evidence. But interesting. What about the concealed communication?"

She held a little notebook aloft triumphantly. "I went back to Professor Fanger's room and found this among his things. He was always writing in it, and I thought it might give us a clue. Look here—on the very last page, in his handwriting. *Invite to room, confirm tritan.*"

"Tritan? What's that?"

"Well, he spelled it wrong, I guess, but Triton is a mythological creature having the body of a man and the tail of a fish—sort of a male version of a mermaid. That would imply a good swimmer, wouldn't it? And seeing them all around the pool, I can tell you Northgate is the best swimmer of the lot."

"Fanger was going to confirm this in his room? How—by flooding the place?"

"Well … " She paused uncertainly. "What else could it mean?"

Rand didn't answer. Instead he said, "Come on. Let's go see Northgate."

The American answered the door with sleepy eyes and a growling voice. "Don't you know it's the middle of the night?" Rand held out the shoes for him to see, and he fell silent.

"Going to let us in?"

"All right," he said grudgingly, stepping aside.

"These are your shoes, aren't they?"

There was little point in denying it. "Yes, they're mine."

"And you were in the room after Fanger was murdered?"

"I was there, but I didn't kill him. He was already dead. He'd invited me up for a nightcap. The door was unlocked and when I went in I found him dead and the room a terrible mess. I was afraid I'd be implicated so I left, but I discovered later I'd stepped in some orange paint. When you got us all out by the pool to search for paint spots I panicked and threw the shoes away."

Rand tended to believe him. The real murderer would have done a better job of disposing of the incriminating shoes. "All right," he said. "Now let's talk about the conference. Jeanne Bisset has already told me its real purpose—to work for nuclear disarmament in your five nations. Did Fanger have any idea of this?"

"I think he was onto something," the American admitted. "That's why he wanted to see me. He wanted to ask me about one of the others in the group—someone he thought he knew."

"Which one?"

"He was dead before he could tell me."

"What damage could a spy do at this conference?" Rand asked.

Northgate thought about it. "Not very much. I suppose if he was in the pay of the Russians or Chinese he could report the names of Rusanov and Dr. Tao to their governments, but that would be about all."

"I may have more questions for you later," Rand said.

"He was probably killed by one of the Arab employees," Northgate suggested as Rand and Leila headed for the door.

Back downstairs, Leila said, "Maybe he's right. Maybe it was just a robbery killing."

"Then why go to such lengths with the paint and the other things? There was a reason for it, and the only sane reason had to be to hide the killer's identity."

Leila took out one of her orange cigarettes. "Splashing paint around a hotel room to hide a killer's identity? How?"

"That's what I don't know." He produced the dead man's notebook again and stared at the final message: *Invite to room, confirm tritan.* It wasn't Triton misspelled. A professor at Cairo University wouldn't make a mistake like that.

His eyes wandered to Leila's cigarette, and suddenly he knew.

D r. Wayne Evans opened the door for them. His hair and beard were neatly in place, and it was obvious he hadn't been sleeping. "Well, what's this?" he asked. "More investigation?"

"The final one, Dr. Evans," Rand said, glancing about the blue suite. "You killed Professor Fanger."

"Oh, come now!" Evans glanced at Leila to see if she believed it.

"You killed him because he recognized you as a spy he used to deal with. He invited you to his suite to confirm it, and when he confronted you with it there was a struggle and you killed him. I suppose it was the beard that made him uncertain of your identity at first."

"Is this any way to talk to a fellow countryman, Rand? I'm here on an important mission."

"I can guess your mission—to sabotage this conference."

Evans took a step backward. He seemed to be weighing the possibilities. "You think I killed him and messed up the room like that?"

"Yes. The room was painted like a rainbow, and strewn with towels and things from the next building. But just a little while ago I remembered there were cigarettes strewn on that floor too, next to the broken ceramic box they were in. There were no cigarettes stored in the next building. I think while you were struggling with Fanger he ripped your pocket. The cigarettes from your suite tumbled out, just as the table was overturned and his own cigarette box smashed. Your cigarettes and his cigarettes mingled on the floor. And that was the reason for the entire thing—the reason the room had to be splashed with paint and all the rest of it. To hide the presence of those blue cigarettes."

Dr. Wayne Evans snorted. "A likely story! I could have just picked up the blue ones, you know."

"But you couldn't have," Rand said. "Because you're color-blind."

That was when Evans moved. He grabbed Leila and had her before Rand could react. The knife in his hand had appeared as if by magic, pressed against her throat. "All right, Rand," he said very quietly. "Out of my way or the girl dies. Another killing won't matter to me."

Rand cursed himself for being caught off guard, cursed himself again for having Leila there in the first place. "Rand," she gasped as the blade of the knife pressed harder against her flesh.

"All right," he said. "Let her go."

"Call Bollinger. Tell him I want a car with a full petrol tank and an extra emergency can. I want it out in front in ten minutes or the girl dies."

Rand obeyed, speaking in clipped tones to the manager. When he'd hung up, Evans backed against the door, still holding Leila. "Can't we talk about this?" Rand suggested. "I didn't come to this place looking for you. It was only chance—what happened, I mean."

"How'd you know I am color-blind?"

"Fanger left a notation in his notebook. *Invite to room, confirm tritan.* He was simply abbreviating tritanopia—a vision defect in which the retina fails to respond to the colors blue and yellow. It's not as common as red-green blindness, and when Fanger thought he recognized you he knew he could confirm it by having you up to his yellow room. By a quirk of fate you'd been placed in the blue suite yourself. And when you dropped the cigarettes during the struggle, you had only two choices—pick up *all* the cigarettes, blue and yellow alike, or leave them all and somehow disguise their presence."

"Make it short," Evans said. "I'm leaving in three minutes."

"If you took all the cigarettes you risked having them found on you before you could dispose of them. Even if you flushed them down the toilet, a problem remained. Fanger was a known nonsmoker. The broken cigarette box would call attention to the missing cigarettes, and the police would wonder why the killer took them away. If your color blindness became known, someone might even guess the truth. But splashing the room with paint, using every color you could find, not only camouflaged the cigarettes but also directed attention, in a very subtle manner, *away* from a color-blind person."

Evans reached behind him to open the door. "You're too smart, Rand."

"Not really. Once I suspected your color blindness, I remembered your momentary confusion on those rainbow-colored paths yesterday, when you started down the blue path to the pool and then changed your mind and took the yellow one to the lounge. Of course both colors only looked gray to your eyes."

"Walk backward," Evans told Leila. "You're coming with me."

"Who paid you to spy on the conference?" Rand asked. "What country?"

"Country?" Evans snorted. "I worked for countries when Fanger knew me. Now I work where the real money is."

He moved down the hall, dragging Leila with him, and Rand followed. Felix Bollinger was standing by the door, holding it open, the perfect manager directing a departing guest to his waiting car.

"Out of my way," Evans told him.

"I hope your stay was a pleasant one," Bollinger said. Then he brought a gun from behind his back and shot Evans once in the head ...

Leila Gaad downed a stiff shot of Scotch and said to Rand, "You would have let him go, just to save me! I must say that wasn't very professional of you."

"I have my weaknesses," Rand admitted.

Felix Bollinger downed his own drink and reached again for the bottle he'd supplied. "A terrible opening for my resort. The home office won't be pleased."

"Who was paying Evans?" Leila asked. "And paying him for what?"

"We'll have to check on him," Rand said. "But I suppose there are various pressures in today's world working against disarmament. In America sometimes they're called things like the military-industrial complex. In other nations they have other names. But they have money, and perhaps they're taking over where some of the governments leave off. When we find out who was paying Evans, it might well be a company building rockets in America, or submarines in Russia, or fighter planes in France."

"Is there no place left to escape?" Leila asked.

And Felix Bollinger supplied the answer. "No, my dear, there is not. Not even here, at the End of the Rainbow."

THE SPY WHO TOOK A VACATION

Rand was waiting at Heathrow when Leila Gaad's plane touched down after the flight from Cairo. When he saw her passing through customs he recognized her immediately, even though they hadn't seen each other in more than a year. She was still the small dark-haired young woman he remembered from their Egyptian adventures, with her high handsome cheekbones and deep dark eyes that seemed always to be mocking him.

"How good to see you again, Rand," she said, giving him a quick sisterly kiss. "It's been too long."

"It has indeed. I hope to make up for it." He helped with her luggage and took her to his car in the airport parking lot.

"Are we going into London?" she asked.

"Only long enough to get you settled. I promised to show you the British countryside and that's what I'm going to do." He gave her a quick smile. "There's no better place to start a Nile mermaid than with a trip down the Thames."

She made a delightful face. "Isn't it all oily and polluted?"

"Not the Upper Thames. We'll motor up to Abingdon and take a boat down as far as Hampton Court, making plenty of stops along the way. It's a fine trip of four or five days and you'll really get to see a charming part of English country living."

"Can Double-C spare you that long?" she asked with a grin.

"I'm on a week's holiday. Concealed Communications is the furthest thing from my mind."

"Good!"

They'd shared three adventures together in as many years, all in Leila's Egypt during those dark days when the Russians were pouring men and money into the region. Though the Russians were now gone, the tensions of the latest Arab-Israeli War remained. Leila finally left her position at the University of Cairo to spend a summer in England, perhaps in hopes of finding a teaching job at a British university.

After a few quick hours at the London flat Rand had rented for her, they were off to Abingdon by car. They were early enough to beat the afternoon traffic, and Rand filled the time with relaxed conversation about British politics and the election the following day. "You'll miss voting if you're away," Leila observed.

"Small loss. There's no real contest in my district. It's quite firmly Tory."

"Tory?"

"Conservative," he explained with a chuckle.

"There's so much to learn about your country."

"It's really yours too. You told me once your mother was Scottish."

"And so she was, but I've spent my life in Egypt."

It was pleasant talking to her, pointing out the familiar sights of the English countryside, seeing them with a new eye because of it. He was a world away from his cluttered office at Double-C, and he almost resented it when she asked, "How is the spying business these days?"

"Terrible, for me. Taz has retired in Moscow, the government has cut our staff, everyone talks of détente."

"In my part of the world men still fight and die."

"Yes."

"But it no longer concerns Britain?"

"It concerns us, but there are so many other problems. We are caught in a very tight economic situation."

She sighed and leaned back on the seat. "Rand—"

"I wish you'd call me Jeffery."

"Very well—Jeffery. But let's not talk shop—not this week. I shouldn't have asked you about the spying business."

"That's all right." He smiled and touched her hand, then braked the car to a halt. They'd arrived. They were in Abingdon.

The boat he'd rented for the week was a handsome old 28-foot inboard of a type known as a Thames Slipper Stern because of the fact that the stern dipped almost to water level. There was a small cockpit, big enough for three, with a canvas top that folded back when not needed. "Like it?" he asked.

"Love it! We're going down the river in this?"

He nodded. "About forty miles."

"I didn't realize the Thames was so narrow up here."

In truth it seemed less than fifty yards wide. "That's what makes it so pleasant. It doesn't really widen out till you're past Windsor Castle."

They cast off the lines and drifted into the gentle current. "What's upstream?" she wanted to know.

"Oxford. Want to go up and see about a teaching position?"

"No, thanks. Not on holiday!"

Her specialty was archeology and she had pursued it from the bottom of the Nile to the top of the Great Pyramid. Now, as they headed down the sun-drenched river at the maximum allowable speed of about file miles an hour, she took a great interest in the big old Tudor and Victorian homes that stood almost at the water's edge.

It was nearly the end of June, and many of the estates had their own crafts in the water, tied to the concrete retaining walls that separated green grass from blue water. Most were modern luxury cruisers of the sort one found at the better clubs and marinas, but a few were refurbished steamboats with great smokestacks coming up through their middle.

"Such a variety of crafts!" Leila marveled. "There's a houseboat!"

"I could have rented one of those, but I suspected you'd rather spend your nights on land, in some of our quaint country inns."

"And right you were."

He pulled in at the next landing and they went to dinner at an inn called The Upper Angler. Over cocktails Leila said, "I'm amazed that the Thames could be so peaceful and lovely. It's rather more like a small canal than a great river."

"It's very much like a canal. In fact, we'll be passing through some locks farther downstream."

There was a brief commotion from the bar area, and a man in a tweed jacket was hustled out. As he passed near their table on the porch he muttered, "I thought there was free speech in this country!"

"What's the trouble, sir?" Rand asked, recognizing the man's American accent.

"They don't want any political comments by foreigners in here," he said. His sandy hair was rumpled and a seam in his tweed jacket had split as the bartender pushed him out.

"The election's heating up," Rand observed with a grin. "Here, why not join us? They shouldn't mind your staying out on the porch."

The man drew over a chair and sat down. "Thanks, old man. Glad to see a few of you people are still civilized. My name's William Sanders. I'm a yacht broker." He fished in a wallet for a business card as Rand introduced himself and Leila.

"I'd say this is the right spot for yacht brokerage," Rand observed.

"Well, yes, except that the big profits come with the big yachts, and the really big ones can't sail on the river this far up. Still, it's a good living buying and selling 'em."

"I'd say it was a very American sort of occupation," Leila commented.

He glanced at her, wondering how she'd meant the remark, but didn't pursue it, saying instead to Rand, "I hope this election is over soon."

"Tomorrow," Rand said.

"Isn't the beginning of summer an odd time for elections?"

"When the government here loses a vote of confidence, a new election is called. It can happen at any time. But at least the campaigns are short."

"Does everyone stay up late to watch the returns on TV, like back in the States?"

"In London they do, but not in some of the towns and villages. In the smaller places the votes often aren't counted till the following morning. The ballot boxes are locked in a cell at the local jail overnight."

"How quaint!"

Rand smiled. "It's England. Here, join us in a drink."

They chatted for a half hour, till the food arrived. Then the American excused himself with a little bow to Leila and vanished into the dusk. "He seemed quite nice," she said after he'd gone. "I can't imagine that mean bartender throwing him out!"

"These country inns like peace and quiet. What they don't like is an American sounding off about local politics."

"That's England too, I suppose."

Rand smiled. "After dinner I'll show you some more of it."

Morning came early to England in late June. It seemed barely four o'clock when the sun was already streaming through Rand's window at the inn. In his London apartment he had a heavy drape to guard against such intrusion, but here he was at the mercy of the sun.

He rolled over, saw that the door to Leila's connecting room was still closed, and thought about her. Finally he buried his head under the pillow and tried to go back to sleep. An hour later he was up, though, and he roused Leila Gaad for breakfast.

"But it's only five o'clock!" she protested.

"We can have breakfast and be on the river ahead of the crowd."

Once up and under way her protests faded. As their craft drifted away from shore and was caught by the gentle current of the river, she said, "This is lovely! Thank you for getting me up for it!"

They traveled downstream past Dorchester and Wallingford, through the Goring Gap to Pangbourne, and then on into the medium-sized city of Reading. Always there were friendly people to wave from the shore, or other boats to honk a greeting. They lunched at another quiet country inn, across the river from a towering Gothic church that might have served as a cathedral in many cities.

After Reading, and before Henley, they chanced on a fellow traveler in distress. A middle-aged man was standing on the deck of his cabin cruiser appealing for aid. "Say there, old chap, I seem to be out of petrol. Quite embarrassing, really."

Rand guided their craft over to his side. "I've got an emergency can of fuel I can give you. It's only two gallons, but it'll get you to town."

"Many thanks, mister." His face showed the beginning growth of a gray beard, and Rand guessed him to be a desk bound Londoner just starting his holiday. So often they grew beards for two or three weeks, only to shave them off when they returned to the office. "My name's Creighton," he said, accepting the petrol can and holding out a greasy hand. "Dave Creighton."

"Jeffery Rand."

"Glad you came along. That's some unusual boat you've got there."

"It's only rented," Rand answered defensively.

"Here, let me buy you and your wife a drink! That's the least I can do to repay you."

At Rand's side, Leila blushed nicely but didn't deny the relationship. "Sounds good," Rand agreed. "You work up a thirst on the river."

Dave Creighton proved an amiable drinking companion, even though his idea of buying them a drink was to invite them aboard his cabin cruiser while he filled plastic cups with some ice and cheap scotch. "I'm a botanist at Corby College," he explained, scratching at the bristle on his chin. "Some teaching, some research. But for the summer I'm just relaxing."

"I'm in civil service," Rand said vaguely. "Desk job in London. My office overlooks the river and I've always wanted to vacation here."

"It's lovely this time of year," Creighton agreed. "I need more ice." He picked up the empty plastic bucket and hopped onto shore, heading for a nearby inn. "Back in a jiff."

When they were alone Leila asked, "Do you think he's a spy?"

"It would be just my luck to run into one on holiday!"

She glanced up and tugged at Rand's arm. "What's that man doing?"

A slim young fellow with long black hair and glasses had intercepted Creighton as he approached the inn. The young man pushed Creighton hard with the flat of his hand and knocked the empty ice bucket to the ground. Rand jumped off the boat and started across the lawn.

"Just get out of my way," the black-haired man was saying.

"Now look here! Keep your hands off or I'll call the police!" Creighton said.

"Call them!"

"What's the trouble?" Rand asked.

"This chap is trying to pick a fight," Creighton answered indignantly.

"We don't want trouble," Rand told the young man. "On your way now."

He peered at Rand from beneath black bushy brows, then took a step forward and swung a hard right fist at him. Rand stepped back, ducking the blow with ease, and grabbed the man's arm as it went by. He twisted and the man went down. "On your way, I said."

Rand waited to see if the man would rise, but he stayed sitting on the grass.

"Tried to pick a fight for no reason," Creighton said. "Just came up and shoved me!"

"You know him?"

"Never saw the bloke before."

"Come back," Rand said. "We can get your ice elsewhere."

They remained with Dave Creighton as the day lengthened into evening. When he finally departed, Leila Gaad summed up her reaction to him. "He's more British than you are!"

Rand smiled. "Many people are."

They had eaten at another of the seemingly perfect country inns, and as they were departing Leila suddenly gripped Rand's arm. "Isn't that the same man who tried to start the fight?"

Rand followed her gaze. "That's him, all right. Wonder what he's up to now."

The dark-haired young man was loitering near the front of the inn, as if waiting for something or someone. Rand paused to watch from a distance, pulling Leila back into the evening shadows. Some people were approaching the inn from the direction of the parking lot. The instant the young man saw them he whirled and hurled something—a rock or a brick—at the front window of the inn. There was a shattering of glass and a moment of general confusion.

"He smashed the window!" Leila exclaimed. "He must be mad!"

"Or high on drugs. I didn't smell any liquor on his breath."

"Should you stop him?"

"That seems already attended to," Rand said. And indeed three men from inside the inn, one of them the manager, had hurried out to seize the vandal. Within a few minutes a police car arrived.

"The excitement's over," Leila said, turning toward the river where they'd left the boat. They'd already decided to go a bit farther downriver before calling it a night.

"Odd," Rand muttered as he fell into step beside her.

"What's odd?"

"That man. The whole business. First he tried to pick a fight with Creighton, and now he breaks a window. There was a Chesterton story once about a priest—Father Brown, it was—who left a trail of petty crimes for the police to follow."

"Well, if he wanted the police he got them! They're taking him off to jail."

"Perhaps that's exactly what he wanted."

"Do you think so?"

"It seems to me he's tried at least twice to get himself arrested. This afternoon he even urged Creighton to call the police."

"But why would anybody want to be arrested?" Leila asked. "A small-town jail can't be the most pleasant place to spend a night."

"Especially not on election night," Rand said.

"What?"

"I'm just remembering something. I mentioned to you that some towns store the uncounted ballots in a jail cell overnight. I wonder if they do that here."

"Does it matter?"

Rand thought about the possibilities. "It just might. Come on, let's go back into town."

They found the small local jail without difficulty and there was no need for Rand to ask his question. As they watched, a car drove up to the door and three metal ballot boxes were removed from the trunk under police guard. A tall white-haired man walked up to watch the proceedings, and Rand guessed that he might well be one of the candidates. He verified it by asking a bystander.

"That bloke? That's Michael Wisbech. He's standing for Parliament in today's election."

"I thought it was," Rand said. "Think he won?"

"I should hope not! I voted for Ramsey."

Rand grunted sympathetically. "Could you point out the Chief Constable to me?"

"That would be Folkestone. I don't see him. He must be inside."

"Thanks."

"What are you up to now?" Leila asked, tugging at his sleeve. "You're supposed to be on holiday, remember?"

"Holiday or not, if I have a suspicion of a crime it's my duty to report it."

"But there is no reason to suspect a crime," she argued.

"That man wanted to be arrested—I'm convinced of it. He wanted to spend the night in jail, and there has to be a reason for it. Suppose he was carrying tools hidden on his body—lock-picks and such. Suppose he plans to get out of his cell and into the cell where the ballot boxes are kept."

"Now you're guessing."

"Sure I'm guessing, but it's certainly a possibility."

"I think we'd best be on our way."

He ignored her and stopped a passing police officer. "Would it be possible for me to have a word with Chief Constable Folkestone?"

"Not unless it's an urgent matter, sir. He's pretty much tied up with this election business. May I be of assistance?"

Rand hesitated, then shook his head. "No. No, it was nothing important."

He caught up with Leila and she asked, "Well?"

"I changed my mind. It's probably a foolish idea."

"Shall we go back to the boat?"

"No," he decided. "Let's see if there's a room at the inn."

In the morning he was up early. Leila stirred on her pillow and mumbled, "You certainly are an early riser."

"I couldn't sleep. I'm going to see the Chief Constable."

"Not that again!"

"Afraid so. I can't let it pass."

She turned over. "Wake me when you get back."

There was more activity at the little town jail than he might have expected. People were already arriving to count the ballots, and the Chief Constable was in his office drinking a cup of steaming tea. He was a gnarled man with a frosty, weatherbeaten face that seemed to reflect a lifetime at sea.

"Constable Folkestone?" Rand asked from the doorway.

"Chief Constable," the man corrected, quietly but firmly. "What can I do for you?"

"I happened to witness the arrest of a man last evening," Rand began, and then went on to explain his suspicions.

Chief Constable Folkestone listened with interest. When Rand had finished he said, "Interesting story. You should have told me last night."

"Can you check it now?" Rand asked. "Can you make certain he hasn't tampered with the ballot boxes?"

Folkestone smiled humorlessly. "No chance of that! The prisoner's name is Edward Brecon, and he never left his cell. In fact, we found him dead in it this morning."

"Dead!"

"He was stabbed. We think the knife was thrown through the cell window from outside."

Over breakfast Leila was sympathetic. "You can't blame yourself for what happened, Jeffery. He might have been killed even if you'd gone to the Constable last night."

"But killed by whom? And why?"

Before she could venture an opinion Leila glanced up and saw a familiar face. William Sanders, the American yacht broker, was crossing the inn's dining room, apparently searching for an empty table. He saw Rand wave and came over to join them. "Did you hear the election results? Wisbech defeated Ramsey. Very close vote!"

"Was he the one you were arguing for the other night?"

"Damned right! I'm trying to sell Wisbech a yacht. That's why I'm here. He didn't want to buy till after the election."

"There was an odd sidelight to the vote counting," Rand told him. "The ballots were stored in the local jail overnight, and one of the prisoners was killed there, in his cell."

The American seemed interested. "You don't say? I hadn't heard about that." He had coffee with them, but seemed anxious to be on his way. "I have to find Wisbech," he explained. "See you both later."

"Do you think he will?" Leila wondered.

"What?"

"See us later?"

"Who knows? It's a small river."

"Are we ready to shove off?"

He thought about it. "Not quite yet. I'm going back to the jail. Something happened there last night and I'm curious to know what. Go down to the boat and work around it as if we're getting ready to shove off. I won't be too long."

There was still much activity in the jail area. Rand recognized the tall white-haired figure of Michael Wisbech, who emerged from the building to the scattered cheers of onlookers. As he passed close by, Rand said, "Congratulations on your victory."

His intent blue eyes turned to Rand. He studied him for just an instant before replying with a simple, "Thank you."

When Wisbech had been driven away in a long black Rolls-Royce, Rand entered the jail, going directly to the Chief Constable's office. "It's you again," Folkestone said, looking up from his work. "What is it this time?"

"The same matter. The killing of this man Brecon." Rand decided to show his identification. "It may be a national security matter," he said, though he knew he was exaggerating.

Folkestone stroked his chin. "Well now, just how can I help?"

"I'd like to see the dead man's belongings—everything he had on him at the time of arrest."

"There was no identification. He gave his name and a London address when we arrested him. The only thing he was carrying was this little notebook, and we didn't even find it till after he was dead. Otherwise, there was only some money and a handkerchief."

Rand flipped through the little notebook. There was no name in it—nothing to show ownership. It seemed to be a record of financial transactions, of payments made or received. Near the back, on some blank pages, a few notes had been scrawled. The most interesting one read: *Cryptogams due Tuesday*. Despite the misspelling, there could be no doubt of the meaning. Perhaps this was a job for Concealed Communications after all.

"I'll want to keep this," he told Folkestone.

"Have to sign a receipt. We do things by law here."

Rand signed for the notebook and left the jail, walking quickly down the front steps to the street. Then, as an afterthought, he strolled around the side of the building. He wanted to see if it was really possible to throw a knife through one of the barred windows. If it wasn't possible, he might have some more questions for Chief Constable Folkestone.

The window itself was easy to spot. It was on the ground floor, near the back of the building, and the broken glass had been boarded over. It was about eight feet above the ground, but Rand was willing to concede that the killer could have broken the glass with a stone to lure Brecon near the bars and then hurled the knife. It could have been done that way. Or it could have been done by someone in the cell with him.

"Mr. Rand?"

He turned at the sound of his name and confronted a bland, smiling young man wearing an open-necked sports shirt and carrying a copy of the London *Times*. "Yes?" Rand answered.

"There's someone wants to talk with you. I have a car." Before Rand could refuse he saw the folded newspaper raise a bit, just enough to show the muzzle of a pistol pointed at him. "Please, Mr. Rand. You won't be hurt."

"I seem to have no choice."

He preceded the young man to a small waiting car. Another man, almost a duplicate of the first, sat behind the wheel. "No tricks now, Mr. Rand," he said. "We're friends."

"Sure you are." Rand leaned back on the seat. It was too soon to be really worried.

The little car sped through the morning sunlight, passing occasional farmers at work in their fields. They were traveling east, toward London, but before they'd gone very far the driver turned off onto a little-used side road. Another car was waiting some distance ahead, sheltered from the sun by a large shade tree.

"We're here," the driver said. "He's waiting for you."

Rand got out alone and walked toward the waiting car. A man was sitting in the rear seat. He opened the door and got in next to him.

"Well, Rand," a familiar voice said. "I hope you'll excuse all this hocus-pocus."

It was Hastings—Rand's immediate superior in the complex structure of British Intelligence.

"This is certainly a surprise," Rand said, meaning it. "What are you doing here?"

"I could ask the same of you. I thought you were on holiday."

"I am—cruising down the Thames with a friend."

"Ah! Then it's just by chance you stumbled onto this thing?"

"It is. In fact, I have no idea what the thing is. A man attracted my suspicions yesterday by going out of his way to be arrested. When I checked on him this morning I found he'd been killed in his cell during the night."

"I know," Hastings said glumly. "He was one of our men."

"One of *yours*?"

"I have other concerns besides overseeing your work in Concealed Communications, you know. My duties include internal security."

"Why did Brecon—or whatever his real name was—want to be arrested?"

"I have no idea," Hastings answered.

"Was it something about the election?"

"His assignment concerned one of the candidates. That's all I can say."

"You mean a British Intelligence agent was put in that jail overnight to tamper with the election results?"

"No, no, nothing like that!" Hastings quickly assured him. "All right, I see I'm going to have to tell you the whole story. Or at least as much as we know. Brecon—we'll call him that—was on a special assignment. One of the candidates in yesterday's election is a businessman with somewhat shady connections. As you know, American companies are forbidden to sell certain strategic goods to Russia. This man buys them through a dummy corporation here in England, then resells them to the Russians. We can't arrest him for it, since he violates no British law, but he could become an embarrassment if he served in Parliament."

Rand remembered the man who had studied him outside the jail. "It's Wisbech, isn't it?"

"Yes," Hastings replied.

"And he won."

"He won," Hastings agreed, "and our man Brecon lost. Lost the hard way, with a knife in him."

"What about Ramsey, the other candidate?"

"He knows nothing about all this."

"You could have slipped him the information during the campaign."

Hastings flashed his eyes. "That wouldn't have been sporting."

"I see." It was the same old British way. "How did you learn I was in town?"

Hastings motioned toward the car behind them. "They spotted you at breakfast. You're quite well known in the business, you know."

"Did they have to use guns?"

"I suppose it was easier than an explanation. I said I was sorry."

"Now that I'm here, what do you want from me?"

"You're good at these things, Rand. As long as you're on the scene anyway, see what you can learn."

He thought of the notebook in his pocket. "Wisbech would need a contact—someone working for the Russians."

"Yes."

"And your man might have been onto him. If Wisbech couldn't be touched, his contact could be—as an unregistered agent of a foreign power."

"Does that explain why he got himself arrested?"

"It could. If he wasn't trying to stuff the ballot boxes himself, maybe he got arrested so he'd be there to prevent someone else from stuffing them."

"Someone else? That Constable fellow?"

Rand shrugged. "Tell me something—did anything about Brecon's mission involve cryptograms? Codes, ciphers, any sort of secret messages?"

"Not that I know of. Cryptograms are your department."

"They seem to be," Rand agreed, "even on holiday. Will you be staying in the area or returning to London?"

"Oh, it's back to London for me. I can leave you a man if you think you'll need him."

"No, thanks." He started to leave the car. "What about Brecon? Did he have a family?"

Hastings looked blank. "Don't really know. Have to check his dossier. We'll handle that end. Phone me when you find something."

"If I find something."

They shook hands and Rand walked back to the other car. The young men drove him back to town, and now the guns were out of sight. "Nice day, isn't it?" one of them said.

Leila was waiting on the river bank near their boat. "Where have you been? I was frantic!"

"It's a long story." He glanced toward the boat, seeing someone move in the cockpit. "We have company?"

"Dave Creighton. He stopped by to chat and I can't get rid of him."

Rand smiled. "He probably wants a return on that Scotch he gave us." He walked to the river's edge and called a greeting.

Creighton poked his head up. "The lady was worried about you."

"I got tied up. There's some excitement at the jail. Remember that fellow who tried to pick the fight with you?"

"Sure do. Long black hair. Looked like a Commie."

"He got himself arrested last night and someone killed him in his cell."

"I'll be damned!" Creighton jumped ashore and joined Rand. "What do you make of it?"

"We saw him deliberately get himself arrested by throwing a rock through the window of the inn. My first thought was that he wanted to get himself arrested to be in the jail overnight with the uncounted election ballots."

"That so?" Creighton motioned downriver toward his own cabin cruiser. "Come aboard, old chap, and bring your wife. There's still some of that Scotch left over."

They followed him onto the boat and Leila relaxed in a convenient deck chair while he poured the drinks. "I thought you'd be far away by now," Rand said.

"Came back," Creighton answered with a grunt, handing Rand a glass. "But what about this man who was killed? Anything to do with the election?"

"As I said, that was my first thought. Because why does someone go to all that trouble to spend the night in a little village jail?"

"Why indeed?" Creighton put down his glass and started the boat's motor. "Let's go for a bit of a spin. I'll bring you back here." He reached over the side to cast off the mooring lines.

"Well, I thought about it and I came up with another possibility," Rand admitted. "It explains everything—why he picked the fight with you and why he broke the window."

"Why?"

The boat was drifting slowly away from shore, catching the current of the river. "He broke the window to get himself arrested, all right—simply for protection. He knew someone was after him, and jail seemed the safest place. Unfortunately, it wasn't safe enough."

"But why start the fight with me? Same reason?"

Rand shook his head. "The fight with you was the key to the whole thing, once I tumbled to it. You see, the whole reason for it was so that he could pick your pocket—steal this little notebook you were carrying."

Dave Creighton's face hardened. "I'll just take that," he said. A gun had appeared as if by magic in his hand. "I've killed once for it, and I'll kill again, if need be."

Leila was out of her chair in a flash, but not quite fast enough for Creighton. He hit out with his free hand, catching her on the shoulder and tumbling her to the deck. "Stay there!" he warned. Then, to Rand, he repeated, "Give me the notebook."

Rand held on to it. "You'd hardly let us live now, in any event."

"Do you know what's in it?"

"I've got a pretty good idea. A list of money payments involving the just-elected Member of Parliament, Mr. Michael Wisbech. He's been dealing with the Russians, transshipping American strategic goods, and you've been the go-between, the paymaster."

"Smart," Creighton said. "You're smart for a civil servant."

"Perhaps I didn't describe my position fully enough," Rand answered with a grin. "I'm with a branch of British Intelligence. You chose the wrong boat to stop for gasoline."

They were still drifting downstream, the motor purring softly but the throttle unopened. Rand wondered if he planned to throw them overboard. "I was unlucky," Creighton admitted. "Still, how did you know the notebook belonged to me?"

"It could have been the dead man's own, but I ruled that out quite quickly. He wasn't carrying a pencil, pen, or other writing implement. So why would he carry a notebook? I decided he'd gotten the notebook from someone. It was important to him, because he didn't surrender it when he was jailed. He kept it hidden on him. I think he figured the jail was the safest place for him and the notebook, till the next day.

"If he knew his killer would come after the notebook, that meant he'd stolen it. I remembered his tussle with you, and now I see the reason for it. You killed him with a knife through the barred window of the jail, hoping to recover the notebook later. Perhaps you posed as a next of kin this morning and the Constable told you I had the notebook. That's what brought you back to us. When I arrived just now you looked suspiciously as if you were searching our boat."

The cabin cruiser rode over a swell and suddenly another boat was cutting in front of it. "What's that?" Creighton rasped, swinging around.

"Just some friends," Rand announced. "Take him, Leila!"

She tackled him around the ankles as Rand dove for the gun. The other boat was alongside now, and Hastings' two young men were aboard. Rand could feel Creighton struggling beneath him still, and he caught the man's sleeve, feeling the hardness of steel there.

"Have you got him?" Leila asked.

"Get this knife out of his sleeve. It's probably a mate to the one that killed Brecon at the jail."

As the cabin cruiser edged into the shore, the young men came aboard to take over. Rand was startled to see Hastings with them too. "I thought you'd gone back to London."

"They told me what you were up to, so I decided to stay around. You should have mentioned Creighton when we talked."

"I got the idea while they were driving me back to town, and we stopped at the library to look up cryptogam. If the notebook belonged to Brecon's killer, I figured that might tell me something. It did. Cryptogams have nothing to do with codes or ciphers. They're an old botanical division meaning plants without seeds, like ferns and mosses." Rand showed him the notebook. "This was a note for Creighton's botany class, and it told me the notebook was his for certain."

"You should have mentioned the notebook too," Hastings said darkly.

"We all have our secrets," Rand answered with a grin. Then, dropping his voice, he added, "There's an American around here trying to sell Michael Wisbech a yacht. Now he wouldn't be one of your people too, would he?"

Hastings cleared his throat. "You took care of Creighton. Leave Wisbech to us." Then, turning toward Leila, he beamed and said, "And this must be Leila Gaad! Jeffery's told me so much about you from the Egyptian days. I do hope you're enjoying our river."

THE SPY AND THE CATS OF ROME

R and felt vaguely uneasy sitting in the familiar chair in Hastings' office at British Intelligence. He'd sat there on a thousand prior occasions over the years, but this time was different. He'd retired from the Department of Concealed Communications the previous autumn, and though he'd been involved in one or two cases since then, this was his first visit back to the old building.

"Good to see you again, Rand," Hastings said. "How's your wife?"

"Leila's fine. Teaching archeology at Reading University."

"You live out that way now, don't you?"

"That's right. We have a house west of London, about halfway to Reading. It's an easy drive for her."

"And yourself?"

Rand shrugged. "Writing a book. What everyone does when they retire from here, I suppose."

"I wanted you to know how much I appreciated your help on that Chessman toy business a few months back."

"You told me so at the time," Rand reminded him. "What is it now?"

"Does it always have to be something?"

"You're too busy a man to invite me down for a mere chat. What is it?"

At that instant Hastings seemed old and bleak. "The sins of our youth catching up with us, Rand. It's Colonel Nelson."

Rand stiffened. That had been—how many years ago? —ten at the very least. Colonel Nelson had been in charge of certain international operations for British Intelligence. He'd lied to Rand about the nature of a Swiss assignment, and some good people had died. Shortly afterward Colonel Nelson suffered a nervous breakdown and was retired from the Service. Even after ten years Rand had never forgotten the man and what he did. He'd thrown it up to Hastings in moments of anger, and had cited the affair to younger members of Double-C as a glaring example of what could go wrong if an overseas agent was not in possession of all the facts.

"What about him?" Rand asked.

"We have reports from Rome that he's stirring things up, recruiting white mercenaries to fight in Africa."

"Not on behalf of British Intelligence, surely!"

"No, no, of course not. And I doubt if he's working for the Americans, either. Frankly, we don't know what his game is. But it's most embarrassing at this time."

"Where do I come in?"

"Could you fly down to Rome for a day or two? Just see what mischief he's up to?"

"Oh, come on now, Hastings! I'm out of the Service. I helped you on that toy business because——"

"I know, I know. But I don't want to send anyone officially. You know Colonel Nelson. You'd recognize him, even after ten years."

"And he'd recognize me."

"That might be enough to scare him off what he's doing, or at least make him assume a lower profile. You'd be strictly unofficial, but he'd get the message."

"I don't want to be away——" Rand began, still resisting.

"Two nights at most. Certainly your bride could spare you that long."

Perhaps it was the enforced bleakness of the winter months, or the simple need for activity. Perhaps it was a gnawing sense of unfinished business with Colonel Nelson. Ten years earlier Rand had wanted to kill him. Now, perhaps if he saw the man, he could write a finish to it, finally forget it.

"All right," he said, "I'll go."

Hastings smiled. "I thought you would. I have your plane ticket here."

Rand phoned Leila at the University and explained, as best he could, that he'd been summoned to Rome for two days. "Back at it, aren't you?" she asked accusingly.

"Not really. It's some unfinished business. A fellow I used to work with."

"Be careful, Jeffery."

"Don't worry. I'm through taking chances."

He gathered up some things into an overnight bag and flew to Rome that evening. It was a city he'd visited only briefly in the past, and perhaps his impressions of it were different from most. To him it was not so much a city of churches as a city of fountains and cats.

This night, having settled into a hotel room not far from the Spanish Steps, he took a taxi to a restaurant near the Forum, where the cobbblestoned street was cluttered with cats of all sizes waiting to be fed the scraps from the kitchen. Some said the cats had been there since the ffth century B. C., when they were imported from cat-worshipping Egypt. They ran wild in many parts of the city, often simply sitting and watching a passerby with a regal indifference that made one believe they might well have inhabited the city for 2500 years.

The restaurant itself was unspectacular. It was called Sabato—

Saturday—and perhaps that was the only night it did any business. Certainly on this Thursday night there were plenty of empty tables. Rand saw a few men at the bar—young Italian toughs of the sort that might make good mercenary material. If Colonel Nelson did his recruiting here, business might be good.

A young woman wearing a tight satin skirt and scoop-necked blouse appeared from somewhere to show him to a table. She asked him something in Italian and he answered in English, "I'm sorry. My Italian is a bit rusty."

"Do you wish a menu?" she asked, speaking English almost as good as his.

"Thank you, no. My name is Rand. I've come in search of a friend. I understood I could find him here."

"What is his name?"

"Colonel Nelson."

"Ah! The man with the cats!"

"Cats?"

"He feeds them. They trail him down the street when he leaves."

"Does he come here every night?"

"Usually, but you have missed him. He's been and gone."

"I see. You wouldn't happen to know where he lives, would you?"

She shrugged. "Ah, no."

Rand glanced at the line of men standing by the bar. "Any of his friends around?"

"Colonel Nelson's friends are the cats."

"But if he comes in here he must drink with somebody."

"Ask them," she answered, indicating the men at the bar.

"Thank you, Miss——"

"Anna."

"Thank you, Anna."

The first man Rand approached spoke only Italian, but his companion had a knowledge of English. He also had a knowledge of Colonel Nelson. "I take you to him if you want. He lives not far from here."

"Fine. Does he work around here?"

"No, no, he's an old man. He feeds the cats, that is all."

Rand figured Colonel Nelson to be in his early sixties, but the effects of the nervous breakdown might have aged him. Still, it seemed odd that a neighborhood character who fed the stray cats of Rome would be seriously recruiting mercenaries to fight in Africa.

"All right, take me to him."

The man gestured with his hands. "I must pay for the drinks I have."

Rand took the hint and put down a couple of Italian bills. The man smiled, pocketed one of them, and left the other for the bartender. Then he led the way outside, heading down a dim alley lit only by the curtained glow from the restaurant windows.

"How far is it?" Rand asked.

"Not far from here," the man said, repeating his earlier words, and Rand wondered if he was being set up for a trap. But presently they reached a seedy stone building that obviously contained small apartments, and the man motioned him inside. "I leave you. Sometimes he does not like visitors."

Rand checked the mailboxes—some standing open with their hinges broken—and found one for *Col. A. X. Nelson*. Ambrose Xavier Nelson. Rand hadn't thought of the full name in a decade. He glanced around to thank the man who'd brought him, but the man had already vanished into the night.

The apartment was on the third floor and Rand went up the dim steps with care. The place smelled of decay. Not all that quiet, either, he decided, hearing the noise of a family quarrel from one of the second-floor apartments as he passed it. There was a man's body sprawled on the third-floor landing, and he thought for an instant it was Colonel Nelson, cut down by enemy agents. But it was only a drunk, wine bottle empty at his side, who opened his mouth and snored when Rand turned him over.

He knocked at the door of Colonel Nelson's apartment and waited.

Nothing happened. After a moment he knocked again, harder this time.

Finally a voice reached him from inside. "Who is it?"

"And old friend, Colonel Nelson. I'm in Rome and thought I'd look you up."

The door did not open. "Who is it?' the question was repeated.

"Jeffery Rand, from London."

"Rand. Rand?"

"That's right. Open the door."

He heard latches being undone and bolts pulled back. The heavy oak door opened a crack and a white kitten squeezed out. Then it opened farther, revealing a wrinkled face and balding head. Tired eyes peered at Rand through thick glasses. "I'm Colonel Nelson," the man said. "Why did you come here?"

"To see you. May I come in?"

"All right. The place is a mess."

Two more cats came into view, running across the floor in Rand's path. He lifted a pile of newspapers from a chair and sat down. The place was indeed a mess. "Do you remember me?" Rand asked.

The man opposite him waved his hand. "The memory comes and goes. The old days are clouded sometimes. But I think I remember you, yes."

"That surprises me," Rand said, almost casually, "because I've never laid eyes on you before. You're not Colonel Nelson."

The old man smiled then, showing a missing tooth. "Didn't think I could fool you, but I had to give it a try, right?"

"Who are you, anyway? Where's Nelson?"

"He's away. Hired me to take care of his cats and things. My name's Sam Shawburn."

"You're English."

"Sure am! There's a great many of us in Rome, you know. I was with the British Embassy in my younger days. That's how I met old Nelson."

"But this place—!"

"Isn't very tidy, is it? He's fallen on bad times, Colonel Nelson has. Gets a small pension, you know, but not enough to live on."

"Yet he can afford to pay you to stay here while he goes off traveling. That doesn't make sense."

"He was called away on business. He expects to make scads of money and then he says he's going to move to a better place. Maybe take me with him, too."

"I see. Are the cats his?"

"Sure are! They're not mine, I can tell you that. He feeds them in alleys and sometimes they follow him home. He's got close to a dozen around here, maybe more."

"I really would like to see him while I'm in Rome. When's he due back?"

"Who knows? He's been gone a week now."

"I understand he has business connections in Africa."

Sam Shawburn's eyes narrowed. "Where'd you hear that?"

"The word gets around. I heard he was recruiting mercenaries to fight in Africa."

"Old Nelson's a sly one. I wouldn't want to say what he's up to. But I never heard anything about Africa."

"All right," Rand said. "Good talking to you, anyhow. And be sure to tell him I was asking for him."

"Sure will!" the old man said.

Rand left the apartment and went back downstairs. The drunk was gone from the landing now, and he wondered what that meant. Was Colonel Nelson's apartment being watched, and if so by whom? Rand hadn't noticed a telephone in the shabby quarters and once he reached the street he decided to wait a few minutes and see what happened. If anything.

Luck was with him. Within five minutes Sam Shawburn left the building and headed down the street, followed by a couple of cats. He might have been taking them for a walk, but Rand was willing to bet he was headed for a telephone.

The streets in that section of the city were all but deserted at night, and it was difficult for Rand to follow too closely. Once or twice he thought he'd lost the trail, but finally he saw Shawburn enter a little tobacco store and make for a telephone in the rear. The cats waited outside, scanning the street for some unseen prey.

He waited until the old man emerged from the shop and started back down the street. Then Rand crossed quickly to intercept him. "Hello again, Mr. Shawburn."

"What?"

"It's Rand. I wonder if you've been in touch with Colonel Nelson."

The old man took a step backward, as if frightened by the sudden encounter. "No, no, I haven't talked to him."

"Who'd you just call?"

"When?"

"Just now, in the tobacco store."

"My daughter. I called my daughter."

"Here in Rome?"

"Yes. No—I mean, near here."

"You phoned Colonel Nelson, didn't you?"

The old man's head sagged. "I sent him a telegraph message. I thought he'd want to know."

"Where did you send it?"

"Moscow."

"Colonel Nelson is in Moscow?"

"Yes."

Rand cursed silently. What in hell had he got himself into? The brief favor for Hastings was opening before him like an uncharted swamp. "What's he doing there?"

"I don't know. Business, I guess."

"Where's he staying?"

"I don't know."

"You had to send the telegram somewhere."

Shawburn seemed to sag a bit. "The Ukraine," he replied at last. "He's staying at the Ukraine Hotel in Moscow."

There was never any doubt in Rand's mind that he'd be going to Moscow. He phoned Hastings in London to tell him the news and then made arrangements to catch a flight the following morning. As Hastings had quickly pointed out, the possibility of establishing a link between the Russians and the recruiting of African mercenaries was too good an opportunity to be passed over.

Rand had been in Moscow before, in 1970, and he was surprised to see the fresh coats of paint on buildings that had long been neglected. The city was spruced up; it was more modern and lively than he remembered it, and riding down Kalinin Prospekt in the taxi from the airport he might have been in any large city of western Europe. He could see the Gothic spires of the Ukraine Hotel in the distance, looking like some sort of medieval anachronism, contrasting sharply with the modern offices and apartment buildings that lined the thoroughfare. And he couldn't help wondering if his chances of finding Colonel Nelson were any better in a grand Moscow hotel than in the cat-filled alleys of Rome.

The desk clerk at the Ukraine spoke some English, and he knew of Colonel Nelson. "I think he is in the dining room," he told Rand.

The difference in time between Rome and Moscow had made it the dinner hour without Rand's realizing it. He thanked the room clerk and entered the dining room. It was long and fairly wide, with a raised bandstand at the far end and balconies running the length of either side. A huge chandelier hung from the center of the ceiling, adding a surprisingly ornate touch. Most of the side tables were set for large parties, but at one of the small center tables he found Colonel Nelson dining alone. This time there could be no mistake, even after a decade.

"Hello, Colonel."

The old smile greeted him, though the face around it had aged and the eyes above it had taken on a slightly wild look. "Well, Rand—good to see you! I trust your flight from Rome was a pleasant one."

"So Shawburn sent a second telegram."

"Of course! Did you think he wouldn't? The old man is quite faithful."

"Mind if I join you?" Rand asked, already pulling out a chair.

"Not at all!"

"How's the food here?"

"Predictable. And the service is slow, as in all Moscow restaurants. But I can recommend the soup. It's so thick your fork will stand in it unsupported."

"I'll try some," Rand said with a smile. "What brings you to Moscow, Colonel?"

"Business prospects. Nothing of interest to Concealed Communications, I shouldn't think."

"Oh, I'm retired from there," Rand said casually.

"Are you, now? Then why are you tracking me across Europe?"

"I was in Rome and thought I'd look you up, see how you're doing. I'll admit when I heard you were in Moscow my curiosity got the better of me. Not changing sides after all these years, are you?"

Colonel Nelson glanced around nervously, as if fearing they'd be overheard. "I have no side in London any more. Surely you remember how I was booted out of the Service."

"I remember how you lied to me about that Swiss assignment and caused the death of several people."

"We are in the business of lying, Rand. You know that. Didn't Hastings ever lie to you?"

"Not to my knowledge."

"Ah, the good gray Hastings! A knight in shining armor! But he's the only one of the old crowd left, isn't he? You and I are out of it—and I hear that even some of the Russians like Taz are gone."

"Taz was blown up in a car shortly before I retired. He made the mistake of coming out of retirement."

Colonel Nelson smiled. "I hope you don't make the same mistake."

Rand leaned forward. "What are you doing here, Colonel?"

"A business matter."

"You're playing a dangerous game. Your apartment in Rome is being watched."

"No doubt by British Intelligence."

Rand decided to lay his cards on the table. "They know you're recruiting mercenaries," he said quietly. A small combo was tuning up on the bandstand, and he doubted if even a directional microphone could have picked up his words.

Colonel Nelson merely shrugged. "There is very little for an aging man to do in my line of work. One must make a living."

"Are the Russians paying you?"

Nelson thought about the question for a moment, then said, "Look here, Rand, come with me tomorrow morning and see for yourself. It will save you the trouble of following me all day."

"Tomorrow morning?"

"At ten, in the lobby. We're going to Gorky Park. It's the first warm weekend of spring and there's certain to be a crowd there."

He'd been right in his weather prediction, at least. The temperature had climbed to 22 degrees on the Celsius scale, and the park was crowded with strollers. Gorky Amusement Park was located on the Moscow River, a few miles south of the central city. Rand had never been there before, and somehow the sight of the giant Ferris wheel startled him.

"They come here in the winter to ride the ice slide," Colonel Nelson said, "and in the summer to sun-bathe on the hillside. It is a park for all seasons."

"A good place for a meeting," Rand agreed. "Especially on a mild spring weekend."

"The man I'm to meet is named Gregor. Make a note of it if you wish, for

Hastings."

"That won't be necessary."

They strolled deeper into the park, past the amusement area to the bank of the river. There were people resting on its grassy shore, and Colonel Nelson said, "It's too cold for swimming except in mid-summer, but they like to wade."

"You know a great deal about Moscow."

"After so many trips it's like London or Rome to me. But come, there's Gregor now."

Gregor was a heavy-set Russian wearing a dull gray suit that seemed too heavy for the weather. Rand's unexpected presence made him nervous, and after a few words in Russian the two of them moved off out of earshot. "You understand, old chap," Colonel Nelson said.

Rand found a bench and sat down, watching some children at play with a fat yellow cat. He couldn't help thinking that the cats of Moscow seemed better fed than those of the Rome alleys. Presently he saw the two men part and Colonel Nelson joined him on the bench. He bent to pet the cat, then sneezed suddenly and sent the creature scurrying into the bushes. "That was simple," he said. "My business in Moscow is finished."

"You handed him an envelope."

"Down payment. In three weeks' time he will deliver five hundred Russian and East German weapons, mainly automatic rifles."

"You're buying arms here?"

"Of course! What else would bring me to Moscow?"

"For your African mercenaries?"

"Yes," Colonel Nelson answered smugly. "Then if the arms are captured it appears the Russians supplied them"

"Who really supplies them?"

"You know as well as I do, Rand. The British are footing the bill, perhaps with the CIA's help. I'm still with British Intelligence, you see. I never really left."

"I can't believe—"

"Can't believe what? That Hastings didn't tell you? Good clean Hastings who's always so aboveboard? Hastings knows what I'm doing, all right. He sent you on a fool's errand, going through the motions in the event anyone asked questions later on. I'm working for the British, supplying guns and men to various African factions. You might as well accept it, Rand, because it's true."

Rand was stunned by the words. He didn't want to believe them, didn't want to believe that Hastings had lied to him just as Colonel Nelson had done a decade earlier.

But before he could speak, a man wearing a black raincoat detached himself from the nearby strollers and headed toward them. Rand's first thought was that the man looked vaguely familiar. Then he saw the gun come into view and he thought they were under arrest.

But the gun was a 9 mm German Luger, and it was pointed at Nelson's chest. "Volta, Colonel Nelson!" the man shouted, and fired three quick shots.

Rand saw it all as if in slow motion. He saw Nelson topple backward as the bullets tore into his chest, saw the assassin drop the weapon at Rand's feet and disappear into the bushes.

Then Rand was running—knocking screaming women and frightened men from his path, running after the gunman who'd already melted into the crowd on the next footpath. It was impossible to find him, and to most witnesses Rand must have looked like the killer himself. He saw a policeman coming his way, guided by the pointing fingers of the crowd.

He ducked behind a signboard as the officer approached, and quickly bought a ticket on the Ferris wheel. As soon as he began his ascent, he spotted the policeman still searching the crowd for him. And higher up, with a view of the entire park, he could see the crowd gathered around the spot where Colonel Nelson's body lay. It was hard for him to believe that the tiny figure at the center of that crowd was Nelson, who'd survived a dozen intrigues to die like this in a Moscow amusement park.

He thought about that, and about Hastings back in London.

Had Hastings really lied to him? Was Colonel Nelson working for British Intelligence all this time, financing his African venture with money from England and possibly from America?

And had the killing of Colonel Nelson been part of the ultimate double-cross?

Rand left the Ferris wheel after three more trips around. The view hadn't answered any of the questions for him, but at least he'd seen Colonel Nelson's body being carried off and he knew the police had stopped searching the immediate area. He took a taxi back to his hotel and was just entering the lobby when he noticed the two men in belted black raincoats talking with the room clerk. This time there could be no mistake. These really were Russian police.

He went back out the revolving door without pausing.

They were looking for him and they knew where to find him.

He was being nicely framed for the murder of Colonel Nelson.

As Rand saw it, there were only two courses of action open to him. He could attempt to leave the country by the first available airliner—and no doubt be stopped and arrested at the gate. Or he could go to the British Embassy and try to get help there. The embassy seemed the better bet. Once inside a Russian prison, he knew he'd be a long time getting out.

He was only a few blocks from the embassy building, and he went on foot. The entrance seemed clear as he approached, but almost immediately two Russian detectives emerged from a parked car to intercept him. "Could you state your business, please?" one of them asked in good English.

"My business is with the British Embassy."

"Could we see your passport?"

"I've lost it. That's why I've come to the Embassy."

"You must understand we are looking for a British citizen wanted in connection with a murder. We must ask for identification.

"Are you denying me entrance to my own Embassy?"

The Russian shrugged sadly. "Only until you produce identification. You are still on Russian soil here." He pointed to the ground at his feet, as if daring Rand to step past him.

"All right. I have some identification in my car. I'll go get it." He held his breath as he turned, wondering if the Russians would follow. But their instructions had been to remain at the Embassy entrance, and they only followed him with their eyes. He walked down to the next cross street, where a small Moskvich automobile sat at the curb, its front end hidden from the Russians by a projecting building. Rand bent and pretended to try unlocking the door, then straightened up, shrugged, and made as if to walk around the front of the vehicle to the other side.

As soon as he was out of sight of the Russians he started running, heading down a narrow alley between buildings. He didn't think they'd desert their post to follow him too far, but he wasn't taking any chances.

Finally, panting for breath and fearful of attracting attention, he slowed to a walk as he emerged onto a busy avenue. No one stopped him. For the moment he was safe.

But what should he do now?

Hunted in a strange country for a murder he didn't commit, unable to leave the city or reach the British Embassy, knowing very little of the language, it seemed only a matter of time before he was taken into custody.

He descended into one of the ornate Moscow subways with its gilded chandeliers and sculptured archways and rode to a point not far from the American Embassy. But as he approached he saw a familiar-looking car with two men inside. He kept on walking, wondering how many embassies in Moscow had teams of police watching their doors.

Next he entered a small shop and asked for a public telephone. When he finally made his message clear, the woman behind the counter led him to a telephone—but there was no phone book. He remembered reading somewhere that telephone numbers were hard to come by in Moscow. With some difficulty he might reach the British or American Embassy by phone, but then what?

They would hardly risk an international incident by coming into the street to rescue an accused killer. The best they'd offer would be a visit to his prison cell after he was arrested.

And what if he was arrested? Even his friends back in London might half believe the charge against him. He'd hated Colonel Nelson for ten years, and that hate might have boiled over into a murderous attack. And though several strollers must have seen the real killer in Gorky Park, Rand was not deceiving himself into believing that any of them would dare come forward to testify. If the government said he was guilty, he was guilty.

He wondered about the man who had really shot Colonel Nelson. Was he in the pay of the Russian, Gregor, who'd accepted his down payment for the weapons and promptly ordered Nelson killed? Or was it a more complex plot than that?

Someone had told the Russians his name, and only Hastings in London had known he was going on to Moscow. Was it possible that Hastings was in on it after all, as Colonel Nelson had insisted?

No. Rand refused to believe that.

The British hadn't been financing Nelson for all these years. He'd bet his life on it.

In fact, he'd bet his life on Hastings.

He took a trolleybus to the Central Telegraph Building and addressed a message to a cover address Hastings maintained in London: *Negotiating early landing shipment of new diesel engines at desirable seaport. Eastern nations don't pose any serious supply problem or route trouble.* He signed it *L. Gaad* and indicated a reply should be sent to him at the Central Telegraph Building.

Rand was certain Hastings would recognize Mrs. Rand's maiden name signed to the wire. And he was betting Hastings could read the very simple steganographic message hidden in it.

But he knew it would be morning before he could expect a reply.

A hotel would ask to see his passport and might even want to keep it. He couldn't sleep in the subway because they closed for maintenance from one to six in the morning. And he knew from his last visit to Moscow that the streets would be empty by ten o'clock. After that there'd be no crowds in which to hide.

Finally, as night was falling, he took the subway out to the end of the line, beyond Gorky Park, and went to sleep on a park bench.

In the morning, hoping his overnight beard wasn't too noticeable, he returned to the Central Telegraph Building. Yes, the woman clerk informed him, there was a reply for Mister L. Gaad. She handed over the form and Rand read, with rising spirits: *News of our negotiations received. Every dealer should quote under amount received elsewhere.* It was signed with Hastings' code name.

Rand almost shouted. Hastings had come through. The passport was on its way. He would meet the man and—

Unless it was a trap.

Unless Hastings was setting him up for the Russian police, or for the man who had shot Colonel Nelson.

It was a chance he'd have to take.

The message from Hastings had instructed him to be in Red Square at noon, so he assumed the agent bringing him the fake passport would know him by sight. Red Square at noon, with its lines of tourists waiting to visit Lenin's tomb, could be a very busy place.

There would have been time for an overnight flight from London, Rand knew—or the agent meeting him could be someone from the British Embassy. In any event, they would have to find each other in the crowd.

He reached Red Square a little before noon, wandering aimlessly along the fringes of the crowd waiting at Lenin's tomb. Though he kept his head down, his eyes were alert, scanning the faces he passed, looking for someone familiar.

At ten minutes after twelve he was still looking.

Perhaps Hastings had meant noon of the following day. Perhaps—

"Jeffery," a soft voice said at his shoulder.

He spun around, trying not to appear too startled, and looked into the face of his wife, Leila. "What are you—?"

"Hastings sent me. He knew it had to be someone you trusted. I have a passport in the name of Lawrence Gaad for you. And tickets on an evening flight to London."

"My God, he thought of everything!"

She smiled up at him, and at that moment they might have been the only people in the center of Red Square. "He said to tell you he expected something better from the former head of Double-C than a steganograph with the first letters of each word spelling out the message."

"Sometimes the simple things are the easiest to sneak by. And I had to have something that could be read almost at once. But I don't like the idea of his sending you here."

"Jeffery, I once swam the Nile to a boatload of Russian spies! A midnight flight to Moscow is really nothing."

He rubbed the stubble on his face. "Come on. If you don't mind dining with someone who needs a shave, I'll buy you lunch."

They arrived at Sheremetyevo International Airport in the late afternoon to find the usual scene of confusion and delayed flights. Rand asked Leila to check the departure time while he went off to do some checking of his own. He was remembering the words of Colonel Nelson's assassin: "Volta, Colonel

Nelson!" It had sounded half Russian then, but he now realized it could have been Italian. *Time, Colonel Nelson!* A time to die.

And if the assassin was Italian—someone who had followed Nelson here from Rome—might not he be returning to Rome?

He confirmed at the information booth that the flight to Rome was six hours late in departing. There was just a chance that—

And then he saw the man.

There was no mistaking him, leaning against the wall smoking a cigarette. He even wore the same black raincoat.

Rand slipped a retractable ballpoint pen from his inner pocket and walked up to the man. Quickly, before he was noticed, he pressed the pen against the skin of the man's neck. "Don't move! Do you understand English? There's a needle in here that could poison you in an instant. You could be dead within a minute. Understand?"

The man was frozen in terror. "Yes. I understand."

"Why did you shoot Colonel Nelson?"

"I—"

Rand pressed harder. "Why?"

"I was paid to."

"By whom? The British?"

Suddenly Rand felt something hard jab him in the ribs, and he realized his mistake. There'd been two of them booked on the flight to Rome. "Let him go, Rand, or you're a dead man," a familiar voice said. "Turn around slowly and drop that pen."

He turned around and stared into the deadly eyes of old Sam Shawburn.

It was then Rand remembered where he'd seen the gunman before. "He was the drunk on the landing outside your apartment!"

Sam Shawburn smiled. "Tony here? Yes, that's right. He was just leaving when he heard you climbing the stairs, so he went into his act. We work well together."

"And you had Colonel Nelson killed."

"A matter of necessity. The African business was becoming too complex—and too profitable to share with a partner. One of us had to go, and I simply acted first, before he got the notion of killing me. I thought murdering him in Moscow was a stroke of genius. It presented so many more possible suspects, including yourself, than did Rome."

"I should have known. Someone tipped off the Russian police and I thought of Hastings. But you knew I'd come to Moscow too—you'd even warned Colonel Nelson of my arrival. You followed me here, had Tony shoot Nelson, and gave the Russians my name. It was easy for them to locate my hotel and to place guards at the embassies."

"Very good!"

"And that wasn't Colonel Nelson's apartment. Those weren't his cats," Rand said, remembering the sneezing in Gorky Park. "Colonel Nelson was allergic to cats."

"True."

"You fed the cats and you recruited the mercenaries for Africa, using Nelson's name."

"His business was buying the guns in Moscow, but I found it safer to use his name for the entire operation."

"How will you get the guns now?"

"Gregor will still deliver. He has contacts and he likes money."

Rand had to know one more thing. "The British? Are they financing the operation?"

"The British?" Shawburn laughed. "Not a chance! Did Nelson tell you that? It was his daydream that he still worked for British Intelligence. He couldn't face that he was living a grubby existence in the back streets of Rome. We were in it on our own."

"What now? Will you try shooting me within earshot of five hundred people?"

"Outside," Shawburn decided. "Walk between Tony and me. No tricks now!"

They were almost to the outer doors, walking fast, when Leila was suddenly upon them. There were two burly Russian policemen with her and she was yelling, "Stop those men! They're kidnaping my husband!"

Shawburn tried to pull the pistol from his pocket but he was old and slow. The Russians were on them, and it was over.

R and and Leila didn't catch the London plane that evening. It took two days and several telephone calls to London, plus a visit by the British ambassador, to free them from the endless rounds of questioning. By that time the Russians had found Gregor's address in Sam Shawburn's wallet and learned all about the illegal arms deal. They seemed more interested in that aspect of the case than in the murder of Colonel Nelson, but it was enough to insure that Shawburn and Tony would be spending a long time in Russian prisons.

Finally, flying back to London, Rand said, "You saved me twice in one day. I'm beginning to think I should have had you around all my life."

Leila smiled and leaned her head back on the seat. "If you're going to keep on doing little favors for Hastings, you'll need me around."

THE SPY IN THE LABYRINTH

The first thing a traveler usually noticed about Egyptian belly dancers was that they wore body stockings—a holdover from the puritanical rule of President Nasser. At least that was the first thing Scotty Jung noticed as he lounged at the bar of Sahara City, a night club exotically located in a giant tent just beyond the pyramids. Seeing Sahara City and remembering his own pyramid adventures of some years back, Jeffery Rand would have been startled and just a bit dismayed. Scotty Jung had no such problem. He was only 26 years old and this was his first visit to Egypt. He accepted the tented night club in the desert just as he accepted the pyramids themselves.

Scotty had become something of a world traveler since he'd fled from the United States in the closing days of the war protests. He'd got in deeper than he'd ever planned when he set a bomb in a Florida draft board that killed the building's janitor. The fact that Scotty hadn't meant to kill anyone, that he'd been physically ill for three days after realizing what he'd done, would have carried little weight with the authorities. He was a fugitive now, a hero among the underground groups, though with the coming of peace and the resignation of Nixon the general public had almost forgotten his name.

Some others had forgotten too, like Linda, the girl he'd been living with at the time. When he fled to Canada and then on to the Middle East, she promised to join him. He waited a whole year believing that promise until someone in the underground sent him a newspaper clipping announcing her marriage to a young systems engineer at IBM.

This past year, first in Turkey and then in Jerusalem, Scotty had managed to live by his wits. He'd stayed out of Turkish prisons and had spent several months living with a charming young typist who was quite willing to support him. When that broke up he'd drifted to Cairo. He had no doubt that the next adventure was no farther away than the pretty blonde now sitting at the bar.

"Your first time here?" she asked suddenly, perhaps aware that his eyes were on her.

"Yes. I've only been in Cairo a few days."

"Oh, you're American!"

"And you're British. I guess there's no hiding it."

They laughed and he offered to buy her a drink. She seemed about his age and said her name was Atlanta Chessman. She also said yes to the drink.

"Atlanta.   Back in the States I lived in northern Florida not far from Atlanta."

"I was named after the ocean," she said with a smile, "not the city."

"Are you here alone?" A tent in the middle of the desert hardly seemed a likely singles bar.

"I'm traveling with my brother. We had a toy business back in England, but we fell on hard times."

"Happens to everyone," he assured her. "What sort of toys?"

"Dolls, games—almost anything."

After a second drink he asked, "Can I drive you home from here? I have a rented car outside."

She threw back her head and laughed. "Only Americans would be foolish enough to rent a car in Cairo! It's almost suicidal, the way Egyptians drive. For a few extra dollars you could hire a car and driver."

"I didn't know that. But the offer's still open."

Her eyes seemed to be searching the crowd. Suddenly she said, "There's my brother—come to meet him."

Richard Chessman was tall and slim, with deep-set eyes that gave his face an aggressive appearance. Scotty Jung disliked him almost at once, though Richard was pleasant enough to him. "Enjoying the belly dancers?" Richard asked as they shook hands. "Of course they're better in Beirut."

"And in Istanbul," Scotty agreed. "These are a bit hefty for my taste."

"You men!" Atlanta complained, leading him away. "Have you seen the sound-and-light show at the pyramids yet?"

"I haven't seen anything, but I'd certainly like a guide."

"Very well," she agreed willingly. "Come on, then. We should be just in time for the English-language commentary. They do it in English, French, German, and Arabic each night."

Scotty followed her outside and then stood for a minute watching the lights playing on the nearby pyramids. "It's still a bit far to walk," he decided. "Let's take the car."

But when they were inside she stayed his hand on the ignition. "Let's just watch the lights for a while. We've got time."

"Sure. Whatever you say."

She turned her lips to his and kissing her he thought about driving her back to his room near Ramses Square. The pyramids could wait for another night.

Suddenly the door opened and Richard Chessman slid into the car with them. "There's something we want you to do for us, Scotty," he said quietly.

For the first time since Rand's retirement from Concealed Communications, he and Leila were having his former superior, Hastings, to dinner. Thinking back to their telephone conversation, Rand couldn't quite remember how it had come about, but he had half a suspicion that somehow Hastings had managed to invite himself.

"Lovely place you have here," the intelligence chief said over coffee, "and the dinner was delicious. I should visit you more often."

Leila and Rand exchanged glances. "We're so far out in the country," she said. "I'm afraid we're losing touch with all our London friends. With my teaching and Jeffery's writing—"

"Ah, yes—how is the book coming, Rand? Giving away all our secrets?"

"Hardly." Rand shifted uneasily in his chair, knowing that the real reason for Hastings' visit was about to be revealed.

"There are two weeks yet before the autumn term begins. You two should get away somewhere."

"Oh?" Leila perked up. "And where would you suggest, Mr. Hastings? Moscow again?"

"No, no! That Moscow business was unfortunate. I was thinking of Cairo. You haven't been back since your marriage, have you, Leila?"

Rand saw the flicker of pleasure mixed with suspicion cross her face. He knew she'd half regretted not going to Cairo on their honeymoon, and they'd talked casually about making the trip earlier this summer. The damp autumn weather had set in sooner than was expected this year, which was another reason for Leila to wish for the warm sands of her homeland. And yet—

"Give it to us straight," Rand said, voicing her suspicions. "What's in Cairo?"

"It's *who*, not what."

"Then who's in Cairo?"

"Richard Chessman and his sister. Remember that business with the toy company last winter?"

"How could I forget!" Rand poured some more coffee. "They got away from you that time. What are they up to now?"

"That's just it—we don't know! I can't send anyone officially, but you're in a unique position to help us, Rand."

"They both know me."

"But they don't know Leila."

"Let's keep it that way. You seem to forget that when we married I retired from Double-C—she didn't join up."

Hastings sighed and took a sip of coffee. "Just once more, Rand, and I won't bother you again. You'll both get a free trip to Cairo."

Rand turned to his wife. "It's up to you, Leila. What do you think?"

She looked into his eyes, found her answer there, and said, "I'd like to see Cairo again."

"Good!" Hastings exclaimed. "How soon can you leave? Tomorrow?"

Rand smiled and shook his head. "Still the same old Hastings, aren't you? Give us forty-eight hours at least."

"Thirty-six. I can get you on a plane Thursday morning. And you'll be back in plenty of time for the autumn term, Leila."

"I hope so. I'll admit it will impress my archeology students to tell them I'm just back from the pyramids."

"Where will we find Chessman and his sister?" Rand asked.

"She's been seen with an American fugitive named Scotty Jung, wanted back in the States for a terrorist bombing. He has a room off Ramses Square and it seems they're living there together."

"Why don't the Americans have him arrested?"

"Extradition is always difficult from those Middle-Eastern countries, even when they recognize it by treaty. Besides, we're more interested in the Chessman connection just now. They're up to something."

"We'll see," Rand said. His thoughts were already in Egypt, where he and Leila first met years ago.

Scotty Jung awakened and opened his eyes, immediately aware that he was alone in the bed. Though it was barely daylight, Atlanta was up preparing breakfast. He listened to her moving around the tiny kitchen, imaging how she looked in the sheer silk kaftan he'd bought her with his advance from Richard. Thinking of Richard, he suddenly remembered what day it was. "How's it going?" he asked, coming out to the kitchen.

She glanced up from the toast she was buttering. "Good morning. I didn't want to disturb you, but I must be on my way. I'm meeting Richard at eight."

"When will you be back?"

She hesitated. "I'm not certain. Tonight or tomorrow."

After breakfast she was gone and he had the whole day ahead of him. He decided to spend it at the pyramids again. They'd gone to the sound-and-light show twice in the week he'd known Atlanta, sitting through all four performances with successive narrations in English, French, German, and Arabic. This was because Richard had told Atlanta he wanted Scotty to spy on a certain Ali Zamal, who presented the nightly taped commentaries and sometimes gave special talks in Arabic. Zamal was a short swarthy man who wore a business suit and a red fez. Scotty might never have looked at him twice had not Atlanta pointed him out. "That is Zamal," she whispered on the first night at the show. "He's a dangerous man."

He considered his situation often in the days that had followed. Richard and Atlanta had recognized him from some old newspaper photos and arranged to meet him. They knew he'd killed a man back home, and knew they could use him for their own purposes. There was little danger of Scotty's turning them in to the police, even after Atlanta told him they wanted him to kill Zamal. But he still looked forward to his eventual return to America at some time when past events would have drifted into the forgotten pages of history. Now Richard wanted him to kill a man, and he wasn't at all certain he could do it.

He spent most of the afternoon wandering around the pyramids, watching groups of American tourists being photographed. Some climbed bravely onto the back of a tired-looking camel while the camera clicked, and Scotty felt a special fondness for them. Foolishly dressed in their garish sports shirts and bulging pants suits, they were still his countrymen.

"That camel looks mean," a young woman at his side remarked.

"He looks more tired than mean," Scotty said. "You know when they're mean."

She tossed the dark hair out of her eyes and smiled at him. "I see you're a camel expert. And an American too."

"Does it show?" Somehow this reminded him of his meeting with Atlanta Chessman only a week before. He studied the young woman intently. She was older than Atlanta, perhaps around 30, and certainly not British. Egyptian, he guessed.

"I like Americans," she replied. "Is this your first time in our country?"

"It is. And you're Egyptian?"

"Partly. I teach at the University." She held out her hand. "I'm Leila Gaad."

He accepted the hand, finding it soft but strong. "Scotty Jung," he said, certain the name would mean nothing to her. "What brings a native out here on a hot afternoon?"

"Archeology is my subject. I like to come here for a bit of a refresher every few months."

He smiled at her. "Speaking of refreshers, Sahara City's just down the road and their bar is open. Can I buy you a drink?"

She consulted her watch, hesitated, then said, "That would be lovely."

The restaurant beneath the huge tent was crowded for the cocktail hour, with tourists mingling freely among a scattering of local residents. Leila Gaad said, "I don't usually drink this early in the day, to say nothing of drinking with a stranger."

He smiled. "We introduced ourselves, didn't we?"

But there was something about the woman that made him uneasy He'd picked up girls in bars and on street corners all through the Middle East, and he knew the way it was supposed to go. This wasn't going right. He was sorry he'd told her his real name.

After a half hour of aimless chatter she excused herself. "I have to make a phone call but I'll be right back. Don't go away."

"I won't."

He watched her cross the empty dance floor and thread her way between the tables. Whoever she was going to call, he had a hunch it wouldn't be good for him. He paid the bill and started for the opposite entrance. Ali Zamal, the man in the red fez, was standing there watching him. Scotty glanced the other way as he walked past. He drove back toward the city, going over in his mind the instructions for that evening which he'd received from Richard. It took him an hour to accomplish what he had to do.

It was dark by the time he returned to his apartment, having made his way through the city's back alleys to shake off any possible followers. He went quickly up the steps and unlocked the door. Inside, he realized he was not alone. There was a sob from a darkened corner of the room. Scotty froze, wishing he had a weapon.

"Who's there?" he asked softly.

The sob came again, and as his eyes became accustomed to the dark he saw Atlanta Chessman hunched in a corner. He ran to her and knelt down. "What is it? What are you doing here, Atlanta? I thought you were away."

She clung to him, her face terrified and tear-streaked. "They've shot Richard," she sobbed out at last, "I think he's dead."

"Where is he?"

"Downstairs—in the car. I was afraid to stay with him. They're after us both."

"Who is?"

"Ali Zamal's people."

"Stay here. I'll go down and have a look."

Scotty went down the back stairs, moving cautiously when he reached the street. The little car was in the place she always left it, and he went to it at once. Richard Chessman was crumpled on the floor of the back seat, his shirt soaked with blood. He was more dead than alive and Scotty drew back helplessly, not knowing what to do.

Suddenly a man he'd never seen before was at his elbow, shoving him aside. Scotty wanted to run, but if the man was a police officer he knew it was too late for that. "Chessman!" the man said, bending over the crumpled figure on the car floor. "Can you hear me?"

Scotty saw the dying eyes flicker open. "What ... ? Rand, is that you? Am I back in London?"

"You're in Cairo, Chessman, and you're dying. Who shot you?"

Chessman gasped and tried to speak again, but his mouth filled with blood. The words wouldn't come. With a final gesture he tapped the breast pocket of his shirt, then sagged back as if crushed by a great weight.

"He's dead," the man named Rand said. Already he was reaching for the pocket that Richard had indicated. He took out a folded piece of paper, glanced at it in the dim light, and pocketed it.

"Who are you?" Scotty asked. "Police?"

"I knew Chessman in London. I think we'd better talk. You could be in big trouble."

Rand had gone searching for Scotty Jung as soon as Leila reported losing him. Finally he'd staked out the apartment near Ramses Square. He hadn't seen Atlanta go in the back door, but when Scotty arrived he saw that. He'd been checking out the rear parking area when Scotty emerged again and went to the car. Rand knew it was some sort of luck that had brought him to the dying Chessman, but he didn't know if it was good luck or bad.

Atlanta faced him now in the upstairs apartment, her face puffy and tear-streaked. "You again! Was it you who shot Richard?"

"Hardly."

"What is all this?" Scotty demanded. "Who is this guy?"

When Atlanta didn't answer, Rand replied for her. "Their father operated a private intelligence-gathering organization in London until he was killed. I'm retired from British Intelligence and they hired me for a time as a cipher expert."

"What are you doing here?"

"On holiday with my wife."

"And doing a little snooping for British Intelligence?" Atlanta asked, beginning to recover herself.

Scotty Jung interrupted. "He's after me. He came to my apartment."

"I'm not after anyone," Rand tried to convince them. "I just want to know what's happened. Who killed your brother, Atlanta?"

"Probably one of Ali Zamal's men. He was shot by a sniper as he was getting into our car at the airport parking lot. We'd just flown back from a meeting—" She broke off suddenly, aware that she was saying too much.

"You have to tell me," Rand urged. "Richard is dead downstairs. You could be next."

"I can't say any more."

"You and Richard are still working for the highest bidder, aren't you? Who is it this time—the Arabs or Israel? And who is Ali Zamal?"

"He works at the pyramid sound-and-light show," Scotty answered.

"That's enough, Scotty," she warned.

"You should know," Rand told her, "that the Egyptian police can be very hard on murder suspects—especially when espionage is suspected."

"Do you think I killed my own brother?"

"They might ask why you drove around while he bled to death in the back seat."

"I was terrified, hysterical! I was afraid to stay at the airport and afraid to drive to a hospital. I came here to find Scotty."

"Where had the two of you been?" Rand asked.

"We flew to Amman," she said at last. "To meet a man named Rangoon." Turning toward Jung she added, "I wasn't sure when Richard planned to come back. I thought he might want to stay overnight."

"But when you did return this evening a sniper was waiting at the airport?"

"Yes. I believe he meant to kill us both."

"Tell me about Rangoon."

She shrugged. "He's paying us a great deal of money."

"For what?"

Another hesitation, and a glance at Scotty Jung. "To kill Ali Zamal. That's where Scotty fits in. We told him first that it was only a spying job, but then we told him the rest of it."

"I see." Rand felt tired. There was always someone new, someone young like Scotty, who could be hired to do the killing. "Where will it all end now, Atlanta?"

"With Ali Zamal. I won't need Scotty. I'll kill him myself."

Rand remembered the piece of paper he'd taken from Richard's pocket. He opened it and studied it again in better light. On it were four lines enclosed in a maze-like frame:

LABYRINTH
LABYRINTHE
LABYRINTH
82

"Any idea what it means?" Rand asked her. "Richard was indicating it when he died."

"It's only doodling," she replied. "It means nothing."

"What is the labyrinth?"

"I don't know."

"What does 82 mean?"

"If it means anything he didn't tell me."

Rand turned over the slip of stiff paper. The message was on the back of Richard's airline boarding pass, but that told him nothing. "All right. Call the police and tell them about your brother. I don't care what sort of story you make up, but leave me out of it. And stay away from Ali Zamal for now—both of you."

Scotty Jung nodded, but Atlanta only turned away.

Rand returned to their hotel room to find Leila on the sofa. "I'm such a failure, Jeffery. Were you able to locate him?"

He poured them both a drink and told her about it. "He and Atlanta were at his apartment. Richard's there too, but he's dead."

"Dead!"

"Someone shot him at the airport. Atlanta let him bleed to death in the back of their car. I found him just in time to get this before he died."

He showed her the slip of paper. "Some memo or note in his pocket. He pointed to it just before he died. Know any labyrinths around here?"

"Of course," she replied, surprising him. "The labyrinth at Arsinoe is just south of here." She studied the paper and smiled. "About 82 kilometers south of here, in fact."

"Interesting. Do archeologists do their digging there?"

"Not any more. Only the foundations survive. The most interesting fact about it is that the ancient name for Arsinoe was Crocodilopolis. Isn't that a wonderful name for a city?"

"Not exactly the sort civic boosters would suggest."

"It was probably the most famous labyrinth of antiquity. Herodotus said it contained twelve courts and 3000 chambers, half of them below ground for the tombs of kings and the sacred crocodiles. It was most likely built as a tomb, though some historians believe it may have served as a secret meeting place for political leaders."

"If we decided to drive there could you find it in the dark?"

She smiled at the question. "Unless it's moved after 4300 years. It's about an hour's drive from here."

"Richard was trying to tell me something about the labyrinth. But what? You say nothing's left of it but the foundations."

She picked up the slip of paper again. "Why did he write the word three times—and once with an *e* on the end? And the *82* at the bottom. It all must mean something."

"You told me that was the distance to the labyrinth."

"Yes, but why did he write it at the bottom like—" Her frown gave way to a slow smile. "Oh, Jeffery, it's wonderful! I should have worked with you at Concealed Communications!"

"You mean you see something that I'm missing?"

"Of course! He's written the word *labyrinth* in three languages—English, French, and German. It's nearly identical in all three."

Rand still didn't get it. "And the number?"

"He wrote down the number—the distance to Arsinoe—because he didn't know the Arabic word for labyrinth. Don't you see? It's an *Arabic* number, like all our numbers! Four lines, four languages—English, French, German, and

Arabic. And what does that bring to mind?"

"The sound-and-light show at the pyramids!"

"Exactly."

"Come on," Rand said. "There's still time to catch the end of tonight's performance."

The order of the multi-lingual narrations was changed nightly and they arrived to find that the French commentary was just ending. The spotlights that played on the pyramids were dimmed and the audience was filing out. A short man in a red fez was changing the lettering on the announcement board, indicating that the German commentary would be coming next.

"Let's go in," Rand said.

They took their seats amid a scattering of tourists. He noticed two Japanese gentlemen in the row ahead and wondered if they understood German. Presently the man in the fez took his place at the microphone and turned on some soothing Eastern music. Then he began to speak rapidly in German.

"Something's wrong here," Leila whispered in his ear. "They usually just play a tape of the lecture in the appropriate language."

"Can you understand what he's saying?" Rand asked, but even he had caught the word *labyrinth*.

The two Japanese men sitting ahead of them suddenly rose and headed up the aisle toward the rear exit. "What do you think is happening, Jeffery?"

"This show is being used as a staging area for some purpose. The spoken narration before the tape recording tips them off as to where they're going next—in this case, the labyrinth at Arsinoe. That was the meaning of Richard's memo. He'd noticed the word *labyrinth* used by the speaker in all three languages he understood."

They left their seats and moved up the darkened aisle after the two Japanese men. But by the time they reached the parking area it was only to see a little car disappearing down the highway. "We'll never catch them at night," Leila said. "They could turn off anywhere."

"Is that the road to the labyrinth?"

"They could go that way, yes. It lies near the city of Al-Fayyum."

Rand was aware that the voice of the German narrator had changed, but it didn't occur to him that the tape was now playing until he saw the short man in the red fez coming up behind Leila. "You departed from my show with great haste," he said. "We should speak of this."

He held out his hand as if to shake Rand's in greeting, and too late Rand saw the spring knife shoot from his sleeve. It moved toward him like an adder, striking for the kill, when suddenly another shadowy figure appeared from the darkness and collided with the man in the fez. There was a brief tussle as they hit the ground together, then stillness. As the light show began, Rand saw the face of his rescuer in the reflected glow from the Great Pyramid. It was Scotty Jung.

"Good to see you again, Scotty." He glanced down at the ground. "Did you kill him?"

"No, only knocked him out." Jung turned and recognized Leila at once. "I should have known you were with him."

"She's my wife. Now suppose you tell us who this fellow is."

"Ali Zamal, the man they wanted me to kill."

"I see."

"I guess I'm not much at killing—at least not with my bare hands. Let's get out of here."

Rand made a quick decision. Whichever side Jung was on, it was better to keep him in sight. "Come with us," he urged. "We're driving to the labyrinth at Arsinoe."

"Tonight? What for?"

"To find out, among other things, why Ali Zamal tried to kill me just now."

Leila drove, because she knew the roads, while Rand and Jung sat in the back seat where they could crouch down out of sight quickly if another car overtook them. "Where is Atlanta?" Rand asked when they'd been on their way abut ten minutes.

"She took the car somewhere, with her brother's body."

"To the police, I hope."

"I don't know."

"How do you fit into this whole picture?"

The American leaned back and closed his eyes. "Sometimes I wonder about that myself. I killed a man back in the States, with a bomb. It was part of an anti-war protest and I didn't mean to injure anyone, but that didn't matter. I've been running ever since, living by my wits, taking on a few dirty jobs just to stay alive. Cairo seemed as good a city as any, until I met Atlanta. Oh, she was fine but her brother was trouble. Right away he tried to recruit me for some dirty work. He wanted me to spy on Ali Zamal and find out what he was up to. Then Atlanta asked me to kill him for them."

"Did you agree?"

"Not at first, but Atlanta was wearing me down. They knew all about my background—they'd recognized me from a photo—and knew I couldn't turn them in. It was a kind of blackmail, I suppose."

"What about this trip to see a man named Rangoon?"

"Rangoon is the CIA's chief undercover agent in the Middle East. He was supposed to return to Cairo with the Chessmans tonight but he changed his plans."

"I see. Then Atlanta and Richard were working for the CIA?"

"For whoever paid them the most. Richard told me sometimes they worked for both sides at the same time."

As they drove on through the darkness, heading south across the desert toward Al-Fayyum and the ruins of Crocodilopolis, Rand imagined another car with Atlanta Chessman at the wheel, bearing her dead brother toward some unmarked grave. Sudden death was a hazard of the game, Rand knew, but that didn't make the danger any more acceptable.

"Soon," Leila said presently. "We're at the outskirts of Al-Fayyum now."

Rand could see little but darkness out the car windows, broken now and then by lamplight from some house they passed. Presently the houses became more numerous, but Leila avoided the center of town to take them a little to the west. It was almost midnight when she finally parked the car and announced, "The ruins are just over the next rise. I'd suggest we go the rest of the way on foot if you expect to spy on anyone without being seen."

Rand and Jung followed her advice, leaving the car and trailing behind her on foot as she led the way up a sand dune. The moon was almost full, and from the top of the dune they could look down at a stretch of palm trees lit by the moon's silver glow. "The ruins of the labyrinth are just beyond the trees. You are standing now in the ancient city of Crocodilopolis."

"Where were the crocodiles?" Rand asked. "Are we close to the Nile?"

"The Nile is nearly forty kilometers to the east, but several streams and a canal flow through here, connecting the river with Lake Moeris to the north. Yes, there were sacred crocodiles in the lake at one time. There still are, occasionally, though the Aswan Dam has pretty much ended the seasonal flooding of the Nile at this point."

"Crocodilopolis," Scotty Jung said, speaking the name softly. "The City of Crocodiles."

Suddenly Leila's hand was on Rand's shoulder. "Look there, in the moonlight!"

He followed her gaze and saw two men moving among the trees. One of them carried what might have been a rifle. "You two stay here," he said. "I'm going down."

Before Leila could protest he was gone, slipping along the sand to the shelter of the palm trees. As he drew closer the moonlight revealed a low man-made structure, half buried in the ground. He could see a sign by an entrance, printed in the usual four languages. With some difficulty he read the lines in English, using a match to augment the moonlight: *Opening soon—a modern reconstruction of a portion of the labyrinth at Arsinoe. Made possible by funds from the Egyptian State Tourist Administration.*

The match flame singed Rand's fingers and he let it drop. Almost at once a voice behind him said, "We meet again, Mr. Rand. But this time I have a gun instead of a knife."

Rand turned slowly to face Ali Zamal and the sten gun he held steadily in one hand. There was no arguing with it. "I thought I left you back in Cairo."

"The journey is very swift by helicopter. Now please raise your hands and step inside ahead of me. You'll find a friend of yours already present."

Rand opened the door and stepped down into the reconstructed maze. The place was a long, dimly lit corridor with passages and rooms going off on either side. Glancing in as they passed, he could see more doorways, more passages, leading in all directions. They passed a niche where a realistic stuffed crocodile waited to greet tourists with its gaping jaws.

"To the left," Ali Zamal instructed as they reached a corner. "Then to the right."

"You know your way through here."

"I helped design the reconstruction. In here now."

Rand entered and found two other Arabs standing beside a chair. Atlanta Chessman sat in it, tied hand and foot. She raised her eyes when she saw him. "Rand."

"Atlanta! How did you—?"

Ali Zamal snorted. "She tried to kill me because she thinks I shot her brother. I brought her along in the helicopter."

"What is all this?" Rand asked. "What's going on here?"

It was Atlanta who answered. "A meeting—a meeting of terrorist leaders from around the world. Germans, Japanese, Irish, Palestinians. All the bombers and plane hijackers and assassins. He wants to unite them into a worldwide terrorist network."

Ali Zamal stared down at her. "Shut up," he said quietly.

"That's why Rangoon was coming—to try and break it up. But something happened at the last minute. He was tipped off there'd be an assassin waiting. There was—only he killed my brother instead."

Ali Zamal slapped her across the face with his open palm. "You've said enough. As for your brother, you'll soon be joining him."

Rand took a step forward and one of the Arab guards raised his weapon. That was when they heard the first explosion.

Ali Zamal wheeled and shouted something in Arabic. The guards took off, running. There was the clatter of machine-gun fire, echoing through the labyrinth's corridors, and then another explosion.

Suddenly Scotty Jung appeared with a sack of grenades over one shoulder and a sten gun in his hands. "Let's get out of here!" he shouted to Rand. Ali Zamal raised his own weapon but he was too slow for the American. The sten gun's bullets cut through his middle and he toppled against the chair where Atlanta was tied.

Rand knelt to cut her free, and then they were running with Scotty, making their way back through the maze. "How can we find our way out?" Atlanta gasped.

"I left a trail of sand. We're following it now," Scotty told her.

"Where'd you get the gun and grenades?" Rand asked.

"Your wife and I found a helicopter behind the dune. The stuff was in there, and I figured you might need help."

"You figured correctly."

Atlanta twisted her ankle and fell. Rand paused to help her up just as a Japanese rounded the corner behind them. Scotty fired a short burst from his weapon. "You two go on," he said. "I'd better stay here."

"You can't—"

"There are probably twenty of them in this maze. It's better if none of them gets out. Go on now! Leila's waiting outside."

Rand put his arm around Atlanta and helped her the rest of the way. The last he saw of Scotty Jung, the American was hurling another grenade into the depths of the labyrinth. They just made it into the moonlit night when a quick series of explosions seemed to rip the place apart, throwing them to the sand.

L eila found them a few seconds later. "Jeffery! Are you all right?"

"Good enough, I guess. Atlanta twisted her ankle, but she's all right."

Atlanta Chessman stood up uncertainly, gazing back at the smoke and fire so close behind them. "Scotty."

"I'm sorry," Rand said. "He didn't make it. Let's get back in case there are more explosions."

They went a little farther but then she dropped to her knees in the sand, sobbing for Scotty as she had for her brother.

"He said to give you this," Leila told Rand. "It was a note he wrote just before he went in after you. I don't think he planned to come out."

"No," Rand said. "He wouldn't have."

"Aren't you going to read it?"

"I think I know what it says, Leila. Richard Chessman knew about the labyrinth—remember the writing on his boarding pass?—so there was no reason for him to want Scotty to spy on Zamal, then to kill him. It was only a cover story so his sister wouldn't know the truth—that he was working for both sides. He knew about the labyrinth and the messages in the sound-and-light show because Zamal told him. And what about Scotty? He supposedly didn't know when Richard and Atlanta were getting back from Amman—but in the back seat tonight he told me the CIA man named Rangoon was supposed to return to Cairo with them this evening. Don't you see? Rangoon got lucky, and Richard died instead, probably thinking Zamal killed him."

"What do you mean, Jeffery?"

He unfolded Scotty's last note and they read it together by the light from the burning labyrinth.

Rand—You're a good guy, so I'm leaving you this. Richard hired me to assassinate Rangoon, the CIA man, at the airport tonight. Ali Zamal was paying for it, but Richard didn't want Atlanta to know. He wanted me to do it instead of some hopped-up Arab who might hit her with a stray bullet. Only I was the wrong guy for it. I don't really know if I would have shot Rangoon or not. The longer I waited there with the rifle, the more Richard became the real villain in my mind. When they went to the car, Rangoon wasn't with them and I shot Richard instead.

THE SPY WHO WAS ALONE

On this afternoon in late September, when summer still lingered under the pressures of the approaching English autumn, Jeffery Rand drove into the yard of his little country house without a care in the world. He'd been retired from British Intelligence for nearly a year, and was settling down at last to writing the book he'd always planned to do. His wife Leila was beginning her second term of teaching archeology at nearby Reading University, having extracted a promise from him never again to be lured into government service, even on a temporary basis.

"I'm home!" he shouted to Leila as he came through the door, expecting to find her relaxing in the living room after her first day back at the University. When she wasn't there he tried the kitchen, and then called upstairs. There was still no answer.

He glanced out the rear door and saw the empty garage. She wasn't yet home—delayed, no doubt, by her first-day duties. He sighed and went to the sideboard to pour himself a drink. That was when he noticed the missing statue. It was a reproduction of an Egyptian cat—one of Leila's favorites—and it had always stood on the coffee table.

Odd.

He began to notice a few other missing things as well—a small silver vase, a set of books on ancient Egypt, a framed photograph of Leila at the pyramids. All were her possessions.

And all were missing.

He went upstairs, convinced now that something was wrong. In the bedroom he opened her closet and his heart skipped a beat.

All her clothes were gone.

Every last stitch.

What was this? What was happening?

He ran back downstairs and looked in the kitchen. Her favorite cookbook was missing.

"Leila!" He called her name again, then went out to the garage. It seemed exactly as it had been this morning, when he watched her drive off to the University.

The University!

Rand hurried back inside to the telephone and dialed the number that had

103

been hers during the last term. It rang for some time before an unfamiliar voice answered. "Is Leila Gaad—Leila Rand—there, please?"

"Leila Rand?" the woman repeated. "I'm afraid not."

"This is her office, isn't it?"

A pause, and then, "I understand Leila Rand is not teaching this term. I believe she has resigned."

"Resigned! Why, that's impossible!"

"I'm sorry. You'll have to speak with the Dean for any further information."

The connection was broken and Rand was left holding a dead telephone. Impossible!

Yet so was what he found here—the clothing and the other things just ... gone! The whole thing was impossible!

He sat down and tried to think. Then he got up and paced. There were no near neighbors, and Leila hadn't made any new friends living out here in the country. Her old friends were back in Egypt, where Rand had met her. Where could she possibly be?

He decided to search the house.

It was not that large and the search took only ten minutes. He discovered a few other missing items, all small and all Leila's personal property. And in the upstairs bathroom, the last place he looked, he found the note taped to the mirror.

His eyes blurred as he read the words, seeing them all at once in a rush of disbelief: *Jeffrey— It's better we part. Noways try to find me. —L.*

She had left him.

For what? For another man?

His mind refused to grasp the fact. They'd been married less than a year, and he could swear it had been a wildly happy year for both of them. Except for some assignments forced on him by British Intelligence, they'd been together all the time. Leila had even journeyed to Moscow to get him out of a particularly tight spot.

And now she had left.

Without a word except for this note.

No, he couldn't believe it.

Something was wrong, terribly wrong.

But where was she?

Later that evening he thought of Hastings, his old boss when Rand was in charge of the Department of Concealed Communications. He still had Hastings' unlisted home telephone number and he called him there.

"Well, Rand! Good to hear from you! I've been meaning to ring you up about the fine job you did for us in Amman."

"Hastings—"

"What is it?" Suddenly his voice reflected Rand's tenseness.

"Leila's gone. She's left me."

"Leila? But you two seemed so happy."

"We were happy. I don't know. It doesn't make any sense to me."

"Is there anything I can do?"

"I don't know. I suppose I thought she might have contacted you."

"No, not a word from her. Look here, Rand, why not drive into London tomorrow for lunch. We can talk about it."

"I was just in London today, seeing my publisher about the book."

"How's it coming?"

"What? Oh, the book. Well enough, I suppose—until now."

"Get a good night's sleep. Maybe things won't look quite so glum in the morning."

"But there was no reason for her to leave, Hastings! Don't you understand? No reason in the world! Everything was fine!"

"Yes. Well, ring me up at the office, Rand. Let me know about lunch. And try to get some sleep."

Rand hung up and started pacing again. He went back and read the note once more.

Noways try to find me.

He couldn't remember Leila ever having used the word *noways*.

But it was her handwriting. Of that there was no doubt.

Sometime after midnight he fell asleep in his chair.

He awoke early in the morning, when the first rays of sunlight brought the birds chirping to activity. It took him a moment to remember about Leila, and what he was doing sleeping in the chair. When he stood up his shoulder and neck were stiff. He rubbed them a bit and made a quick breakfast for himself, as he had so many times during his bachelor existence.

Then he drove to Reading.

The house that Rand and Leila had chosen for their married life was a little country place near Bracknell, on the edge of Windsor Forest. It was about halfway between the western edge of London and the city of Reading, where Leila had been teaching at the University.

It was just a bit over ten miles from their house to the University, and even with the heavy morning traffic Rand drove it in less than twenty minutes. Reading was a small city of barely 132,000 people. The medium-sized University had been affiliated with Oxford in its early days but had been independent for more than 50 years. Leila seemed to like it during her first term there, and Rand thought she'd been eager to return in the autumn.

He drove into Reading on the London Road, but had to detour around some street construction before reaching the University. The city had the usual array of shops catering to the student population. There were bookstores, fast-food outlets, boutiques, and even an oyster bar. But he paid little attention to any of them. Presently he reached the University itself and parked in the visitors' lot.

Rand remembered just one name from those Leila had mentioned—a fellow instructor named Isabel Skrech. Her husband was a professor doing research in stress detection, and Leila had helped him out earlier in the summer by taking some psychological tests. Rand located Isabel just a few minutes before her first morning lecture, puffing on a cigarette as she studied her notes. "Mr. Rand—how nice to meet you at last! Leila mentioned you often. How is she?"

"I was hoping you could tell me. She seems to have disappeared."

"Disappeared? How odd!"

"I was told on the phone that she'd resigned."

"That's what I heard too. I believe the Dean received a letter over the weekend, or yesterday morning. I know he was quite disturbed by the short notice she gave."

"I would like to see that letter."

"I suppose I could ask him," she said after an instant's hesitation. "Come along."

After giving her students a brief reading assignment she led the way across the courtyard to a nearby building. The Dean was a flustery man with a red face who wasn't pleased to see Rand. "You must understand that a resignation on such short notice raises great problems for us, Mr. Rand."

"I'd like to see her letter if I may. Leila told me nothing of this, and I was under the impression she came here to begin the new term yesterday. When I arrived home from London last evening she was gone."

The Dean looked all the more unhappy. "We really can't concern ourselves with family difficulties."

"Could I see her letter of resignation?"

"Certainly."

He produced it from a folder on his desk and Rand read the brief lines: *I am sorry that personal problems preclude my teaching at Reading this term. Please accept my resignation. Leila Rand.*

"When did this arrive?"

"In the first mail yesterday morning. I tried phoning her for some sort of explanation, but there was no answer."

"No. I was in London and she was—" Where?

The letter was typewritten, not on their machine at home, and Leila's signature could easily have been forged. The apprehension that had played in his mind now took a firmer hold.

"I'm afraid that's all I can tell you," the Dean said.

Rand handed back the letter. "I don't believe she wrote this."

"My dear chap, I received the letter and your wife did not appear for the beginning of the term. That is all I know. Now if you'll excuse me—"

Outside, Isabel Skrech tried to comfort him. "Don't mind old Bosey. He's like that with everyone."

"Do you believe she's disappeared?"

"Well, she's certainly disappeared as far as you're concerned. But the question seems to be whether that disappearance is voluntary or not."

"I can't believe she'd leave me."

Isabel took out one of her cigarettes. "Stranger things have happened. Leila always struck me as a very secretive person."

"No," Rand said, shaking his head. "Something's happened to her. I know it!"

"You mean you think she was kidnaped?"

"I don't know. There's been no ransom demand." *Not yet*, he added silently. There were a good many people interested in his former position with British Intelligence. Someone might well have taken Leila as a way of forcing him to deliver information.

If that was the case, they'd be making contact with him soon.

"I'd better get back home," he decided.

"If there's anything I can do—"

"Certainly. I'll call you if I hear any news."

He drove back home and arrived just as the postman was delivering the morning mail. There were the usual advertisements and a letter from an old friend in Dublin.

There was nothing from Leila.

He waited patiently through the afternoon, expecting a phone call at any moment. Once he thought of putting through a call to her relatives in Cairo, but he dismissed that as counterproductive. They would not have heard anything from her, and he might only worry them needlessly.

By early evening he'd lost hope that he would hear anything form her. He got out the note to read it again, because it was the last concrete link he had with their life together.

Jeffrey—It's better we part. Noways try to find me. L.

Noways.

That word stuck out again, as it had before.

And then for the first time he noticed something else. Though he spelled his first name J-E-F-F-E-R-Y, she'd used the more common spelling of R-E-Y.

Why would she spell his name wrong in a note saying goodbye?

To tell him something.

But what?

His whole adult life had been devoted to codes and ciphers. If she wanted to communicate with him, wouldn't she have used a code, knowing he'd break it? He remembered the message he'd sent from Moscow, using only the first letters of each word. That was worth a try.

J-I-B-W-P-N-T-T-F-M-L

Nothing.

With only one vowel the letters couldn't be jumbled to form words. Even leaving off the *Jeffrey* and the final *L* was no help.

And yet, that *noways* was there for a reason, to make up something she needed for her cipher. He was sure of it.

The more he thought about it the more excited he became. A secret message meant she hadn't really left him, not of her own free will.

She'd spelled his name wrong for a reason, to attract his attention to the message and to tell him—what? That the letters were reversed?

That she was using the last letters instead of the first?

Leave off the *Jeffrey* again and—

S-R-E-T-S-Y-O-D-E

Still nothing.

Reversed. Try it backward.

E-D-O-Y-S-T-E-R-S

Ed Oysters?

Or with the final *L*, Led Oysters?

No, he liked Ed Oysters better.

Half of a lifetime in Double-C, working on enemy ciphers, had taught him many lessons. He knew that real words sometimes formed themselves by chance, leading code-breakers on a merry chase down the wrong path.

Ed Oysters might be just such a chance formation, meaning nothing.

And yet, she'd used that word *noways*. And she'd misspelled his first name. For a reason.

All right, all right. He would proceed on the assumption that the note contained a secret message and that the message was *Ed Oysters*. If the words meant nothing to him, what might they have meant to Leila?

A person's name? A man named Ed who ate oysters? A man named Ed who was somehow connected with oysters? This last seemed the most likely.

Oysters. He'd seen the word somewhere recently, this very day. An oyster bar in Reading, that was it, near the University.

It was a slim lead, but he had no other.

He got out the car and drove into Reading for the second time that day. It was growing dark when he arrived, and the streets were crowded with university students still exploring the city that was their new home. Several of them, men and women, stood in a group at the corner of Duke Street and Mill Lane, by the multi-story car park. The Reading Gaol Oyster Bar was just across the street and it was obviously a student meeting place. Though Rand didn't remember Leila's mentioning it, he expected that the faculty went there on occasion too.

The inside was dim and crowded, reminding Rand of a smoky London club. On the walls near the entrance were the framed stanzas of Oscar Wilde's *The Ballad of Reading Gaol*, the city's main claim to literary immortality.

A smiling man with a handful of menus approached Rand. "Would you like dinner, sir? We have a special seafood platter this evening—"

"I'm looking for Ed. Is he around?"

"Ed?" There was a flicker of hesitation on the man's face. "I don't believe I know him."

"I think he works here."

The man shook his head. "No, you must be mistaken."

"Is there another oyster restaurant in Reading?"

"We're the only one."

"All right. Sorry."

Rand turned to leave. The man might be lying, but there was no way of proving it. Rand was at a dead end. But as he was going out the door he decided on one more try. He wheeled around and made for the liquor bar near the front of the restaurant.

"What'll it be?" the bartender asked him.

"I've got a message for Ed. It's important."

"Ed the waiter? He's off this week."

"Do you know where he lives?"

"Couldn't tell you. Ask the boss." He nodded toward the man with the menus.

"What's his name?" Rand asked.

"Griffin. Joe Griffin."

"Thanks."

A crowd of young people entered at that moment, and Rand was able to slip out the door. He didn't want another run-in with Mr. Griffin, not just yet. There was an Ed who was a waiter at the oyster restaurant, and he was away this week. And the owner of the place was quick to deny his existence.

Rand sat in his car and thought about it. The fact that a man named Ed was connected with the oyster bar tended to confirm his decoding of Leila's note. And if she had left a note with a hidden message it meant she had not left willingly. She'd been kidnaped, or somehow forced to go along with this man Ed. She'd left for the University and been intercepted. They'd gone back for her things, and he forced her to write the note.

But why? Why did they want her?

The plot, whatever it was, was not directed at Rand. There had been no ransom demand, no request for information. And they'd gone out of their way to make it appear that she'd left him of her own free will. They did not want to arouse his suspicions. That meant two things—they wouldn't be contacting him in the near future, and they wouldn't be returning Leila right away. In fact, the plot only made sense if they never intended to return Leila.

If they didn't want her because she was married to Rand, why did they want her? Was there something in her past, something in those Egyptian years before Rand knew her?

But if this was some sort of revenge, wouldn't an assault be more likely than a kidnaping?

They needed her for something. But for what?

His eyes fell on another group of students entering the restaurant. Leila's only connection with Reading was the University. If she'd met this waiter named Ed it was only because of her position as a lecturer at the University. Somehow the University was the key to her disappearance.

He found a telephone booth and looked up Isabel Skrech's home phone number. He called it but there was no answer. Returning to his car he drove down Queen's Road to Watlington Street and turned right. When he reached the London Road—the route back home—he could see the shadowed towers of the campus among the trees across the street. There were still lights in many of the buildings and he decided it was worth a stop.

Isabel Skrech shared her office with another instructor who said Isabel might be found in the library if she hadn't gone home. Rand mounted the steps of the old building and made his way down a silent corridor to the reading room. Most of the faces at the tables were young but luck was with him. He spotted Isabel at one of the side tables, poring over the illustrations in a book on the treasure of King Tut's tomb.

"You startled me!" she said, jumping a bit as he spoke her name.

"I'm sorry. I wonder if we could talk some more, Isabel. It's quite important."

She closed the book and stood up with a smile. "Certainly. Is it about Leila?"

Rand nodded. "Where can we talk without disturbing anyone?"

"Outside would be best. I was finished here anyway."

They strolled across the inner courtyard toward the parking area and Rand asked, "Tell me, Isabel, did you and Leila ever have lunch or dinner together off campus?"

"Oh, we might have, once or twice."

"At the oyster bar on Duke Street?"

"I think so, yes. A great many of the students go there."

"Did she ever talk to the waiters? Especially one named Ed?"

"Ed … I remember him. A stocky fellow with a broken nose. Leila wondered if he was an ex-boxer."

"Do you know his last name?"

"I don't think we ever heard it."

"Did he talk to her about her personal life?"

"No, just idle chatter about the students and such. Never anything personal."

They'd reached her little car by then and as she opened the door the inside light went on. Rand caught a glimpse of something familiar. "Isn't that Leila's scarf?" he asked, reaching suddenly inside to snatch the Nile green square of cloth from the seat. It still bore the tag of the Cairo shop where he'd bought it for her. "What are you doing with it?"

Isabel Skrech looked him in the eye. "She left it in the car last term. I brought it along to give her yesterday. You certainly don't think I'm connected with her disappearance, do you?"

He could not specifically remember Leila's wearing the scarf during the summer months—but she wouldn't have worn it then anyhow. Isabel could be telling the truth. It might have been missing since the spring term. "Of course not," he apologized. "You'll have to excuse my jumpiness."

"I understand Leila's going off has upset you. But maybe you're seeing plots where none exist. Maybe you have to face up to the most likely explanation—that her note meant exactly what it said."

"I know. And you're right to remind me. But I have to keep looking for her. This man Ed—the waiter with the broken nose—can you tell me anything more about him?"

She thought for a moment. "No. Except that Ed is probably only a nickname. He's swarthy, dark-skinned. I'd guess him to be from the Middle East."

"He speaks with an accent?"

"A slight one, yes."

"Interesting. Was there ever a hint that he might be Egyptian?"

"No—I think Leila asked him that, in fact. He's not Egyptian."

She slipped behind the wheel of the car. "Thank you, Isabel. You've been a big help."

She looked up at him and smiled. "I hope so. I hope you find her."

He drove back to the oyster bar and parked across the street. All the restaurants in Reading closed by 10:30, so he knew he wouldn't have too long to wait. It was a few minutes before eleven when the last of the customers had departed and Griffin left with one of his bartenders, turning out the lights and locking the door behind him. The two men parted at the car park nearby and Rand followed the restaurant owner.

If he'd hoped that Griffin would lead him to Leila, he was disappointed. The man drove directly to a modern country home a few miles out of town and went in. Rand could see a woman and two teenage children watching TV in the family room next to the garage.

He got back on the London Road and headed home, feeling depressed. He was more certain than ever that Leila was being held prisoner somewhere, but there was still no concrete evidence he could present to the police. His only lead now seemed to be the waiter, Ed, and he'd have to pursue that in the morning.

Five miles out of Reading, traveling along the narrow highway, Rand suddenly became aware of a larger, heavier sedan coming up fast behind him. He moved over to let it pass, but the car came up next to him and started edging into his vehicle.

"Damn fool!" Rand muttered, hitting his horn, but the other car kept edging over. It was deliberately trying to run him off the road.

In the last instant before he hit the ditch he saw a glimpse of the man at the wheel—a man with a broken nose silhouetted against the glow of the rising moon. Then Rand's wheel spun out of control and he felt a sickening grind as the car lurched over, half on its side ...

In the morning Rand phoned Hastings in London again. Hastings listened patiently to his story and finally said, "You're telling me they tried to kill you last night?"

"That's right. I believe it was this same man Ed—the one who kidnaped Leila."

"But you still don't have a motive? No effort has been made to contact you?"

"None whatsoever. In fact, after last night I'd say just the opposite. They'll go to great lengths *not* to speak with me."

Rand could hear Hastings sucking in his breath. "I don't know," Hastings muttered, "even if your suspicions about Leila's being kidnaped are correct, it's an internal thing—Scotland Yard's baby, not ours."

"This man Ed is a Middle Easterner of some sort. It could be tied in with espionage or terrorism, and that would get you into the picture, wouldn't it?"

"Perhaps," Hastings hedged. "It would depend on the circumstances."

"You mean which country was involved?"

"The government wouldn't want a diplomatic incident."

"For God's sake, Hastings, we're talking about my wife!"

"Leila is half-Egyptian, Rand. This could all be something from her past."

"Half-Egyptian and half-British. Will you at least help me rescue the British half?"

There was a pause and then, "Let me get back to you."

Rand slammed down the phone in disgust. His car had been towed home, barely capable of operation, his body was bruised and battered, and his wife was now missing for two days. And Hastings would get back to him!

He went out to the car, pried open its dented left door, checked the headlights, and tried the motor. At first it wouldn't start, and he had visions of a broken fuel line; but finally the engine turned over and started.

All right. Maybe things weren't as bad as he thought. At least Ed hadn't come back to take a shot at him after his car hit the ditch.

Maybe they didn't really want to kill him. Maybe the man in the car wasn't Ed at all. Maybe Rand was imagining the entire plot.

Maybe Leila had simply walked out on him.

No. No more thoughts like that.

He got out of the car on the driver's side and checked the paint scrapes on the right door. There was no doubt that he'd been hit several times. It was no accident, but a deliberate attempt to kill or maim him.

He was debating his next move when he heard the phone in the house ringing. He ran to answer it and heard Hastings on the other end. "Still thinking about it?" Rand asked sarcastically.

Hastings sighed, sounding like the tired warrior whom Rand had known for so many years. "The waiter's name is Edim el Baiz. He's in our computer."

"For what reason?"

"Affiliation with known terrorists."

"Egyptian, is he?"

"Turkish citizenship, but that doesn't mean much."

"What would he want with Leila?"

"I've no idea."

"Do you have an address for him?"

"Berkeley Avenue, in Reading. But I don't want you going there alone."

"What's the number?"

Hastings gave it, reluctantly. "Be careful, Rand."

The house was a big brick place set back from the busy avenue. The grass was tall in the front yard and Rand knew at once what he would find inside. It was empty, and judging by the grass it had been for some weeks.

Edim the waiter was in the computer, so he'd gone into hiding before the operation commenced. They'd have Leila at some other house, a safe house even the computer didn't know about.

He sat in the car for a long time, thinking about what little he knew. Why would anyone—especially Middle East terrorists—want to kidnap Leila?

Because she was married to Rand? No, they'd made no effort to contact him.

Because she was Egyptian? Unlikely—there were many Egyptians living in London who'd make bigger headlines than Leila. Because she was an archeologist? That wasn't a subject to interest terrorists.

Rand sat tapping the steering wheel of his car. There was just a possibility—

He turned the car around in a driveway and headed back to the center of town. It took him only a few minutes to reach the University and to learn that Isabel was off that day. He obtained her address from the faculty directory and headed out toward Gosbrook Road on the north side of town.

Isabel Skrech's house was a pleasantly large place with a colorful garden running down to the road. Someone—she or her professor husband—spent a great deal of time in it. It was the husband who came to the door when Rand rang. He blinked his eyes behind dark-framed glasses and asked, "Can I help you?"

"Professor Skrech? My name is Rand. Your wife Isabel is a friend of my—"

"Oh, yes! Come in, Mr. Rand! Isabel has been telling me about your wife's disappearance."

He led the way into a large living room decorated in a subdued modern style. Isabel entered from the kitchen and seemed surprised to see him. "What is it? Have you located Leila?"

"No, not yet."

Professor Skrech hovered over him solicitously. "May I get you a drink?"

"No, no—nothing." Rand was looking at Isabel. "I wonder if I could speak to you alone."

"I have no secrets from Max. Is it about Leila?"

Rand nodded. "I accused you falsely about that scarf. I don't want to make another mistake."

Professor Skrech sat down, looking concerned, but Isabel continued to stand. "What is it now?" she asked a trifle petulantly.

"You said I should face up to the possibility that her note meant exactly what it said. But I never told you she left me a note, Isabel."

"Well … Maybe I just assumed that she had." But the color had drained from her face.

"And what were those psychological tests you tried on her, Professor? It all ties in, somehow. You two have got her, haven't you?"

Max Skrech looked annoyed. Without moving from his chair he spoke one word. "Edim."

Rand tried to turn but he wasn't fast enough. The man with the broken nose had come through the door behind him and suddenly Rand's arms were pinned to his sides.

"Tie him up," Professor Skrech ordered. "If he gives you any trouble, you know what to do."

Silently cursing his stupidity, Rand allowed himself to be tied to a straight-backed chair. The man named Edim worked silently and efficiently. When he'd finished, Isabel walked over to stand in front of Rand. "I'm sorry it happened this way. We were trying to keep you out of this."

"Where is she?"

Isabel's husband answered. "Upstairs. She hasn't been harmed— only given something to make her sleep."

"You need her for something. You need her knowledge for something."

"That's quite correct," Professor Skrech said. "It is a devious plot involving a great many other people in America and in Europe. We needn't bore you with details."

"I like to be bored. If I'm going to die, I'd like to know the reason."

"Who said anything about dying? As a matter of fact, you're just what we need to make Leila more cooperative."

But Isabel Skrech must have seen the foolishness of the charade. "For God's sake, tell him, Max! You know we'll have to kill them both."

He shot her a black look, then turned back to Rand. "We are associated with a group trying to bring about an equitable solution to the Middle East problem."

"Terrorists!"

"I never use that word. Nevertheless, it is a group that needs a great deal of cash for its endeavors. In recent weeks several of this group have slipped into America. They are going to raise the money in a special way—through what you might call a caper. At this moment fifty-five items from the tomb of King Tut are touring American museums and attracting record crowds."

It was all clear to Rand now. "That book in the library, Isabel! You were so startled when I found you reading it!"

"What's this?" Skrech asked his wife.

"Nothing. I was glancing through a book on Tut and he surprised me."

"Foolish!" he muttered, but then turned back to Rand. "While the exhibit is en route between cities tomorrow, several of the smaller items will be stolen and replaced with copies. They will be flown over here, hidden in a shipment of machine parts. And that is where Leila comes in."

"You need her to verify the authenticity of the pieces."

"Exactly. She's an archeologist with close ties to the Cairo Museum. We couldn't ask for a better person."

"And she won't be missed afterwards, when you kill her," Rand added. "A famed art expert or museum director would create too great a stir if he disappeared. But how will you know if she's telling the truth about the pieces?"

Professor Skrech smiled broadly. "You mentioned the psychological tests she helped me with, and you know my field of study is stress detection. The tests were to verify that your wife would be a good subject for lie-detection machines and—if needed—the so-called truth serum. It doesn't matter if she lies or not after she inspects the stolen objects from the Tut collection. We'll know the truth.   And if our American friends haven't pulled a double-cross, the authenticated treasures will be passed on to wealthy collectors in Switzerland and elsewhere."

"The Egyptian government will discover the theft sooner or later."

"Certainly. But we hardly care about them. They have already proved themselves traitors to our cause."

Rand took a deep breath. He could wait no longer. "Let me see her."

"You will, soon enough," Isabel said. "Having her leave the note was my idea. We'd forged her resignation letter in advance, of course, and Edim intercepted her on the London Road after she left you Monday morning. But we thought she might need her books on ancient Egypt to verify the pieces from the Tut collection, and decided to bring her clothes and other things too, so you wouldn't notice that just the books were missing. I had her write the note to strengthen the idea that she'd left you."

"I noticed the missing books, but I didn't think about them. You were clever."

"So was she. I let her use her own wording in the note and she slipped a message in, didn't she?"

Rand nodded. "She couldn't get *Isabel* in so she had to settle for *Ed Oyster*. Now are you going to let me see her?"

Max Skrech motioned to Edim. "Untie him but keep your gun ready. If he tries anything shoot him."

Edim pointed a small pistol at Rand's head while he untied the rope. Then he ordered him up the stairs. The door at the top was locked and Rand waited, hands raised, while the waiter opened it. Edim motioned with the gun for Rand to enter first and when he did he saw the tiny shape under the blanket on the bed. He ran to her, pulling back the covers, but there was only a puffed-up pillow there.

Then he heard the thud and turned to see Edim el Baiz topple to the floor. Leila, beautiful Leila, was standing behind the door with an upraised flower pot.

"I thought you'd never come," she said.

Rand scooped up the fallen weapon and pointed it at Isabel and her husband in the doorway. Then he told Leila, "Call the police and then phone Hastings in London. I'll keep these two covered."

She blew him a kiss as she went for the phone. "It's good to have you back, Jeffery."

THE SPY WHO WASN'T NEEDED

Whenever Hastings came to dinner Rand was apprehensive. Ever since his retirement as head of the Department of Concealed Communications he'd found himself being lured, cajoled, and coaxed back into intelligence work by the irresistible appeals of his former superior. Often the appeals began over the dinner table at the little country house of Rand and his wife Leila.

"No business tonight," Rand cautioned as he poured the wine one January evening. "I hope you haven't come all the way out here with another one of your projects."

Hastings smiled. "Not at all. Purely a social call to see how you two are doing. After all, I haven't laid eyes on either of you since that Reading business last September. Have a nice holiday?"

"A quiet one," Rand acknowledged. "When one leaves the Service it's sometimes necessary to cultivate a whole new group of friends."

"The old ones still remember you. Parkinson's doing a fine job running Double-C. He especially asked to be remembered to you."

"Good man, Parkinson."

Leila served a meal of roast beef done up in her special style, and even Hastings was hard pressed for superlatives. "Delicious, my dear! Your cooking is only exceeded by your beauty."

Leila glanced sideways at Rand. "He wants something," she said with a smile.

Rand wiped his mouth with the napkin and refilled their wine glasses. "Yes, Hastings, isn't it about time you broke down and told us? You can talk all you want about this being only a social call, but Leila knows you better than that."

"And I won't let you pull Jeffery away from me one more time!" she insisted.

Hastings was suddenly serious. "I didn't come for Jeffery, Leila. As far as he's concerned this is a social visit just as I said. It's you we need, my dear woman."

"Me?" Leila simply stared at him. "Whatever for?"

"Because you're brave and beautiful and intelligent. And because you're an expert Egyptologist."

Leila had been teaching a course in archeology at the University of

118

Reading, and Rand was always pleased when her talents in this area were recognized. Still, he didn't want her involved in anything Hastings might have in mind. "She'll write you a paper on it," he said. "Will that do you?"

Hastings merely smiled. He'd had long experience dealing with Rand. "We need her in New York. It's very important."

"New York! Why New York?"

"It's a favor to another department, really. They need a woman Egyptologist who can meet with some shady characters in New York. Of course the word's gotten round about that business a few months ago when Leila was kidnaped as part of a plot to steal the King Tut treasures, so naturally her name came up. We know from past experience that you can take care of yourself, Leila, and you're just the person we need on this mission."

"But—what would I be expected to do?"

"These people in New York are offering certain Egyptian pieces for sale, supposedly taken from a newly discovered tomb along the Nile and smuggled out of the country for sale to museums. It's surprising how many reputable institutions are willing to acquire art objects in this manner."

Leila listened, but when he finished she shook her head. "I'm afraid I can't see why all this should concern me."

Hastings smiled like a kindly uncle. "Before you moved to England and married Rand you worked at the Cairo Museum, didn't you?"

"I worked there while I was teaching at the University of Cairo." Leila was frowning, intent on the conversation. "That's why those people were so sure I could identify the King Tut objects when they kidnaped me."

"And we need you for the same sort of reason. We believe these people in New York are attempting to sell objects stolen from the Cairo Museum."

"Could that be possible?" Rand asked her.

"Anything's possible, I suppose, but there've been no reports of missing artifacts in the press."

"We believe they're being replaced by copies," Hastings answered. "I understand that might be possible at the Cairo Museum."

Leila agreed readily enough. "The place needs a great deal of renovation. The last time I was there, pigeons were actually getting in through broken skylights. Many objects are displayed in dark, cluttered hallways—often without labels. The lighting is especially bad in some areas, and it's quite possible that reasonably good copies would pass undetected."

"Then you'll help us with this?"

She spread her hands helplessly. "I've never been to New York. And the new University term begins the middle of the month."

"You may be back here by the start of the term, and if you're not we'll clear it with the University. As for never having been to New York, I seem to remember, Leila, that you functioned quite well on your first trip to Moscow last year."

"Exactly what would she have to do?" Rand wanted to know.

"Simply pose as an interested buyer representing a British museum. Inspect the objects and verify to us whether you remember them from the Cairo Museum. The police in New York will do the rest."

"It sounds simple enough," Leila told Rand.

"I'll go along," he decided.

"No," Hastings said. "You're too well known. That would give the game away."

And so, with a minimum of discussion, Hastings recruited Leila for a flight to New York and an undercover assignment. It was not until she was already on her way across the Atlantic that Rand started wondering why British Intelligence was so interested in possible thefts from an Egyptian museum.

But by that time it was too late to stop her.

L eila Rand stepped off the plane at Kennedy Airport and passed through customs with no delay. By the time she'd reached her Manhattan hotel she was already in love with the city, marveling at the way the afternoon sun reflected off the glass-walled buildings. Her only regret was that Jeffery wasn't along to share it with her. "I'm only as far away as the telephone," he'd said. "You can direct-dial our house on your New York phone."

His words added confidence to her lone journey, though she was already having second thoughts about the speed with which she'd agreed to Hastings' request. The plan, as he'd outlined it, was simple enough. A man named Grazer would phone the hotel room shortly after her arrival and give her the address of the place she was to visit. There she would inspect the articles offered for sale and report back to Grazer if any of them were items from the Cairo Museum.

She'd just phoned down for room service, calculating that it was nearly ten o'clock back home, when there was a knock on her door. "Who is it?" she asked.

"Grazer," a man's voice answered.

She opened the door to admit a stocky, rumpled man wearing a tweed overcoat and carrying a briefcase. "You were supposed to telephone," she admonished.

The man named Grazer merely smiled. "Yes, well, there's been a slight change of plans. You are to see a Mr. Chando tomorrow morning at ten, and give him this envelope." From the briefcase he extracted a large manila envelope, its flap sealed with wide tape. "It's a catalogue of the collection at the Cambridge Museum of Egyptology, together with a letter from the director authorizing you to arrange purchases on their behalf. Here's a copy for you to look through, just so you're familiar with it."

"Is Chando the man who's selling the artifacts?"

"That's right. He's a minor official at the Egyptian consulate here. We believe the art objects were brought over in diplomatic pouches. He has a shop on upper Madison Avenue and that's where you'll meet him. Phone this number after nine for an appointment."

"Very well."

Grazer seemed to realize the abruptness of his visit. As he turned to go he said, "I hope you had a good flight."

"I did, thank you."

"Good luck. I'll phone here tomorrow afternoon for your report."

Then he was gone, buttoning his overcoat as he strode down the hall toward the elevators.

Tired as she was from the long flight, Leila drifted off into a dreamless sleep, thinking of Jeffery back home.

Still suffering from jet-lag, she awakened early and breakfasted in the room. By nine o'clock she was showered, dressed, and ready to go out. But she waited another fifteen minutes before phoning Chando at the number Grazer had given her.

"May I speak to Mr. Chando?" she asked the youngish male voice that answered. His accent was distinctly American and she knew he was not Chando.

"Just a moment," he replied.

The line went dead momentarily and then another voice came on, perhaps from an inner office. "Mr. Chando?"

"Is this Leila Rand?"

"That's right. I'm calling for an appointment to view the Egyptian artifacts you have for sale."

"Whom do you represent, Miss Rand?"

"The Cambridge Museum of Egyptology. I've taught at the University of Cairo."

"I see. Could you come up here this morning?"

"I can be there by ten o'clock. I have a catalogue of our collection and a letter from our director."

"That will be most helpful," Chando said. "I will see you at ten."

Leila picked up the envelope Grazer had given her and went downstairs to get a cab. She arrived at the Madison Avenue address within ten minutes but spent a half hour window shopping in the area until it was ten o'clock. The address was that of a small gallery between 75th and 76th Streets. She studied the single painting in the window before entering. It was a water color of a mosque in Alexandria, and she wondered if it was displayed as a signal of some sort.

Inside, a slim young man in a gray suit came forward. "May I help you?" he asked, and she recognized the voice on the telephone.

"I'm Leila Rand. I've come to see Mr. Chando."

He smiled and extended his hand. "Ron Janus. I manage the gallery for Mr. Chando. His work at the consulate takes a great deal of his time, you understand. Step this way, please."

He led the way into a small outer office and Leila handed him the envelope. "This is for Mr. Chando. One of our catalogues."

"Fine." He put it on his desk. "Chando's on the telephone but he should be free in just a minute." He relaxed and lit a cigarette. "Are you enjoying your visit to our city?"

"I really can't say. I only arrived late yesterday afternoon. It's a good deal colder than England, though."

"But not as damp. And it's supposed to get warmer tomorrow." He gestured with his cigarette, reminding her of an affected British actor she'd once met at a party. "On the wall there behind you is a painting of Hyde Park. It should remind you of home."

She glanced at the water color, which showed the same style as the one in the window. "My home is really Egypt," she explained. "I only moved to England when I married, though my mother was British. Is this by the same man as the one in the window?"

Ron Janus smiled. "Actually they're both by Chando. See his name in the corner? He's very good really."

"I didn't know he painted."

"You can talk to him about it. He's off the phone now."

Janus picked up her envelope and led the way into the inner office. Mr. Chando was a short man with dark wrinkled skin, older than she'd expected. He rose and held out his hand. "What a pleasure this is, Miss Rand. Or is it Mrs.?"

"I'm married," she said simply.

"A lucky man." Janus handed him the envelope and left them alone. "What's this—the catalogue you promised?"

She nodded. "And a letter of introduction from our director."

"You're a charming young lady to be so knowledgeable about Egyptian antiquities." She watched his fingers undo the clasp and lift the flap of the envelope.

"Egypt is my home," she explained. "I was raised on—"

The words froze in her mouth. She saw him pull the layers of cardboard from the envelope, saw the quick snap of something like a mousetrap, and then

Mr. Chando seemed to vanish in a blast of light and sound that sent her spinning backward out of her chair.

"No broken bones," the emergency room doctor told her less than an hour later as he finished his examination. "You're a very lucky young lady. We'll get those cuts tended to. You'll be a bit bruised and sore for a few days, but nothing serious."

"Thank you, Doctor," she said, trying to move her right leg to a less painful position on the examining table.

"There's a detective waiting outside to see you."

"That doesn't surprise me. I suppose I'd better see him."

The detective was a friendly middle-aged man named Feeley. "Detective Sergeant George Feeley, ma'am. I'm investigating the bombing."

"Is Chando dead?"

"I'm afraid so. The bomb wasn't awfully powerful, but at that range it was deadly. A sheet of plastic explosive, detonated by a mousetrap arrangement when the envelope was opened. A letter bomb, to use the simple terrorist term for it."

"I thought it was a museum catalogue," she said slowly.

The detective smiled disarmingly. "Obviously you wouldn't have remained in the room had you known the envelope contained a bomb. Even though you were seated some ten feet away you could have been killed or seriously injured."

"I still can't believe it," Leila said. "I slept with that envelope next to my bed last night."

"Who gave it to you?"

She was on dangerous ground here, she knew, and she answered carefully. "A man named Grazer. He's some sort of New York representative for the museum that employs me."

"Where can we find him?"

"I don't know."

"Can you give me a description?"

"Stocky, around forty. Dark hair, glasses. Nothing special about him except that he had a rumpled look."

"Any idea why he'd want to kill Chando?"

"None at all."

"What was the nature of your business with Mr. Chando?"

"I—it concerned the purchase of Egyptian antiquities for a collection in England."

Feeley was still smiling when he asked his next question. "I don't know too much about these things, but isn't the exporting of antiquities against the law in Egypt?"

"Not these, certainly. You can't suspect that an employee of the Egyptian consulate was engaged in anything illegal!"

The smile disappeared. "Lady, the man got himself blown apart. That much is illegal to start with. And I see consulate and U.N. employees engaged in something illegal every day of the week. Most of them park illegally, just as an example. If you're keeping anything from me you'd better think twice about it. You survived that bomb, but you could still be in big trouble unless you can produce this mysterious Grazer."

"Are you saying I'm under arrest?" Leila asked.

"I'm saying you could be held as a material witness."

"Am I allowed one phone call?"

"To your lawyer? Sure."

"Not to my lawyer, to my husband. He's in England."

It was a dreary January afternoon in London, and the weather fitted Rand's mood perfectly. He strode into Hastings' office with only a passing word to the secretaries and others who'd once been his co-workers.

"Well, Rand," Hastings said, rising to greet him. "You sounded quite disturbed on the telephone."

"I have reason to be disturbed. Leila may be in a New York jail at this very moment."

"No, no—it's nothing like that. I'm afraid her telephone call upset you needlessly. I've checked with our people there."

"Who? This man Grazer who gave her the letter bomb? Just what in hell did you get her into?"

Hastings held up his hands, almost as if he expected Rand to strike out at him. "My God, Rand, you must know me better than that! Do you think I'd send Leila into an assassination plot?"

"All I know is what happened. And the more I think about it the more unlikely your first story sounds. British Intelligence doesn't do favors for other departments—not unless it's in your field somehow. What was the real reason you sent Leila to New York?"

"It was pretty much as I stated," Hastings answered defensively.

"Pretty much, but not exactly."

The older man sighed. "You know how it is in the Department, Rand. You were in it long enough yourself. An agent is only told as much as he or she needs to complete the mission."

"Need to know. My wife didn't need to know she was carrying a letter bomb that could have killed or mangled her!"

"I swear to you, Rand, I didn't know about the bomb!"

"Just what did you know?"

"Everything I tell you is highly classified. You're no longer a member of the Department, and you have no—"

"Just tell me!" Rand commanded.

"Well, it was a joint operation with the Americans. You must know that the seemingly endless Middle East peace talks have been the subject of great concern and not a little sabotage by various intelligence agencies. There are some in the Egyptian government itself who still oppose peace with Israel, and who have taken steps to prevent it. Chando was one of them."

"He was in the pay of the Russians?"

"More likely one of the more militant Arab states."

"So you decided to kill him."

"No, no! You don't understand, Rand. We really have changed our ways since the old days, and so have our American friends."

"I'll bet!"

Hastings smirked. "You're sounding like one of them now. We did want to remove Chando from the scene, but not by killing him. It came to our attention that he might be involved in these museum thefts, exactly as I told Leila. We needed her to pose as a buyer and verify that the objects had indeed come from the Cairo Museum. Then we planned to get rid of him—either by having him arrested in America or by informing the Egyptian authorities and having him shipped back there for trial. Either way he'd have been removed from the scene. So everything I told Leila and you was true. I was only secretive about the true motive for our interest in Chando. It was indeed an intelligence operation from beginning to end."

"Who is this man Grazer, the one who brought Leila the letter bomb?"

"Well," Hastings admitted, "there's a problem. Grazer isn't exactly a person."

"Isn't a person! Do you think Leila imagined him? You told her yourself that he'd contact her."

"Of course Leila didn't imagine him! What I mean to say is that Grazer is a code name for agents operating in friendly countries. The man who came to see your wife using the name Grazer could be any one of six different agents in the New York area."

"Surely she could identify his picture!"

"That's one of the problems. It would be a violation of security to produce pictures of all six men. Leila, and presumably the police, would then know the identities of our entire New York bureau."

"What difference does it make? You said yourself that America is a friendly country. You're certainly not spying on them!"

"We're protecting British interests," Hastings replied, a bit testily.

"And I'm protecting Leila's interests. I want a seat on the next Concorde to New York."

"That's out of the question, Rand! You're not needed there."

"My wife needs me."

"Calm down a bit, will you? We're trying to get through to our New York people and the Americans right now, to find out who authorized the killing. At least wait until we have more information about this whole business."

"I'll wait, but I'll wait right here in your office. We can have dinner sent in."

Hastings glanced unhappily at the clock. "It's not even one o'clock yet in the States. This killing of Chando happened less than three hours ago. We might have a long wait for any news."

"We'll wait all night if we have to," Rand answered grimly.

L eila had telephoned Rand from the hospital shortly after eleven o'clock. Now, at one thirty, she was hurrying back to her hotel in the company of a grim-faced detective named Burke. Sergeant Feeley had agreed to her request that she be allowed to replace her torn and blood-spattered dress before questioning was resumed at police headquarters. Still, the presence of Burke at her side was a constant reminder that she was far from free. Sergeant Feeley obviously had no intention of turning her loose until he had the full story, or until the man named Grazer was safely behind bars.

"I'll wait here," Detective Burke told her when they reached the door of her room. "Make it fast."

Inside, Leila got the first good look at herself in the mirror. Bandages covered the cut on her forehead and the one on her neck, and a larger bandage had been applied to her forearm. The green wool dress she liked so much was torn in one place and spotted with blood. Seeing the blood, she was reminded again of that scene in the office—Chando unfastening the clasp of the envelope, lifting the flap, and pulling out the cardboard. Then the snap of the mousetrap detonator and the flash of the explosion. She thought the memory of it would stay with her the rest of her life.

She was starting to pull the green dress over her head when the man named Grazer stepped out of the hotel bathroom, holding a silenced pistol pointed at her chest.

" A ll right," Hastings said when he'd finished the transatlantic call on the scrambler phone. "At least now we have a little more information. The killing of Chando was not authorized, either by our people or the Americans. Grazer acted on his own."

"How is that possible?" Rand wanted to know.

"You were in this business long enough to know the troubles we occasionally have with rogue agents, Rand. There's no way of controlling completely every man on our payroll, especially in the case of overseas assignments."

"All right. What about Grazer?"

"We've narrowed it down to two agents. One was assigned to meet Leila, but he was taken ill and they seem to think the second man might have substituted for him."

"Convenient."

"Seems so, doesn't it? In any event, both Grazers have dropped out of sight since this morning. If he knows we're after him our man may have gone into hiding."

"Leila can identify him. She may be in danger."

"I'm assured the police won't let her out of their sight. They have too many questions to ask her, and they'll have a great many more when word reaches them about the international interest in Chando."

"I still think I should be there with her."

"It'll all be over before you could reach New York, even by Concorde. It's only a matter of hours before our people locate the right Grazer."

"Or the wrong Grazer."

"Yes." It was dark outside by then, and Hastings turned in his chair to look out over the river. Rand wondered if he could see anything out there besides the pale reflections of their own troubled faces in the glass windowpanes.

Leila Rand stood very still, staring at the gun with its ugly black silencer. "You said you'd call," she remarked, trying to keep her voice casual.

"I was searching your room," Grazer said. "You came back unexpectedly."

"Searching? For what?"

"Don't play dumb with me!"

"Look here, there's a detective right outside that door. If I scream he'd be in here in a second."

"And you'd be dead."

"I'll take that chance."

Grazer raised the pistol a fraction of an inch. "I've no time for games. Who's paying you?"

"I thought we were on the same side until a few hours ago."

"What happened at the gallery—"

He was interrupted by a knocking on the door. Detective Burke was growing impatient. Either that, or he'd heard the sound of their voices. "Open it!" Grazer commanded, stepping quickly behind the door.

Leila did as she was told. She saw Burke's face as the door opened, saw Grazer's silenced pistol raised, and then she acted. She brought the door back hard, catching Grazer in the abdomen with the knob. He gasped and the pistol coughed close to her head, sending its bullet across the room. Then Burke had his service revolver out. They struggled at close quarters for a few moments until the detective got an arm free and hit Grazer a glancing blow with the gun butt. Burke backed off, covering Grazer as he slumped to the floor.

"No tricks now," he warned Leila. "I thought I heard voices."

"Tricks! I was helping you! This is the man who gave me the letter bomb!"

Burke stepped to the telephone and dialed the operator. "Police officer requests assistance in room 532," he said brusquely.

"Can I finish changing my dress now?" she asked.

Grazer was barely stirring on the floor. Burke glanced into the bathroom, perhaps to be certain no one else lurked there. "Go ahead, but be quick about it."

It was while she was removing the dress that she thought again of the way Chando died, and suddenly realized that she'd made a terrible mistake.

"I have to talk to Sergeant Feeley right away," she told Burke as she came out of the bathroom.

"And that's right where I'm taking you, as soon as somebody arrives for our friend on the floor here."

But it was another hour before Leila found herself once more with George Feeley. He smiled again as he greeted her, and ushered her into his tiny cubicle in the squad room. "Burke said you were anxious to talk with me."

"I am. They've arrested Grazer."

"The man in your hotel room." Feeley nodded. "That was good work on your part, Mrs. Rand."

"But don't you see? It's all a mistake! Grazer is innocent!"

Feeley's smile turned slowly into a frown. "He's the man who gave you the letter bomb, isn't he? And he did threaten you with a gun in your hotel room, didn't he?"

"He was in my room searching for more explosives and detonators. Don't you see—he thought *I* made up the letter bomb and killed Chando!" She was exasperated with herself, searching for the right words. "He thought I was trying to frame him for the murder."

"How do you know it wasn't Grazer?" Feeley asked.

"The envelope he left with me had a wide piece of tape across its flap. But just before the bomb went off I saw Chando open the envelope. He undid the clasp and lifted the flap. He couldn't have done that if there was tape over it."

"Which means—?"

"That it was a different envelope! A substitution was made!"

"By whom?"

"The only person who could have made it is Ron Janus, the gallery manager. The envelope was on his desk, and he called my attention to a painting on the wall behind me. When I turned my head he switched envelopes. I'd told Chando on the phone that I was bringing a catalogue. Janus must have been listening in, and decided it was the perfect opportunity to frame someone else for Chando's murder. He could easily guess the catalogue would be in a standard-sized clasp envelope, and the tape was a minor detail that didn't seem to matter. Even if I noticed in the last instant that it was a different envelope, he probably figured the explosion would kill me too."

"What if your envelope was pink, or green? What if you handed over the catalogue without an envelope?"

"Then he'd simply leave the letter bomb in his desk and wait for another and better opportunity."

"You know so much, what would be his motive?"

"Chando was importing stolen art objects in diplomatic pouches from Egypt. I imagine Janus decided he wanted the deal all for himself. It was a case of thieves falling out."

Sergeant Feeley waited no longer. He walked to the door of his cubicle and called out, "Burke, get a car around front. We're going back to that gallery and talk with Ron Janus again."

It was close to midnight when the telephone rang on Hastings' desk. Rand knew it was an overseas call when the scrambler was switched on. Hastings listened with intense interest, giving only brief monosyllabic replies. Finally he hung up and looked at Rand.

"She's all right. And neither of our Grazer agents was involved after all."

Rand's mouth was dry. "What happened?"

"It seems that one of Chando's partners in crime switched envelopes and killed him. When the police returned to the art gallery to question him they found him trying to move some of the stolen goods out of the building's basement."

"And Leila?"

"I told you she was all right. In fact, she's the one who solved it. She's flying home tomorrow."

Rand let out his breath. "I suppose I wasn't needed after all."

"Leila's the one who was needed. Damn it, Rand, we might be able to find a place for her in—"

"No!" Rand said, and that was the end of the conversation.

THE SPY AND THE HEALING WATERS

Ever since Hastings retired from British Intelligence and moved to Scotland, Rand and his wife Leila had promised to visit him. Thinking about it now, Rand was somewhat ashamed to realize that three full months had passed with no attempt to make good on the promise. He turned to Leila one evening after dinner and said, "The weather's supposed to be good this weekend. What say we drive up to Scotland and see old Hastings?"

She put down the archaeology text she was reading and said, "I never thought you'd bring yourself to it."

"I know I've been dragging my feet," Rand admitted. "I'm afraid of what this retirement might have done to him."

Months earlier, Hastings had come under suspicion as a traitor, a Russian mole operating at the highest levels of MI6. Rand had been instrumental in clearing his name, but the ordeal had been too much for his former superior. Hastings felt he could never again do an effective job, even though there'd been apologies all around. He'd called it quits and retired to a little holiday home he'd maintained east of Edinburgh along the Firth of Forth.

"He must be very lonely up there," Leila speculated. "It's too bad he never married."

"I think he did, in his university days, but it was short-lived. Ever since I knew him he devoted himself entirely to his work. When I was heading up Concealed Communications he took an almost daily interest in the department, even though it was only one of his many responsibilities."

And so it was that Rand and his wife set out for the east coast of Scotland on a Friday morning in May.

They'd phoned Hastings to tell him they were coming, and the bald man had obviously been watching out the window of his cottage. He came out at once as they turned in the little gravel driveway, smiling and extending a hand of greeting to Rand. "So good of you both to drive all the way up here!"

Hastings had aged in the three months since his retirement. He walked a little slower and watched the ground, as if fearful of a tumble. In his office overlooking the Thames he'd always been sure of himself.

"It's a lovely house!" Leila marveled as he showed them through the four small rooms.

"Small, though. Very small."

"It's all the space you need."

"Well," Hastings replied, "I have my books, and all my fishing gear. The fishing has always been a delight around here. And my niece in Edinburgh drives out to see me every couple of weeks. It's not a bad life."

Leila had promised during the drive up that she'd be bright and cheerful the whole time of their visit, even though she'd grown to resent Hastings in the years before his retirement. "At least he won't be calling on you with his problems two or three times a year," she'd said.

"No, those days are over." Rand was surprised that the thought of it made him a little sad, for Hastings but also for himself.

Now, seeing Hastings here in his little retirement cottage, Rand felt a little better. His former superior went on about the region at some length, and it was only when Leila went off to use the bathroom that he asked, "Have you been in the Double-C or the other departments since my departure?"

"No, I've had nothing to do with any of them."

"I thought Parkinson might ask you for help."

"He never did before. You're the only one I ever did work for." Parkinson, who'd moved up to director of Concealed Communications when Rand retired more than a decade ago, was a by-the-books professional who rarely asked help from anyone. Rand couldn't entirely dislike him, though. It was Parkinson who'd tipped him off that Hastings had been taken to a safe house for questioning on suspicion of treason.

Hastings sighed and gazed out at the water, perhaps following the progress of a large yacht under full sail. "I guess we're both retired then, after all these years."

"No shop talk, you two!" Leila cautioned, returning in time to overhear their remarks. "Have you decided how to entertain us for the weekend?"

Hastings took on an impish expression Rand hadn't seen in years. "We might drive over to Foxhart tomorrow. It's not far and there's a rather strange phenomenon there—a spring whose waters are said to heal the infirm."

"You sound like a non-believer."

"Well, I think I'll reserve judgement until I see it. I don't believe the priests at Lourdes need worry about competition from Foxhart quite yet."

Leila and Rand slept well in the big double bed Hastings kept for guests. Rand suspected they were the first ones who'd used it, at least since the retirement. It was doubtful if any of his former co-workers wanted to be seen visiting Hastings, even though he'd been cleared of all suspicion. That was the way things were in intelligence work.

Hastings himself prepared breakfast, seeming more relaxed than at any time since their arrival. They set off for Foxhart in Rand's little car and Hastings warned, "I understand it's crowded on weekends, even though there's been little national publicity about it so far."

"If it's too crowded we'll drive down along the coast," Leila suggested.

When they reached Foxhart shortly before noon Rand found the traffic being diverted onto a grassy field. A local constable seemed to have things well under control and directed them down a path toward the little stream that was the central attraction. The path itself was crowded with people moving in both directions, some reverently silent while others laughed and chatted like typical tourists. Foxhart had become just another stop to them.

At the stream itself Rand was surprised to see a tall, dark-haired man in clerical garb facing the people like some sort of tour guide. "Come, place your hands in this healing water," he told them. "The miracle has happened once, it can happen again. Don't be afraid! Here, Granny, let me give you a hand."

"Is he real?" Leila whispered in Rand's ear.

"Let's see if he takes up a collection."

Most of the people did dip their hands into the swiftly flowing stream, and one elderly man even took off his shoes and socks to immerse his feet. The clergyman spoke again. "I am the Reverend Joshua Fowler. As you leave you will note that bottles of the healing water are available for your purchase. All monies raised through their sale goes to continue the Lord's work. Thank you, thank you. Please keep moving. There are other pilgrims anxious to bathe in these waters."

Rand saw that Hastings was no longer looking at the Reverend. Instead his gaze had shifted to an attractive woman standing near the edge of the crowd. She wore a fashionable tan raincoat and had a scarf to protect her hair from the breeze. Tall, brown hair, probably in her mid-thirties. Rand judged her to be a business type and wondered what had brought her to this place. Hastings must have wondered too, because suddenly he left Rand's side and edged his way through the crowd toward her. Rand followed along, never one to avoid meeting an attractive woman.

"Hello, Karen," Hastings said as he reached her.

She glanced sideways at him and said, "My name is Monica. You must be mistaking me for someone else." She spoke with a strong American accent.

Hastings hesitated and then tipped the plaid cap he was wearing. "I'm sorry. You looked just like her."

She edged away immediately and hurried back up the path to the parking lot. "Who did you think it was?" I asked.

"A young woman I met in London last year. Karen Hayes."

"But you were mistaken."

"No, it was she."

"She's one of ours?"

"CIA, actually. One of their specialists."

"Oh?" That interested Rand. He'd had some personal contact with the Americans during his own tour of duty.

Leila joined them then. "What are you two up to, huddled here like a pair of thieves! Are you plotting to steal the receipts from the sale of the healing water?"

"Hastings thought he saw someone he knew," Rand explained. "Shall we be on our way?"

"I'm sorry I dragged you out here," Hastings murmured apologetically. "There wasn't really much to see."

They were passing a small glass-enclosed concession stand when Leila decided she wanted a souvenir. "I'll catch up with you," she promised.

"Just don't bring back a bottle of water," Rand warned her.

He and Hastings strolled on toward the parking lot, where a minor traffic jam seemed to have developed. "I suppose she might be on assignment," Hastings said, as if thinking aloud.

"What?"

"That woman we saw. Karen Hayes."

"You miss the job, don't you?"

"Didn't you, when you retired from Double-C?"

"Well, I had Leila, and I did some writing. And of course you kept me busy over the years."

"I'm not lonely, Rand, if that's what you mean. I just miss knowing what's going on from day to day."

"Surely you could have stayed on. After all their mistaken accusations they could hardly have forced you out."

"I didn't feel comfortable being back. Parkinson and the others were most friendly and solicitous, but there was still something in their eyes that hadn't been there before. I was only two years away from mandatory retirement anyway, and I found that I could leave now with severance pay and my full pension rights. It seemed the wise thing to do."

Leila came running up the path to join them, carrying a small plastic bag. "The water is three pounds per bottle! Can you believe that? I settled for a laminated color photo of the stream, with the Reverend Fowler standing beside it."

"I hope you're not planning to hang it in our living room," Rand told her.

A number of cars were lined up in the car park attempting to get out. Rand heard the constable blowing his whistle, and then he heard another sound, off to his left, of almost the same pitch.

It was a woman screaming.

They reached her at the same time as several others. She was a gray-haired lady who looked like somebody's mother. At her feet lay the sprawled body of a woman in a tan raincoat. Blood was already soaking through the coat from an unseen wound.

It was the woman Hastings had identified as Karen Hayes.

Neither Rand nor Hastings had been in the line of work where one volunteered information to the police, so they remained on the sidelines merely as interested observers during the brief turmoil that followed. Constable Stebbins, the officer who'd been directing traffic in the parking lot, was summoned by several local people. He made a perfunctory examination, pulling back the raincoat enough to reveal a wound just beneath the left breast. Then he hurried to his patrol car to summon reinforcements on the police radio.

"Keep back, everyone," he urged, using his traffic baton as an extender for his widespread arms. "There's nothing to see here. Keep moving, please!"

Leila tugged on Rand's sleeve. "We don't need to get involved in this, do we?"

"Hastings thinks he knows her," he replied quietly. "Let's just wait till the investigating team arrives."

The Reverend Joshua Fowler had arrived on the scene by that time, and was exhorting the faithful to remain calm. "A woman has been struck down in the prime of her life! Join me in a prayer for her, and a prayer for her attacker, that the Lord might show him some mercy that he denied his victim."

Rand took Hastings aside. "You said she was a CIA specialist. What was her field?"

"If that was Karen Hayes, as I believe, she was a disguise technician. Washington loaned her to us last year to help with a particular operation. I assumed she'd gone back by now."

"What sort of operation?"

"That's top secret, Rand. You know I can't—"

Their conversation was cut short by the arrival of two police cars. If Rand had expected them to remain on the sidelines, he was sadly mistaken. The first detective out of the unmarked second car spotted Hastings at once and headed right for them. "Well, Mr. Hastings, are you involved in this?"

"Not at all. I'm just showing my friend some of our tourist spots. Jeffery Rand, this is Detective Sergeant Scott Winston."

They shook hands and Winston said, "Stay around. I'll want to see you two later about this business." Then he hurried off to view the body.

"Now what?" Leila asked.

"He's a friend of Hastings. He wants to talk with us."

Hastings himself came over to join them. "I've known Sergeant Winston for as long as I've had my place. I'd see him when I came here to fish. He's a good sort, and this will probably become his case unless he has to ask for help."

"Don't the local police usually summon Scotland Yard for help in murder cases?" Leila looked toward where the police were grouped around the body. "I assume she didn't commit suicide."

Hastings grunted. "Despite its name, Scotland Yard's jurisdiction does not normally extend to Scotland. The Scottish courts and legal system are quite separate from ours."

Rand observed that the Reverend Fowler was deep in conversation with Sergeant Winston, gesturing with both hands as he spoke. Perhaps he was disturbed about the business he was losing. "Tell me some more about this place," he urged Hastings. "And about Fowler."

"Well, this is my first visit, but I've read about it in the local papers, of course. It seems that Fowler leased this property from the owner about a year ago. Within months, a young woman who'd limped for years because of a hip problem claimed she'd been cured by daily bathing in the stream. This was followed by an elderly man reporting that his arthritis had been cured. That was when Fowler started building the souvenir stand and bottling the water."

"The world is full of charlatans," Rand observed. "What would bring a CIA technician to this place?"

"I can't imagine."

Leila, who'd been listening enough to grasp the flow of their conversation, suggested, "Perhaps she just had a tennis elbow or some such thing. She might have come for the waters themselves."

"Then why deny her identity when I greeted her?" Hastings asked.

Leila shrugged. "She was embarrassed," she suggested, "or you were mistaken."

Sergeant Winston sent the constable to summon them as the body was being removed. "Never had anything like this in Foxhart," Constable Stebbins grumbled. "I lived here all my forty years and I told them when the tourists started coming in to see the waters there'd be trouble of some sort. Any time you get this many people, you get trouble."

There was no disagreeing with that, and Winston's refrain was not much different. "It's people from the city who do these crimes," he argued. "Country people would never stick a stranger with a knife for no reason at all."

"How do you know it was for no reason?" Hastings asked.

"The woman was an American, traveling alone. We've located her rented vehicle in the car park. Apparently she'd been touring England and Scotland, judging by the route maps we found spread out on the passenger seat. She just arrived here this morning. In her bag we found a hotel bill for a single room in

Edinburgh last night."

Rand nodded. "She was alone at the hotel, and the maps on the passenger seat indicate she was alone in the car as well."

"Exactly," the sergeant confirmed. "A stranger in a strange land, and someone killed her."

"What sort of weapon?"

"A dagger with a very thin blade, I'd guess. We'll know more after the autopsy." He turned his attention to Hastings. "Now tell me what you saw."

"Nothing, really. I had noticed the woman earlier, down by the stream when Fowler was speaking. I suppose she caught my eye because she was younger and more attractive than most of the other visitors."

The detective agreed. "I could see there were a great many people with canes and crutches. Did any of you notice someone watching or following her?"

"No one," Hastings said. Rand could read in his troubled face the realization that his speaking to Karen Hayes, calling her by name, might have caused her death.

"What about this man Fowler? Know anything about him?"

"Not a thing, except what little I've read in the newspapers. About the cures."

"Yes," Sergeant Winston muttered. "Well, he didn't cure this woman."

As they were leaving, Rand asked, "Has she been identified yet?"

"She was carrying quite a bit of identification, including an American passport, in the name of Monica Camber, and an MI5 courtesy card, the sort they issue people on special duty involving travel."

"Interesting," Rand murmured.

Driving back to Hastings' cottage, Rand had to suggest the most logical explanation. "Perhaps you were wrong. She said her name was Monica, not Karen. She might have been telling the truth. I read once that everyone in the world has a double. This might have been Karen Hayes's double."

"If she was an innocent American tourist, why was she killed?"

"A random act of violence, just as the police believe."

"Hogwash!" Hastings exploded. "I just keep fearing it was my fault that she died."

"Then you're certain it was this person Karen Hayes?"

"As certain as I've ever been of anything. I spent two entire days with the woman just last year, and I have a very good memory."

"What are you going to do?"

He sighed, as Rand had heard him do so many times in the midst of a particularly troublesome operation. "I suppose I should tell London, pass the word on to the Americans."

"It's none of your affair any more," Rand reminded him.

"The woman is dead, for God's sake! Someone cares about her—not just the people who employed her but her family and friends."

"She'll be identified through that MI5 travel card."

Hastings was silent for a moment and then said, "No, I have to tell them now. Otherwise they won't know before Monday."

They arrived at the cottage and he went directly to the telephone. Rand knew he was dialing a private number of London Central, one that would be manned even on weekends. When he came back to them he said, "Well, I left a top priority message for Parkinson. It's not Double-C's responsibility but he's always been decent to me."

They waited, expecting the telephone to ring at any moment, but no call came. Finally Leila walked to the window and stared out at the lush green countryside. "It's so lovely, so peaceful. Why would the CIA have any interest here?"

"I can't imagine," Hastings said. "There's an inactive RAF base near here, but it was mothballed years ago. It's not likely to reopen, either, with peace breaking out across Europe. The cold war is over."

"And the spies are all out of work," Rand said with a smile.

"It's no joke. You know how much of our work has already been taken over by spy satellites, and even those may become obsolete if Russia becomes a completely open society."

"There'll always be spies, Hastings. There'll be little wars and government-backed terrorism."

Leila was growing restless. Her dark hair had streaks of gray in it now, but she was still as lovely as when Rand had first met her down along the Nile River at the height of the cold war, when Russian troops were actually based in Egypt. He remembered his first sight of her small body, and the high-cheekboned beauty of her face. Had that really been eighteen years ago? Yes, it had. Leila had turned forty-two this year.

"Well, the healing waters were certainly exciting," she told Hastings. "What have you got to show us next? Something without another body, preferably."

"Would you care for a bite to eat? It's still several hours till dinner."

They agreed on a sandwich, and then a drive into Edinburgh for dinner at a fancy restaurant. It was to be Rand's treat. On the way they would stop at Inveresk Lodge, a tourist attraction.

As it turned out, their plans were due for a change. They were just walking out to the car when a black sedan pulled up in front of the cottage. Rand recognized Parkinson at once, accompanied by a slightly overweight American he'd never seen before. "Glad we caught you!" Parkinson said. "Flew up as soon as I received your message, Hastings. Mr. Camber here is quite concerned about his daughter."

So it's to be more games, Rand decided. The Americans loved games, but no more so than the British. "My name is Rand, Mr. Camber. Haven't we met before?"

The American frowned at him. "I don't believe so, unless it was back in Richmond. I'm Hugh Camber, Monica's father. I have a construction business back there."

"You're the one who saw his daughter?" Parkinson asked Hastings.

Rand and Leila both looked at Hastings, who gave one of his sighs and said, "I think we'd better go back indoors."

When they were seated in Hastings' cramped living room, he looked at Camber and said, "The woman I saw this morning at Foxhart was Karen Hayes, a CIA disguise technician. She was not a field operative and to my knowledge never had been. She was a sweet young woman with a particular talent for disguises. Whoever sent her to Foxhart sent her to her death. Which of you is prepared to take responsibility for that?"

The American shifted uneasily. "I think you must be mistaken—"

"Like hell I'm mistaken! You're CIA and everyone in this room knows it. Parkinson here doesn't sacrifice his weekend at home to fly to Scotland with a worried father searching for his daughter."

The man who'd been Hugh Camber got to his feet. "Just tell us what you know, please," he said, his voice softening a bit.

"What's your name?"

"Camber is good enough. Tell me."

Hastings seemed to make a decision. He nodded and started talking, telling them everything that had happened. When he'd finished, Rand took over. "Now it's your turn, Mr. Camber."

The American gave him a distasteful look. "Does this man have clearance?"

"He was my predecessor at Double-C," Parkinson explained. "I'll vouch for him."

"And the woman too?"

Leila started to leave but Rand waved her back to her chair. "My wife stays."

Camber decided not to press the point. "Very well. Does the name Oleg Penkov mean anything to you?"

Rand had been gone too long for the name to register, but Hastings immediately said, "The Limping Man."

"Exactly. And an expert with makeup. They say he can disguise everything but his limp." He showed them a photo of a white-haired man.

"He was at Foxhart?"

"We believe he came to London two weeks ago on some sort of mission."

Rand interrupted the dialogue between Camber and Hastings. "I thought the cold war was ending. Why would Moscow send someone over here?"

"It's not ending as far as industrial espionage goes. They want every secret they can put their hands on."

"Not much industry or espionage in Foxhart," Hastings observed dryly.

Camber ignored him and went on. "We brought over Miss—"

"Hayes."

"Well, yes. Miss Hayes was a better disguise technician than anyone London could supply. She knew what to look for, and we felt sure she'd see through Penkov's makeup, even if he dressed himself as an old lady. She's been on his tail for the past ten days, ever since he left London."

"Making contacts?"

"Yes. A school teacher in Bath, a magistrate in Newcastle, a postman in Blackpool. No one of obvious importance, and no one on any list of suspected agents."

"Perhaps he's selling magazine subscriptions," Rand suggested.

Camber glanced at him distastefully. "Please, Mr. Rand. I'm trying to conduct a briefing."

"Sorry."

"She called London early this morning and told us she was in Foxhart. Penkov seemed interested in the healing waters here, and she was certain he would make another contact. That's the last we heard."

"I spoke to her," Hastings confessed. "I called her by name. It may have blown her cover."

Parkinson pursed his lips. "I doubt if her name would have meant anything to Penkov, unless she was known to the person he came here to contact."

"But she was dead within minutes."

"A coincidence, possibly," Hugh Camber agreed.

Still, Rand could see that Hastings was deeply bothered by it. The thought that he might have been responsible for this woman's death, however inadvertently, was beginning to haunt him. "She wasn't an agent, you know," he argued, more to himself than the others. "I had no reason to believe she might be up here doing field work—and at the Reverend Fowler's healing waters, of all places!"

"It's all a bit bizarre," Camber agreed.

Parkinson went to the telephone. "They promised they'd have a preliminary autopsy report by now. Mind if I use your phone?"

"Go ahead."

Parkinson spoke briskly to someone on the other end, asked one or two questions, and then hung up. He returned to report, "Karen Hayes was killed by a single stab wound with a thin-bladed weapon. It penetrated to a depth of about seven inches, entering beneath the left breast and going straight to the heart. She died within seconds."

"A thin-bladed weapon," Rand repeated. "And what's the one fact we know about Oleg Penkov's appearance? The single thing he could not disguise?"

"His limp!"

Rand nodded. "If he limps he probably uses a cane. And that suggests a sword cane."

Parkinson shrugged. "He's probably on his way back to Moscow by now, complete with sword cane."

"Not necessarily," Rand argued. "The limp makes identification fairly easy, especially if he's trying to flee. I'm sure that helped Miss Hayes a great deal while she was on his trail. The safest place for him might be right here in Foxhart, at Fowler's miraculous stream."

"You think he'd return there?" Camber asked.

"Perhaps he never left."

It was after six when they returned to the site of the healing waters, but this far north in late May there were still hours of daylight remaining. The crowd at the little wooded stream seemed even larger than before, swelled no doubt with curiosity-seekers attracted by news of the killing. The two teenagers working the concession stand were selling bottles of the healing water as fast as they could ring up sales on the cash registers, and Constable Stebbins was doing his best to keep the traffic flowing, jabbing his baton first one way and then another. As they entered the grounds they spotted Joshua Fowler himself on the path leading to the stream.

"We'd like to ask you a few questions," Parkinson told him. At Rand's side Leila was scanning the faces as they passed by, searching for someone she might remember from earlier.

"I've already talked with the local police," Fowler said, recognizing them as strangers up from the south. Unfamiliar with jurisdictions, he might have mistaken them for Scotland Yard investigators. "I have nothing more to contribute."

"It's not directly about the killing," Rand explained. "You've been here all day. We're looking for a man with a limp, using a cane, who may have lingered here throughout the afternoon, or left and returned later." For the moment he'd discarded the possibility that Penkov might be dressed as a woman.

"I didn't notice anyone like that," he said.

Rand believed him, even if the others had doubts. Oleg Penkov hadn't gained his remarkable reputation for disguise by making foolish mistakes. He'd be seen once and only once. If it was necessary to return to the scene, he would do so in an entirely different guise.

Suddenly he felt Leila tugging at his sleeve. "That man over there!"

"What about him?" Rand asked, following her gaze to a distinguished-looking white-haired gentleman with a walking stick, just starting down the path to the stream.

"Don't you see it? That's the photograph we were just looking at! That's Oleg Penkov without his makeup!"

"My God!"

He moved forward, stepping between the lines of pilgrims, cutting in front of a blind man and his guide dog. The gentleman with the walking stick was moving faster now, limping only a little. He was almost to the stream before Rand intercepted him.

"Pardon me, Mr. Penkov?"

The face turned toward him, smiling uncertainly, and Rand almost missed the sudden swing of the stick. It was only Leila's shouted warning from behind that alerted him in time, and he lifted his right arm to ward off the half-seen blow, twisting away from it as he did so. Then both of them were locked together, toppling down the last few feet of the path, into the healing waters of the stream.

It took Camber and Parkinson to pry them apart, restraining the Russian while he and Rand were hauled from the water. Hastings, whose mind had always run to management matters, quickly arranged with Fowler for the use of a small storeroom at the back of the concession stand. It was there that they tried to dry out while awaiting Sergeant Winston's reinforcements and a change of clothes.

"You English are mad!" Oleg Penkov insisted. "What are you trying to do?"

Hugh Camber glowered at him. "Your leaders talk of peace and a new beginning, yet they send you to spy on us."

"No, no! You don't understand. My mission is to dismantle a network of sleeper agents. Some have been in place for twenty years or longer. I am calling on each of them personally, telling them we no longer have a need for them."

"A likely story!" Camber snapped. "Then what about the young woman? Why did you kill her?"

"I didn't."

The American picked up the walking stick in a burst of fury and broke it over his knee.

It was only wood. There was no thin metal blade within.

Hastings and Rand exchanged glances. Parkinson said, trying to keep his voice calm, "Give me the names of the agents you have contacted."

The Russian shivered in his wet clothes. "That would hardly be fair, would it? They have taken no action against your country, and now they will not. Most were recruited during their university days and never used. Why punish them for what might have been?"

"Who killed Karen Hayes?" Camber asked.

"I have no idea. I didn't know the woman."

"She's been on your trail since London."

The Russian's eyelids raised slightly. "Oh?"

"What about the person you were to meet here?" Rand asked.

"There was no one. I stopped off on my way to Edinburgh."

"To take the waters."

"My leg—"

"I know." Rand sighed and went outside, hoping the evening sun would help dry his clothes. They would get nowhere with Oleg Penkov.

It was, of course, just possible that he was telling the truth about the purpose of his mission. The cold war was over. Only people like Camber and Parkinson and the man with the sword cane hadn't heard about it yet.

Hastings followed him out. "What do you want to do?"

"It's not up to me. Parkinson and the American seem to be running things."

"They need you, Rand. They're backed into a corner. If they tell Sergeant Winston to arrest the Russian he'll do just that, and we may have an international incident on our hands."

He watched the lines of people moving toward the healing waters. They were looking for something to believe in. Maybe everyone was, even the Russians. He still didn't know why it had happened, but he thought he knew who had murdered Karen Hayes.

"I'm going to my car," Rand decided. "Stay here with Leila and back me up."

"What do you want us to do?"

"You'll know when the time comes."

Rand strode quickly across the busy parking lot and climbed into his car. He backed out of the space and edged into the exit line heading toward the highway. Camber and Parkinson had come out to watch now too, and ahead on the highway he saw the flashing lights of Detective Sergeant Winston's vehicle arriving at last.

There was a pause in the line to allow the patrol car to enter, and Constable Stebbins directed it with a flourish. Then he turned back to the exiting line, directing Rand to follow the car ahead. Rand's little sedan almost brushed against the constable as it passed, and it was a simple matter for Rand to reach out the window on the driver's side and grab the traffic baton with his right hand.

He saw the color drain from the constable's face, and then Stebbins turned, breaking into a run through the rows of vehicles.

Hastings and Parkinson caught him just as he reached the highway.

Later, at the local police station, it was Detective Sergeant Winston who explained the charges against him. "You understand, Stebbins, that we're concerned here strictly with the murder of the American woman, Karen Hayes. Anything else is a matter for these gentlemen. I'm waiting only for the blood test on the grooves of your baton."

"I understand, sir," the constable said, staring at his hands.

Winston nodded and began filling out forms. "But I'm sure we'd all like to hear from Mr. Rand how he was able to deduce that the murder weapon was hidden in your traffic baton."

"That was something of a guess," Rand admitted, "though an educated one. If we believe Penkov's story, and there was no reason to doubt it, he was in this country to contact various sleeper agents, men and women in deep cover who might have surfaced in the event of hostilities between Britain and Russia. These agents were being cut loose, freed of any commitments. Karen Hayes had followed Penkov and recorded his contacts in other cities. Whom did he see? A teacher, a magistrate and a postman—all civil servants or public employees of one sort or another. Then he journeyed to Foxhart, specifically to Joshua Fowler's healing waters, to inform the next person on his list. Was there anyone at Foxhart today who could be classed as a civil servant? Someone working at the healing waters who could be met nowhere else? Certainly not Fowler nor the teenagers he employed to sell the bottled water. Only Constable Stebbins, stationed there to direct traffic, seemed to qualify."

Parkinson still shook his head in disbelief. "What would the Russians have done with a local constable in a place like Foxhart if war broke out? The idea is ridiculous."

"Is it? Hastings told me earlier of a nearby RAF base in mothballs for years. In the event of war that base could have reopened. Then would a police constable with a long and perfect record be quite so ridiculous? He might have been just the sort of agent the Russians needed up here."

"Still, you have no proof he killed the Hayes woman."

"No proof at first, only a vague memory. As we were leaving the stream after Fowler's little talk this noon, I was aware of a traffic jam in the parking lot. I thought no more about it at the time, especially after the body was discovered, but what caused that pile-up of cars? We've all seen how efficient Stebbins is at directing traffic. Could it be that he'd left his post for a few moments, to murder Karen Hayes back among those trees? I thought it more than likely. The weapon didn't have to be as long as a sword cane. After all, it had penetrated only about seven inches. Constables in Britain don't carry guns, but we'd seen Stebbins with his short traffic baton. Suppose it unscrewed to reveal a thin-bladed dagger, like a sharpened knitting needle. He could have walked by Karen Hayes and stabbed her virtually undetected. That was when I decided to get a look at that baton. It was the perfect weapon for a sleeper agent like Stebbins. He might never need it, but it was always with him."

"How did he know about Karen Hayes?" Hastings asked quietly. "He was nowhere near when I spoke her name."

It was Constable Stebbins himself who finally answered, in a voice full of resignation. "She drove in right after Penkov and wanted to park near him. When I directed her down to the other end of the lot she flashed a courtesy card from MI5 giving her permission to travel anywhere within Britain without delay. I knew she was following him then, and I knew she was after me. I had to kill her."

"What about your meeting with Penkov?"

"I'd received a message that he was coming, but I was on duty today. They assign a constable on weekends to handle all the traffic at Fowler's place. Penkov came there to speak with me when I took a break. After the killing he went away, but he came back. That was when you recognized him."

"He wore no makeup when he returned," Camber said.

"He said once that sometimes no disguise is the best disguise."

"It would have been," Rand agreed, "except that my wife never read the disguise manual. She just looked at the picture and recognized him."

EGYPTIAN DAYS

It was in the Old City section of Cairo, the thousand-year descendant of al-Qahirah, that Rand first encountered the Egyptian astrologer Ibn Shubra. He had wandered the crowded streets for an hour before finally locating the narrow alleyway he sought, part of the elaborate labyrinth of fragile old structures of wood and brick. A century ago rich and poor had lived together in the Old City, but now only the poor remained among the piles of rubbish and leaking sewers.

Rand had been told to look for a weathered wooden sign with a half-moon on it. He located it near the end of the alleyway, where a bearded man wrapped in rags was asleep on the bottom step. Then he made his way up to the top floor of the building, knocked and waited until a tall man in black answered.

"I am looking for Ibn Shubra," Rand said. "I was sent by Max Zeitner, a bartender at the Nile Hilton."

The faint aroma of jasmine reached his nostrils as the tall man stepped aside and motioned him to enter. "I am Shubra. Have you come for a reading?"

"In a way, but not for myself. Max said you could tell me more than anyone about the Egyptian Days."

"The Days. Yes, I can. Come in." He switched on a dim light by a small table. The room was growing dark in the late afternoon, lit only by the sun filtering through the fine latticework of a mesheebeeyeh bay window. "Have a seat please, Mr. Rand."

"You know my name."

"Max Zeitner called to say you were coming. I had expected you sooner, but the alleys are like a maze to the uninitiated. Might I offer some tea or a glass of wine?"

"Tea will be fine. I admit to a thirst after my search for you."

Shubra disappeared through beaded curtains and returned in a moment with a cup of strong tea, obviously already prepared. "What do you wish to know about the Days?" he asked, seating himself across the table from Rand. Perhaps for some customers he produced a crystal ball as well as a cup of tea.

"What are they? What effect do they have on people?"

He placed his hands together as if in prayer. Rand could see that the apartment, and perhaps the whole house, once had been the domain of a

145

wealthy merchant or perhaps a lawyer. Had this man lived in such luxury, or had he only acquired the place during its present days of decline?

"I am an astrologer," Ibn Shubra began, speaking in the soft, precise voice of a teacher who begins by stating the obvious. "It was a long time ago that my native predecessors named the unlucky days, days on which no business should be transacted. These became known as the Egyptian Days. Astrologers named two in each month."

"Max was able to tell me that much," Rand persisted, "but I understand that three days each year are especially unlucky. Even people who ignore the others view these as especially baneful."

The tall man nodded. "They are the last Monday in April, the second Monday in August, and the third Monday in December. The worst days of all. The Egyptian Days."

"Next week is the last Monday in April."

"I know that," he replied with a slight smile.

"What can be done to ward off the evil influence?"

"Nothing." A shrug. "True believers will remain at home and do no work."

Rand leaned forward. "Are you a true believer, Mr. Shubra? Will you be casting horoscopes next Monday?"

The eyes raised to meet his. "I do what must be done, Mr. Rand, for the good of my people."

It was almost evening when Rand returned to the Nile Hilton where he was staying with his wife Leila. It was a return visit for them both, more than twenty years after they'd first met there. In those days Leila had been in graduate school, Rand had been in British Intelligence, and the Russians had been in Egypt. His first sight of her had been in his hotel room. She was 25 years old, studying archeology at Cairo University.

Now, as he entered their room and found her resting on the bed, it all came back to him. "Been out shopping?" he asked.

She opened her eyes and nodded. "It's hot for late April. And I don't remember the city being this crowded." Then she sat up on the bed. "I was just resting. Are we going out to dinner?"

"How about eating downstairs? They have a nice dining room. It's a bit late and the other good restaurants might be crowded on a Friday night."

Leila gave her sardonic chuckle. "And besides, you hate Egyptian food. Here at the hotel you can dine just like we were back in London."

"I suppose so," he admitted with a smile. She was still the small, dark-haired woman he remembered from that first night in a different Cairo hotel room, with the pleasing Middle Eastern features that came from her father rather than her Scottish mother.

"What about the astrologer?" she asked after a moment, perhaps only just remembering where he'd been. "Did you locate him?"

Rand nodded. "It took me forever in those Old City alleyways. I was almost ready to give up. His name is Ibn Shubra and he lives in a fancy old place that's been carved up into apartments. There was a ragged man asleep on his doorstep."

"What about the Egyptian Days?"

"Monday is the next one."

"Does that mean Rynox—?"

"I don't know."

"Are you going to call London?"

"I don't work for them any more," he reminded her, though in truth he'd done so several times since his early retirement. This job had come about not in London but in Cairo, when he'd been recognised by a belly dancer named Emira at Sahara City. It was Emira who'd told him about Rynox and the Egyptian Days.

"Did we come back to Egypt just so you could flirt with a belly dancer?" Leila had asked that night on the way back to their hotel.

"She's almost your age," he said, trying to reassure her.

"What's that supposed to mean?"

He leaned over and kissed her in the back of the taxi. "She met me once in Athens, years ago. She just happened to remember."

"You do make lasting impressions, Jeffery."

"She didn't know I was retired. She wanted to tell me about a man called Rynox." He remembered the taxi driver and lowered his voice. Later, in their hotel room, he'd continued the conversation. "This fellow Rynox, according to Emira, is bringing a shipment of plastic explosives from Europe to sell to terrorists here. She thought I could stop him."

"Don't get involved. We're here on holiday."

It was good advice and he might have heeded it except that the very next morning a terrorist bomb went off on a tourist bus, killing three people.

The belly dancer had mentioned a bartender at the Nile Hilton, Max Zeitner, and it was no inconvenience for Rand to seek him out. He was a scowling German who worked the afternoon shift in his own version of the hotel's bartending uniform—an open red jacket worn over a hairy chest and tight jeans. Rand guessed him to be in his late thirties, though trying to appear younger.

"Emira over at Sahara City said you might be able to help me," he said when Zeitner had poured him a beer.

"The dancer?" His eyes showed immediate interest. "Haven't seen her around in a while. How is she?"

"Well enough. I'm looking for a fellow named Rynox and she said it might be difficult to find him this weekend because of the Egyptian Days, whatever they are."

The German snorted. "Superstition, nothing more! You need an astrologer to tell you about the Egyptian Days. I've been here ten years and I still don't understand which ones are important."

"What about Rynox?"

Max Zeitner studied him for just a second before replying, "Never heard of him."

When Rand had finished his beer he asked about an astrologer. The bartender gave him the name and address of Ibn Shubra. Leila was out shopping and he'd left her a note in the room telling where he'd gone, in case he didn't get back. It was a habit of too many years in the trade.

Now, as she prepared to accompany him down to dinner, Leila asked, "Do you really think this man Rynox is a menace?"

"You read about the bombings. If he's really supplying explosives he's a menace."

"Why would she tell you about it rather than the police?"

"The Egyptian police can be corrupt. They have a reputation for torture and people like to avoid them. The British, on the other hand, had troops here until 1951. Some Egyptians still view us as their guardians. Remember the war—we kept Rommel out."

Leila said no more about it during dinner, and when Rand suggested later that they pay another visit to Sahara City she didn't seem surprised. Neither did she seem too agreeable. "Wasn't one night enough? That's the worst sort of tourist trap."

"Perhaps that's what Cairo has become, only with these terrorist bombings there soon won't be many tourists to trap."

"You go without me," she suggested.

"I'd look suspicious. Together we're just two more middle-aged tourists."

"Why don't you just call London and be done with it?"

"There may be nothing to call about. I have to speak with Emira again."

"All right," she agreed finally, reluctantly.

Sahara City was one of Cairo's best-known nightspots, famous for its belly dancers. It was really an open-air complex of nightclubs located just south of the Giza Pyramids, its name spelled out in garish lightbulbs in both Arabic and English. The place held a bizarre fascination for Rand and he always included it on his Cairo itinerary. Perhaps it was the outlandish mix of customers, or the haze of cigarette smoke that hung in the night air, or the sweaty flesh of the dancers.

This night the place was packed with a Friday crowd, tourists and locals. Leila took one look at them and muttered, "So much for a pleasant night at the hotel."

"I promise we won't stay long. I just want to speak with Emira again."

After they were seated in a row of tables a few back from the dance floor, Rand excused himself and circled around to the backstage curtains. A dozen women of varying ages, all voluptuous and heavily made up, waited for their turns to perform. Rand knew from his last visit that they would dance separately and in various combinations, vying for tips from men at the ringside tables.

"Emira!" he called out, spotting her near the back. She stepped forward quickly, wearing a bright green costume with matching tassels.

"What are you doing here?"

"I have to speak to you again about Rynox."

"Not tonight! Do you want to get me killed?"

"What—"

"Get out, the show is starting!"

"I've seen Max Zeitner. He sent me to an astrologer—"

That stopped her. "What astrologer?"

"A man named Ibn Shubra."

She closed her eyes and sighed. "It was a mistake talking to you. Get out—someone is here!"

One of the other dancers passed her and said, "Tell him to give us some *kunafah*, honey."

Emira ignored the remark and turned quickly away. She sought shelter among the other girls and Rand could do nothing but retreat as the first dancer went into her act.

"Did you find her?" Leila asked back at their table.

"Yes. She's too frightened to talk. I'll try to see her later."

The first dancer was undulating to the music, weaving slowly like a snake emerging from a basket. As the music increased in tempo she began to twirl her tassels and move among the ringside tables. Like the others she wore a tasseled bra and low-slung gauzy skirt that seemed about to slide off her hips with every violent undulation. The appreciative males at the front tables were stuffing folded Egyptian pound notes and other currency into the band of her skirt as she danced by.

Rand and Leila watched two other dancers perform before Emira finally appeared. Her bright green costume caught the light, shimmering like a wave over her breasts and hips. The crowd roared its approval.

From every side men reached out to stuff folded bills into her waistband. She seemed to shake more vigorously with each one, flashing a smile that dazzled. Completing her circuit of the ringside tables, she moved back toward the rear of the stage. It was then that her hand dropped toward her waist, and Rand thought later that she must have felt something rather than seen it.

There was a blinding flash and roar that seemed to come from her gut, and instantly everyone was screaming, running, tumbling over each other in blind panic. The sound of it drowned out the final terrible screams from Emira in the seconds before she died. For her, the Egyptian Days had arrived early.

Leila stood staring out the window of their hotel room at the black serpent that was the Nile by night. "My God, I don't think I'll ever forget that for as long as I live," she said, as much to herself as to Rand.

"Nor will I."

"What was it? What killed her?"

Rand had been trying not to think about it, but now he forced himself. "Probably a thin layer of plastic explosive, molded to the size of a credit card, and with a radio-controlled detonator embedded in it. One of the men at ringside wrapped a pound note around it and slipped it into the band of her skirt. Then when she was far enough away from him he pressed a tiny transmitter in his pocket and the thing went off. It was not a very big explosion, just enough to—" He saw her face and left the sentence unfinished.

"Who would do such a thing?"

"The killer obviously escaped during the panic following the explosion. It might have been this man Rynox but more likely it was someone he hired. When I spoke to her earlier she seemed afraid of someone, but I doubt if she'd seen Rynox himself."

"Will you call London now, or talk to someone at the embassy?"

"And tell them what?"

"You can't just ignore what happened to that poor woman!"

"Believe me, I won't ignore it." He started pacing the floor. "It might have been my presence there that caused her death, or the fact that I visited the astrologer Ibn Shubra. Someone knew she was talking, and they shut her up in a way that would be a lesson to others."

"But you know nothing about this Rynox. What can you do?"

"I know some key facts about him. He's bringing in a large shipment of plastic explosives, he's superstitious about these so-called Egyptian Days, and if he killed Emira he's utterly ruthless."

"You think he'll wait till after Monday to complete his deal?"

"More likely he'll move before Monday. There's a sense of urgency now that Emira's been killed."

In the morning Rand was awakened by the ringing of the bedside telephone. He glanced at his watch before answering it, noting the time as two minutes after eight. "Hello?"

"Mr. Rand?" A woman's voice, speaking softly.

"Yes. Who is this?"

"I was a friend of Emira. I saw what happened last night. I must talk to you."

He hesitated only an instant. "When?"

"This morning? In an hour?"

"Where?"

"In front of the Egyptian Museum. That's in Tahrir Square, very close to your hotel."

"I know," he assured her. Beside him in bed, Leila had come awake. "I'll be there in an hour. How will I know you?"

"I'll find you," she told him and hung up.

"Who was that?" Leila asked sleepily.

"A friend of Emira's. She wants to meet me in an hour."

"Jeffery—"

"I'll be careful."

The museum was a large stately building more than a hundred years old. It shared the square with the city's central bus terminal where hundreds of people waited along strips of concrete for their crowded but inexpensive transportation to appear. On Saturday morning there was not the bustle of weekdays but Rand still found the elevated walkway that circled the area to be the fastest way around the square to the museum. From above he tried to pick out the woman who had phoned him but it was impossible among the variety of faces and skin tones, with Mediterranean and Levantine types mingled with the darker Sudanese immigrants.

When he descended to street level and paused by the museum steps he quickly realized that the woman on the phone had been none of these. She appeared at his side almost at once, young and lithe and with the pale skin of the Turko-Circassians who had once been Egypt's ruling class. "I phoned you, Mr. Rand," she said simply, falling into step beside him.

"Do you want to go inside?" he asked.

"Let us walk down to the river," she suggested instead. "The museum is not quite open yet."

As they walked he suddenly recognized her. "You were a dancer with Emira. You came on just ahead of her last night."

She barely nodded. "My name is Pasha. Emira was a good friend, almost an older sister to me. I saw you come backstage last night and she told me your name."

"How did you know where I was staying?"

"I phoned Shepheard's first. When you weren't there I tried the Nile

Hilton."

"Good guess. I'm terribly sorry about last night. No one should die like that."

They neared the river and he could see the Cairo Tower on Gezirah Island across the way. A hollow cylinder of lattice walls, it carefully hid its utilitarian purpose as a television mast and revolving restaurant. "It was Rynox who had her killed," Pasha said quietly. "He knew she was talking about his business."

"Who is Rynox? Where can I find him?"

"She didn't tell me that. She told me a lot, but not that. The bombings of tourists horrified her. Somehow she learned he was supplying them with plastic explosives from a plant in Europe—it might have been Czechoslovakia or whatever it's called now. Then she recognized you the other night and asked for your help."

"I'm retired now. I told her that."

"You still have ties to those people. I've heard no one ever really retires from intelligence work."

Rand sighed. She was still young enough to imagine the glamour of it. "I talked to a couple of people. She told me of a bartender at my hotel named Max Zeitner."

"Max was an old friend of hers."

"He sent me to an astrologer named Ibn Shubra to learn about the Egyptian Days."

Pasha frowned. "That's odd. I'm sure Max knows what they are."

"Monday is one of them, isn't it?"

"Yes," she agreed.

"Tell me something. How did Emira know about this man Rynox?"

"I don't know. They were friends, I think, but these recent bombings were more than she could stand. After she spoke to you she told me that maybe you could do something about it."

Rand smiled sadly. "I was a glorified cipher clerk, heading up something called the Department of Concealed Communications. I was never a field agent except by accident a few times."

"Maybe she didn't know what else to do," Pasha suggested. "Can you bring Rynox to justice for what he did to her?"

"I'll try," he promised, wondering what justice had become in the Middle East. Sometimes it was whatever suited the politics of the moment. "Tell me one thing. Did Rynox, or someone who might have been Rynox, ever visit her at Sahara City?"

"Not that I know of. Certainly there are always male customers wanting to have a drink with us between shows. Usually we don't, unless it's someone we know. Of course Emira had been working a long time. She knew more people than I did."

Rand thought about it. "I'll do what I can," he promised. "Whoever killed her deserves to be punished. I may contact you again if I need more help."

They parted at the river and he headed back to the hotel. Leila was already gone from the room, planning a few hours of shopping before they met again in mid-afternoon. Rand breakfasted alone in the hotel's dining room, reading about the Sahara City outrage on the front page of one of the city's English-language newspapers. He was surprised when a bulky man wearing an open shirt asked to join him. When he saw the hairy chest he recognized the hotel bartender, Max Zeitner.

"Sit down," Rand gestured. "You've seen the papers?"

"About Emira, yes."

"I was there," Rand told him. "I saw it happen."

"Terrible, terrible!" He leaned forward, lowering his voice. "I knew her only slightly, hadn't seen her in months. We moved in different circles." It was as if he was distancing himself from the crime, or perhaps from her life.

"She told me to contact you about Rynox," Rand persisted.

A shrug. "I know him by reputation only. A camel trader with a mean streak."

"I think something more."

The bartender ordered breakfast from a hovering waiter, then said, as he had about Emira, "We move in different circles."

Rand finished his eggs but remained sipping his coffee while Max Zeitner ate breakfast. But the conversation shifted to the unusually warm April weather and the influx of tourists. "The bombings haven't had too much effect," Rand observed, trying to steer the conversation in the direction he wanted.

"Not yet," Zeitner agreed. "But if the attacks are stepped up, the result could be disastrous for tourism."

"Some say Rynox is selling explosives to the terrorists."

The German's eyes shot up. "Who says?"

"That's the word I hear. The astrologer, Ibn Shubra, says he cannot work Monday because of the Egyptian Days. If a deal is in the works, it must be completed before then."

"Never believe everything astrologers tell you."

"I was sent to him by you," Rand reminded the man.

They paid their checks and walked out to the lobby together. Max Zeitner had the day off from his job but he was working a wedding reception in the upstairs ballroom at one o'clock. They stood looking at the cantilevered staircase that rose dramatically from the foyer to the upstairs ballrooms.

"That staircase is the reason this hotel is so popular for weddings," Zeitner explained. "Everyone can see the arrivals making their grand entrance. We often have two or three wedding receptions or engagement parties on the same day—more than four hundred a year."

"That's a great deal of extra work for a bartender."

"It is indeed! Some don't drink, of course, because they're strict Muslim, but others want it at their weddings. Come by here about one o'clock and you'll see a real sight. The bride and groom will be escorted in by bagpipers."

"Really?"

"It's something left over from British colonial days. The people really like it for special occasions. The entertainment often includes a belly dancer too. That's how I met Emira. She sometimes earned extra money performing at weddings."

"I'd like to see one of them."

"Come ahead! If anyone questions you, tell them you're from the newspaper. They won't bother you."

Rand followed him up the impressive staircase to the ballroom floor, then into one of the large rooms where preparations for the wedding reception were already under way. A huge wedding cake, five tiers tall, was being placed carefully on a low table which raised its top at least seven feet off the floor. "How will they reach it?" Rand wondered.

The caterer who'd supplied the cake, a small Egyptian with a mustache and glasses, was busy positioning it just right on the table. "This is Sher Wahba," the bartender said by way of introduction. "Mr. Rand here is writing about your wedding customs."

Wahba turned his eyes toward Rand, always eager for publicity. "How will they reach it, you wonder? With a short step-ladder, of course!" He bustled around to the other side of the cake, checking it out. "A large confection like this is a sign of wealth. The groom's family pays for the weddings here and they want the guests to know nothing is too good for them. There will be two hundred here this afternoon, and I have another wedding tomorrow."

"Two hundred!" Rand stared up at the cake. "This would feed a thousand!"

The caterer chuckled. "The center core and every other tier are artificial, made of cardboard and a bit of plaster decoration. Everyone does it with large cakes."

Rand only shook his head. "Everything is illusion these days!"

Promptly at one o'clock the sound of bagpipes and drums was heard from the staircase. The happy couple entered the foyer and made their way up the stairs to the ballroom. Rand mingled with the invited guests as the pipers were dismissed and a twelve-piece orchestra took over on the bandstand. The room was decorated with hundreds of balloons with the bride and groom presiding over the festivities from a ceremonial dais at one side of the dance floor.

Rand found a spangled belly dancer preparing to perform after the singer. Her name was Mustafa and she admitted to sometimes working at Sahara City. "Emira?" she repeated. "I've met her. I read what happened. But she never went out with the other girls."

"Did she know an astrologer named Ibn Shubra?"

"I do not believe in astrologers. Some of the girls go to them. I do not."

"Thank you for talking to me," he said, though he'd learned nothing from her.

As he turned away she said, "Emira didn't come with the other girls because she had a lover."

"Who was he?"

"I do not know. She would go to meet him sometimes after work."

R and met Leila as planned, and looked over the things she'd bought. One, a replica of the painted limestone bust of Nefertiti, had become a symbol of ancient Egypt throughout the world. "I have just the place for it at home," Leila promised. "What have you been up to today? Did you meet that woman who phoned?"

He told her about it, and about the wedding reception at the hotel. "I talk to these people and I get nowhere," he admitted.

"I still think you should call London."

"Who? Parkinson? I don't owe him anything."

There was a show at a Parisian nightclub that Leila wished to see, and they went there in the evening. He spent the time trying not to think of Emira and the man known as Rynox, but by the end of the evening he had decided to pay a return visit to the astrologer on Sunday morning. Leila intended to attend mass at one of the Coptic Christian churches in Cairo, and he planned to go then.

Sunday was another day of mid-80s temperatures and sunny skies, more suited to summer than the last week in April. Some shops were closed, others open, and as he made his way through the twisting alleys of the Old City he wondered why anyone would choose to live there when so many more colorful areas of Cairo were available. The inhabitants, like many of the houses, had seen better days.

At the house where Ibn Shubra resided, Rand could see on his approach that the latticework screens on the upper windows were open, indicating the astrologer was probably at home. A beggar in rags sat across from the entrance to the house, perhaps the same one who'd been sleeping there on Rand's first visit.

The tall astrologer, dressed in black as he had been earlier, answered his knock and stepped aside to let him enter. "I have been expecting your return,

Mr. Rand. Our first conversation was not completely satisfactory."

Rand took the same seat he'd occupied on his earlier visit, and once again accepted a cup of tea. "Tomorrow is one of the Egyptian Days," he said. "I thought I should visit you before then. I am seeking a man named Rynox who may be closing an important business deal before tomorrow."

"Rynox— An odd name."

"A dealer in contraband."

"How did you learn of him?"

"From a dancer at Sahara City. She was killed Friday night. You may have seen it in the papers."

Ibn Shubra looked away. "A woman named Emira."

"That's right."

"What is your connection with her? You were sent to me by Max Zeitner."

"She referred me to Max. I'm looking for Rynox, now more than ever."

The astrologer closed his eyes as if deep in thought, and put his fingers together as he had on the previous visit. Finally his head jerked up as a telephone rang in the next room. "Pardon me a moment," he said, and went to answer it.

Rand was left alone. He glanced toward the bookcase and walked over to inspect its contents. There was a large mixture of British books and some foreign-language ones, mainly on various aspects of astrology and necromancy. He glanced through one or two, working his way down the bookcase. In the next room he could hear the astrologer's low voice on the telephone, but could make out none of the words.

On the bottom shelf were a dozen or so British detective novels from the 1930s. Most had shabby and torn jackets if there were jackets at all. Rand recognized some but not all of the titles: *The A.B.C. Murders* by Agatha Christie, *The Beast Must Die* by Nicholas Blake, *Murder Must Advertise* by Dorothy L. Sayers, *The Rynox Mystery* by Philip MacDonald—

Rand held his breath as he slid that last title from the shelf and glanced through it. Rynox was the name of a corporation. It was not a book Rand had ever read, so he was unfamiliar with the plot. But that didn't matter. It was the title that mattered.

He heard a noise behind him and turned to see the Mauser pistol in Ibn Shubra's steady hand. "Yes, Mr. Rand," he said quietly. "You have found him. I am Rynox."

R and let his breath out slowly, weighing the odds if he made a dive for the gun. At the moment they didn't seem too good. "Why did you kill Emira?" he asked. "Or have her killed?"

The tall astrologer held his position. "Whatever you choose to believe about me, I had nothing to do with Emira's death. I loved her."

"What?"

"Emira and I had been lovers for the past two years."

Rand shook his head, unable to put the pieces together. "You were the one she met after work?"

"Yes. She often stayed here with me. Do not look so disbelieving, Mr. Rand. Emira was only ten years younger than me, and even astrologers are entitled to love."

"It's not that. It's— She betrayed you. She told me Rynox was selling plastic explosives to Egyptian terrorists."

"Emira strongly objected to some of my business dealings. She told me once she'd like to stop them if she could do it without hurting me."

"Put down that gun," Rand said. "Let's talk about this. If you didn't kill her, one of your business partners did!"

"No, no, Mr. Rand. The gun is necessary. Explosives and weapons are only a small part of my business. I do not intend to sacrifice everything because you were rash enough to be browsing on my bookshelf."

"Tell me who killed her."

"If I knew, I would let you die with the knowledge. But I truly don't know. Certain radical Muslim groups who want to tear down the pyramids and sphinxes for being idolatrous are also opposed to belly dancers. Her death might have been meant as a warning to others. It could have nothing to do with my business dealings."

"You don't believe that any more than I do. The delivery is being made today, isn't it—before the bad-luck day tomorrow?"

Ibn Shubra nodded slightly. "But you will neither find nor prevent it, Mr. Rand. A cubic meter of plastic explosives is too valuable in this part of the world to be bartered away lightly. If Emira died because of it, I mourn her death. I will not mourn yours."

Rand could wait no longer. He hurled the book he still held just as the astrologer squeezed the trigger, then followed it across the space between them, feeling the burn as the bullet creased his arm. Then he was onto Ibn Shubra, wrestling him to the floor, clawing for the gun before the man could get off a second shot. It had been years since Rand engaged in any sort of prolonged bodily combat, and he felt the strength oozing out of him quickly.

Gasping, he felt Ibn Shubra roll over on top of him. He gave a mighty shove as the man stood, aiming the Mauser, and sent him backward into the latticework screen. Rand heard a breaking of glass but the astrologer righted himself, still holding the gun.

Rand managed to kick out at his legs as he fired again, missing Rand's head by inches. Then they were tussling again and the weapon flew free, hitting the floor a few feet away. Ibn Shubra broke loose of Rand's grasp and aimed a kick to his head, then dove once more for the pistol. The kick dazed him and he was unable to bring Ibn Shubra into focus. He only saw a blurred outline reach for the gun and take a steady aim with both hands.

He had a flash of realization that this man Rynox was about to end his life, here in a dingy Cairo apartment where he might never be found. He thought of Leila as the roar of a gunshot filled his ears, somehow louder than the rest.

Then Ibn Shubra fell dying across his legs and he looked up to see the short-barrelled riot gun held in the hands of the ragged beggar from the street outside.

The man who'd fired the shot identified himself as Sergeant Hani Fahmy of the Cairo Police anti-terrorist squad. As he tended to the bullet graze on Rand's arm, others were already arriving downstairs. "When I heard the first shot I called for assistance," the sergeant explained. "We wanted him alive for questioning, but when I broke in here and saw him about to shoot you I didn't have much choice."

"I'm eternally grateful," Rand admitted.

"What was going on in here? We've been watching the house for weeks. Saw you visit him on Friday."

"I came looking for a man named Rynox. I'd been told he was selling plastic explosives to terrorists."

"Ibn Shubra was Rynox," the sergeant confirmed. "We've known that for some time. But we've never been able to catch him or any of his associates with explosives. He brings it in from Eastern Europe and somehow it finds its way into the hands of terrorists."

There were other police in the apartment now as Fahmy explained what had happened. Rand was hustled away for a ride to the hospital, though he insisted he was all right. At the hospital they thought differently, examining the bruise on his head where Shubra's kick had landed and speaking darkly about the possibility of a concussion.

Soon after that, Leila arrived at the hospital. "You weren't careful," she greeted him, and he could almost hear the relief in her voice. He didn't look as bad as she'd feared.

"No, I wasn't." He tried to shrug but that made his head hurt.

"What happened?"

"The Cairo police came to my rescue."

"Someone from the British embassy is waiting to see you."

"I don't have time for that. The transfer of explosives is being made today. Shubra admitted as much before he died. I have to get out of here."

"We'll see what the doctor says."

Rand lay back on the bed, frustrated. Before he knew it he was being interviewed by a British civil servant from the embassy who asked endless questions and promised to contact London the following morning. It was Sergeant Fahmy who brought them the good news at mid-afternoon.

"The doctors say you can go now, Mr. Rand. Just take it easy for the next couple of days." He nodded to Leila and said, "I'll drive you both back to your hotel." He had changed his beggar's rags for a white shirt and pants, possibly part of a police uniform.

They were driven to the hotel in an unmarked car which Fahmy insisted on parking so he could accompany them inside. "We appreciate your help, Mr. Rand," he said with a smile, "but I think we'll be able to handle it now."

"Not unless you can find a cubic meter of plastic explosives that's being transferred today."

"That much?" he asked, doing some quick mental calculations. "It's worth a great deal of money on today's market."

"A cubic meter could weight hundreds of pounds," Leila commented.

The sergeant nodded. "But it could be in several packages, and probably is."

They were crossing the hotel lobby when Rand spotted a familiar face. It was the dancer Pasha, who'd met him Saturday at the museum. She was hurrying toward the elevator, carrying a canvas bag. "What are you doing here?" he asked.

She glanced uncertainly at Leila and the sergeant. "Emira was supposed to dance at a wedding reception this afternoon. I'm taking over for her."

Rand's head was buzzing. He remembered someone mentioning another wedding today. It meant nothing to him at the time, and still shouldn't have meant anything. They had weddings at the Nile Hilton almost every day, often two or three at a time. The bartender had told him that. So why should this one be so important?

Was it important enough that Emira had to be killed to keep her from dancing there?

"I'm going up with you," he decided suddenly, following her onto the elevator. Leila and Fahmy exchanged glances and followed along. "Whose wedding is it?" he asked Pasha.

"The son of a Cairo banker. He is marrying a French woman."

The wedding reception was well under way and Rand was surprised to realize it was almost four in the afternoon. Max Zeitner was working with another bartender, pouring drinks as fast as he could, and Wahba the baker stood proudly near his latest five-tiered confection. A young woman was singing traditional Egyptian songs on the bandstand, receiving warm applause from those who took time out from their celebrating to listen.

"I'm late now," Pasha said. "I have to change into my costume." She ran around the back of the bandstand.

"She's lovely," Leila commented, gazing up at the dark-haired French bride on her dais.

"Nothing's going to happen here," the sergeant insisted, "in full view of over two hundred people."

Rand didn't reply. He was remembering that Emira had been killed in full view of several hundred people.

The singer finished with a flourish and it was Pasha's turn. She came through the beaded curtains like a dervish, whirling and undulating to the native music, bringing cheers from the wedding guests. She was faster, younger and more aggressively sensual than Emira had been, prompting Leila to lean over and whisper in his ear, "That's the girl you were with yesterday?"

"She looks different with all her clothes on," Rand assured his wife.

Even in the slower parts of her dance Pasha was careful to avoid getting too close to the tables. There was no opportunity to stick currency in the band of her shimmering skirt. She was taking no chances.

When she'd finished her dance and the singer had done another set of songs, it was time to cut the cake. Both bride and groom climbed a short step-ladder to slice the top tier as cameras and videos recorded the scene. Everyone cheered and trays of other confections were brought forth to supplement the thinly cut pieces of cake.

"What are these?" Leila asked Sergeant Fahmy, helping herself to a sticky confection from the tray.

"Ah, *kunafah*! It's an Egyptian sweetmeat, flour paste rolled up with honey, nuts and raisins—very popular at holidays and festive occasions. Bakers often supply them at weddings along with the cake."

Rand tasted it at Leila's urging and agreed it was quite good. But his mind was elsewhere. "Do you use bomb-sniffing dogs?" he asked Fahmy.

"Of course! We have them trained to detect all sorts of explosives."

"How long would it take you to get one here?"

"It is a Sunday. I would need to get authorization."

"See what you can do. Tell them it's important."

When the sergeant had gone off, Leila asked, "Do you know what you're doing, Jeffery?"

"I hope so. Come on, let's get a drink."

Max Zeitner was enjoying a respite at the bar. He winked at Rand and asked, "Enjoying yourself? The drinks are free. A bit of French champagne, perhaps?"

They settled for Egyptian beer, which Leila had always liked. Rand leaned toward the bartender and said, "You sent me to Ibn Shubra because you knew he was Rynox."

Zeitner only smiled and said, "Maybe."

Rand's eyes scanned the room. Almost all the wedding cake had been distributed to the guests. By six o'clock many people were beginning to leave, but there was still no sign of Sergeant Fahmy. "How long do you want to stay?" Leila asked. "We weren't invited, after all."

"A few minutes longer."

Rand caught sight of some white-jacketed men entering the ballroom. Sher Wahba was speaking to the groom's father and gesturing toward the stand for the wedding cake, where everything edible had been transferred to paper plates on the serving tables. As the new arrivals prepared to remove the cake stand, Rand strode forward.

The baker turned, surprised to see him "Ah, Mr.—"

"Rand. We met here yesterday."

There was a deep-throated growl from the door and the few remaining guests turned in panic. Sergeant Fahmy had returned with his dog, a big German shepherd who headed directly for them. Wahba the baker grabbed for something beneath his tunic and Rand hit him smashing blows with both fists, sending him to the floor.

"That's for Emira," he said, breathing hard. "I wish it could have been more."

It was Sergeant Fahmy who brought them the news a half-hour later, while Rand was soaking his hands. "I hope I broke his jaw," he said as Leila opened the door for Fahmy. "I almost broke my hands."

"You did some damage," the sergeant confirmed. "And my dog sniffed out the plastic explosives hidden inside that cake stand—carefully wrapped packages filling the tall center core and the alternate tiers between the layers of real cake. You'd better tell me something I can put in my report, though."

"Before you killed him, Shubra insisted he hadn't been responsible for Emira's death. He had no reason to lie, since he was about to kill me anyway. And yet I felt sure one of his confederates had killed her. The use of plastic explosives, even just a couple of ounces, tied it too closely to his contraband operation. And Emira was frightened by someone she knew in the audience Friday night. You see, the main reason she had to die wasn't just that she was threatening to tell about the delivery of plastic explosives. It was that she was scheduled to perform at today's wedding. With a shipment that large it was safer to kill her than to risk her revealing everything today. You see, Sher Wahba delivered the wedding cake plus the explosives, and the terrorists were to take away the cake stand, with the explosives still in place. I suppose it was easy for him to smuggle the explosives into the country in a shipment of flour or other bakery supplies."

"They had enough *plastique* in there to blow up the entire hotel! Why would they risk such a thing?"

"It was so unlikely as to be above suspicion. And without a detonator the material is relatively benign. It can be molded into any shape, remember. Terrorists are used to working with it."

"How did you know it was the cake?"

"What else did Wahba bring that was big enough?"

"But how did you know it was Wahba who killed the girl?"

"When I was backstage with her Friday night, Emira implied she was afraid of someone at the club that night. Another dancer overheard her and obviously knew whom she meant. The dancer told her to ask him for some *kunafah*. I had no idea what the word meant until tonight, when I ate some and you told me bakers supplied it. The dancer knew the man Emira feared was a baker. The only baker at this wedding, the wedding where Emira would have danced had she lived, was Sher Wahba."

Rand and Leila slept late the following morning. The remainder of their holiday seemed rather bland, but perhaps it was just as well. The Egyptian Days had come and gone.

WAITING FOR MRS. RYDER

It was a continuing fascination with the Indian Ocean and the east coast of Africa that led Rand to remain in Cairo after his wife returned to her spring semester of lectures at the University of Reading. "I want to spend a week or so on the islands off the coast," he told Leila. "Then I'll head back home."

"It's the rainy season there," she warned him. "They call it the Long Rains."

"I know. It comes and goes."

"Like some husbands."

Rand's destination was the island of Lamu off the coast of Kenya. He learned he could reach it by flying to an airstrip on Manda Island, only a couple of kilometers away, and taking a diesel-powered launch across the channel. He did exactly that on a Monday afternoon in late April, arriving in the middle of one of the Long Rains his wife had warned him about. Leila had studied archeology in Egypt and traveled frequently in East Africa. He had wanted to bring her with him but her lecture schedule prevented it.

The motor ferry was waiting for him at the dock and by the time it had taken him and the other two passengers across the channel the rain had started to let up. "Damned nuisance," the stout man with the white mustache muttered. "Been coming here for ten years and the rain's always the same in the spring."

"Are you British?" Rand asked, though the accent didn't sound quite right to his ear.

"Australian, actually." He held out his hand. "James Count. I write travel books. Just now I'm updating our volume on East Africa. Lived a good bit in London, though. That's probably why you mistook me for British. You're a Brit, aren't you?"

"Yes, that's right."

"Not many people come to Lamu in this season. You here on business?"

"No," Rand assured him with a smile. "I'm a retired civil servant. This is just a holiday for me."

"Do you have a hotel?"

"Someone back in Cairo recommended the Sunrise Guest House."

"That's a good place," James Count agreed, stroking his mustache. Rand guessed him to be in his fifties. "Especially in this humidity. The rooms have ceiling fans and mosquito netting."

"Sounds fine to me."

The third passenger on the motor launch was a man in a white Muslim cap and full length white robe, carrying a closed umbrella against the vagaries of the weather. He did not speak, and Rand suspected he did not understand English. When the ferry docked on the Lamu side of the channel he was the first one off.

"The Sunrise is at the top of this street," James Count told Rand as they came off the jetty. "After you pass through customs go up to the fort and turn right. You'll see it there."

Rand found the place without difficulty and booked a room for three nights. It seemed like a clean, well-run guest house with a good view of the harbor. A sign in the reception area informed him that drugs and spirits were prohibited and prostitutes and homosexuals were not allowed in the rooms.

He turned on the overhead fan as he unpacked his single suitcase. Then, seeing a bug in one of the bureau drawers, he decided to leave most of his clothing in the suitcase after all. The shuttered windows opened wide to the afternoon breeze off the Indian Ocean. It was a pleasant place despite the bugs and the humidity. Leila would have liked it.

When it was time for dinner he went off along the ancient, narrow lanes in search of a likely restaurant. He passed several Africans and white-clad Muslims on the way, some leading donkeys and carts. Private motor vehicles were not allowed on the island and donkey carts were obviously a common form of transportation. The white-walled fort with its battlements, nearly two centuries old, had been used as a prison through most of the current century, according to a brochure Rand had picked up in the guest house reception area. It was closed now while being converted into a museum.

There were women in the narrow lanes along with the men and he was surprised to see that they wore the traditional black wraparound garments without the usual Muslim face veil. He was even more surprised at the café he chose for dining to find a pair of waitresses serving the food. His waitress was named Onyx, a brown-skinned woman with western features, possibly in her forties. She spoke fair English, enough to understand his order.

"Bring me a bottle of beer, too," he said after ordering his food.

"We have Tusker, a local beer."

"That's fine."

"Chilled or warm?" When she saw his expression of distaste she explained, "Most Africans like it warm."

"Not me. Chilled will be fine."

The food was passable and the tables were mostly filled by the time Rand finished eating. He was thinking of phoning Leila back in Reading when he thought he spotted a familiar face at a corner table. Walking over there on his way out, he saw that he was correct.

"George Ryder, isn't it? I'm Jeffery Rand. We met in London some years ago." He kept his voice low, though the next table was empty.

Ryder was a handsome gray-haired man in his early fifties. He'd been a decade younger when Rand met him in the offices of Concealed Communications, overlooking the Thames. Rand was already retired from British Intelligence by that time, but Ryder was still quite active in the American CIA.

He looked up from his food and smiled. "You must be mistaken. My name is Watkins."

"Pardon me." Rand continued on his way out of the café. If George Ryder was in Lamu on an assignment, he had violated a cardinal rule of espionage in calling him by his real name. Still, Ryder had never been a case agent to his knowledge. He sat at a desk in Langley, Virginia, and shuffled papers around.

Rand thought about it ·as he strolled around the town, taking in the waterfront and its surprising sights. One of the most unexpected was the large number of dhows, small sailing vessels used by Arab traders. Rand had seen them before on the Arabian and Indian coasts, but never in such profusion. Staring at them in the twilight as they rode at anchor close to shore, he was not aware of the white-robed Muslim until he spoke. "The dhows are built and repaired at nearby villages. That is why there are so many here."

Rand recognized the man who'd been on the ferry that afternoon. This time he carried no umbrella. "Do you live here?" he asked.

The man nodded. "I am Amin Shade. I buy and sell these boats."

Rand introduced himself and they shook hands. "This is an unusual place, more Arab than African."

"It has a long history as an isle of fantasy and romance. It is both remote and unique, which is why it attracted your so-called hippies in the early 1970s."

Rand was staring out at the boats. "I'd like to ride in a dhow," he decided, admiring the sleek craft with their distinctive sails.

"That is easily arranged. Tomorrow morning I must sail to Matondoni, one of the villages where they are built. I would be pleased to have you as a companion."

"That's very kind of you," Rand murmured. "What time do you leave?"

"Around ten o'clock," Amin Shade replied. "It is well to travel before the heat of the day, though the journey is brief. I will conduct my business, we will have a barbecued fish lunch and return in the afternoon. I will meet you right here at ten. And bring an umbrella. It is sure to rain."

Rand left him and continued along the shore. The people of the island certainly seemed friendly enough. After a time he left the shore and headed back north, the way he had come. Almost at once he heard the laughter of a young woman and somehow knew she was British. Hurrying along the street he caught up with her and saw that she was accompanied by James Count, the travel writer who'd been his other ferry companion.

"Rand, for God's sake!" Count put a heavy arm around his shoulders and Rand could smell the beer on his breath. "Laura, this is the British chap I told you about. Laura Peters, Jeffery Rand."

She was much younger than Count, probably still in her twenties, with the fresh attractiveness of an outdoor person. "Hello, Jeffery Rand. You must come with us! I'm taking my uncle to see where I work."

"Your uncle?"

"Don't you think we look alike?" she asked mischievously. "If I had that mustache we'd be dead ringers!"

"Where are you two taking me?" Rand demanded with a smile.

"To something you've never seen before," she assured him, starting down the narrow lane toward the waterfront. "The Donkey Sanctuary!"

Even before they reached it the braying of the animals could be heard. If Rand had thought she was jesting he was proven wrong by the first sight of pens filled with injured, sick and tired donkeys. "What is this? Do you round them up off the streets, Miss Peters?"

"They are brought here by their owners or we find them ourselves. We offer rest and protection until they are well."

"But whom do you work for? Who pays you for this?"

"The International Donkey Protection Trust of Sidmouth, Devon. I've been working for them the better part of a year and there's nothing like it."

"I don't imagine there is," Rand agreed.

She showed them around the place. The donkeys were interesting, but when Rand spotted a copy of the London *Times* in her small office he was more interested in that. "I haven't seen one in weeks," he admitted.

"Take it!" Laura said. "I'm finished with it. They fly them in every week with my supplies. If you don't mind reading week-old news—"

He folded it and stuck it under his arm. "Not at all. Thank you. Can I buy you people a beer or something?"

"A capital idea!" James Count agreed. "I've already had a few but there's always room for one or two more."

"Where shall we go?" his niece asked.

Count made a face. "Only place in Lamu that serves cold beer is the Harmony Café. It's just a few blocks away."

"I know it," Rand told them. "I ate dinner there."

They paused at the outdoor pens while Laura petted some of her favorite donkeys, then left the Sanctuary to set off for the café. When they reached it Rand was pleased to see that the man who denied being George Ryder was no longer present. The owner of the place, a fat Arab named Hegad, was going over the menu with Onyx, the waitress who'd served Rand earlier. "On Tuesday evenings we serve special Indian dishes," he told her. "Some traders sail up from Zanzibar for them."

Somehow the thought of dhows docked by the jetty at Lamu like yachtsmen on the Thames was more than Rand could imagine, but until an hour ago he'd never imagined a Donkey Sanctuary. The three of them chose a table near the door and Onyx came over to take their order. It was past the dinner hour, with only one other table occupied.

"Just beer," Count told her. "Three cold Tuskers."

Onyx went off to fill the order and Rand asked about the local economy. "What does one do for a living on Lamu?"

Laura Peters grinned. "Tend to the donkeys. Seriously, though, there is dhow building and repairing in the villages, and fabulous tourism at the right times of the year. Shela, a village south of here, has a magnificent beach. All of that brings in money. The local police will tell you illegal currency exchange is a thriving business too, but I think they exaggerate."

Over the second beer James Count and his niece turned their conversation to family matters and gossip about relatives in England and Australia. Rand glanced at the front page of the *Times*, skimming an article on the royal family. That was when his eye fell on an item at the bottom of the page. The headline read: *CIA Official Charged in Espionage Case.*

Rand quickly read the news report out of Washington. George Ryder, longtime CIA bureau chief, and his wife Martha were both indicted on multiple counts of espionage by a federal grand jury. They are assumed to have fled the country and a worldwide search is underway. It is believed that Ryder and his wife were paid more than two million dollars over the past decade to supply CIA secrets to Moscow.

Rand lifted his eyes from the page and found himself staring at the empty table where George Ryder had been seated just a few hours earlier.

On the way back to the Sunrise Guest House Rand pondered the trick of fate that had brought him together with George Ryder at this remote outpost of civilization. They'd hardly known each other, and in truth Ryder might not even remember him. Now he was a wanted man, and Rand since his retirement was something of an unwanted man.

At the Sunrise Rand climbed the stairs to his second-floor room and inserted the key in the lock. As he entered the darkened room he was aware of the slight swish of the ceiling fan above his head. He'd turned it off when he went out. He dropped quickly and quietly to the floor, knowing it was already too late. The red line of a laser gunsight had split the darkness and targeted the wall next to his head.

"Can't we talk about this?" Rand asked. There was a muffled sound like a dry cough and a bullet thudded into the wall above him. He slid forward under the bed, yanking off his shoe, throwing it against the side wall. The laser beam followed it, just for an instant, and Rand was out the other side of the bed, ripping the mosquito netting from its fastenings and wrapping it around the gunman before he could fire again.

He picked up the fallen gun, an awkward thing with its laser sight and silenced barrel. "Who did you expect to kill with this, Ryder? I'm retired but I'm not crippled. How'd you find me?"

"I followed you from the ferry this afternoon."

"One thing to remember, no matter how hot it gets you never turn on the ceiling fan when you're waiting in the dark to kill someone."

"Give me back the gun and we'll forget about this. It was a mistake."

"And you made it. I read your press notices in the London *Times*. I gather the Russians paid quite well."

He sighed and glared at Rand. "So you know what they're saying."

"I assume it's true since you took a shot at me. I didn't come here looking for you, Ryder. I'm retired from British Intelligence and I certainly have no connection with your CIA."

"Then what are you doing on Lamu?"

Rand relaxed his grip on the mosquito netting but kept holding the pistol. He sat down on the edge of the bed. "I was curious about the area. An American writer, Walter Satterthwait, called Lamu the most beautiful place he'd ever seen in his life. What are *you* doing here?"

"Waiting for my wife. She was supposed to meet me three days ago."

"An odd place to meet, not exactly like Waterloo Bridge or the top of the Empire State Building."

"We were here together once, years ago. Its very remoteness made it the perfect meeting place."

"And it's on the way to Russia."

"I doubt we'll be going there. Frankly I don't know where we'll be going." He turned his gaze on Rand, his face momentarily bathed in moonlight through the window. "Are you planning to turn me in?"

"Is there any reason why I shouldn't? If the reports are correct the Russians paid you more than I earned in my entire career with Concealed Communications. How did you and your wife get into it, anyway?"

George Ryder shifted uneasily. "If we're going to chat I wish you'd remove this netting you've got me tangled in."

Rand turned on the light and closed the window shutters. Then he allowed Ryder to unwrap himself. "No tricks, or I'll see how this gun of yours works."

"No tricks," the CIA man promised. He sat in the room's only chair, a white wicker thing that looked uncomfortable. Rand remained seated on the bed. "Martha and I met when we were in college," he began. "I was in a play and she helped with the makeup. We started going out and were married soon after graduation. I was taking a pre-law course but in my senior year I was recruited by the CIA. We moved to Washington and took up with other young couples in government service. I like to think we were popular then. People kidded us about being George and Martha, like Washington and his wife. The 1970s were a glorious time. I was advancing at the company and Martha had a nice job at a travel agency. Then came the '80s."

"What happened?" Rand asked quietly.

"I don't know. Maybe we were bored with our lives. Maybe it was simply like that spy in an Eric Ambler novel. We needed the money."

"What were you giving them for it?"

"The names of Russian double agents. I never betrayed an American."

"And your wife?"

"Martha used her position at the travel agency to arrange side trips for me. When I was out of the country on company business I'd hop over to a nearby city or country and meet with my Russian contact. That's how I delivered the material and how I was paid. The money went into a Swiss account in Martha's name, and she drew from it as we needed it."

"They never suspected you?"

"Oh, sure. I was routinely questioned a few times, especially during the great mole hunt of the mid-'80s. But things always quieted down. I managed to satisfy them and even passed the polygraph tests."

"Now you've been indicted."

He stood up and Rand shifted his grip on the pistol. "I'm being frank with you because we're in the same business, Rand. Or we were. Maybe you can understand how it is these days, with the cold war over and the superpowers at peace with one another. Do you want to know how Martha and I managed to escape? The only close friend I still had in the company phoned me at a hotel two weeks ago and tipped me off. He said they'd been watching me and tapping my home phone for the past year. When I returned home Martha and I would both be arrested."

"What did you do?"

"I sent a fax to Martha's travel agency, tipping her off in a prearranged code. She dispatched a ticket to Lamu, with a message that she'd join me here."

"How do you think the CIA found out about you?"

"That's the damnedest part of all. My friend said my name came down a year ago from the highest level. It just took them twelve months to prove the charges were true."

"The highest level?"

"No one will admit it. Maybe fifty years from now when the top secret files are declassified, historians will learn about it. By that time it won't matter to anyone, especially not Martha and me. Remember what happened about a year ago? A new president of the United States met with a new president of Russia who was desperately seeking aid. The cold war was over. Our president wanted a new beginning and the Russian president owed nothing to the former Soviet government. He owed nothing to the crumbling KGB."

"What are you telling me?" Rand asked.

"I can't prove it, but I know what happened. They held a brief private meeting without even their advisors present. The Russian president made a final appeal for more aid, and my president asked, 'What can you give me in return as a gesture of good faith?' and the Russian said, 'I can give you the name of the top Soviet agent in the CIA,' and he slipped a piece of paper across the table—a paper with my name on it."

"You really think that happened?"

"It happened. The word came down to start an intensive investigation. It took them a year, but they finally nailed me. And Martha."

"If she's not here yet she may not be coming."

"I'll wait a while longer. Every day when the ferry comes in from the airstrip I watch for the new arrivals. I saw you today, of course, but I hoped you wouldn't run into me, or remember me. I hoped you weren't the one sent to bring me in."

"They'll only know where you are if they have Martha."

"Yes. I'm betting she's still free and on her way here by some sort of roundabout route. If anyone can shake them Martha can."

"And meanwhile you wait, and try to kill people like me. If there is an enemy here, Ryder, it could be anyone. It could be an Arab leading his donkey through the narrow lanes, or a trader sailing in on his dhow."

"I know that."

"You'll be running the rest of your life. That's why you're reluctant to go to Russia, isn't it? It's because you think the Russians betrayed you."

"I'm going," he said. "Give me back my gun."

Rand emptied the magazine onto the bedspread and cleared the chamber of the final round. Then he passed the weapon to George Ryder. "You may need it, but not against me." He returned the bullets too.

The American stuck the weapon in his belt, beneath his shirt, and left the room.

In the morning it was raining, a sudden downpour that woke Rand from a troubled sleep. He shaved and dressed and went out, borrowing one of the black umbrellas the guest house management kept in a stand by the front door.

Although the Sunrise Guest House provided morning tea, he decided to walk to the Harmony Café for a full breakfast. The rain was still falling as he reached his destination and he left his umbrella inside the door. The waitress Onyx was not yet on duty but Hegad, the owner, was waiting on customers. Rand ordered banana pancakes with honey and a cup of tea. The pancakes were quite tasty but the tea was far too milky and sweet for his taste. He finally settled for a Coke.

"Has the American gentleman been around this morning?" he asked Hegad.

The fat Arab shook his head. "No Americans today. They wait for the rain to stop."

A few others drifted in and finally the waitress arrived, leaving her umbrella with the others. "You are back again," she said with a chuckle. "Does our food deserve a second or third chance?"

"This was my first time for breakfast. Those pancakes are quite good."

Onyx cast an eye on Hegad. "Sometimes he lets me make them. They are even better."

The rain was finally stopping and Rand remembered his ten o'clock appointment with Amin Shade at the dhows. He would worry about George Ryder later. He paid his bill and picked up the umbrella by the door. The humidity outside was high as the sun broke through the clouds and water vapor rose from the puddles along the lanes.

It was just before ten when he reached the mooring area for the dhows, south of the jetty. There was no sign of Shade, but he was surprised to see Laura Peters tugging on the reins of a recalcitrant donkey. She was trying without great success to urge him north along the shore to her Sanctuary a few hundred meters away.

"Need some help?" he asked.

"A great deal, Mr. Rand. This creature just doesn't realize what I'm doing is for its own good! Could you give me a hand, push from the rear while I pull?"

He put down the umbrella and got into position. "It's not every day I get to push donkeys."

But it seemed to work and the beast was soon under motion without even a parting kick. "Thank you!" she called back to him. "I'll give you a job any time you need one!"

He laughed and waved, turning back to the mooring area. There was still no sign of Amin Shade. Finally he asked an old man who seemed to be in charge of renting the dhows, "Has Amin Shade been here this morning?"

The man peered at the boats bobbing on the water. "He is out there on his vessel. He waits for you."

The dhow he indicated was moored about fifty meters offshore. Rand could see a white-robed figure hunched over one of the two masts, but there was no rowboat riding alongside. He borrowed one from the old man and rowed himself out to meet Shade.

"Did you forget your invitation?" he asked as he pulled alongside and climbed over the railing.

The figure at the mast didn't move. It was indeed Amin Shade, but he wouldn't be traveling to Shela or anywhere else. He appeared to have been shot once in the throat. There was a great deal of blood all around, attracting the flies, and Rand could see that he was dead.

Before summoning help he looked closely at the deck in front of the sagging body. Shade had not died instantly from the neck wound. He'd lived long enough to print a half-dozen letters in his own blood. *CAMERI*, it said, or possibly the final *A* was incomplete and it was meant to read *CAMERA*.

Rand searched around for a camera but there was none on the vessel. In fact there was nothing at all that might have belonged to Amin Shade. If he'd had anything with him, the killer had taken it. Although the deck was wet from the morning rain it had not washed away the man's dying word. That meant he'd been alive during the last twenty minutes, after the rain had stopped, though the shooting could have been earlier.

Rand rowed back to shore and told the old man what he'd found. "Amin Shade is dead. We must call the police." The man's eyes widened. "Did you hear a shot while you were here?"

"No, no shot! He go out to the boat with another Arab."

"Did you see the man's face?"

A shake of the head. "Raining. Shade covered the other with his umbrella. I went inside and did not see the other man row away."

Presently, as word spread and a crowd gathered on the shore, the District Commissioner arrived—a towering black man wearing portions of a military uniform and driving a Land Rover, the only motor vehicle allowed on the island. He listened intently to Rand's story and noted down his name and address in Lamu. "We will talk to you further," he promised in perfect English. "Do not leave the island."

That afternoon when the ferry arrived from the airstrip on the adjoining island, he found George Ryder standing in a nearby lane watching the new arrivals. Rand could see that Martha Ryder was not among them. "Hello, Ryder," he said. "Do you still have the gun?"

The American looked at him distastefully. "Are you planning a bit of blackmail, Rand?"

"No. Someone was killed today, possibly with a silenced pistol. No shot was heard. Can you imagine two silenced pistols in a place like Lamu?"

"I can imagine ten silenced pistols if I put my mind to it. I had nothing to do with any killing. I don't even know who died."

"An Arab named Amin Shade who bought and sold dhows."

"The name means nothing to me."

"If you were watching yesterday's ferry, he got off with that travel writer and me. He was wearing a white robe and cap, carrying a furled umbrella."

"I may have noticed him but I didn't know him."

"Has there been any word from your wife?"

"None. I am beginning to fear she's been arrested. She would be here by now otherwise." He started to turn away.

"Do you know anything about a camera?"

The American shrugged. "Tourists and spies always carry them. Sometimes the tourists have more expensive cameras than the spies."

Rand watched him walk away. Then he went back to the Sunrise Guest House and dug the bullet out of the wall of his room.

The District Commissioner was named Captain Chegga and he remembered Rand from their morning encounter at the scene of Shade's murder. He used a small room at the post office when official business summoned him to Lamu, and in the confined space he seemed hemmed in and uncomfortable. "It's much too humid here on the coast," he grumbled. "Do you have more information about the killing of Mr. Shade?"

"Perhaps," Rand answered. He took an envelope from his pocket and removed the bullet from it. "You might try matching this with the slug that killed him. I assume it was recovered?"

"It will be. There was no exit wound. Where did this come from?"

"First tell me if it came from the same gun that killed Shade."

The District Commissioner smiled sadly. "There are no facilities here in Lamu. The bullets must be sent to the mainland."

"How long will that take? A few hours?"

"Ah, you Englishmen! You expect everything to happen instantly."

"How long?"

"Twenty-four hours, at the very least. It will be morning before the bullets arrive for comparison, and afternoon before I receive a report, even by telephone."

"I'll come back then. Meanwhile what about Shade's background? Was he involved in anything—"

"Shady?" Captain Chegga laughed at his own humor. "We are looking into it, never fear. Go now, Mr. Rand, and enjoy your vacation. Or whatever it is that has brought you to Lamu."

James Count was having a beer at the Harmony Café when Rand arrived there. "The only place you can get a cold one," he said, holding up his bottle of Tusker. "Come join me."

"How's the travel book going?" Rand asked, pulling out a chair for himself.

"Revisions, revisions. Even places like Lamu never stay quite the same. The guest houses and cafés must be reevaluated, the prices adjusted."

Rand told him about encountering Laura with the balky donkey that morning. "It was just before I found that dead Arab, Amin Shade."

"I heard about that," the Australian said. "Crimes against tourists are usually limited to confidence games or muggings." He signaled to Onyx and she brought them two more cold beers. "But then Shade was not a tourist."

"Might he have been a smuggler?"

"Anything is possible."

Rand saw the body again, lying in its pool of blood on the deck of the dhow. In his mind's eye he was trying to see something else, something that wasn't there—

"They say the killer was dressed like an Arab, in white robe and cap—*khanzus* and *kofia*, I guess they're called."

"That proves nothing," Count said.

"No, I suppose not." Rand thought of something else. "Is the ferry the only way onto this island?"

"Well, yes, but there are three ferries from various points on Manda Island, where the airstrip is, and another from the mainland. In addition, of course, there are always private dhows for hire."

In the end Rand was no closer to learning anything than he'd been before. He declined Count's invitation to dinner, deciding he needed to be by himself. His long conversation with George Ryder the previous night had cut drastically into his sleeping time and he was beginning to feel the effects of it. He went back to his room and put in a call to Leila, trying not to alarm her with too much detail about the journey.

"It's beautiful here," he said. "A little paradise."

"Will you be home soon?"

"I'm only booked here for three nights. We'll see what happens then."

He thought about telling someone in London or Washington about George Ryder's presence in Lamu but decided against it. He was beginning to suspect that too many people knew about it already.

R and spent Wednesday morning exploring the quaint little shops of the island, choosing a gift for his wife from among the native crafts and imported Asian items. In the afternoon he encountered George Ryder again, down by the ferry dock. James Count had told Rand that boats arrived at different times of the day, but obviously it was the ferry airline connection that interested Ryder. Today the plane had brought no one at all. The ferry carried only a man from the neighboring island with two donkeys to sell.

"No word from her yet?" Rand asked the American.

"Nothing. If they have arrested her they will be coming for me next." He glanced nervously at Rand. "You seem to be keeping an eye on me."

"You tried to kill me two nights ago," Rand reminded him. "That makes us practically brothers."

"If they come for me, could I look to my brother for help?"

In that instant Rand almost felt sorry for the man. He didn't answer directly, only asked, "Where are you staying?"

"Yumbe House, a hotel at the north end of town, a few blocks inland from the Donkey Sanctuary."

"I'll find it." The safest place for George Ryder might be a jail cell, but he didn't tell him that.

After they parted Rand left the jetty and walked to the nearby post office. Captain Chegga was in his office, relaxing beneath the slowly turning ceiling fan. "It is Mr. Rand, isn't it?"

"That's right. I came to see you yesterday. I brought you a bullet."

"I remember."

"Does it match the bullet that killed Amin Shade?"

"Yes, the bullets match, but it appears that the body does not match. The real Amin Shade is alive and well on Zanzibar."

"Then who—?"

"The dead man was an Italian ex-convict named Giacomo Verdi, a confidence man and occasional government informer. He had been known to indulge in blackmail in the past. He may have tried it again. Apparently he assumed Shade's identity to help pull off some sort of swindle involving the sale of used dhows."

"Then he wasn't an Arab at all?"

"No, no." Captain Chegga played with the papers on his desk. "Now if you will please tell me where you obtained that bullet—"

"It was fired at me two nights ago by a sneak thief I discovered in my room at the Sunrise Guest House. He escaped before I could raise the alarm, and since he took nothing I didn't report it. That was the bullet I dug out of the wall."

"Interesting. The thief could have been an accomplice of Verdi's. They may have had a falling-out."

Suddenly the rain was back, with drops dancing against the windows of the little office. They reminded Rand of what he'd forgotten earlier. "Did you find Shade's umbrella anywhere?"

"It was onshore. His initials were on the handle. He must have left it there when he rowed out to the dhow."

"And now I find myself without one," Rand said, looking out at the rain.

"It never lasts long, but you may borrow one of mine if you wish. I'm sure I'll be seeing you again, Mr. Rand." It sounded more like a threat than a promise.

The District Commissioner had been right. The rain stopped within five minutes and Rand closed the borrowed umbrella. Up ahead he saw the man with the two donkeys who'd been aboard the ferry. He'd been joined now by James Count's niece from the Donkey Sanctuary, who was attempting to examine the animals.

"Need any help pushing?" Rand asked with a smile.

"No, but I'm trying to tell this man these animals are sick. I want to treat them at my place before he sells them."

There was more talk in a language Rand did not understand, then Laura Peters seemed to end the discussion by taking a small camera from the pocket of her jeans and snapping a picture of the donkeys' heads. The trader was furious, trying to grab it from her, but Rand intervened. Finally he relented, and Laura smiled as she put away the camera and took hold of the donkeys' reins.

"Thank you for your help once again!" she told Rand. She set off toward the Sanctuary with the trader following meekly along.

Rand smiled and went on his way. He'd almost reached the Sunrise Guest House when an African man wearing a uniform similar to the District Commissioner's appeared from a side lane to intercept him. "Mr. Rand, Captain Chegga wishes to see you."

"I just saw him less than an hour ago. Is he worried about getting his umbrella back?"

The officer did not smile. "You will come with me."

Rand saw that he had no choice and he fell into step beside the man. "Where are we going? Back to the post office?"

"To Yumbe House."

Rand recognized the name. It was the hotel where George Ryder was staying. He asked no more questions. It was a five-minutes walk through the narrow lanes and when they reached the little hotel the District Commissioner's Land Rover was parked in front. They went up to the second floor where Captain Chegga was standing grim-faced with several others in the hall outside an open door.

"May I go in?" Rand asked.

The Commissioner nodded. "Touch nothing. We are waiting for the photographer."

George Ryder was seated in a chair by the window. There was a bullet hole in his right temple and the gun was lying on the floor beneath his right hand, minus its silencer and laser scope. "Did anyone hear the shot?" Rand asked.

"No one. The maid found him. When did you last see Mr. Ryder?"

Rand knew the question was a trick. He'd never mentioned Ryder to the Commissioner, but anyone might have seen them conversing at the jetty. "Just before I stopped at your office. He was meeting the ferry from the airstrip."

"Was there someone he knew on it?"

"No, only a trader with a pair of sick donkeys. The woman from the Sanctuary has them now."

"Do you have any ideas about this?" Captain Chegga asked, gesturing toward the body in the chair.

"Just one. It wasn't suicide."

"How so?"

"This place has thin walls, yet no one heard a shot. If you'll look closely at the barrel of that gun you'll see scratch marks where a silencer was attached. If he shot himself with a silenced gun, where's the silencer? Without the silencer this gun would have made more noise and left more powder burns around the wound."

Chegga was impressed. "You have done some detective work back in England, Mr. Rand."

"Not this sort. A bit of work with codes, but I suppose in a way it's all the same."

"Do you know who killed him and the other one?"

"Yes." He did know, now that it was too late.

"Will you tell me?"

"Suppose we discuss it over dinner tonight, Captain."

"Where would you suggest?"

"The only place in Lamu that serves cold beer."

Rand was not surprised to see James Count and his niece Laura at one of the tables when they entered the Harmony Café a couple of hours later. The owner, Hegad, hurried over to take their order, obviously a bit intimidated at having the District Commissioner as a customer. Rand waved to Count and Laura and ordered a Tusker. Captain Chegga chose a glass of wine.

"I have spent too much time in Lamu," the captain complained. "There are duties on the mainland."

"I was told nothing happens in a hurry here."

"That is part of Lamu's charm," Chegga agreed. "But it can be carried too far. Will you tell me what you know?"

"All in good time."

The beer tasted fine. Rand ordered from the chalked menu on the wall, choosing a beef dish as the safest. The captain ordered mutton. Onyx served them both in a reasonable time and Rand could see Hegad relax behind his cash register. "Now will you tell me?" the captain asked.

Rand nodded. "I think the time has come."

Onyx had cleared the table of dishes and returned with the check. That was when Rand gripped her wrist and held it tight. "What is this?" she asked.

"Captain Chegga, let me introduce you to the killer of Amin Shade and George Ryder—the elusive Mrs. Ryder."

Later, back at the little room in the post office, Rand told Captain Chegga, "There were at least five clues pointing to Onyx as Mrs. Ryder and the double killer of Shade and Ryder. For dramatic effect I might call them the clues of the borrowed gun, the wrong umbrella, the dangerous rain, the menu lesson and the dying message."

"I think you Englishmen sometimes read too much of Sherlock Holmes, but go on."

"First, the borrowed gun. We established through the bullet comparison that Amin Shade, whatever his true name, was killed by George Ryder's gun. He'd tried to use it on me less than twelve hours earlier, and it was back at his side this afternoon. Conclusion: either Ryder killed Shade and then himself or he loaned the weapon to someone else. Since I'd shown that he didn't kill himself we can conclude that he loaned the weapon to someone. Obviously that would have to be someone very close. Martha Ryder, as his co-conspirator, was the most likely person."

The Commissioner grunted. "Except that she wasn't yet here on the island."

"I had only his word for that, the word of a spy and traitor. He had a very good reason for keeping her presence on the island a secret. If I or someone else had come here to arrest him for extradition back to America, we'd be most likely to wait until Martha Ryder arrived too. So long as he went through the daily charade of waiting for her at the ferry dock, he was safe."

"Go on."

"The clue of the wrong umbrella. I had an umbrella with me yesterday morning. I left it by the door at the Harmony Café where I had breakfast. While I was there the waitress Onyx came in with another umbrella and left it by the door. I took an umbrella, thinking it was mine, when I left and went down to the dhow moorings to meet Amin Shade. I left the umbrella on shore to row out to his vessel and discover the body. The man who rents the dhows told me Shade was carrying an umbrella when he went out to his vessel, obscuring the face of his companion. Yet there was no umbrella on the dhow. There was nothing belonging to Shade. Obviously the killer took it as protection against the rain. You told me you found it on shore, with his initials on the handle. Had the killer left it there? No, the umbrella would have provided virtually no protection while he was rowing the boat to shore. It was taken because it was needed after landing, so it would not have been left on shore. I brought it there myself, because I picked up the wrong umbrella at the Harmony Café—the umbrella Onyx brought in with her."

"But how could Onyx be Martha Ryder? Her skin color—"

"Which brings us to the clue of the dangerous rain. Why was an umbrella so necessary to the killer? Because the rain was dangerous. It would cause her body makeup to run! Ryder told me earlier he met his wife while performing in a college play for which she helped with the makeup. She used body makeup to give herself a brown skin and a perfect disguise. Onyx was not young, remember. Even in her makeup she was clearly middle-aged, with western features. Something else—my clue of the menu lesson. Monday at the Harmony Café I overheard the owner explaining to Onyx that they featured special Indian dishes on Tuesday nights. The implication was that Onyx had been employed at the Harmony for less than a week."

"She was new," the Commissioner confirmed. "But your final clue, the dying message—"

"*CAMERI.* I thought he was trying to write *camera* until you told me that Shade wasn't Shade but an Italian confidence man named Verdi. In his dying moments he reverted to his native tongue. He was trying to write *CAMERIERA*, the Italian word for waitress. Because she was new he didn't know the name she was using. He only knew that Martha Ryder was posing as a waitress, and when he tried to blackmail her she took her husband's silenced pistol and shot him."

"Why would she kill Ryder?"

"There could only be one reason. When he escaped arrest his continued freedom was too embarrassing for the governments involved."

Rand went to the jetty a bit later when the Commissioner and his Land Rover were leaving the island. He watched while Martha Ryder was led to the ferry in handcuffs. With the makeup gone she seemed simply a lonely middle-aged woman. He walked over to meet her and said, "Tell me one thing, Mrs. Ryder. Which side paid you to kill your husband?"

She stared at him for an instant before replying. "Does it really matter? It's all politics."

THE OLD SPIES CLUB

Rand had been retired from British Intelligence for a good many years, but it was not until he turned sixty that he was invited to join the Old Spies Club. That was not its official name, of course, but around London's Clubland it was often called that, especially by nonmembers who may have been a bit envious of its exclusive status and impressive membership.

The club itself occupied three floors of a Late Victorian building on St. James's Street, just a short walk from Piccadilly. The main floor was given over to the gentlemen's lounge and the dining room, with billiard room, card room, smoking lounge, library and the other amenities one might expect. On the second floor were rooms for meetings or private dinners, along with the club's offices. The third floor was given over to three dozen residential rooms where members might stay for a day or a year. These were often occupied by members in the city on a visit, although some also found them useful when death or divorce suddenly changed their marital status.

Rand had taken a good deal of kidding from his wife Leila about being elderly enough for the Old Spies Club, and in truth he had never been much of a joiner. He was a bit dismayed the first time he took the train up from Reading and stopped in the place one warm July afternoon. The first person he met, just inside the door, was Colonel Cheever, a blustering old man who could have starred in any number of film comedies about the army. It was hard to imagine he'd ever been engaged in any sort of intelligence work.

"Rand! How are you, old chap? I saw your name come up on the new member postings. Good to have you aboard." His gray mustache drooped around his thick lips and he had a habit of spitting when he spoke quickly, but Rand had to admit he seemed trim and in good health for his age. Cheever had been in army intelligence, far from Rand's own sphere of activity. Their paths had only crossed a few times at government functions Rand couldn't avoid.

Now, in trying to be politely friendly, he asked Cheever, "Do you come here often, Colonel?"

"I'm here for the meeting at two o'clock. I expect you are too."

"No," Rand admitted. "I was just in the city for the day and thought I'd acquaint myself with the place."

Colonel Cheever smiled. "Let me give you the tour."

Rand admired the comfortable leather armchairs in the lounge, wondering if he'd ever be elderly enough to pass his afternoons in such a place. "The air in here used to be blue with cigar smoke," the colonel explained, "but now the smokers have been relegated to a smaller lounge down the hall. Times do change."

He led the way through the spacious billiard room and the card room, where green-shaded lights hung down over felt-covered tables. "I imagine there are some wicked card games in here," Rand commented.

"Wicked indeed! I prefer bridge, but most players like faster methods of losing their money."

The dining room with its rows of neatly arranged tables was quite inviting and Rand made a mental note to dine there sometime with Leila. When they'd reached the second-floor meeting rooms it was two o'clock, time for the colonel's meeting. Rand started to excuse himself but saw another familiar face among those entering the meeting room. "Harry! Harry Vestry!"

The slender smiling man turned at the sound of his name. "Well, if it isn't Rand! Good to see you, old chap. How long have you been gone from Concealed Communications now?"

"Too long, Harry. I'm old enough to qualify for this club, after all. And Double-C doesn't even exist any more under that name."

Vestry chuckled. Rand had been a close friend of Vestry's when they were recruited together for intelligence work, but the vagaries of overseas assignments had separated them after a few years. "Look, why don't you sit in on our meeting, Rand? It's nothing really secret and you may have some good suggestions to toss in."

"I don't even know what it's about," Rand protested mildly.

Vestry smoothed back his thinning gray hair. "Finding the truth, old chap. That's what it's about." Then, acknowledging Cheever for the first time, he urged, "Bring him along, Colonel. It's an open meeting."

Cheever placed a hand on Rand's shoulder. "You heard the man. Come along and join us."

There were a dozen of them around the long oval table, though seats had been provided for twice that number. Rand had already decided that like most London clubs this one had not yet progressed to admitting women. Harry Vestry took his place at the head of the table, ready to conduct the meeting, and it was obvious he'd been within his rights when he invited Rand to sit in. Looking around the table at the other men, all about his age or slightly older, Rand was surprised that he knew so few. Cheever and Vestry were the only two he could have named, though a tall man with a red face and bald head like a bullet seemed familiar.

"I think we all know the purpose of this meeting," Vestry began when the others had quieted their conversations.

Rand raised his hand. "I'm afraid I don't."

"Of course, Jeffery. I forgot. Well, you probably read in the papers last winter about the death of Cedric Barnes during heart surgery. He was the author of all those books on famous British spies, double agents, MI5, MI6, and Air Intelligence. I believe he even did a volume on Concealed Communications, your old department."

Rand remembered. He'd read it when it came out, feeling a perverted sense of pride when he found sixteen references to himself in the index. Even in a top secret organization it was nice to achieve some level of recognition. Oddly enough, he'd thought of Cedric Barnes just a few days earlier, reading a news account from America that the CIA had agreed to no longer employ journalists in the gathering of intelligence data. "I had lunch with the man once," Rand said. "He wanted an interview but it was forbidden by the Official Secrets Act. I don't know where he obtained all his information."

"It hardly matters now," Vestry said. "What matters is that his daughter Magda intends to auction off the furnishings from his country house. Barnes's wife has been dead about ten years, so everything went to the daughter. The auction is scheduled here in London next week, at Sotheby's. Many of us believe grave danger can be done to the country if that auction is allowed to go forward."

Rand was a bit surprised when he allowed his gaze to circle the table and saw that the others were taking this seriously. "Do you really think he had some top secret papers hidden in a piano leg?"

"Such things are possible," the tall red-faced man said. "He worked at home with his daughter's help, and we already know certain well-placed journalists will be bidding on select pieces. A diary or journal could be invaluable."

Harry Vestry continued. "My proposal, gentlemen, is that we stop this auction by placing a preemptive bid for the entire offering. I have already spoken to Magda Barnes about the possibility and she is agreeable."

"How much does she want?" Colonel Cheever asked.

"One million pounds."

There were sighs and groans from around the table. "The club doesn't have that sort of money," someone said.

"We may be able to negotiate a lower figure," Vestry tried to reassure them. "But certainly we must all realize the importance of this matter."

Rand spoke again. "If it's so important why doesn't the government step in and take action?"

"We understand they have done all they could on an official basis," Vestry answered vaguely. Rand wondered if he was implying the government had appealed to the Old Spies Club for financial backing in the matter.

It was Colonel Cheever who seemed most vocal in opposing Vestry. "Are you saying you expect the members in this room to come up with the million pounds necessary to cancel the auction? Such a suggestion borders on the ridiculous!"

Vestry tried to remain calm against this attack, but the members around the table quickly chose up sides. After most of them had spoken it seemed obvious he was in the minority. "The money just isn't there," the red-faced man said.

"Do you have any other suggestions, Shirley?" Vestry asked.

At first the use of the feminine name jarred Rand, but then something clicked in his memory. Shirley Watkins, the man with a woman's name. During his years of covert government service Shirley's job had always been assassination. Few knew his name and fewer still had seen his face. Rand had met him just once in Berlin, twenty years ago, but supposed him long dead. Could this possibly be the same man?

"Let me talk to the daughter," Shirley suggested. "Maybe I can make her see reason."

It might have been an innocent remark, but coming from this man it could also have been a death threat. Rand knew his imagination was running away with him but still he raised his hand and spoke. "If you'll excuse me, I wonder if I might be of service, gentlemen. As I said, I had lunch with Cedric Barnes a few years back when he wanted an interview for the Double-C book. His daughter might remember my name if she helped him with the book."

"That's very good of you, Rand," Colonel Cheever said at once. "What say you all? Shall we take Jeffery up on his offer?"

There were assents from around the table, and perhaps a sense of relief. Rand wondered what he was getting himself into.

Sotheby's London auction rooms were located on New Bond Street, in a remodeled four-story building that probably dated from Georgian times. The building ran through the block to St. George Street, and the main entrance was around the back. It was here that Rand entered, stopping to purchase a pricey full-color catalogue of that week's lots to be auctioned. The one that interested him was titled simply *Items from the Country House of an Author and Journalist.*

He went upstairs to the second-floor exhibition hall and spent the better part of the next hour inspecting an array of furniture including antique desks, chairs, tables, lamps, even a four-poster bed with a canopy. Barnes's old manual typewriter was there with a shiny new plastic ribbon in place. A pile of books, neatly tied in manageable bundles of twenty or so, was being sold as a separate lot. Glancing over the titles, Rand recognized some of the Cold War classics plus a few books on espionage in general and World War II in particular. David Kahn's thick volume *The Code Breakers* was there, along with *Hitler's Spies* and Robert Harris's recent novel *Enigma*. There was also a complete set of Cedric Barnes's own books, many in foreign language editions, leaving little doubt as to the identity of the "Author and Journalist." An array of office supplies, a camera and a tape recorder completed the lot.

Rand spent the rest of his time studying the others who roamed through the exhibition hall. One that he recognized at once was Simon Spalding, a columnist for the *Speculator*. He was an expert at digging up dirt on the Royal Family, and perhaps now he was widening his horizons.

On his way out Rand stopped in the office and requested a ticket to the auction itself. The young woman behind the desk informed him that no tickets were necessary. "Anyone may attend our regularly scheduled auctions," she said. "However if you think you might be bidding you should register at the door and receive a numbered paddle which you hold up to signify a bid."

"I wonder if you could help me with one other matter. Could you put me in touch with a family member regarding this auction?"

Apparently she was accustomed to such requests. "You may place an early bid with us for any item you wish."

"This is more of a family matter," he said, purposely vague.

She glanced toward the closed door to an inner office. "Just a minute, please." She tapped lightly on the closed door and then entered.

After a moment she emerged with a dark-haired woman, perhaps in her middle thirties, wearing a bright summer dress that looked expensive to Rand's untrained eye. She smiled and extended her hand. "I'm Magda Barnes. The items to be auctioned are from my father's house. I came by today to see how they were being displayed. May I be of service?"

He accepted the hand, which was surprisingly soft. "Is there somewhere we could talk in private, Miss Barnes?"

"I was using their conference room to review the catalogue. Perhaps we could talk in there." She glanced at the secretary who nodded permission.

Inside the small room Rand introduced himself and came right to the point. "Your father was a respected journalist. I met him once and you may recall I was mentioned several times in his book on the Department of Concealed Communications. Some of us, now retired from the Service, are concerned that your father's possessions might contain some hidden notes that could fall into the wrong hands."

She smiled at the thought. "No, no—I've been over everything being offered at auction. I examined and searched each item at least twice. There are no hidden notes or journals. All his personal papers and manuscripts will be given to Cambridge University."

"Miss Barnes, the feeling is that he might have come into possession of material he could not publish under the Official Secrets Act. Do you know what he was working on at the time of his death?"

The smile faded as she began to comprehend the people he represented. "Did that man Vestry send you?"

"I have spoken with Harry Vestry. He did not send me."

"He knows my price."

"One million pounds is beyond our resources."

"Then the auction will go on as planned, even though I realize I won't come close to that figure. Men like Vestry fought my father all his life. I owe him nothing."

"When I was looking over the items just now I spotted a familiar face. Simon Spalding. You certainly don't owe him anything."

The news didn't seem to bother her. "He knew my father years ago. I remember him visiting the house once around the time of Sadat's assassination. It's not surprising he'd be interested in the exhibition. Perhaps he might even bid on something."

"Has he approached you about any particular piece?"

"No." She stood up from the table and said, "I really must be going, Mr. Rand. We have nothing further to discuss. Tell Harry Vestry the auction will go on as planned."

He sighed and left the room after a few polite words. Then he went downstairs into the warm July afternoon. He'd walked about a block when someone fell into step beside him. It was the bullet-headed former assassin, Shirley Watkins. "Didn't do so well, did you, Mr. Rand? I could have told you that. She's the sort of woman needs a little fright before she sees reason."

The following morning as she was leaving to deliver one of her summer lectures on Egyptian archeology at Reading University, Rand told Leila he'd be going into London again. "Two days in a row?" she asked, somewhat surprised.

"Maybe three. There's an auction at Sotheby's tomorrow that I should attend. It's part of Cedric Barnes's estate, the fellow who wrote those insider books about British Intelligence."

"I hope you're not going to buy anything."

"I'll try not to," he said with a grin.

This time only three of them were in the meeting room on the second floor of the Old Spies Club. Vestry and Colonel Cheever listened intently as Rand told them what had transpired the previous afternoon. "When I suggested contacting Magda Barnes I had no idea that Shirley would be dogging my steps.

Did one of you send him after me?"

"Hardly, old boy," Cheever answered. "You know Shirley. He has a mind of his own."

"Look, the auction is taking place tomorrow morning. Shirley can't stop it. You can't allow him to threaten that woman in any manner."

"Nothing could be further from our minds," Vestry assured him.

"We're out of the game now, retired. I don't break codes any more and Shirley Watkins doesn't kill people. Is that understood?"

Colonel Cheever snorted. "I doubt that he ever did kill people. It was probably all a scare campaign to intimidate the other side."

"Maybe he started believing the campaign himself. He spoke of Barnes's daughter needing a little fright to see reason. I told him to leave her alone."

"Did you look over the auction items?" Vestry asked. "Any likely hiding places for notes or a journal?"

"A desk or coffee table could have a hidden drawer or a false bottom. If it's on microfilm or a microdot the possibilities are endless." Rand decided it was time to bring things out in the open. "Look here, there's something about this whole business you're not telling me. You talk of spending upwards of a million pounds, of threatening Barnes's daughter, of keeping the press away. From what? What's in this journal that makes it so valuable?"

Vestry maintained an uneasy silence until Colonel Cheever started to speak. Then he interrupted to say, "You might as well know, Rand. Rumor has it that Cedric Barnes once interviewed a double agent, someone working for us, who was on the verge of defecting to Moscow. This was to be the man's swan song, his public rationale for his actions, not to be published until he was safely out of the country."

"And—?"

"And at the last moment something changed. The double agent never defected, and Cedric Barnes kept his word. He never published the interview."

"How long ago is this supposed to have happened?" Rand asked.

Harry Vestry shrugged. "In some versions it was 1985. Other versions have it way back in the '70s when Barnes was still a relatively young man. Your guess is as good as mine."

"And yet the dozen men around this table yesterday all believe it happened. Not only that, they believe the interview still exists somewhere. Why would Barnes keep it all these years? Why not simply destroy it?"

"Unfortunately, he was a newspaperman," the slender man answered. "I imagine he kept it all these years on the off-chance that the man might defect after all. The cold war ended, the Berlin Wall came down, and still he kept it."

"You have no way of knowing that with any certainty," Rand pointed out.

"Simon Spalding knows it, and he's after the journal."

Someone else knew it too, Rand suddenly realized. The man who had given the interview. Naturally he would have begged Barnes to destroy it after he decided to remain in England. Naturally he would know or suspect if it was still in existence. He would have been most anxious to keep it out of Spalding's hands.

Rand found himself asking the obvious question. "Which of the club members first brought up this matter? Who was it that wanted the auction stopped?"

Colonel Cheever answered. "We'd all heard the rumors, of course. They say Barnes dropped hints himself on nights when he'd had a few too many brandies. When the auction was announced, several of us were concerned. I suppose Harry and I took the lead in it, but it was Shirley who talked it up and arranged for the meeting. He claimed to have two dozen of the old boys, but as you saw only half that number really appeared when the time came."

"Eleven of us, really," Vestry corrected. "Rand was an addition, you'll remember. I'd say you and I and Shirley were the organizers. The other eight were lukewarm to the idea."

"Could you give me a list of their names?"

"What in heaven's name for?" Vestry still possessed the field agent's reluctance to commit anything to paper.

"If there's any truth to the rumors, the mysterious double agent could be retired now. He could even be a member of this club. If so, he would have been especially interested in attending your meeting yesterday."

"Nonsense!" Cheever blustered. "I've known these people for most of my life. I'd vouch for any of them."

Rand ignored him and asked Vestry, "Where can I find Shirley Watkins?"

The slim man considered his question. "If he's not here he's most likely at the Moon and Stars. It's a pub down by the river, near Canary Wharf."

The two worlds of Shirley Watkins were vastly different from one another. The quiet luxury of the Old Spies Club was only some eight kilometers from the Moon and Stars Pub at Canary Wharf, but they were separated by more than distance. Once a haven for seamen off the nearby docks, now it was a meeting place for office workers from the tallest building in England. Even a recent IRA bombing had done little to frighten people out of the area. On this summer Wednesday the place was crowded and the aroma of beer mixed with a haze of cigarette smoke.

Rand spotted Shirley Watkins at once, seated in a booth with a middle-aged woman wearing too much makeup. He had on a suit and tie, and his bald bullet head seemed to reflect the overhead lights as he drank from a pint of stout. A decade or so older than the other male customers, he could still have been an executive from one of the Canary Wharf firms. When he saw Rand heading for him he told the woman, "Here's business. I'll talk to you later." She gave Rand a sour look and exited the booth.

He slipped in to take her place. "I want to speak with you about the auction," he began.

Shirley eyed him, sizing him up. "How'd you find me down here?"

"Harry Vestry said you might be at this place."

"Yeah, Harry. I think he still spies on all of us, just to keep his hand in."

"Did you take my advice about Magda Barnes and stay away from her?"

He held up his hands in a gesture of surrender. "Whatever you say is fine with me. I was always one for obeying orders."

Rand deliberately avoided making eye contact, fearing he might detect a touch of irony in the words. "I was talking with Vestry and the Colonel this afternoon. They told me about the rumors."

"What rumors?"

"The interview that Barnes is supposed to have done with a double agent before he defected."

"Yeah, that." Shirley Watkins downed the rest of his pint. "Do you believe any of it?"

"I don't know. I heard it for the first time about an hour ago."

"Well, I've got my doubts but I'll do whatever they want."

Rand frowned at the words. "What do you mean by that?" he started to ask, then cut himself short. Another familiar face had just entered the Moon and Stars.

"What's the matter, Rand?"

"That reporter Spalding just came in. He must have followed me."

"Say the word and he'll be feeding the fishes."

Rand gave a dry chuckle. "Did you ever in your life really kill anyone, Shirley, or has it all been an act?"

"I've done my part."

"Haven't we all?" He slid out of the booth. "I'd better go talk to Spalding."

The columnist was nursing a half-pint, trying to avoid looking in the direction of the booth, when Rand joined him. "You're Simon Spalding, aren't you? I don't think we've ever been formally introduced. I'm Jeffery Rand."

Spalding was a slender man in his early fifties with thinning brown hair and a crooked nose that might have been broken in his youth. "Oh, yes. One of the retired spies. There are a great many of you around these days, aren't there? You must have hated to see the cold war end."

Rand already knew from his columns that he didn't particularly like the man. "I retired from the Service long before the end of the cold war," he said, and then asked, "Were you a friend of Cedric Barnes? I saw you at Sotheby's yesterday."

Spalding shrugged. "A fellow journalist. I was interested in what was being offered. I think I only met him once, at some awards dinner."

"I suppose his daughter has already removed anything of special value."

He shot Rand a glance that seemed an unspoken question. "We don't know that. Sometimes people have clever hiding places for their valuables. They even sell fake beer cans now so you can hide your money and jewelry in the fridge."

"Good idea, so long as the thief doesn't have a thirst. I gather you'll be at the auction tomorrow morning?"

"Sure. I'd like to pick up a souvenir of the old guy."

"There are legends about him, about the stories he didn't publish."

Simon Spalding laughed. He was warming a little toward Rand. "We all have stories that don't get published for one reason or another, same as you blokes. I remember back in 1981 when the *Speculator* took me off the European desk and gave me the column to write, I passed along some great story leads to my successor but nothing ever happened."

"Tell me something, just between us," Rand said with a smile. "Who are you following this evening—me or Shirley?"

"They say that man is a government-authorized assassin."

"Does he look like one?"

"Damn right he does!"

"Then he's probably not. Not any more, certainly. He's retired, same as the rest of us."

A sly look came over the columnist's face. "Member of the Old Spies Club, is he?"

"What's that?"

"The place on St. James's Street where you all go. That's what they call it, don't they? I'd do a column about it if I wasn't afraid of getting sued."

"Stick to the Royal Family," Rand advised. "It's safer."

He moved away from the bar and headed for the door, waving goodbye to Shirley Watkins.

Rand had to catch the early train into London for the auction the following morning. He was up before Leila because he wanted to clean and oil the little Beretta pistol he hadn't fired in years. Just seeing him with it would have upset her, he knew. But catching sight of himself in a mirror he realized how foolish he looked. He was too old for these things. Deadly weapons were not for Sotheby's, and certainly not for the Old Spies Club.

The first familiar face he saw as he entered the auction house and registered for his plastic paddle was Harry Vestry, standing near the door and glancing at his watch. "I was hoping you'd be here, Rand." He glanced at the paddle. "Number 77! Sure to be lucky if you care to bid. If Cheever and Watkins get here too I'd like to position us in different parts of the hall where we can keep track of the bidding. I know it's often impossible to identify the high bidder, especially if it's made by phone, but we can try."

Still playing the old spy, Rand thought. "Simon Spalding is sure to be here, bidding on something. I'll keep an eye on him."

"Good! I saw him go in a few minutes ago. He took a paddle so he plans to bid."

But when Rand entered the large high-ceilinged auction room with its twin chandeliers and rows of folding chairs, the first person he saw was Magda Barnes, immaculate in a white summer suit. "We meet again, Mr. Rand."

"So it seems."

"Will you be bidding on any of my father's items?"

"I may." He lifted number 77 and gave it a little twirl. "Good luck! You have a nice crowd." Then he went off to find a seat.

The auction had already started and they were on the fifth item. Rand estimated there were about a hundred and fifty people in the room. Some, apparently the high bidders, were in glass booths above floor level. They seemed to be connected by telephone to their agents on the floor. Above the stage where the auctioneer stood, a large electronic sign gave the latest bids in pounds sterling, dollars, francs, yen and other currencies. As each item was announced for bidding it was shown on a turntable next to the auctioneer. Spotters along each side of the room watched for bids that the auctioneer might miss.

Rand could see that the prices were running fairly high for the antique items. Personal items and office supplies brought less, although Simon Spalding, seated a few rows ahead of Rand, paid two hundred pounds for Barnes's old manual typewriter. Rand was surprised when Colonel Cheever suddenly appeared, raising his paddle from a back row to bid on the collection of books. The bidding was lively but Cheever finally lost out.

The canopied four-poster bed, too large for the turntable, was wheeled onto the stage. It went to a dark-complexioned man who may have been an Arab. Barnes's writing desk fetched a good sum from a neatly dressed young couple. Finally Rand spotted Shirley seated on the aisle near the rear. He held a plastic paddle with the number 68 on it. That probably meant he'd come in before Rand, yet Harry Vestry at the door hadn't noticed him. It signified nothing, of course. Vestry might have stopped in the men's room for a moment.

The collection of Cedric Barnes's own books, in various languages, was the last item to be auctioned. This time Colonel Cheever tried again, with better results. He took the lot for eleven hundred pounds.

Several of the winning bidders went to the office to settle up and claim the items if they were small enough to carry. Rand was on his way out when he ran into Simon Spalding at the St. George Street entrance. "Did you bid on anything?" the columnist asked.

"Not a thing. But I see you picked up that old typewriter."

Spalding hefted it in its leather carrying case. "It's worth about a tenth of what I paid, but I wanted a remembrance of the old guy. He was one of the tops in the business."

Rand smiled in agreement. "He certainly was that." He glanced at his watch. "Look here, Spalding, it's nearly one o'clock. We both could stand a spot of lunch. The Old Spies Club, as you referred to it, is only a few blocks away, just across Piccadilly. Come along with me and I'll treat you."

Spalding quickly accepted. "That's very generous of you, Rand. I'll admit to being curious about the place."

As they entered the club he suggested that Spalding might want to leave the typewriter in the checkroom, but the columnist clutched it firmly. "Oh, no! This cost me two hundred pounds and I'm hanging onto it."

Rand chuckled and led the way into the dining room. After an exotic luncheon of roast beef and blood pudding, topped with red wine and finished off with trifle for dessert, Spalding took out a cigar and they adjourned to the gentlemen's smoking lounge. It was deserted at this hour of the afternoon except for one man sleeping in an armchair, his bald head visible over its top. The columnist lit his cigar, offering one to Rand who declined. Then they settled back in the comfort of the overstuffed leather armchairs.

"I can see why you chaps like this place," Spalding said. "It's a perfect setting to wile away one's retirement."

Rand smiled slightly. "Now that we're comfortable, suppose you show me the typewriter."

"What? This thing?"

"The very same."

"What for?"

"So I can confirm my suspicion as to the identity of the fabled double agent."

Simon Spalding laughed. "You think this old manual typewriter of Barnes's will tell you that?"

"I know it will, and so do you. Who ever saw a shiny plastic ribbon on a manual typewriter? They all used fabric ribbons." He reached down and unzipped the leather carrying case. The columnist made no attempt to stop him. "It's a bit narrower than the quarter-inch plastic ribbons that electric typewriters use. There was all this talk of a journal, but Cedric Barnes used a

192 THE OLD SPIES CLUB

tape recorder for interviews, didn't he? They even auctioned one off today." Rand removed the ribbon from the machine. "It's a tape, masquerading as a typewriter ribbon. The tape of Barnes's infamous last interview with the double agent."

"It's going to make me a rich man," Simon Spalding said.

"Or a dead one. Suppose I get a machine and we play this tape right now."

"Here?"

"We're alone except for that fellow sleeping in his chair. We won't disturb him. Don't you want to know the size of the fish you've landed?"

"I'd rather find out back in the office."

"Funny thing," Rand said, keeping his voice light. "You told me yesterday you only met Cedric Barnes once, at an awards dinner. But his daughter said you were at their house, back around the time of Sadat's assassination. That would have been 1981, wouldn't it?"

"You have a better memory for dates than I do."

"There were rumors about Barnes's unpublished interview with a double agent, a defector who changed his mind at the last minute. Rumors of a journal Barnes kept of the interview. Only Barnes didn't keep journals, he used a tape recorder. One person would have known that for sure, would have known exactly what to look for among the items to be auctioned, would have spotted that recording tape disguised as a typewriter ribbon. The man Barnes interviewed, the double agent himself."

"Damn you, Rand!"

"If I'm wrong, play the tape for me."

Spalding's hand came out of his pocket holding a small automatic pistol. Rand remembered his own gun and wished now that he'd brought it.

"I'm a journalist, remember, not one of you spy boys!"

"You don't look much like a journalist with that gun. I suppose the British and Russians used journalists from time to time, just as the CIA is sometimes accused of doing. Your job on the European desk was the perfect place to gather information. As for that interview, a journalist would be the most aware of a good news story, and the most likely to tell Barnes his side of the story before he defected."

Simon Spalding held the gun very steady. Behind him, Rand thought he could hear the sound of the bald man snoring. "If what you say is true, why would I change my mind after giving Barnes the interview?"

"Because the *Speculator* gave you a column."

His face had become a frozen mask. "How could you know that?"

"Magda Barnes remembers you at the house in 1981, around the time of Sadat's assassination. You told me last evening they took you off the European desk and gave you the column in '81. Did you desert Communism for a newspaper column, Simon?"

"That's what Barnes asked me! I should have killed him before his tongue got loose and he started those rumors. I thought I'd put it all behind me, especially after the collapse of the Soviet Union."

Rand reached out his hand. "Give me the gun. It's much too late in the game to be shooting people."

Spalding raised the pistol, to fire or to surrender it. Rand would never know which. There was a low cough from behind the man's chair and a flower of blood burst from his chest. His head went back and he lay there dead.

The bald man was Shirley Watkins, and the silenced pistol was out of sight before Rand ever saw it. "Thought you might need help from that bastard," he said. "Hated to put a hole through the chair, though."

"You were already here when we entered," Rand protested.

"Saw him waving his cigar around the dining room. Knew you'd head this way."

He stared at the body, and then at Shirley. "You really are an assassin."

"I was once, in my younger days."

Rand stared at the body. "What do we do now?"

"Forget it ever happened. I'll handle everything. If that tape is what you say, the whole thing will be hushed up. This is the Old Spies Club, remember?"

Rand caught the evening train home.

ONE BAG OF COCONUTS

The sun-tanned man with the wild hair passed through customs at Heathrow Airport without difficulty, carrying a single suitcase and a burlap sack clearly marked *Coconuts*. Both had been checked through from Madagascar to avoid having them pass through airport security. After glancing in the suitcase and feeling a few of the coconuts through the burlap, the inspector waved him on. After all, the man had come from a place where coconut palms were commonplace. Hurrying through the waiting crowd, knowing no one would be meeting him, the wild-haired man headed outdoors toward the line of London taxis in the covered loading area. A driver stepped out to take his suitcase and the man was just opening the back door to enter the cab when his body seemed to jerk and tumble forward. A blossom of blood grew suddenly in the center of his back.

The bag of coconuts landed on the pavement next to the taxi. That bag of coconuts was to summon Jeffery Rand out of retirement.

Rand had visited the American Embassy in Grosvenor Square before, but this was his first meeting with Mr. Ralph Coir of the United States Fish and Wildlife Service, Division of Law Enforcement. "I'm retired, you know," he said after the amenities had been dealt with.

Coir was a bald man running to overweight. He wore thick glasses and must have been near retirement age himself. "Mr. Rand, you were recommended by a high government official as being the perfect man for this job. You would be paid on a per diem basis, plus expenses. I understand that you did a good bit of intelligence work during the cold war, and in recent years you've been invaluable in certain African matters."

Rand laughed at the suggestion. "I'm hardly an African expert."

Ralph Coir flipped through the pages of a report on the desk in front of him. "It says here you met your future wife in 1971 while on assignment in Egypt. You returned there in '72, '74, '94 and '96. In 1993 you were on a ship in the Red Sea, and in '94 you performed an invaluable service on an island off the east coast of Africa."

Rand smiled slightly. There was no point in growing angry about this combing through his life. "I believe you missed some of the Egyptian visits. My wife is from Cairo and we return there frequently."

Coir folded his hands on the papers, signifying they had served their purpose. "I'm especially interested in the East African islands because this concerns Madagascar. I stopped there myself recently, on my way back from South Africa. The flora and fauna of that island are fantastic. It's a thousand miles long and a nation all by itself since the French granted independence in 1960. The people are more Malayan-Indonesian than African or Arab."

Rand shrugged. "How does all this concern me?"

Coir showed him a head-and-shoulders photograph of a man with a deep tan and unruly hair. His eyes were closed. "This is Telga Toliara. IIe was killed at Heathrow Airport two days ago."

"Killed? How?"

"Shot. Scotland Yard thinks it was a silenced weapon which may have been concealed in a cane. At least no one heard or saw it happen. He was just entering a taxi, carrying this." He reached beneath the desk and brought up a burlap bag marked *Coconuts*.

Rand felt them through the bag and then untied the top, reaching inside. He gave a yelp of pain and surprise as something alive nipped at his finger. "What in hell—?"

"I'm sorry," the American said. "I should have warned you." He tipped the bag and emptied a dozen medium-sized turtles onto the desktop. "We cleaned and fed them, of course. I only returned them to the burlap to give you some idea of how they slipped through customs."

"Turtles?" Rand stared at them in amazement, clutching his bitten finger.

"To be exact, they're radiated tortoises, very rare. Females are worth about ten thousand dollars each on the black market when they're fully grown. They were being smuggled from Madagascar to Florida by way of London. The dead man was changing planes at Heathrow. They ended up on my desk, as do all smuggled animals bound for America." He smiled slightly. "Of course with the coconut label on the bag the embassy people thought they were being funny presenting it to me."

"You want me to investigate a case of animal smuggling?" Rand asked in a skeptical tone of voice.

"That, and murder. You know the east coast of Africa, even if not Madagascar itself. More than that, you've had a lifetime of intelligence work."

"Certainly there must be Americans who—"

"An American in this area would rouse too much suspicion. That's why we asked for your government's help. It's an illegal ten billion dollar business, Mr. Rand."

"What do you want from me?"

He indicated the tortoises. "Trace these back to their source, find us the people behind the smuggling operation and Toliara's murder, and we might be able to shut down at least the Madagascar part of this operation."

That was how Rand came to arrive in Antananarivo, called Tana, the centrally located capital city where more than a million and a half people suffered daily in the tropic heat. The city itself sprawled over the sides of a dozen red-dirt hills, and the slanted roofs on many of its low native and French colonial buildings hinted at heavy seasonal rains. At this time of the year, late spring, it was merely hot.

Why Rand had taken on the contract work for the United States Fish and Wildlife Service was something he had a hard time explaining to Leila, his wife of more than twenty years. But she was still teaching at Reading University and would be for another few weeks until semester's end. At least the trip to Madagascar should keep him from growing bored.

Someone once called Tana a city of dusty beauty. It was all of that, but Rand soon determined that the dust which filled the air was really smoke, drifting in from burning forests and grasslands far away. The roads were cluttered with carts drawn by zebu, Indian beasts of burden that resembled oxen. As he passed a man carrying a live chicken over his shoulder, no doubt for an evening meal, he decided it was not a city he would like to call home.

On the lengthy plane trip Rand had read about the island's unique wildlife in a government report Coir had given him. Madagascar was the only place on earth where lemurs lived in the wild. There were three-foot-long chameleons and various other unique reptiles, including the valuable radiated tortoise. The free-market democracy that had replaced the country's Communist dictatorship in 1993 was still working out its kinks, and smugglers had found that the illegal trade in exotic pets was one of the few dependable businesses around. It was also one of the safer ones. Customs officials, on the lookout for cocaine, often missed a smuggled supply of cockatoo eggs from Australia or radiated tortoises from Madagascar. Even if the smugglers were caught and convicted, a first offense might not even bring prison time.

Rand had been given the address of Toliara's house near the downtown area. Hiring a taxi to take him there, he found a square two-story building with a gated passageway leading to an interior courtyard. It was one of the better sections of the city and he was surprised that the gate was unlocked. He asked the driver to wait and stepped inside. The first thing he saw in the courtyard was a large shade tree with a bright green lizard scurrying toward him along one branch. He drew back in alarm and heard gentle laughter from somewhere behind him.

"Don't worry. Max won't hurt you," a woman's voice reassured him.

For a moment he still could not see her. Then a flash of red on an upstairs balcony caught his eye and he observed a young woman with blond hair descending an iron staircase from the second floor. She wore a long housecoat and as she drew nearer he saw that she was barefoot. "My name is Adelaide Toliara, and you are Mr.—?"

"Rand. I'm British."

"I could tell," she said with a smile. Her accent was British colonial and it took him a moment to place it.

"And you're Australian."

"Very good, Mr. Rand."

"Adelaide. Named after the city."

"Of course." She'd come up to him now and even without shoes she was almost his height. "What do you want? Have you brought home my husband's ashes?"

"I'm sorry, no. I imagine his death was a great shock to you."

"Not especially. The only shock was that he died at the London airport rather than in a Tana brothel."

Rand glanced uncomfortably at the lizard, which hung from a branch directly over his head. "Might we go inside for a chat?"

"It's too hot in there. Come over in the shade. We have a table and chairs."

He followed her across the courtyard to a green wrought-iron table with four matching chairs. The lizard made no attempt to follow. Adelaide picked up a small bell on the table and rang it. A native servant appeared and she asked Rand what he'd like to drink.

"Something cool would be nice," he admitted.

"The water isn't fit to drink but I have some Tusker from the mainland."

He'd drunk the African beer before. "That'll be fine."

"Two Tuskers," she told the servant, who retreated in silence.

"Do you live here alone?" Rand asked.

"When my husband is away. I guess now he's away permanently." She thought about that, then added, "But I have a great many friends. Sometimes they stay overnight. And my servant Janje has a room downstairs."

"I wanted to talk to you about Telga's business," he said as the servant returned with glasses and two bottles of Tusker.

"The animal business."

"Yes."

She sighed and poured herself a beer. "I came here from Australia three years ago to work as a teacher. Telga was virtually the first person I met on the island. I knew he was in the export business but I didn't learn about the animal trade until after we were married. It seemed harmless enough." For the first time she allowed her pale blue eyes to meet Rand's.

"The smuggling and selling of exotic animals is big business these days.

Those tortoises your husband was carrying could be worth ten thousand dollars each when grown."

"That much?"

"I need to know where he obtained them, Mrs. Toliara."

She tilted her head slightly, as if thinking about the question and how to answer it. Finally she said, "I'm told the jungles of Madagascar are full of exotic animals. As our population increases, more and more of those jungles are being burnt away, not unlike the rain forests of the Amazon. Telga told me that if the animals weren't captured and exported they'd die."

"I suppose there's some truth to that," Rand agreed. "But the fact remains that this animal trade is illegal, and a great many people are profiting from it. Was your husband capturing the animals himself?"

"No, no!" She scoffed at the idea. "He bought them from a middleman, someone named Frier at the Ice Cream Bar. It used to sell ice cream, now it sells whisky and women."

"Do you know Frier? Could you introduce me?"

She hesitated only a moment. "I could, but what's in it for me?"

"You might help find your husband's killer."

A slow smile curled her lips. "I could do that, yes. Finish your beer and we'll go for a walk. The Ice Cream Bar is only a half-mile down the road."

Rand sent the waiting taxi on its way and walked with her. She had not bothered with shoes, and he realized now that the red housecoat was really some sort of native dress. "Don't your feet get dusty?" he asked, watching the sand gradually coat her red toenails.

"I don't like shoes. My feet sweat in this climate."

The Ice Cream Bar no longer catered to children. Though it was still mid-afternoon a half-dozen men loitered at the bar and a few others sat at a table playing some sort of gambling game with matchsticks. They seemed to be Malaysians, though Rand couldn't be certain. A couple of dusky women sat together at one end of the bar, ignored by the men.

Adelaide spoke quietly to one of the men at the bar and he glanced over at Rand. He was dressed better than the others, in a shirt with epaulets that might have indicated a ship's officer, but his thin body and sallow complexion hinted at some recent illness. He sauntered over and joined them at a table. "This is Captain Frier," she said. "Mr. Rand."

Frier smiled, showing a gold tooth, and shook hands. "You're interested in animals?"

"At the moment, radiated tortoises."

"Very rare. Each one is different, you know."

"Mrs. Toliara's husband was killed smuggling them into Heathrow Airport."

"I was sorry to hear that. Such things are rare. It's not a violent game."

"What do you deal in?" Rand asked.

"Reptiles. Snakes and tortoises. They're the best because they can survive long trips without food or water. Birds and monkeys are tough. Only ten percent of the birds survive."

"Aren't the customs agents on this end watching for them?"

Frier raised a hand and signaled the bartender. "Another rum here. You want anything?" Rand and Adelaide both ordered Tuskers. "When things are tight we take the animals off the island in speedboats. Madagascar has no Coast Guard."

"But Telga left from here, planning to change planes in London for a flight to Orlando, Florida."

Captain Frier shrugged. "That means he paid someone at the airport. It's often done. A safer way these days is to transport the animals by boat to the French island of Reunion, east of here, or to South Africa. There the animals are supplied with fake documents indicating they've been bred in captivity, making their shipment legal."

"Do you have a boat for this?" Rand asked.

Frier squinted at him and grinned. "I could find you one."

Adelaide was getting nervous. "He's an investigator, Frier, not a customer."

"I'm trying to learn about the business," Rand admitted. "For example, which is easier to smuggle, snakes or tortoises?"

"Snakes," Frier answered at once. "They can fit into almost any shape of cavity and stay there. I can introduce you to a couple of the boys, if you're looking for a boa."

"I want to know where the tortoises come from."

"One good place is Tulear, on the southwest coast. Ask around for a woman named Gin. She is known as the tortoise merchant."

When Rand and Adelaide left the Ice Cream Bar he asked if she'd be staying on now that her husband was dead. "Of course," she answered. "Where else would I go?"

"But what is there for you here?"

She shrugged. "I like the animals."

The plane ride from the capital to Tulear was in a small propeller craft that seemed to cruise along barely above the treetops. He saw a great deal of the country during the two hours of the flight, passing over burning grasslands and once flying straight through a cloud of smoke rising from a jungle river basin. The airport at Tulear was smaller than Tana's, but flying over the town's harbor he was impressed by the blueness of the water. As soon as he stepped from the plane he felt a cool breeze that offered welcome relief from the oppressive heat of the capital city.

It was a poor town, with a sense of desperation about it. Along the beach fishermen caught what they could, and tropic winds sent eddies of sand into the air. Still, there was a beach hotel for tourists and Rand took a room there. The first man he asked about Gin, the tortoise merchant, spit on the ground and walked away. He had better luck with a teen-age boy, offering him money before asking the question. "Gin Gin," the boy answered with a grin, grabbing at the folded bill. "She lives with the tortoises. Down that street to the end, a small house with a tin roof." Then .

Rand walked quickly down the street, careful to avoid the occasional groups of young men who stood watching him. It was not a place he'd like to be after dark. There was only one house with a tin roof, and he knocked at the rickety door. After a moment a native woman appeared. "I am interested in tortoises," he told her.

"Come in," she answered in French. It was a language Rand knew moderately well. He was surprised to hear it spoken here until he remembered the island's former ties with France.

"You are Gin?"

"Yes. I will show you tortoises."

She was slim and moderately attractive, with dark hair and eyes. Her age was impossible to guess. It might have been thirty or fifty. He followed her into the tin-roofed shack and she showed him a pen piled two and three deep with radiated tortoises. There were easily two dozen of them, a fortune to this woman if she was halfway around the world in Florida. Rand reached out to touch their shells, marveling at the grooved black lines broken by designs of white and beige, no two alike.

"What do you sell these for?" he asked.

She mentioned a figure in Malagasy francs about equal to one pound, far from the ten thousand American dollars these would bring at their final destination. "That is for local people, for food. Three times that much for others like yourself."

At three pounds they were still a fantastic bargain. "Do you know a man named Telga Toliara? Is he a customer?"

"He comes in a boat, buys many tortoises at a time. I have not seen him in a few weeks."

"He's dead," Rand told her, "killed in London."

"A dangerous city."

Rand glanced out the door where the young men loitered. "It's not exactly safe around here."

"They protect me," she said simply.

"Where do these tortoises come from? I'm seeking the source."

"Up the coast. The natives catch them and bring them to me in outrigger canoes."

"When is the next shipment due?"

Gin shrugged. "Maybe tonight. But they will not trust you. Your clothes are too new. They always expect the gendarmes."

"I needed something to wear in the jungle," Rand explained. "The rest of my things are at the hotel."

"Why bother with a hotel when you can sleep on the sand under the stars?"

"My aging bones cry out for a mattress," he told her. "I will come back after dark."

"Perhaps around ten," she suggested as he handed her some francs.

The town seemed to take on a new life after dark, with the sound of an Indian sitar being played somewhere in the distance. There were bonfires along the beach, and groups of people Rand could barely make out, some kneeling for rites he could only imagine. Somewhere far out over the water the glowing trail of a skyrocket streaked across the heavens and then arced into the sea. He moved cautiously, aware of the possibilities for trouble. Once he passed a man in a white suit carrying a furled umbrella, looking completely out of place. But then he no doubt looked out of place himself.

The woman Gin was waiting for him. "They are coming tonight, soon," she told him. She carried a large woven basket, as if for shopping.

"How do you know?"

"Did you see the rocket a few minutes ago? That is Kriter's signal. His canoe will be here soon."

They walked down to the water together, watching the waves dash against the sand. He loved seeing it, remembering his boyhood visits to Brighton beach where there was nothing but pebbles waiting for another ten thousand years of erosion to grind them into sand.

The outrigger canoe was on them before Rand realized it, and a bare-chested young Malaysian leapt out to pull it onto shore. "Only nine tonight, Gin," he said in French. "They're all busy mating."

She flipped back the burlap covering and shined a small flashlight on them. Rand could see the radiating lines of the tortoise shells, as different as fingerprints. "I'll take them," she said quickly.

Kriter motioned toward Rand. "You got a buyer here already?"

"Maybe." She hoisted the sack full of tortoises onto the sand and took several Malagasy franc notes from her pocket.

"There'll be more next time," he promised, pushing off in the outrigger. The entire transaction had taken only a few minutes.

Gin shook her head in disgust. "He usually has seventy or eighty for me.

I think he's selling to someone else up the beach."

Rand remembered the man in the white suit. "Is this the rainy season here?'

"No rain until next month," she told him.

"Have you seen any strangers lately? A man in a white suit with an umbrella?"

"There are always tourists."

He took the bag full of radiated tortoises from her, careful not to put his fingers in it. "I may want to buy these from you later. First I'm going to take a walk up the beach. If Kriter landed somewhere else first, where might it have been?"

"Perhaps Ankil Cove, two miles north of here."

"Can I walk along the beach?"

"At night?"

"Right now."

She shrugged. "It is safer than through the jungle. There is a small village there, but the natives are friendly." He wondered if she was mocking him.

After carrying the sack of turtles back to her shack, he returned to the beach and set off up the coast. The stars seemed different from those he saw in London, brighter and more numerous without the glare of city lights. In spots the beach narrowed as the jungle reached out, but for the most part it was an easy, pleasant walk, his way lit by a full moon. Finally, ahead, he saw more bonfires on the beach and knew he'd reached the village at Ankil Cove. That was when he saw the man in the white suit again.

He turned as Rand approached, almost in slow motion, and raised his furled umbrella. Rand dove sideways into the sand, but not quite quickly enough. The silenced bullet creased the side of his head and everything went black.

When he awakened it was morning, and by the light from the sun he could see small octopuses hung out to dry on racks, already caught by the dawn fishermen. Crouched next to him on the sand, staring into his face, was a lizard he'd seen before.

"Back among the living, Mr. Rand?" a voice asked, and he turned his head slightly to see Adelaide Toliara standing there in a short beach jacket, her legs bare beneath it. She put her arm down to Max and the lizard ran up to her shoulder, its long tail swishing from side to side.

"What happened to me?" he managed to ask. The side of his head hurt a bit, but otherwise he seemed all right.

"You were shot. Luckily the bullet only grazed your skull. I bathed it with some palm oil."

"It was the man in the white suit. Where is he?"

"I don't know. He thinks you're dead."

"He's the one who killed your husband."

Her eyes closed for just an instant and then she opened them and asked, "Why do you say that?"

"Scotland Yard suspected Toliara was killed with a silenced gun hidden inside a cane, because no one heard or saw it. It isn't the rainy season here, yet this man was carrying a furled umbrella. He was certainly out of place, and when I saw him point that umbrella at me I dove for the sand. You know him, don't you?'

"I know him, yes."

Rand tried to sit up. It made his head hurt. For just an instant he was seeing double and it seemed as if the lizard's head were on Adelaide's body. "What are you doing here, anyway? And what's that lizard doing around your neck?"

"Max is a Madagascan day gecko. Very rare. Most geckos found elsewhere are nocturnal. As for what I'm doing here, I'm completing my husband's work."

"You bought the tortoises from Kriter last night."

"Is there anything wrong with that?"

"A woman called Gin was waiting for them on the beach in Tulear."

Adelaide snorted. "She is nothing. She swindled Telga out of a whole shipment once."

"Where is the man in the white suit now?"

"Stop calling him that! His name is Sidney Moullion. He's South African."

"Why did he kill your husband?"

"He had no reason to kill him," she said, reaching back to stroke Max's head.

"But he came here to help you smuggle tortoises."

"One last time. Telga had another trip on his contract."

"What's Moullion's part in all this?"

"Ask him yourself. He'll be coming back for me soon."

"Back here? What for?" Rand was immediately on alert.

"He has some work to do. Then we'll leave together. I've got sixty-five radiated tortoises in sacks."

"Are you going to carry those through customs? More bags of coconuts?" He stood up, shakily, and surveyed the area in all directions. If Sidney Moullion was coming back, he wanted to be ready this time.

"I'll get them through," she assured him.

Off in the distance Rand heard the sound of an approaching speedboat. Adelaide's smile vanished. "You should take cover somewhere. I don't want any more shooting."

"It's him, isn't it?"

"Might be." She dropped the gecko to the ground and motioned Rand into the jungle.

"If you're taking the tortoises, what's he coming back for?"

"I don't know." She seemed distracted. "He does something to them."

"Does something?"

The boat came into view, heading directly for the beach. Rand quickly retreated from view, taking cover at the edge of the trees. He could see Moullion at the wheel of the sleek craft, killing the engine and gliding to a gentle halt in the surf. Adelaide Toliara ran to meet him. The South African waded through the shallow water, looking a bit foolish as he clutched his umbrella.

The woman was speaking to him, carrying on a conversation perhaps meant to distract him from questions about Rand. But as they came closer he heard Moullion ask, "Where is the body?"

"I dragged it into the jungle," she answered.

He studied the sand for a moment and then grabbed her by the arm. "The truth! There are no drag marks in the sand!"

"I—"

"He's alive, isn't he?"

All her pent-up fury seemed to explode then. "Damn it, Sidney, why did you have to kill Telga?"

"That's none of your business." He dropped his umbrella and swung his fist at her.

Prudence might have told Rand to flee deeper into the underbrush, but there was the woman to be considered. He burst from his hiding place and shouted, "Here I am!"

Before Moullion could reach for the umbrella, Rand was on him, toppling him, tussling in the sand. They rolled over once, and Rand already knew he was no match for the younger man. The South African was on top, closing his hands around Rand's throat, when there came a gentle cough behind him. Rand recognized the sound of a silenced gunshot even before the man's hands loosened on his throat.

"I had to do it," Adelaide said, holding the smoking umbrella.

Moullion had rolled over onto his back, gasping for breath. Rand leaned close and said, "You're dying. Tell me what's behind this."

He opened his mouth but at first no words came out. Then he patted the breast pocket of his white jacket and mumbled something. Rand strained to hear it. "Diamonds to coconuts," Moullion said, and then he was gone.

"Did I kill him?" Adelaide asked.

"You did, and saved my life in the process." He reached into the dead man's breast pocket and took out a folded envelope sealed with tape. "Do you know about this?" he asked her.

"What is it?"

Rand tore a corner off the envelope and poured the contents into the palm of his hand. "Diamonds, and fair-sized ones at that. There must be fifty of them, at least."

She nodded. "From South Africa. I should have known."

"His dying words were *Diamonds to coconuts.* But how was he smuggling them?"

"Inside the tortoises," she said. "Telga told me once that he seemed to be force-feeding them with some sort of baster. We never knew exactly what he was doing."

"Smuggling diamonds inside of smuggled tortoises. That's a new one on me," Rand admitted. "But it still doesn't tell us why he killed your husband."

"What will I do now?" Adelaide asked, more to herself than to Rand.

"I'd suggest you leave the body here. Turn the tortoises loose and go home. I'll take care of things in London." He picked up the fallen umbrella gun from where she'd dropped it.

"It's over, then?"

"For you. I have one more bit of business."

It had suddenly occurred to him what Moullion's dying words meant.

R alph Coir welcomed Rand like some 19th century explorer who'd located the source of the Nile. "I read your report, Rand. That was a magnificent piece of work. With Moullion's death this entire smuggling operation seems to have been closed down. I know it's only one of many, but an important one."

"The umbrella gun?"

The bald man nodded. "Ballistics says it's the weapon that killed Telga Toliara, just as you suspected. And the diamonds were a great surprise to everyone." He smiled at Rand. "Your report says Moullion was shot accidentally as you struggled over the weapon."

"That's more or less how it happened."

"Did he ever say why he shot Toliara at Heathrow Airport?"

"No, but I think I can answer that question," Rand said. "You see, there was something staring me in the face from the very beginning and I didn't see it."

"What was that?" Coir asked.

"If Toliara was changing planes at Heathrow for a flight to Florida with the tortoises, why had he passed through customs? Why was he outside the building entering a taxi?"

"Perhaps he had a layover of several hours."

"Even if he had, why double his risk by passing through customs twice, here and in Florida? He could have remained in the transit lounge and allowed his checked luggage and sack of coconuts to be loaded directly onto the Florida plane. The truth was he never intended to continue on to Florida. He was going to find a buyer on his own in London. Moullion must have been at Heathrow to guard against just such a possibility, and when he saw it happening he killed Toliara."

Ralph Coir shifted uneasily at his desk. "What did he accomplish by that? The coconuts—the tortoises—were still lost to him, along with their hidden cargo of diamonds."

"I asked myself the same question. He might have acted instinctively, without weighing the consequences of his act, but that seemed highly unlikely. There was another possibility. He may have known that by killing Toliara he wasn't abandoning the prize but actually saving it. This could only be true if he knew that the sack of smuggled tortoises, once found by the police, would eventually end up on the desk of his partner in crime—yourself, Mr. Coir."

"That's ridiculous!" the bald man sputtered. "What are you trying to do, Rand?"

"Just get at the truth. You hired me, remember? I suppose you needed some sort of investigation for the record, and never thought I'd get as far as I did. You told me yourself that seized animals bound for America ended up here. If you couldn't arrange somehow to keep them yourself, you could still remove the shipment of South African diamonds they'd been fed. I remember you told me you'd visited South Africa recently."

He stared at Rand with fiery eyes. "It's too bad Sidney Moullion isn't alive to back up your assertions."

"He talked about it before he died," Rand said blandly.

"Talked? What did he say?"

"His exact words were *Diamonds to coconuts*. It meant nothing to me at first, but then I remembered your mentioning that the embassy staff thought they were being funny presenting you with a bag of coconuts. It's your name, Mr. Coir. Coconut fiber, used in rope and matting, is called coir. To Moullion *coconuts* was a code name for Sidney Coir, and it was the word he spoke as he was dying."

The American actually snickered. "Wow! I'd like to see that one get laughed out of court!"

"Oh, I doubt if it will come to court. I have filed a report on my suspicions with your superiors, however. I think it's time you got out of the exotic pet business and the diamond business too, Mr. Coir."

Ralph Coir stood up. "I believe we've talked long enough, Mr. Rand. Good day, sir."

"Good day," Rand said with a smile. "I'll submit a bill for my expenses."

THE MAN FROM NILE K

Though they returned frequently to Egypt over the years since they met and fell in love there, Leila had rarely spoken to Rand about the years before their marriage. She was a young archeologist exploring the Nile River for Cairo University when they met, at a time when Russian technicians were strongly entrenched in the city. Though that seemed a lifetime ago she was barely fifty now, still a handsome, vigorous woman.

"You're as lovely as the first time we met," he told her one night in bed.

"I was all wet in those days," she reminded him, "swimming in that polluted Nile River. They claim now it's worth your life to swim there."

"Sometimes what we don't know won't hurt us."

His joking words, spoken in the dark, brought no immediate response from her. He thought she'd dozed off until she finally spoke, a full two minutes later. "There's something you don't know that might hurt you, Jeffery."

Her voice was suddenly so serious that he propped himself up on one elbow and turned toward her. "What's that?"

"In Egypt, before we met, I had a brief encounter with a man. I never told you about it."

"Encounter? You mean an affair?" He was wide awake now.

"I suppose you'd call it that. The man was Victor Constantine, a Russian. He had the most wonderful thick black hair."

The memories of his days in Egypt came flooding back. "He was one of the technicians?"

"Yes. More than that. He was an intelligence officer. That's why I never told you about him. He was one of the men you were fighting against, and the affair had been over for months by the time we met."

"What was his position?"

"You remember the houseboats along the Nile that the Russians used for their radio transmitters?"

"How could I forget? That's just what the Germans did during the war when Rommel was on Cairo's doorstep."

"Victor was stationed on one of those houseboats. It was code-named Nile K."

"And you never told me?"

"Our relationship was over. There was no point in bringing it up."

Rand's eyes were becoming accustomed to the dark. He could almost make

207

out her face full of anguish. "Then why did you bring it up tonight?" he asked.

"Because Victor Constantine came to see me at the University yesterday afternoon."

After that they got up and went into the kitchen. Leila poured them some juice and they talked about it. "I've been wanting to tell you since last night," she admitted. "I couldn't find an opportunity till just now in bed."

"And he showed up at Reading University yesterday?"

She nodded. "I had a message after my archeology lecture that there was a man waiting to see me."

"After more than twenty-five years," Rand marveled.

"He noticed my name on that article I wrote last winter for the *Journal of Archeology*. He wanted to see me again. He still has the accent and the black hair, though I suspect it's a dye job now."

Rand snorted. "If you used your married name it wouldn't be so easy for old boy friends to find you." He was trying to keep the conversation as light as possible.

"I told him I was married and that you were retired from government service. He said he'd like to meet you sometime."

"Did you invite him to dinner?"

"Hardly! We had coffee together at the faculty club and then he went on his way. It couldn't have lasted more than an hour."

Rand took a sip of juice. "But you didn't tell me about it yesterday."

"I was wondering if I should tell you at all. But then I decided I would. It was so far in the past, what difference could it make?"

"Is this man Constantine living in England now or just visiting?"

"I gather he's in London for a couple of weeks. He didn't tell me where he was staying, but he said he might call me before he left the country. I told him our number is in the book."

"Good," Rand said, somewhat sardonically. "Perhaps we can all get together."

He said nothing more to Leila regarding Victor Constantine in the days that followed. There was nothing more to be said, really. She was at the University three days a week and he had resurrected his long-delayed book about British Intelligence after the Second World War. In view of the Official Secrets Act it was a difficult volume to write. He had to rely on previously published sources rather than his own inside knowledge.

It was midway through the following week when the telephone rang around ten in the morning. The voice on the other end asked for him by name. "Am I speaking with Mr. Rand?" Somehow he knew at once that it was Leila's former lover.

"Yes," Rand answered carefully.

"You do not know me. My name is Victor Constantine. I worked for the Soviet government in Egypt back in the early 1970s. I would like very much to meet you for lunch, if that is possible."

"For what purpose?"

"Merely conversation. I knew your wife back in Egypt and—"

"She mentioned seeing you last week," Rand said, letting him know Leila had no secrets from him.

"I thought we might reminisce about the old days. I have very few friends in England."

And I'm not one of them, Rand thought. But he had to admit to a certain curiosity about Leila's lover from a quarter-century ago. "Were you thinking of today?"

"Yes, if you are free. Otherwise—"

"Today would be fine. Where shall we meet?'

"I'm at that new hotel on London Road, quite near the university. They have a nice dining room downstairs where we can pick up something light, if that is agreeable."

"Fine. Twelve o'clock?"

"I will see you then, Mr. Rand."

After he hung up, Rand considered phoning Leila with the news. But he knew she'd be giving her morning lecture at that time. He could wait and tell her all about it in the evening. He showered and changed into the casual jacket and pants he often wore around the city when he wasn't going into London.

The hotel was one of those modern American chains that beckoned tourists but did little for the British landscape. Rand spotted Victor Constantine as soon as he entered through the revolving doors. At the moment he was the only man in the lobby of the right age, and there was about him a certain foreign appearance. Perhaps it was his suit, dark and double-breasted in the style of those Russian leaders at the May Day parades.

"Mr. Constantine?"

"Ah, Mr. Rand! So good to meet you at last!"

Rand had to admit the man was still handsome, even with his gray hair and furrowed brow. He was tall and carried himself well, with a firm grip as they shook hands. He led the way into the hotel dining room, where a few business people from the area had already arrived for lunch. When they were seated and had ordered drinks, Rand asked, "What brings you to Reading, Mr. Constantine?"

"Please call me Victor. And you are … Jeffery?" He spoke perfect English, without a trace of an accent.

Rand nodded. "Leila mentioned seeing you a week or so back at the University. Have you been here all that time?"

"No, no! I came down from London that day and returned the same evening. This time I come to see you, to talk of the old days when we were on opposite sides. I am a journalist now, you see." He passed Rand one of his business cards which read: *Victor Constantine – East European News Service.* It gave a Warsaw address.

The drinks arrived and Rand took a sip of his. "Leila told me you were a communications specialist on board one of the houseboats on the Nile River."

He nodded. "That is correct. Nile K."

"We were aware there was at least one in operation, but I don't believe we ever knew about the others."

"We had a very elaborate operation in those days. But I suppose British Intelligence was just as elaborate."

"Oh, yes." Until that moment Rand had assumed that Constantine's purpose in suggesting lunch was that of a former lover wishing to meet Leila's husband. But now he wasn't so sure. Her name had barely been mentioned and now the conversation was moving into uncharted territory. Was this man hoping to pry some sort of information from him after all these years? And to what purpose?

Their food arrived and the conversation shifted to London restaurants. Rand suggested a few good ones he knew, and Victor Constantine mentioned a favorite place in Paris. "The food in Cairo was terrible during the time I was there," he said. "Leila took me to some local restaurants, but I never developed a taste for it." He stared at Rand across the table. "Of course even then there was still a strong British influence in the city. I don't suppose you had any difficulty in dining."

"I can eat most anything," Rand told him.

"Were you ever a field agent for them?"

"Not officially."

"The Department of Concealed Communications. You were its director for a time, no?"

"I was," Rand acknowledged. He wondered how much Leila might have told Constantine about his work, either then or now. But admission of his connection with Double-C revealed no secrets. That fact had been published in various accounts of British Intelligence work.

"In the early 1970s I reported to a man named Taz."

"I knew him. I was in Switzerland when he died there, some years later."

"You killed him, perhaps?"

"No. He was killed by a car bomb. Not exactly a car bomb, but it's a long story."

Constantine nodded. "I have heard the story. But some thought you were responsible for his death."

"Far from it. I tried to save his life. I believe we came to respect one another toward the end."

The conversation drifted into discussions of the weather, world politics, and the state of the economy. Victor Constantine was knowledgeable on many subjects, but the conversation never returned to either of their Cold War roles in intelligence gathering. When lunch ended with an affable handshake, Rand was left to wonder what it was all about. Neither Leila nor the Cairo years had been discussed in any detail. He drove home through the afternoon sunshine, wondering how he was going to describe the luncheon to her.

The first thing he noticed upon reaching their house was that the front door was slightly ajar. Certainly he hadn't left it that way. He entered carefully, aware that something was wrong, and saw at once what it was. When they'd married and moved to Reading following his retirement, Leila had set aside a spare downstairs bedroom for his office. One wall was lined with filing cabinets holding the non-secret papers and correspondence he'd been able to take with him, along with Leila's notes on her early archeological digs. Though he kept the cabinets locked at all times, one drawer was standing open. He could see the lock had been tampered with.

First Rand checked the rest of the house to make certain he was alone. Then he used a handkerchief to carefully open the file drawer. In his old business one thought of everything, even booby traps. But there were no hidden trip wires or springs. The open file drawer covered the year he'd met Leila in Egypt. It contained nothing secret, yet it appeared someone had entered his house to go through it.

Entered while he was away, having lunch with Victor Constantine.

He saw now that he'd been set up, lured to that meeting while Constantine sent someone to break into the house.

Rand went upstairs and retrieved the Italian automatic pistol he kept hidden in the linen closet. The clip was full and he slipped the weapon into his pocket. Then he went out to his car and drove back into the city to the hotel on London Road. Whatever Victor Constantine had taken, he intended to get it back.

At the hotel's front desk he showed the business card Constantine had given him. "I seem to have forgotten my room number," he told the clerk.

She checked the computer. "That's 607, Mr. Constantine."

"Thank you."

He took the elevator to the sixth floor and knocked at the door. No one answered. Feeling frustrated, he glanced around, noting the chambermaid's cart at the other end of the hall. He approached her, smiling. "I'm Mr. Constantine in room 607. I seem to have left my key card in my room. Could you open the door for me, please?"

She appeared hesitant and he showed her the business card. "All right, but it's not one of my rooms," she said finally, leading the way down the hall with some reluctance. She used her card to open the door and he gave her a one-pound coin.

212 THE OLD SPIES CLUB

Once inside he glanced at the made-up bed and the closed suitcase on the luggage rack. That seemed to be the most likely place to begin his search. The bathroom door was almost shut and he pushed it open as he passed.

That was when he saw the body of Victor Constantine lying on his back in a pool of blood by the bathtub.

Rand's first thought was of Leila. He would have to tell her that her long-ago lover was dead. His second thought was the realization that the killing must somehow be linked to the theft from his files. His third thought was that someone was knocking on the hotel room door.

He peered through the peephole and saw a man in a business suit wearing a nameplate that read *Security*. Opening the door a crack, he asked, "Yes?"

"Sorry to bother you, sir, but the maid reported she let you into this room. I just need to see some identification."

"I—I was about to call you. There's a body in here by the bathtub." He swung the door open to let the man enter. There was nothing else he could do.

The security man glanced at the body. "Do you know this man?"

"He's Victor Constantine. I lunched with him downstairs. This is his room."

The grim-faced man motioned toward a chair. "Please be seated, sir. I'm going to have to notify the police and they'll want to question you."

"I'd like to phone my wife at the University. She lectures there."

"You'd better wait for the police, sir."

The extent of his situation was beginning to dawn on Rand. "I should tell you I'm carrying a firearm."

The security man's face, already grim, seemed to harden into granite. "Please raise your hands above your head."

Rand did as he was told. "It's a small automatic pistol, in the left-hand breast pocket of my jacket. The safety's on."

The man carefully removed it with two fingers and placed it on the bedspread. "Now sit over there and don't move."

He called downstairs to report what he'd found, and within minutes another security man arrived to join him. "What have we got here, Jennings?"

"The chambermaid phoned that she let this gentleman into the room. I came up to check and he showed me the body, then said he had a handgun. It's there on the bed."

The second man peered in at the body. "It's a bloody mess! Was he shot?"

"Can't tell without moving him, and I figured that was a job for the police."

They arrived a few minutes later. Detective-Sergeant Herbert Squires was known to Rand from various community meetings they'd both attended. While the others bent to examine the body he came over and asked, "What happened here, Mr. Rand?"

"It's a long story. Before I tell it, I wish you'd let me call my wife at the

University. She may be worried when she finds I'm not at home."

Sergeant Squires nodded. "Of course. I'll find an empty room for you to use. The fingerprint boys will want to dust the phones in here."

A constable accompanied Rand to an unoccupied room just down the hall and he phoned Leila's office, hoping to catch her at her desk. He was in luck and when she answered he told her he had bad news.

"Have you been in an accident?" she asked immediately.

"No. Your friend Constantine has been murdered in his hotel room and I found the body."

"What were you—?"

"I'll tell you about it later. Right now they seem to be holding me for questioning. I'm still at the hotel but they may take me to Police Headquarters shortly."

"I can't believe what you're telling me."

"It's true enough."

"Did you kill him, Jeffery?"

"Of course not! Did you have to ask that question?"

"I'll meet you at headquarters," she said quickly and hung up.

When he returned to Constantine's room, Detective-Sergeant Squires told him, "Death appears to have been caused by a gunshot wound to the back of the head. You'll have to come with us to headquarters while we check out your weapon."

"It hasn't been fired," Rand assured them.

"It doesn't seem to have been," Squires agreed, "but the fact that you came here carrying it opens you to questioning. The security man, Jennings, said you tricked the maid into opening the door for you."

Rand sighed, "I'd better tell you the whole thing from the beginning."

The sergeant listened intently, with barely an interruption, until Rand had completed his story. "Will your wife bear this out?"

"Certainly, as much as she knows. I haven't had an opportunity to tell her that Constantine and I had lunch together today, or that our home was entered and robbed."

Leila was awaiting them at headquarters, and Squires escorted them both into the interrogation room. "What happened?" she asked grimly.

He told his story again, noting her surprise upon learning that Constantine had phoned him and suggested lunch. "Why would he do that?" she wondered.

"As it turned out, his apparent motive was to lure me away from the house so an accomplice could go through my old Egyptian files."

"Those files in your cabinets? There's nothing secret in them, certainly nothing of interest a quarter-century later. The cold war is over. The Soviet Union is over!"

Squires listened to it all with interest. "How well did you know the dead man?" he asked Leila.

"Quite well, back in the 1970s. Before I met my husband."

"Didn't you regard him as the enemy?"

"Not my enemy, certainly. At the time he and the other Russians were in Egypt at the invitation of the Egyptian government. I was there searching for some small tombs from the First Dynasty which might have been submerged when the Nile shifted its course. I was skindiving in the river and Victor Constantine was on one of the Russian houseboats. One day he invited me on board for tea and I accepted. The tea turned out to be vodka but that was all right with me."

"Why did your relationship end?"

Leila shrugged. "I discovered that Victor was spying on some British diplomats in Cairo. I had a Scottish mother and an Egyptian father, and a certain amount of loyalty to my homeland. I broke it off and shortly after that I met Jeffery." She smiled sadly at Rand, as if begging his forgiveness for all she was putting him through.

Detective-Sergeant Squires rubbed his chin in thought. "Did you report this break-in at your home, Mr. Rand?"

"Well, no. My immediate thought was to get down to the hotel and confront Constantine."

He stood up. "I think we'd all better take a ride out to your house and examine the scene."

The street where they lived was quiet and nearly deserted, as it often was before the children came home from school. Rand and Leila drove in their separate cars, with Squires and a constable close behind. The sergeant took only a moment to find scratches on the front door lock indicating it had been picked.

"A man of some skill," he decided. "Probably used one of these new electronic gadgets."

They went inside and Leila led the way to Rand's office. "In here, Sergeant Squires."

"Nice place you've got," the detective commented. "These older homes have a great deal of charm."

"Which drawer is it?" Leila asked Rand, but then noticed the drawer open about an inch. "The thief left it like this?"

"That's right. I haven't looked through it yet."

She shook her head in bewilderment. "It's almost as if he wanted to call attention to what he'd done. This drawer and the front door slightly ajar—" She turned to Sergeant Squires. "Is it all right if we go through it? Do you need to check for fingerprints?"

"Avoid touching the exterior of the cabinet," he suggested. "If there are no prints there, we have little chance of finding any inside."

But the files seemed untouched to Rand. Some that were kept in manila envelopes had remained sealed. As he looked over the dates, starting in 1971, memory flooded back. He'd been young in those days, under forty, discovering the intoxicating charms of Egypt and true love for the first time. "I don't notice anything missing," he said, "but I can't be certain."

"Yet the thief wanted you to know he'd been here," Squires said. "That's very strange."

The uniformed constable took some photographs at the sergeant's direction, then began dusting for fingerprints. When he finished he reported, "The door and the filing cabinet seem to have been wiped clean, Sergeant. Either that or he was wearing gloves."

"What now?" Rand asked. "It seems likely Constantine hired someone to break in here and the man found something valuable enough that he decided to keep it and killed his employer."

"That's a possible explanation," Squires conceded. "There are at least two others."

"What are they?"

The detective smiled. "I have to check into a few things. Would it be convenient for each of you to come to my office in the morning for interviews?"

"What time?" Leila asked. "I have classes at the University."

Rand was about to correct her but he bit his tongue. Obviously she knew Thursday was a free day. If she had misspoken it was for a reason. "Ten o'clock?" Squires suggested.

Leila and Rand exchanged glances. "I suppose we could make it then," she answered.

"It might be best if I spoke with you separately," he said. "Suppose we make it ten o'clock for you and ten-thirty for Mr. Rand."

"What's the purpose in that?" Rand asked.

"It's just routine."

Sergeant Squires and the constable departed then. Rand watched them drive away and turned back to Leila. "You told them you had to teach tomorrow."

She shrugged. "I forgot I was off on Thursday. Is that a crime?"

"Is there something you're not telling me, Leila?"

"No. Is there something you're not telling me?"

"I didn't kill him. I had no reason to kill him. He seemed like a pleasant enough chap. Your name hardly came up in our conversation."

"You must see that Squires believes the break-in and robbery were faked. He suspects you shot Victor out of jealousy and made up the story of the robbery."

"But I didn't. He was after something in the files."

"Let's have a drink while we try to puzzle this out," she suggested.

The morning paper carried a half-column account of the murder ("A man registered at the hotel under the name of Victor Constantine, believed shot to death by a burglar"), which supplied no new information. Happily, the brief story made no mention of the reported robbery at Rand's home.

Detective-Sergeant Squires was waiting when they arrived at Police Headquarters. "Have you come up with anything else that might help us?" he asked as he greeted them.

"Not a thing," Rand told him. "We were talking about it all evening. We even went through the house to see if anything else had been searched or stolen, but everything seemed to be in its place."

Squires smiled sympathetically. "Let me speak to Mrs. Rand alone, please. You can wait out here."

Rand sat down on a hard bench facing a bulletin board with *Wanted* fliers and departmental announcements. He wondered why Squires was questioning Leila separately. Did he seriously believe that Rand might have killed that man out of jealousy over something that happened a quarter-century ago?

"Mr. Rand, isn't it?" a voice asked. He looked up to see Jennings, the security man from the hotel.

"That's right, Mr. Jennings."

"It's Phil. Phil Jennings." He sat down next to Rand. "They got you in for questioning, too? They just finished with me."

"Yes. My wife's in there now."

"I told the sergeant I don't know a thing about it. I never even noticed Mr. Constantine. In a hotel as big as ours, guests come and go." The grim face Rand remembered from the hotel room had softened a bit, and the man seemed younger, probably no more than thirty. "I think he just returned to his room and surprised a burglar, like it said in the paper."

"Someone in your place must have seen him."

Jennings nodded. "I spoke with the chambermaid who made up his room. She remembers him. Handsome older man who spoke with an accent."

"Was he with another man?"

"No, he was alone. On his way down for breakfast, I imagine, just as she arrived to do his room."

Breakfast, Rand thought. That was where he might have met with the man he'd hired to break into Rand's house. Perhaps someone in the hotel dining room would remember them.

Sergeant Squires appeared in the doorway, escorting Leila out. "Mr. Rand, you may come in now."

Leila smiled at him and went to sit down. Jennings said goodbye and went on his way.

As Rand settled into the chair opposite the sergeant's desk, Squires cleared his throat. "First off, I want to tell you you're in the clear on the gun. It wasn't even the same caliber as the one that killed Victor Constantine. I'll return it to you when we're finished here."

"I'd appreciate it. I assure you I took it with me only for self-defense. There was never any intention of shooting the man."

"I know. We've checked into your background, Mr. Rand, and you're highly regarded in government circles. I understand you're retired from British Intelligence."

"An obscure branch of it, yes."

"And your wife tells me she was working in Egypt when you two met."

"That's correct. She met Constantine in Egypt too."

Squires rubbed his chin. "We haven't been able to locate his passport, which seems odd. He had some business cards in his wallet, and the key card to his room, but no passport."

"He was staying somewhere in London. No doubt the passport is in his room there."

"Perhaps. People traveling in a foreign country often like to keep their passports with them."

Rand was growing tired of the seemingly pointless speculations. "Are you trying to get at something?"

"Yes, I am," Squires admitted. "We checked at the University. Your wife had no classes yesterday between noon and two o'clock. She could have gone to your house, opened the door with her key, scratched the lock a bit so it would appear there was a forced entry, and done the same with the filing cabinet."

Rand could hardly believe his ears. "What are you saying, that my wife might have killed Victor Constantine? That's ridiculous! She'd told me all about him last week."

"Did she really tell you all? Is it possible, Mr. Rand, that your wife did some work for Constantine during those Cairo years, spying for the Russians? Perhaps he was blackmailing her about it, threatening to tell you."

"Not a chance. She would have told me. We're completely honest with each other."

"She says she never told you about the Constantine relationship until last week. Was that being completely honest?"

"Look here, Leila didn't kill Constantine or anyone else! If you wish to continue this line of questioning we'd better phone our solicitor."

"No need for that," Squires assured him, backing off a bit. "Certainly I'm open to any new evidence you might present. Perhaps the break-in at your home had nothing to do with Constantine's killing."

But something in the conversation had set off a spark in Rand's memory. "It has something to do with it, all right. I have an idea. Give me a day to follow up on it.

"All right, you may go," the sergeant told him. "Neither you nor your wife is under arrest."

Yet, he seemed to add silently.

Rand didn't speak until he and Leila were clear of Police Headquarters. Then she said, "Somehow he suspects I'm involved."

"I know. He told me."

She turned to him. "You don't believe that, do you?"

"Of course not. Do you have a train schedule in your purse?"

"To London?"

"Yes. We should catch the next train if we can."

"What—?"

"I can't tell you yet. Just trust me."

"Do you know who killed him?"

"Maybe."

He was quiet during the train journey, scanning the copy of the London newspaper he'd purchased at the station. It was not until the last section, when he came upon a listing of the day's events, that he found what he was looking for. "See here," he pointed out to Leila, "there's a conference of the Archaeological Institute of Great Britain all this week at the Barbican Centre. Don't you usually go to those?"

"I haven't been in years. One doesn't discover much in the way of archaeological treasures in a lecture hall at Reading University. I leave that to others now."

"I think we should drop in on it. We might learn something."

"What can we learn?" she asked, and he told her his theory as she sat wide-eyed by his side.

In London they took a cab to the Barbican Centre and entered its stark concrete reception hall. The area seemed crowded, with men and women standing in groups or hurrying off to the next session. "Wait here," he told Leila as they approached the registration desk. He went up and spoke to the young woman wearing an AIGB badge but she shrugged and shook her head. He took a program from her and scanned the list of panels and reports on the schedule for that afternoon.

"Conference Room D, second floor," he told Leila. "Come on."

"Jeffery, are you sure you want to do this?"

"Sure enough," he said. At Room D he stationed her outside. "If something goes wrong, you may need help from the security guards."

"I know what to do," she assured him.

He went in without her, seeing at the far end of the room a dais with a long table and microphones. Four men and a woman were seated there, and a question period seemed to be in progress. Rand walked to the nearest audience microphone and raised his hand. After a moment the moderator called upon him. "Please give your name and affiliation when asking your question."

"Jeffery Rand, retired. I would like to know the progress of the Egyptian archeological dig known as Nile K, and I address my question to our visitor from Russia, Mr. Victor Constantine."

R and hadn't known what reaction his question might bring, but the tall black-haired man rose quickly to his feet and walked off the dais, heading for the room's fire exit off in the corner. He didn't get far. Lcila and two security guards were waiting for him outside the door.

"You knew he'd go for the fire exit?" Rand asked her later, after the City of London police had taken Constantine into custody.

"I knew. He did it once before, a long time ago. But how did you know he was alive? And who was the dead man in his room?"

"I told you a little of it on the train. My first mistake was getting everything backward. You told me he'd located you through a recent article you published in the *Journal of Archaeology*. But how did a former Russian spy happen to be reading such a journal? It's not the sort of reading matter you'd find on the average newsstand or in a doctor's waiting room. No, Constantine was reading it because of a professional interest in the subject. He'd become an archaeologist, or at least a treasure hunter, and because of his early relationship with you he was especially interested in sites along the Nile River. That's how I located him today. We knew he'd come to London for some purpose and when I saw the Conference on Archaeology listed in the paper I took a chance that he'd be here. It was pure luck that we arrived while he was actually on a panel."

"I understand all that, but what about our robbery?"

"My mistake was in jumping to the conclusion that Constantine was after my records from the period. Actually he was after your records of the Nile River searches you carried out for Cairo University. He believed he was close to locating a lost tomb beneath the river, and he needed your records to pinpoint the location. Though he brought along a man to assist him, once he talked to you and established your daily schedules he decided it would be best if he burgled our house himself. He knew exactly what he was looking for, and as a former spy he would have been well trained in picking locks. You probably mentioned to him that our old files were kept together."

Leila nodded. "He was asking about the house, how we lived."

"He went to the house, and since I'd never met him, his assistant assumed his identity and lured me out to lunch. I thought it odd that he didn't talk more about you, or about his days with Russian Intelligence. He mentioned you briefly, and my old enemy Taz, but of course Constantine would have told him that much. Two clues should have tipped me off sooner. You mentioned

Constantine's black hair, probably dyed, and both you and the chambermaid said he spoke with an accent. The man with whom I lunched had gray hair and spoke perfect English with no trace of an accent."

"Why did Constantine kill him?"

"Perhaps he didn't fully trust the man. It must have occurred to him that if he left obvious signs of a break-in I would phone the police or return to the hotel myself. If Constantine killed the man in his hotel room and left his wallet and business cards on the body, the police would assume it was him, especially if I identified him. It might be days, if ever, before you or someone else corrected the error. Of course he couldn't leave his passport on the body because the photo wouldn't match the corpse."

"All this over that research I did more than a quarter-century ago!" Leila marveled. "And I thought Victor came to Reading simply to see me again."

THE WAR THAT NEVER WAS

It was only because Rand missed his usual train home to Reading that he stopped in the Unicorn pub near London's Paddington Station for a quick glass of beer. He paid no attention to the ruddy middle-aged man standing next to him, except to notice that he needed a shave. In fact he had almost downed the beer, thinking about catching the next train, when the man tapped him on the shoulder. "Were you in the war, mate?"

"The Second World War?" Rand answered politely. "I was too young. I did my government service during the Cold War."

"I didn't mean those wars. I meant the war I was in."

Judging his age to be about 45, Rand asked, "Was that the Falklands or the Persian Gulf?"

The man shook his head, and Rand realized he'd had more than a few drinks. His breath surrounded them both in a haze of alcohol. "Neither one. I flew a fighter-bomber in the Ayers Rock War, back in '93."

"The what?"

The man seemed to realize he'd said too much. He shook his head vigorously. "Top secret. Not supposed to talk about it."

"Ayers Rock is in Australia, isn't it? There was never a war down there."

The man had a sly look on his face. He glanced around and dropped his voice almost to a whisper. "They kept it hushed up. Buy me a beer and I'll tell you about it."

Rand glanced at his watch. He had a half-hour before the next train to Reading. This seemed as good a way to spend it as any, and he'd have a funny story for Leila over dinner. "Sure," he responded. "Let's get a booth where we can chat. I've got a little time before my train."

They carried their beers over to a table still damp from the most recent customers, and Rand noticed the man walked with a decided limp. Close up, facing him across the table, Rand was aware of his scarred, battle-weary face. "Name's Chat Wallis. What's yours?"

Rand dismissed the question with a casual, "Jeff. What sort of name is Chat?"

"Short for Chatterton. Family name, all very old school. They thought I'd be Prime Minister one day. Instead I ended up a mercenary, available to the highest bidder."

"Tell me about the Ayers Rock War," Rand urged. "When was it?"

"Six years ago," he replied at once. "The summer of '93. God, it was hot that July. I remember the sweat pouring off me even before I took off. We were flying six Russian jets from the Afghanistan days, with rocket launchers and napalm bombs under the wings."

"What was your target?"

"Well, it wasn't the sheep, I'll tell you that."

"The sheep?"

"Lots of sheep in Australia, so many that they use helicopters to herd them. That was part of the problem, you see."

Rand shook his head. "I believe you'd better start at the beginning. Exactly whom were you fighting against? Australia?"

He leaned forward, lowering his voice still further. "Course not! We were fighting with the Australians, not against them. It was the Aboriginal revolt that started it, over a hundred thousand of them crying for blood. They overran Alice Springs and some of the other interior towns, established their headquarters on Ayers Rock, a sandstone monolith in almost the exact center of the country. It was a sacred place to the Aboriginals. They called it Uluru. The Australians fought them as best they could, but in the end they needed our help."

"Against unarmed natives?"

"Don't fool yourself, man! A lot of the native people had taken jobs, learned skills. Several were sheepherders who learned to fly helicopters. The Australian planes would fly in, looking for revolutionaries, when suddenly a swarm of copters would rise straight up in their path, firing heat-seeking missiles."

Rand merely shook his head. "Funny I never read anything about all this. Six years ago, you say? How long did it last?"

"Fifty hours after we got there. Some people called it the fifty hours war, but in all the top secret dispatches it was the Ayers Rock War."

"Television and the press simply ignored all this?"

"You don't go to the papers and TV to find out what's really happening in the world, mate. Things go on that you'd never dream of. Once in a while the public gets wind of it, but rarely. They say a newspaper publisher who found out about Ayers Rock got pushed off his yacht in the Mediterranean, and no paper would touch it after that."

What struck Rand more than anything else about Chat Wallis was that the man didn't seem crazy or delusional. His eyes lacked the wild look of an unhinged mind. "You're not talking about a political scandal or a sex romp here," he told Wallis. "You're talking about war. There must have been hundreds killed."

"They told us there were over thirteen hundred Aboriginal casualties. We lost forty-four men. By any yardstick it was a successful mission."

"And you flew a Russian fighter plane?"

"Fighter-bomber, war surplus. We carried no markings. The British weren't supposed to be involved. We only came to the aid of the Australians when they needed us to put a quick finish to the thing."

"But you were an RAF officer?"

A shake of the head. "Paid mercenaries, all of us. I earned flight pay of seven thousand American dollars a month. We'd fought in Africa for various nations. But we were trained by our officers, and flew our own planes, usually surplus Soviet MiG-23 fighter-bombers. Some countries were willing to pay a million dollars a month or more for our services."

"Where did Third World nations get that sort of money?"

"Usually it was financed by the International Monetary Fund. They wanted to prevent a long protracted war that would damage a nation's trade and economy."

"Tell me more about Ayers Rock."

"We attacked out of the east just at dawn, when they'd be blinded by the sun at our backs. I remember seeing them clambering like ants up the face of that great rock as it glowed orange in the rising sun. They tried to hide in its crannies but we swept over in waves, strafing them first and then dropping napalm to burn them out of their holes."

Rand could hear no more of this obscene dream. "I have to catch my train now," he decided suddenly, glancing at his watch for confirmation. "Been nice talking to you."

"Come back tomorrow," Chat Wallis urged. "I'll tell you some more."

That evening over dinner he told Leila about the man in the pub. "You should stay out of bars," she advised. "Or out of London."

Involved as she was with her lecturing duties at Reading University, Leila rarely ventured into the city, except to join Rand at some exceptional play or concert they both wanted to attend. She took a dim view of Rand's occasional visits to his London club or to a few old friends. "You get into trouble every time you go there," she'd told him once following the business at the Old Spies Club.

"I'm not in any trouble," Rand assured her. "I had a drink with him in a pub and I'll probably never see him again."

"The Ayers Rock War!" she said with a snort. "Who ever heard of such a thing? Are you telling me the Australians or British or anyone else could mount a major air attack against their own people without the world's press knowing anything about it? That a racial war with over thirteen hundred casualties could pass unnoticed in the 1990s?"

"The middle of Australia is a pretty arid place with very few people. How many would there be out at Ayers Rock?"

"Plenty, Jeffery. Did you ever hear of tourists? They come to Ayers Rock by the busload. And often a number of Australians are camped out there by the rock. There's always someone around. It's a national landmark. The man is just plain crazy. You find them everywhere these days, especially in London." She allowed herself a smile. "I think it has to do with the millennium."

He chuckled along with her and switched to another subject.

But in the morning he found himself still thinking about Chat Wallis, a veteran of the war that never was.

R and didn't tell Leila that he was off to London again. He simply boarded the morning train, leaving her a note saying he might be a bit late getting back. There was no real reason to anticipate another meeting with Wallis, but he had a feeling the man would be true to his word and reappear as promised. Rand was seated in the same booth by one o'clock, having a sandwich and a pint, but the Ayers Rock veteran was nowhere in sight.

Thirty-five minutes later the man appeared in the doorway, still needing a shave. He paused until his eyes became accustomed to the dim light of the pub. Then, as if he'd known all along that Rand would be there, he limped over to his table. "Hello again, mate. Good to see you."

"I've been thinking about what you told me yesterday."

Wallis glanced down at Rand's half-empty glass. "Can't talk with a dry mouth."

"Of course not." Rand signaled to the barmaid, a pert young lady with short brown hair. "You know, there's something about your story that doesn't make sense. Why should you tell it to me rather than one of the tabloids that might pay you for it?"

"I talked to a reporter once. He thought it might make a better story if I could work an alien kidnaping nto it. Spaceship landing on the Rock and all."

"Maybe he was right."

Chat Wallis shrugged. "I told him I was willing to take a lie detector test, but he wasn't that interested."

"Wait a minute. Are you saying you'd take a lie detector test to prove you fought in this Ayers Rock War?"

"I sure would! Hell, it's my life!"

It was a crazy idea, but Rand had to get to the bottom of this. "Look, I know a woman who gives lie detector tests in the private sector, to new employees hired for sensitive positions. If I set it up and paid for it, would you be willing to take it?"

The man squinted at him. "You don't believe me, do you? Nobody ever does."

"Her name is Sophie Gold. Let me give her a call."

Rand went over to the pay phone on the wall and looked up Sophie's number in his address book. He'd known her briefly at Concealed Communications before he retired and the department was shut down. In the years since then he'd talked to her on the phone and had lunch with her occasionally when he was in London. He recognized her voice at once when she answered. "Gold Technologies, Sophie Gold speaking."

"Sophie, this is Rand. How have you been?"

"Can't complain. Are you in town?"

"Just for a few hours. Still in the lie detector business?"

"More than ever. I'm buying a second machine and hiring an assistant to operate it."

"I have someone I'd like to bring over. I don't suppose you have any time this afternoon."

"Is it urgent?"

"Not really, but I'd like to do it before he changes his mind."

"Let me check my appointment book. I may have an opening." She came back on in a moment. "Is four-thirty too late for you?"

"How long does it take?"

"Usually close to an hour by the time I get things set up and ask the subject some test questions first."

"Write me in for four-thirty, Sophie. If he can't make it then I'll call you right back."

Rand went back to the table. "We can do it between four-thirty and five-thirty today if that's good for you."

"Sure, why not? It'll be good to have someone believing me after all these years."

They had over two hours to kill and Rand wasn't about to spend them at the pub. "I have some people to see," he told Wallis. "Can you meet me at this address at four-thirty? It's on Charing Cross Road, just up the street from the National Portrait Gallery."

"I'll find it," he promised. "Four-thirty."

Knowing it might be the last he ever saw of the man, Rand left the pub and hailed a taxi to the nondescript government building overlooking the Thames which had once housed the Department of Concealed Communications. The old crowd was scattered now, dead, retired, or transferred to a world where messages were encoded by microchips and decoded the same way. He remembered the rooms full of young women at rows of desks, toiling to break the latest enemy cipher, because women were better at it than men. It was all gone now, and the building was part of the Ministry of Trade, but he still had one or two old friends left there.

His visit had to be cleared by a receptionist in the main lobby, but otherwise there was none of the tight security from earlier days. The workers here dealt with trade balances rather than codes and ciphers. Brent Foxwell, barely hanging on until retirement, was one of those.

"Well, Rand," he said, getting up from behind his crowded desk. "It's good to see you again."

"Always a pleasure, Brent. I had an hour or so to kill and there's no better way to do it than with old friends."

"How's Leila?" He was younger than Rand, but balding and squinty, beginning to show his age.

"Very good. Still lecturing in archaeology at Reading, of course. Sometimes I think she married me because I looked like a bag of old bones."

They chatted on for about ten minutes, casually reliving the old days, before Rand managed to steer the conversation into the desired channel. "It must be boring working with imports and exports all day, nothing like old times."

"Boring is just what I need," Foxwell said, lighting his familiar pipe.

"Do you handle Commonwealth countries too, like Australia?"

"Certainly. It's all trade."

"I've heard there was quite a disruption during the uprising back in '93."

Foxwell wrinkled his brow. "Uprising? What was that?"

"Something about the Aboriginals as I remember it."

He shook his head with a smile. "There was never anything like that. You probably dreamed it one night after watching *Zulu* on the telly."

"No doubt," Rand agreed. "But I thought I heard it from a fellow named Wallis."

"Chatterton Wallis? The fellow with the limp? The man is off his rocker. Battle wounds, I suppose. Should be locked away."

"You've had contact with him?"

"Not in years. I'm surprised he's still around."

After another twenty minutes of aimless banter he took his leave, pausing only to look out the window at the river. "It was always a great view," he told Foxwell. Once outside he crossed Westminster Bridge and headed up Whitehall to Trafalgar Square, then past St. Martin-in-the-Fields where a craft sale was in progress. At the start of Charing Cross Road he found Sophie Gold's building and was surprised to see Chat Wallis waiting for him, though it was not yet four-thirty.

"I came early," the man told him. "Something you learn in the military."

"Fine. Let's go up."

Sophie Gold had been short and slender when Rand worked with her, an auburn-haired bundle of energy. She'd broadened out somewhat over the years, but still retained the momentum he remembered from the old days. She greeted him with a professional handshake and a glance sideways at Wallis. "Is this my subject?"

"Sophie Gold, let me introduce Chat Wallis. He's been telling me an interesting but unbelievable story, and he's willing to take a lie detector test to convince me it's true." Rand ran quickly through the highlights of Wallis's tale and the man contributed a few personal facts so she could develop the questions to ask him. Then Wallis waited in the anteroom while they wrote out a list of things to ask.

It was five o'clock by the time he was seated in the chair by the machine, entangled in wires like a spider's hapless victim. "Go ahead," Wallis urged. "Let's get this over with."

"Very well." Sophie fiddled with the dials and started down the list of questions while Rand sat on the sidelines, behind Wallis.

"Is your name Chatterton Wallis?"

"It is."

"Were you born in Liverpool on April 25, 1952?"

"I was."

"Have you ever been to Russia?"

"No."

"Have you ever been to Australia?"

"Yes."

"Have you ever been a mercenary in the pay of a foreign government?"

"Yes."

"Have you ever killed a man?"

"Yes."

"Were you ever in the Royal Navy?"

"No."

"Have you been to Africa?"

"Yes."

"As a mercenary?"

"Yes."

"Were you in Australia in July of 1993?"

"Yes."

"As a mercenary?"

"Yes."

"Were you fighting Australian Aboriginals?"

"Yes."

The questions droned on, covering Ayers Rock and the early morning assaults, touching on the number of people killed, on his training and pay, on the unmarked planes. At the end of a half-hour Sophie Gold was still asking questions. It was almost six before they finished. She spent a few silent moments checking the graphs and marking certain answers, then came out to Rand with the results.

"As you know, the lie detector is not a foolproof device. That's why the results have no standing in a court of law. However, based upon what we see here I have to tell you this man is speaking the truth."

"I was afraid you were going to say that."

"Does it make your job more difficult?"

"There is no job," he said, writing a check for her service. "Just a man in a pub with a story. And I had to listen to him. Anyway, thanks for your help, Sophie."

"Any time."

Rand walked downstairs with Chat Wallis. "Did I pass?" the ruddy-faced man asked.

"You know you did."

"Then maybe I can ask the government for a medal."

"I wouldn't advise that." Rand had a sudden thought. "Tell me something. What about the men you fought with, the other pilots? What happened to them?"

"When you're a mercenary you go where the money is. Some of them went back to Africa, a few died there."

"Are you in contact with any of them?"

"Not really. The company didn't want me back after I started talking about Ayers Rock. There's a man here in London I see occasionally, though. Rex Ryan. He retired from the game after a back injury."

"Are his memories of Ayers Rock the same as yours?"

Wallis shrugged. "You'd have to ask him. He didn't talk much about it."

"What's his address?"

"Don't know. I just saw him at the club once in a while."

"What club is that?"

"Soldiers of Fortune Ltd. It's the company that employed us. They have a place on Pembridge Road."

They'd strolled back down to Trafalgar Square and were cutting a path through the pigeons when a short man with bulging eyes appeared directly in front of them, passing out handbills. "Take one, mate. Best show in town," he said as he forced the paper into Chat Wallis's hand.

Wallis glanced at the ad for a Soho strip club, crumpled it and threw it away. "Those places are all alike."

Rand noticed a drop of blood on the tip of his thumb. "Did you cut yourself?"

"Probably a paper cut," Wallis said, barely noticing it.

"I want to see you again. How can I contact you?"

Wallis hesitated and then answered, "Celeste, the barmaid at the Unicorn. We're buddies. If I'm not there, she'll give me a message."

They parted near Charing Cross and Rand took a taxi to Paddington Station. Chat Wallis had given him a great deal to think about. Had the man been living in an alternate universe or was there really a massive cover-up under way? Neither explanation seemed possible, and Rand was beginning to regret he'd ever stopped in the Unicorn for that beer.

It was Leila who called his attention to the small item in the *Times* the following morning. "That man you met in the pub—didn't you say his name was Chatterton something?"

"Chatterton Wallis. Why?"

"He died. Collapsed on the Strand early last evening, apparently of a heart attack."

Rand took the paper from her and read the brief story. Wallis was not further identified. Though no time was given, the location on the Strand made it likely he'd died within minutes after Rand left him. That was when he remembered the drop of blood on Wallis's thumb, and the little man with the handbills. "My God, Leila! They've killed him!"

"What are you saying?"

"A crowded street, a poisoned needle, that's all it takes."

"Why would they kill a man for telling a crazy story like that?"

"Perhaps because the story wasn't all that crazy. Perhaps because I had him take a lie detector test and he passed it."

Leila reached over to take his hand. "Promise me you'll stay out of it, Jeffery. Whatever happened, you can't help him now. If the government's involved—"

"They had him killed, Leila. They were afraid because he was talking to me."

"You're not sure of that."

"I have to find out. Wallis mentioned two people, another mercenary named Rex Ryan and a barmaid at the Unicorn named Celeste. They might be able to tell me something. I have to go back this morning."

"On a Saturday?"

"The people behind this don't keep regular office hours."

"Be careful," was all she could say.

Rand caught the train into London for the third straight morning. This time he went directly to the Unicorn pub, though it was barely open at a few minutes after eleven. The barmaid with the short brown hair was polishing glasses and he wondered if she was Celeste.

"I'll be right with you," she told him.

"I don't want a drink. Are you Celeste?"

She stopped polishing and turned toward him. "You're the bloke who was in here with Chat yesterday."

"I read about what happened."

She nodded. "He had a lot of things wrong with him but I never knew his heart was one of them."

"He told some pretty wild stories," Rand ventured.

"That he did."

"I believe I left him yesterday shortly before his fatal heart attack. He told me if I ever needed to reach him I should come to you. He said the two of you were buddies."

Her large violet eyes clouded over. She shook her head, close to tears. "I can't reach him now."

"I know that, but I have to find out more about him. I don't even know where he lived."

"Sometimes with me," she admitted. "When he wasn't away somewhere or just bumming around the city."

"Did he ever talk about Australia?"

"He told that story to everyone who would listen. Fire-bombing Aboriginals on Ayers Rock! Who would believe that?"

"I would," Rand admitted. "Or at least I believed that he believed it." He decided he had to be frank with her. "Look, Celeste, I think Chat might have been killed by someone because he was talking too much about the Ayers Rock War."

"Killed? The paper said it was a heart attack."

"I've made a study of counter-intelligence work. There are certain drugs that can mimic a heart attack quite effectively. They've been used before."

She shook her head, unwilling to accept what he was saying. "Don't tell me that. I don't want to hear any more."

Rand sighed. "I'm not trying to upset you. I'm only trying to get at the truth. Did Chat ever mention a fellow mercenary named Rex Ryan?"

"Rex, sure! They were good friends. God, I wonder if he knows about it!"

"Could you tell me where he lives?"

She shook her head. "He came in here with Chat a few times, but that's all I saw of him."

"Chat told me yesterday that I could contact him through the organization, Soldiers of Fortune, Ltd."

"Yes, I suppose so. I stayed away from that sort of thing. I hated even hearing about what they did, waging someone else's war for money."

Other customers were coming in, and their conversation ended with his promise to tell her if he learned anything. Rand left the Unicorn and took a taxi to the address of Soldiers of Fortune, Ltd. He'd half expected an efficient modern office with a wall map showing all the countries in which these men had fought. Instead he found more of a clubhouse, with television sets and rooms for card-playing and billiards. There were only a few men in the place during the noon hour, and all were younger than Rand by a decade or more.

"You a member here?" one of them asked. "It's a private club."

"I'm looking for Rex Ryan."

"Not here. Haven't seen him in weeks."

'It's important. It's about Chat Wallis."

"Don't know as I can help you, mate. Rex is probably out of the country."

Rand took out a card with his home phone number on it. "If he turns up, could you ask him to give me a call? Tell him it's most important."

"Right you are!" He stuffed the card into his pants pocket and Rand left the clubhouse doubting if Rex Ryan would ever see it.

There were no cabs in front of the place and he started walking north toward Portobello Road. He hailed a passing taxi and was just getting in when a man shoved him on the shoulder and got in after him. Rand opened his mouth to protest and the man held a finger to his lips. "I'm Ryan," he said quietly. "Why do you want to see me?"

"You were at the clubhouse?"

"Where to?" the cabby interrupted to ask.

"We'll get out at the next corner," Rand decided suddenly. He didn't want the driver to overhear their conversation. But he'd forgotten it was Saturday and they found themselves on Portobello Road, in a sea of shoppers seeking out antiques and second-hand goods of every description at the weekly street market.

Ryan, a scrubby man with a gradually graying brush cut, asked, "Is this your idea of a private conversation?"

Rand smiled ruefully. "Sometimes a crowd is the safest place. Why didn't you show your face at the club?"

"These days I like to stay undercover."

"You heard what happened to Wallis?"

"Yes."

"I think he was killed."

"So do I."

"By whom?" Rand asked.

"The operations people. They can't let the truth get out."

"About the Ayers Rock war?"

Ryan nodded. "That's it."

"But there was no Ayers Rock War!"

"For some people there was."

"Where, in an alternate universe?"

"Stop asking questions, or you'll be next. He talked to you. Last year he was sounding off at the Unicorn and then got struck by a car on the way home. Hit and run. It left him with that limp. I think it was meant as a warning for him to shut up, but he didn't take it."

"His girlfriend Celeste says he talked to people."

"But you're the first one who believed him."

"No," Rand corrected. "I believed that *he* believed. But how could he have fought in a war that never took place?"

Rex Ryan closed his eyes for an instant. Then he said, "I fought in the same war."

"Tell me about it."

The crowd was pressing in on all sides. Families with children fought their way to the stalls alongside teen-age girls with green hair and nose rings. Rand and Ryan threaded their way along as best they could, but conversation was impossible.

Finally they took shelter in a doorway and Rex Ryan began his story. "I never would have told this except for what happened to Chat. He was a good buddy and he didn't deserve to end up like that."

"Tell me."

He sighed and started to talk, and all the time they stood in the doorway watching the people of all races and colors mingling at the Portobello Market, as they did every Saturday. "We'd been fighting in Africa, flying for one of those newly independent nations struggling to survive. Then the contract ran out and Soldiers of Fortune summoned us back to London. It was the summer of '93..."

After they parted Rand put in a phone call to Brent Foxwell at the Ministry of Trade. He wasn't there on a Saturday afternoon but at Rand's insistence the operator patched him in to Foxwell's home number.

"What is it, Rand?" Foxwell asked when he came on the phone, sounding irritated. "They're only supposed to put emergency calls through on a weekend."

"This is an emergency. I've just spoken to Rex Ryan and he told me the whole story."

Foxwell might have cursed softly. "Where are you now?"

"Portobello Road. Can you meet me here?"

"Give me an address and I'll be there."

The crowd had thinned out only slightly by the time Brent Foxwell arrived. He'd parked on the next street and walked the rest of the way, pushing through the strollers and shoppers until he caught sight of Rand. His face was flushed with anger as he approached. "Who gave you authority to meddle in government business?" he asked as soon as he determined there were no eavesdroppers nearby.

Rand allowed himself a slight smile. "I didn't know the training of private mercenaries was part of government business."

"Is that what Ryan told you? He's as crazy as Chat Wallis!"

"Wallis certainly had mental problems, but their root cause was the training your people subjected him to. I knew from my first conversation with Wallis that there was no Ayers Rock War. He described how hot it was in Australia in July of '93. But it's winter in Australia then. Even in those arid areas the temperature would have been barely above 60. Wherever that war was fought, it wasn't in Australia in July."

"None of this involves me," Brent Foxwell said, dismissing it with a wave of his hand. "I'm in trade, remember?"

"You mentioned Wallis's limp but told me you hadn't seen him in years. Ryan says the limp was from a hit-and-run driver just last year. You knew about it, perhaps because you caused it to happen."

Foxwell snorted. "You always were one for rash judgments, Rand."

"This isn't a judgment, this is fact. Rex Ryan told me all about it. Trade with the emerging African nations was important to our country, and you wanted to bring stability to the stronger nations by facilitating the training of the mercenaries they hired to fight their wars."

"Perhaps I did," Foxwell admitted. "Was that so wrong? The mercenaries' contract fees are often financed by the International Monetary Fund that supports these actions. We used standard training techniques."

"Some of them weren't so standard. According to Ryan the mercenary pilots wore special headsets and hand controls for virtual reality scenarios. They seemed to be piloting their fighter-bombers through a three-dimensional environment generated by computer software. It was very real to the senses, too real for someone like Chat Wallis. He came out of the training convinced that he'd fought rebelling Aboriginals at Ayers Rock. Of course Soldiers of Fortune ceased to employ him, but he couldn't be stopped from talking about it. Not unless he died."

They walked on through the crowded street, hearing the occasional shouts of vendors. "These things happen with any sort of training," Foxwell argued. "It was something of a tragedy for Wallis, but there was nothing we could do. If someone started believing him, you can imagine what the press would have done with the story. The racial angle alone—" He shook his head sadly. "Believe me, what happened to Chat Wallis yesterday was the only possible solution."

"But why did you use Australian Aboriginals in your virtual reality scenario?"

The balding man turned to him. "Don't you understand? The mercenaries were killing blacks in those African nations! We needed to perfect their training with a similar enemy. We couldn't use a specific African nation, so we invented an Australian revolt by the Aboriginals."

That was when Rand saw the short man with the bulging eyes approaching them through the crowd of Saturday bargain-hunters. The only possible solution for Chat Wallis, and for himself.

"Take one, mate," the man urged, extending a handbill while echoing the words he'd spoken in Trafalgar Square. "Best bargain on Portobello Road!"

Rand had only an instant to yank Brent Foxwell off balance, pushing him into the outstretched hand of the little man. Foxwell gasped softly, though the pain could not have been more than the prick of a needle.

"Didn't you work once with a Brent Foxwell?" Leila asked him over breakfast Sunday morning as she read the *Times*.

"I think so, yes," Rand answered, sipping his coffee.

"He died of a heart attack yesterday on Portobello Road, the same thing that happened to the other chap you knew."

Rand shook his head sadly. "It seems we live in stressful times."

A JEFFERY RAND CHECKLIST

COLLECTIONS

The Spy and the Thief. New York: Davis Publications, 1971. Contains seven
   stories about Nick Velvet and seven about Jeffery Rand.
Tales of Espionage. Secaucus: Castle Books, 1989. Contains eight stories about
   Rand, seven stories in Hoch's Interpol series, and stories by Robert Edward
   Eckels and Brian Garfield.
The Spy Who Read Latin and Other Stories. Helsinki: Eurographica, 1991. Contains
   five stories about Rand.
The Old Spies Club and Other Intrigues of Rand. Norfolk: Crippen & Landru
   Publishers, 2001. Contains fifteen stories about Rand.

FIRST PUBLICATION OF EACH STORY

1. "The Spy Who Did Nothing," *Ellery Queen's Mystery Magazine* [hereafter,
   EQMM], May 1965.
2. "The Spy Who Had Faith in Double-C," *EQMM*, August 1965. Collected in
   The Spy and the Thief.
3. "The Spy Who Came to the Brink," *EQMM*, December 1965. Collected in
   The Spy and the Thief and *The Spy Who Read Latin.*
4. "The Spy Who Took the Long Route," *EQMM*, March 1966. Collected in
   The Spy and the Thief.
5. "The Spy Who Came to the End of the Road," *EQMM*, July 1966. Collected
   in *The Spy and the Thief.*
6. "The Spy Who Walked Through Walls," *EQMM*, November 1966.
7. "The Spy Who Came Out of the Night," *EQMM*, April 1967.
8. "The Spy Who Worked For Peace," *EQMM*, August 1967.
9. "The Spy Who Didn't Exist," *EQMM*, December 1967.
10. "The Spy Who Clutched a Playing Card," *EQMM*, February 1968.
11. "The Spy Who Read Latin," *EQMM*, August 1968. Collected in *The Spy
   Who Read Latin.*
12. "The Spy Who Purchased a Lavender," *EQMM*, April 1969. Collected in

The Spy and the Thief.
13. "The Spy and the Shopping List Code," *EQMM*, July 1969.
14. "The Spy and the Calendar Network," *EQMM*, November 1969. Collected in *The Spy and the Thief.*
15. "The Spy and the Bermuda Cipher," *EQMM*, June 1970. Collected in *The Spy and the Thief.*
16. "The Spy Who Traveled With a Coffin," *EQMM*, October 1970. Collected in *Tales of Espionage* and *The Spy Who Read Latin.*
17. "The Spy and the Diplomat's Daughter," *EQMM*, January 1971.
18. "The Spy and the Nile Mermaid," *EQMM*, May 1971. Collected in *The Old Spies Club.*
19. "The Spy Who Knew Too Much," *EQMM*, August 1971.
20. "The Spy Without a Country," *EQMM*, February 1972.
21. "The Spy Who Didn't Remember," *EQMM*, April 1972.
22. "The Spy and the Reluctant Courier," *EQMM*, June 1972.
23. "The Spy in the Pyramid," *EQMM*, September 1972. Collected in *Tales of Espionage* and *The Old Spies Club.*
24. "The Spy Who Was Expected," *EQMM*, December 1972.
25. "The Spy With the Knockout Punch," *EQMM*, August 1973.
26. "The Spy and the Intercepted Letters," *EQMM*, January 1974.
27. "The Spy at the End of the Rainbow," *EQMM*, April 1974. Collected in *Tales of Espionage* and *The Old Spies Club.*
28. "The Spy and the Talking House," *EQMM*, November 1974.
29. "The Spy Who Took a Vacation," *EQMM*, April 1975. Collected in *The Old Spies Club.*
30. "The Spy and the Mysterious Card," *EQMM*, October 1975.
31. "The Spy Who Collected Lapel Pins," *EQMM*, March 1976. Collected in *The Spy Who Read Latin.*
32. "The Spy at the Crime Writers' Congress," *EQMM*, November 1976.
33. "The Spy Who Died Twice," *EQMM*, July 1977.
34. "The Spy in the Toy Business," *EQMM*, January 1978. Collected in *Tales of Espionage.*
35. "The Spy and the Cats of Rome," *EQMM*, June 1978. Collected in *Tales of Espionage* and *The Old Spies Club.*
36. "The Spy in the Labyrinth," *EQMM*, December 1978. Collected in *Tales of Espionage* and *The Old Spies Club.*
37. "The Spy Who Had a List," *EQMM*, May 1979.
38. "The Spy Who Was Alone," *EQMM*, September 1979. Collected in *The Old Spies Club.*
39. "The Spy Who Wasn't Needed," *EQMM*, December 17, 1979. Collected in *The Old Spies Club.*

40. "The Spy Who Came Back From the Dead," *EQMM*, June 2, 1980. Collected in *The Spy Who Read Latin*.
41. "The Spy and the Snowman," *EQMM*, November 3, 1980. Collected in *Tales of Espionage*.
42. "The Spy and the Walrus Cipher," *EQMM*, March 25, 1981.
43. "The Spy Who Didn't Defect," *EQMM*, September 9, 1981. Collected in *Tales of Espionage*.
44. "The Spy Who Stayed Up All Night," *EQMM*, November 4, 1981.
45. "The Spy at the Film Festival," *EQMM*, June 1982.
46. "The Spy and the Village Murder," *EQMM*, October 1982.
47. "The Spy Who Sat in Judgment," *EQMM*, April 1983.
48. "The Spy Who Stepped Back in Time," *EQMM*, Mid-July 1983.
49. "The Spy Who Went to the Opera," *EQMM*, April 1984.
50. "The Spy at the Top of the List," *EQMM*, July 1984.
51. "The Spy and the Suicide Club," *EQMM*, January 1985.
52. "The Spy Who Looked Back," *EQMM*, August 1985.
53. "The Spy at the Spa," *EQMM*, Mid-December 1985.
54. "The Spy Who Knew the Future," *EQMM*, July 1986.
55. "The Spy's Story," *EQMM*, December 1986.
56. "The Spy and the Short-Order Cipher," *EQMM*, June 1987.
57. "The Spy and the Embassy Murders," *EQMM*, January 1988.
58. "A Game For Spies," *EQMM*, June 1988.
59. "The Spy and the Guy Fawkes Bombing," *EQMM*, December 1988.
60. "The Underground Spy," *EQMM*, April 1989.
61. "The Spy and the Geomancers," *EQMM*, October 1989.
62. "The Spy Who Went to Camelot," *EQMM*, March 1990.
63. "The Spy and the Healing Waters," *EQMM*, August 1990. Collected in *The Old Spies Club*.
64. "The Spy and the Christmas Cipher," *EQMM*, Mid-December 1990.
65. "The Spy and the Gypsy," *EQMM*, May 1991.
66. "The Spy and the Psychics," *EQMM*, October 1991.
67. "The Spy and the Greek Enigma," *EQMM*, April 1992.
68. "The Spy With the Icicle Eye," *EQMM*, March 1993.
69. "Spy at Sea," *EQMM*, October 1993.
70. "Egyptian Days," *EQMM*, March 1994. Collected in *The Old Spies Club*.
71. "Waiting for Mrs. Ryder," *EQMM*, November 1994. Collected in *The Old Spies Club*.
72. "The Nine-O'Clock Gun," *EQMM*, August 1995.
73. "Train to Luxor," *EQMM*, April 1996.
74. "The Old Spies Club," *EQMM*, May 1997. Collected in *The Old Spies Club*.
75. "One Bag of Coconuts," *EQMM*, November 1997. Collected in *The Old*

Spies Club.
76. "The Liverpool Kiss," *EQMM,* July 1998.
77. "The Man From Nile K," *EQMM,* July 1999. Collected in *The Old Spies Club.*
78. "The War That Never Was," *EQMM,* December 1999. Collected in *The Old Spies Club.*
79. "Season of the Camel," *EQMM,* September-October 2000

THE OLD SPIES CLUB

The Old Spies Club and Other Intrigues of Rand by Edward D. Hoch is printed on 60-pound Glatfelter Supple Opaque Natural (a recycled acid-free stock) from 11-point Baskerville The cover painting is by Carol Heyer and the design by Deborah Miller. The first printing comprises approximately one thousand, two hundred copies in trade softcover, and two hundred seventy five copies sewn in cloth, signed and numbered by the author. Each of the clothbound copies contains a separate pamphlet, *Assignment: Enigma* by Edward D. Hoch. The book was printed and bound by Thomson-Shore, Inc., Dexter, Michigan.

The Old Spies Club was published in August 2001 by Crippen & Landru, Publishers, Inc., Norfolk, Virginia.

CRIPPEN & LANDRU, PUBLISHERS
P. O. Box 9315
Norfolk, VA 23505
E-mail: CrippenL@Pilot.Infi.Net
Web: www.crippenlandru.com

Crippen & Landru publishes first edition short-story collections by important detective and mystery writers. Most books are issued in two editions: trade softcover, and signed, limited clothbound with either a typescript page from the author's files or an additional story in a separate pamphlet. As of August 2001, the following books have been published:

Speak of the Devil by John Dickson Carr. 1994. Eight-part impossible crime mystery broadcast on BBC radio in 1941. Introduction by Tony Medawar; cover design by Deborah Miller. Published only in trade softcover.

Out of Print

The McCone Files by Marcia Muller. 1995. Fifteen Sharon McCone short stories by the creator of the modern female private eye, including two written especially for the collection. Winner of the Anthony Award for Best Short Story collection. Introduction by the author; cover painting by Carol Heyer.

Signed, limited clothbound, Out of Print
Trade softcover, sixth printing, $17.00

The Darings of the Red Rose by Margery Allingham. 1995. Eight crook stories about a female Robin Hood, written in 1930 by the creator of the classic sleuth, Albert Campion. Introduction by B. A. Pike; cover design by Deborah Miller. Published only in trade softcover.

Out of Print

Diagnosis: Impossible, The Problems of Dr. Sam Hawthorne by Edward D. Hoch. 1996. Twelve stories about the country doctor who solves "miracle problems," written by the greatest current expert on the challenge-to-the-reader story. Introduction by the author; Sam Hawthorne chronology by Marvin Lachman; cover painting by Carol Heyer.

Signed, limited clothbound, Out of Print
Trade softcover, second printing, $15.00

Spadework: A Collection of "Nameless Detective" Stories by Bill Pronzini. 1996. Fifteen stories, including two written for the collection, by a Grandmaster of the Private Eye tale. Introduction by Marcia Muller; afterword by the author; cover painting by Carol Heyer.

Signed, limited clothbound, Out of Print
Trade softcover, Out of Stock

Who Killed Father Christmas? And Other Unseasonable Demises by Patricia Moyes. 1996. Twenty-one stories ranging from holiday homicides to village villainies to Caribbean crimes. Introduction by the author; cover design by Deborah Miller.

Signed, limited clothbound, Out of Print; a few overrun copies available, $30.00

Trade softcover, $16.00

My Mother, The Detective: The Complete "Mom" Short Stories, by James Yaffe. 1997. Eight stories about the Bronx armchair maven who solves crimes between the chicken soup and the *schnecken*. Introduction by the author; cover painting by Carol Heyer.　　　　Signed, limited clothbound, Out of Print

Trade softcover, $15.00

In Kensington Gardens Once... by H.R.F. Keating. 1997. Ten crime and mystery stories taking place in London's famous park, including two written for this collection, by the recipient of the Cartier Diamond Dagger for Lifetime Achievement. Illustrations and cover by Gwen Mandley.

Signed, limited clothbound, $35.00

Trade softcover, $12.00

Shoveling Smoke: Selected Mystery Stories by Margaret Maron. 1997. Twenty-two stories by the Edgar-award winning author, including all the short cases of Sigrid Harald and Deborah Knott (with a new Judge Knott story). Introduction and prefaces to each story by the author; cover painting by Victoria Russell.

Signed, limited clothbound, Out of Print

Trade softcover, third printing, $16.00

The Man Who Hated Banks and Other Mysteries by Michael Gilbert. 1997. Eighteen stories by the recipient of the Mystery Writers of America's Grand Master Award, including mysteries featuring Inspectors Petrella and Hazlerigg, rogue cop Bill Mercer, and solicitor Henry Bohun. Introduction by the author; cover painting by Deborah Miller.　　　　Signed, limited clothbound, Out of Print

Trade softcover, second printing, $16.00

The Ripper of Storyville and Other Ben Snow Tales by Edward D. Hoch. 1997. The first fourteen historical detective stories about wandering gunslinger Ben Snow. Introduction by the author; Ben Snow chronology by Marvin Lachman; cover painting by Barbara Mitchell.　　　　Signed, limited clothbound, Out of Print

Trade softcover, $16.00

Do Not Exceed the Stated Dose by Peter Lovesey. 1998. Fifteen crime and mystery stories, including two featuring Peter Diamond and two with Bertie, Prince of Wales. Preface by the author; cover painting by Carol Heyer.
Signed, limited clothbound, Out of Print
Trade softcover, $16.00

Renowned Be Thy Grave; Or, The Murderous Miss Mooney by P. M. Carlson. 1998. Ten stories about Bridget Mooney, the Victorian actress who becomes criminously involved in important historical events. Introduction by the author; cover design by Deborah Miller.   Signed, limited clothbound, Out of Print
Trade softcover, $16.00

Carpenter and Quincannon, Professional Detective Services by Bill Pronzini. 1998. Nine detective stories, including one written for this volume, set in San Francisco during the 1890's. Introduction by the author; cover painting by Carol Heyer.
Signed, limited clothbound, Out of Print
Trade softcover, second printing, $16.00

Not Safe After Dark and Other Stories by Peter Robinson. 1998. Thirteen stories about Inspector Banks and others, including one written for this volume. Introduction and prefaces to each story by the author; cover painting by Victoria Russell.   Signed, limited clothbound, Out of Print
Trade softcover, second printing, $16.00

The Concise Cuddy, A Collection of John Francis Cuddy Stories by Jeremiah Healy. 1998. Seventeen stories about the Boston private eye by the Shamus Award winner. Introduction by the author; cover painting by Carol Heyer.
Signed, limited clothbound, Out of Print
Trade softcover, $17.00

One Night Stands by Lawrence Block. 1999. Twenty-four early tough crime tales by a Grand Master of the Mystery Writers of America. Introduction by the author; cover painting by Deborah Miller. Published only in a signed, limited edition.   Out of Print

All Creatures Dark and Dangerous by Doug Allyn. 1999. Seven long stories about the veterinarian detective Dr. David Westbrook by the Edgar and Ellery Queen Readers Award winner. Introduction by the author; cover painting by Barbara Mitchell.   Signed, limited clothbound, Out of Print
Trade softcover, $16.00

.

Famous Blue Raincoat: Mystery Stories by Ed Gorman. 1999. Twelve detective and crime stories by the author described as "great, possibly one of *the* greats . . . never a word too many, never a word too few, never a word that doesn't come from the heart." Introduction by the author; cover design by Gail Cross. Signed, limited clothbound, Out of Print; a few overrun copies available, $30.00
Trade softcover, $17.00

The Tragedy of Errors and Others by Ellery Queen. 1999. Published to celebrate the seventieth anniversary of the first Ellery Queen novel, this book contains the lengthy plot outline of the final, never published EQ novel, six previously uncollected stories, and essays, tributes, and reminiscences of EQ by family members, friends, and some of the finest current mystery writers. Cover design by Deborah Miller. Limited clothbound, Out of Print
Trade softcover, second printing, $16.00

McCone and Friends by Marcia Muller. 2000. Eight of Muller's recent mystery stories—three told by Sharon McCone and four by her colleagues, Rae Kelleher (including a novella), Mick Savage, Ted Smalley, and Hy Ripinsky. Introduction by the author; cover painting by Carol Heyer.
Signed, limited clothbound, Out of Print
Trade softcover, second printing, $16.00

Challenge the Widow Maker and Other Stories of People in Peril by Clark Howard. 2000. Winner of the Edgar for Best Short Story and five-time winner of the Ellery Queen Readers Award, Clark Howard writes about ordinary people who find the strength, the humanity, to survive. Introduction by the author; cover painting by Victoria Russell. Signed, limited clothbound, Out of Print
Trade softcover, $16.00

The Velvet Touch: Nick Velvet Stories by Edward D. Hoch. 2000. Fourteen stories about Nick Velvet, the choosy crook who steals only the seemingly valueless, including all the tales involving "The White Queen," who claims to be able to do impossible things before breakfast. Introduction by the author; cover painting by Carol Heyer. Signed, limited clothbound, Out of Print
Trade softcover, $16.00

Fortune's World by Michael Collins. 2000. Fourteen classic private-eye stories, including one written for the collection, about Dan Fortune, the one-armed op who investigates cases involving major issues of our times. Introduction by Richard Carpenter; prefaces to each story by the author; cover painting by Deborah Miller. Signed, limited clothbound, Out of Print
Trade softcover, $16.00

Long Live the Dead: Tales from Black Mask by Hugh B. Cave. 2000. Ten classic stories and novelettes from the greatest pulp detective magazine, in honor of the 90th birthday of one of *Black Mask*'s legendary authors. Introduction by Keith Alan Deutsch; prefaces to each story by the author; cover painting by Tom Roberts.

Signed, limited clothbound, Out of Print
Trade softcover, $16.00

Tales Out of School: Mystery Stories by Carolyn Wheat. 2000. Nineteen stories by the creator of Cass Jameson, filled with sympathy for people caught up in the system. Introduction and prefaces to each story by the author; cover painting by Victoria Russell.

Signed, limited clothbound, Out of Print
Trade softcover, $16.00

Stakeout on Page Street and Other DKA Files by Joe Gores. 2000. In 1967, Joe Gores, himself a private-eye, created the first P.I. stories based on the realistic depiction of an investigator's life. The twelve short stories about the Dan Kearny Associates form one of the most distinguished series in the mystery genre. Introduction and prefaces to each story by the author; cover painting by Carol Heyer.

Signed, limited clothbound, Out of Print
Trade softcover, $16.00

Strangers in Town: Three Newly Discovered Mysteries by Ross Macdonald, edited by Tom Nolan. 2001. Macdonald was, *The New York Times* wrote, the author of "the finest detective novels ever written by an American." Macdonald's biographer, Tom Nolan, unearthed three unpublished private-eye stories including two Archer novelettes. Introduction and prefaces to each story by Tom Nolan; cover painting by Deborah Miller.

Limited clothbound, Out of Print
Trade softcover, $15.00

The Celestial Buffet and Other Morsels of Murder by Susan Dunlap. 2001. Seventeen stories by the Anthony-Award winning author of the Jill Smith and Kiernan O'Shaughnessy detective tales. The book also includes two cases of "The Celestial Detective" who investigates crimes in the afterlife. Introduction and prefaces to each story by the author; cover painting by Carol Heyer.

Signed, numbered, clothbound, $40.00
Trade softcover, $16.00

Kisses of Death: A Nathan Heller Casebook by Max Allan Collins. 2001. A novella and six short stories tracing private-eye Heller's changes (and America's changes) from the early thirties to the sixties, with each story investigating a genuine unsolved crime of the past. Introduction by the author; cover design by Gail Cross.

Signed, numbered clothbound, Out of Print; a few overrun copies available, $32.00
Trade softcover, $17.00

The Old Spies Club and Other Intrigues of Rand by Edward D. Hoch. 2001. The Mystery Writers of America's Grand Master presents fifteen stories of espionage involving the man from Double-C, Jeffery Rand, and his wife Leila Gaad. Introduction by the author. Cover painting by Carol Heyer.

Signed, numbered clothbound, $42.00

Trade softcover, $17.00

Forthcoming Short-Story Collections

Adam and Eve on a Raft: Mystery Stories by Ron Goulart.
The Sedgemoor Strangler and Other Stories of Crime by Peter Lovesey.
The Reluctant Detective and Other Stories by Michael Z. Lewin.
The Lost Cases of Ed London by Lawrence Block.
Nine Sons and Other Mysteries by Wendy Hornsby.
Jo Gar's Casebook by Raoul Whitfield [published with Black Mask Press].
The Curious Conspiracy and Other Crimes by Michael Gilbert.
The 13 Culprits by Georges Simenon, translated by Peter Schulman.
The Dark Snow and Other Stories by Brendan DuBois.
One of a Kind: Collected Mystery Stories by Eric Wright.
Problems Solved by Bill Pronzini and Barry N. Malzberg.
Kill the Umpire: The Calls of Ed Gorgon by Jon L. Breen.
Cuddy Plus One by Jeremiah Healy.
Come Into My Parlor: Stories from Detective Fiction Weekly by Hugh B. Cave.
14 Slayers by Paul Cain [published with Black Mask Press].
The Adventure of the Murdered Moths and Other Radio Mysteries by Ellery Queen.
The Mankiller of Poojeegai and Other Mysteries by Walter Satterthwait.
[Untitled collection of Slot-Machine Kelly stories] by Michael Collins.
The Iron Angel and Other Tales of Michael Vlado by Edward D. Hoch.
The Spotted Cat and Other Mysteries: The Casebook of Inspector Cockrill by Christianna
    Brand.
Hoch's Ladies by Edward D. Hoch.

Crippen & Landru offers discounts to individuals and institutions who place Standing Order Subscriptions for all its forthcoming publications. Collectors can thereby guarantee receiving limited editions, and readers won't miss any favorite stories. Standing Order Subscribers receive a specially commissioned story in a deluxe edition as a gift at the end of the year. Please write or e-mail for more details.